FIC Dell'Antonia K.
Dell'Antonia, K. J.,
In her boots /
9780593542460

7/2022

"*In Her Boots* is such a charming, funny, original story that I wished it were a blanket I could wrap myself in. Rhett is a unique heroine, the likes of which I haven't come across in contemporary fiction before, and I felt like I was tagging along with a close friend as I went along on her journey. KJ Dell'Antonia is a fabulous writer, and *In Her Boots* is expertly plotted and full of the perfect little details that make a book sing."
—Elyssa Friedland, author of *Last Summer at the Golden Hotel*

"Both peppy and heartfelt, *In Her Boots* is a tender page-turning romp about running from both your past and your truth, only to discover that, just like real life, you can only run for so long before it's time to turn back home."
—Allison Winn Scotch, author of *Cleo McDougal Regrets Nothing*

"*In Her Boots* is a modern, bighearted, laugh-out-loud-funny novel that reminds us that the only way to find true connection, friendship, and belonging is to fully be ourselves. A joy to read from page one all the way to the very end."
—Louise Miller, author of *The Late Bloomers' Club* and *The City Baker's Guide to Country Living*

"Full of quirky twists and heartfelt humor, *In Her* Boots is a wildly entertaining page-turner about forging your own path and finding your way home again." —Virginia Kantra, author of *Meg & Jo*

Also by KJ Dell'Antonia

FICTION

The Chicken Sisters

NONFICTION

How to Be a Happier Parent

Reading with Babies, Toddlers & Twos
(with Susan Straub)

In
Her
Boots

KJ Dell'Antonia

G. P. PUTNAM'S SONS

NEW YORK

PUTNAM
— EST. 1838 —

G. P. Putnam's Sons

Publishers Since 1838
An imprint of Penguin Random House LLC
penguinrandomhouse.com

Library of Congress has catalogued the G. P. Putnam's Sons trade
paperback edition as follows:
Names: Dell'Antonia, K. J., author.
Title: In her boots / KJ Dell'Antonia.
Description: New York : G. P. Putnam's Sons, [2022]
Identifiers: LCCN 2022006328 (print) | LCCN 2022006329 (ebook) |
ISBN 9780593331507 (trade paperback) |
ISBN 9780593331514 (ebook) Subjects: LCGFT: Novels.
Classification: LCC PS3604.E444637 I52 2022 (print) |
LCC PS3604.E444637 (ebook) | DDC 813/.6—dc23/eng/20220224
LC record available at https://lccn.loc.gov/2022006328
LC ebook record available at https://lccn.loc.gov/2022006329

Library Edition ISBN: 9780593542460

Printed in the United States of America
1st Printing

Book design by Katy Riegel

To Judi, who would totally go on

the *Today* show for me

In Her Boots

1

A Passport

I TRIED EVERYTHING possible to avoid my own thoughts on the flight home, and none of it worked. The movie selection reminded me of nights with my grandmother, who loved her basic cable and would happily settle in for any romance Lifetime had to offer. The voice in the meditation app lulled me into a doze, until I jerked myself awake from a dream of my father reading me to sleep with *The Essential Whole Earth Catalog*. The book I'd chosen for the flight was the worst of all, a memoir by an English sheep farmer about his attachment to the place where he was raised. I thought it would help me wrap my brain around what lay ahead. Instead, the author landed a solid punch to my gut within the first few pages. *People who went away ceased to belong*, he wrote; *they changed and could never really come back.*

I shut my reading app and determinedly launched a game of Candy Crush. I'd gone away wanting to change, and I had, or at least part of me had. But I'd always meant to come back before it was too late.

The flight attendant handed me a package of Oreo alfajores and I leaned down to tuck it into the pocket of my backpack for Grandma Bee before I remembered there was no one to save it for. Instead, I ate them myself and barely tasted them, staring out over the clouds, concentrating on feeling nothing, not when the Manhattan skyline came into view, not when my fellow passengers broke into applause as the wheels touched down on the runway. I was good at pretending to be tougher and stronger than I was. Not just good. I was a pro.

I was playing my part perfectly when the border control agent unexpectedly broke through my determination to pretend this was just any trip.

"Welcome home," he said, handing me my well-worn blue passport along with my nothing-to-declare paperwork.

Home. I turned away quickly, wiping a stinging from the corner of my eyes that could have been from anything. Dust. Pollen. The sharp itch of my new tattoo, a tiny bumblebee on my upper arm in honor of the grandmother who raised me but wouldn't be waiting to greet me when I finally made my way to our farm in New Hampshire. The farm where I learned that animals were more reliable than people. The farm that gave me the skills I needed to make it in the real world, like focusing on the job even when it's raining so hard you can barely see the fence you're fixing or shaking it off when a cow's just knocked you flat on your butt, then getting up and showing that cow who's in charge. My farm, now. I'd be there within twenty-four hours. Then I could cry.

With no luggage to claim, I was outside JFK within minutes, shaking off unwanted emotion and opening my eyes wide to absorb the light and set my internal clock for another season. I'd left behind a mild fall in Argentina. Here, the sharp greens of spring had already mellowed into a glorious May. In a minute I'd plunge back into the crazy and head for the AirTrain and then the subway to Brooklyn and my best friend Jasmine's fancy brownstone, but first I needed a little air, even the exhaust-filled version offered by the ocean of concrete and tarmac that surrounded me. At least there were no mosquitoes.

But there were plenty of distractions, and I welcomed them, even the two men yelling at each other over a stalled sedan parked on the side of the access road.

"Why won't it start?" The shorter of the two, and, based on his Wall Street casual uniform of khakis and button-down, the obvious passenger, sounded to me as if he might have asked that same question more than once already.

The other, long and sideburned in the manner of the hipster part-time driver, part-time whatever–else–New York–had–to–offer, stared down into the open hood as though he hoped the answer might be written there.

"I don't know, man. It was fine on the way here." Hipster driver glanced up nervously at the approaching security guard. "This isn't where I was supposed to pick you up either. I'm going to get a ticket."

"You can't stop here," the officer said, taking out her radio. "I'm going to have to have you towed."

Oof. That tow fee would be no joke. I hesitated—this might

be my chance at a far cushier ride into town than that offered by public transport. If I had the cojones to pull it off.

"Why don't you help him start it?" the would-be passenger demanded angrily. He looked the officer up and down. "That's what a real cop would do. I don't know why they let you even have this job if all you can do is call for help."

That's it, I'd heard enough. *You see a sexist jerk,* said the voice of the Modern Pioneer Girl in my mind. *I see a teaching opportunity.* The mechanical part would be easy. It was the human element that always made me anxious. But almost twenty years of travel and job-hopping overseas had taught me tricks—like what I thought of as my alter ego, the Modern Pioneer Girl—for overcoming those fears. I'd done it for so long it was almost second nature.

Almost.

Channeling my alter ego's confidence, I strolled up to the open hood and slid my backpack off my shoulders. "What seems to be the problem here, gentlemen?"

Business guy snorted with distaste as he took me in. Too tall, with my lanky body clad in the nondescript jeans–and–T-shirt uniform of backpackers everywhere, long, faded red braids stringing out from under my baseball cap. Too old, at forty, too wrinkly from the sun. Too not–New York for the likes of him.

I met his eyes with an intentionally blank face. I knew I didn't look like much. I didn't look like someone who could rig a sail in a storm, round up a thousand cattle from the back of a horse, or, of more interest to him in this moment, hot-wire a truck when my boss dropped the keys somewhere along the trail of a six-mile mushroom-foraging hike. I certainly didn't look like someone who would write a book about those things and find myself newly beloved by an entire generation of would-be feminist adventurers—just in time for the life I'd built to crumble quietly into the dirt of the Patagonian ranch I'd had to leave behind.

That last thought made it hard to face him down, this anonymous dude who was probably compensating for some insecurities of his own. But that was no excuse for his behavior. I stood my ground, refusing to drop my eyes. *More people know my name than he'll ever meet,* I reminded myself.

Well, sort of.

He rolled his eyes and stepped aside, taking out his phone, probably to call another ride and leave the driver to his fate.

There was nothing the Modern Pioneer Girl loved more than being underestimated. I joined the driver in looking under the hood. "How old's your battery?"

"Pretty new," he said, clasping his pale hands together nervously. "Plus, I just drove here and turned off the engine."

"Yeah, it's probably not that." Second–most likely thing, then. I leaned in, avoiding the hot engine, and opened the fuse box. Got it in one. Driver guy didn't look likely to have a spare fuse, though, and this was a pretty old car, so there were none in the fuse box.

My eye fell on the security officer, radio in hand, her hair pulled tightly into a bun at the back of her neck, and I knew I had this. I turned to the driver. "If I fix it, will you give me a ride into Brooklyn? I don't care what you do with this guy."

"Deal," the driver said. "But I can't leave him here. He'll screw my star rating."

"Whatever," I said, and turned to the officer. "Can I have three minutes?"

She nodded, and I pointed to her bun. "And one of the pins in your hair?"

That made the officer grin. She reached back and handed me exactly what I was hoping for, an open-ended hairpin. "Set a timer," I said, feeling more cheerful than I had in days. I slid the burnt fuse out, then rigged up the hairpin to complete the circuit, bending it to anchor it tightly. "Okay, try to start it."

The driver slid into the car, turned the key, and gave it a little gas, and after the faintest hesitation—just enough to allow the business guy to give me a triumphant look—the engine turned over.

The driver cheered, and the officer held up her hand to offer me a high five. "Two minutes, sister," she said.

I grabbed my backpack. "Can I put this in the trunk?" The driver nodded and opened it as the businessman, avoiding eye contact, hurriedly climbed into the back. "I'll sit up front with you, okay? I don't think Smiley here likes me very much."

2

Pluck

LESS THAN AN hour later, the driver sternly instructed to get a real fuse as soon as possible if he didn't want a much more expensive repair, I was standing on Jasmine's stoop in Brooklyn, fist poised to knock. The door opened before my knuckles even grazed the gleaming red wood. Jasmine burst out onto the stoop, still in the chef's pants and tank top she must have worn to her job at the Empty Donut and insanely skinny for someone who made a living baking desserts. She threw her arms around me. "Rhett! You're here!"

Jas pulled me in tight, and all the thoughts I'd been holding in washed over me. She held me, hugging and patting as I gulped and hiccuped in a way I would do with no one but her, saying the words no one else had said to me since I'd heard about my grandmother's death.

"I'm so sorry, I'm so sorry," she said, and I nodded into her shoulder and didn't even try to talk. I'd been alone every minute since I got the news. More than alone. Alone in a crowd, alone in a country I thought I'd made my own, alone and hiking hard and fast and steep and trying not to beat myself up for breaking my own rule and letting another guy get close enough to crush me when he turned out to be as bad as the rest.

It took a minute, but after a couple of deep breaths I straightened up.

"I know," I said. "I'm okay, I really am. I'll be okay."

Jas gave me a questioning look but I managed a smile. She'd know I wasn't ready to talk about it, now or maybe ever. She grinned back, and suddenly I really did feel happier. She held out her phone with one arm and wrapped the other around my shoulder. "Record this moment?"

I nodded, and she took a selfie of our faces squished together, our eyes a little red but both of us looking delighted to be reunited. That was about all our faces had in common. As much as I resisted comparing my hat hair, wrinkles, and dark spots with her blond topknot and glowing, dermatologically enhanced perfection, I was. I always did, for our first ten minutes together—and then it would pass and she'd just be my old friend again, though this version of her demanded far more maintenance on her part.

Personally I missed the old burger-and-fries Jas, but I tried not to say so too often.

"That's for the MPG's Instagram," she said in a teasing tone, surveying the image. "We have to mark your arrival. The MPG is in the house."

"Don't you dare," I said, following her through the doorway and past the staircase and kitchen out to the light-filled living room. "The Modern Pioneer Girl is a woman of mystery." I stopped short as I realized that Jasmine's husband, Zale, was stretched out on one of the white couches, the shoulders and biceps he worked so hard on set off as always by a black muscle tee emblazoned with the logo of the chain of gyms he'd named after himself, Zale's Powerhouse Fitness.

Zale stood up slowly and we exchanged the awkward hug of two people who would never have spent more than thirty seconds in each other's presence without Jasmine to connect us. He was a few inches shorter than I was, and I could feel him, as always, stretching up just a little in an attempt to deny it. "Hey," I said in greeting. "How's business? Still thriving?"

He responded with his usual intensity as he released me. "All good. Clients are loving the new food, telling me they wish we'd do all their meals. The only problem has been sourcing enough ingredients. Everybody wants plant-based meats right now, and the supplement powders I like are having supply-chain issues."

I laughed. "Wouldn't it be easier to just use real food?" It was a familiar dispute, one that went back to the very first time I found him in Jasmine's kitchen five years ago, packing powders and liquids with a list of ingredients as long as my arm into a blender. I threatened to put a banana in it, and I swear he got pale at the thought. Bananas, it seemed, were the devil's fruit. Or something like that.

It started out as just an annoying quirk, along with his multihour-a-day workout habit, but he'd turned his obsession into an empire and he'd done it incredibly fast. I could have respected that, except for the way he rebuilt Jasmine from the ground up after tearing her down first. He constantly demanded "improvements" but I saw nothing to improve. The old Jas was funny. Happy. Gorgeous, but gorgeous in a regular person's body leading a regular person's life instead of spending every minute trying to make herself smaller in the name of "wellness." Every time I saw them together, it got harder to watch her trying and failing to live up to his expectations. Now he had the best baker I'd ever known jumping through hoops trying to create recipes that met the loopy dietary requirements of his acolytes and also tasted of something besides processed sawdust. I'd been hearing about it for a year via WhatsApp, and I had a terrible feeling I was about to have to taste it. If I'd thought of that, I might have gone straight to New Hampshire.

"They like to know their food is produced in an ethical, sustainable way," Zale replied.

The industrial food complex that comes up with this stuff isn't something I'd describe as ethical or sustainable. I started to say so, but Zale, probably knowing what was coming, interrupted me with the faintest of smiles, as if he'd been readying this next sally in our ongoing skirmish. "They also love your book," he said. "We sell it in the gear shops. Last month you sold more copies than Gwyneth's cookbook."

I paused, startled. No one besides me and Jasmine had ever known the real identity of the Modern Pioneer Girl.

"Don't worry," he said. "I know all about it. Jas kept pushing it on people, so I made her tell me what was up. Nice work. People love that armchair adventure stuff, especially when you mix it with some self-love. They eat it up."

I would have glared at Jasmine, but she'd ducked back into the kitchen. I could hear her clattering plates.

I shifted from one foot to the other. I loved my book almost as much as I hated talking about it, and I'd carefully arranged my life so that I never had to, using a pseudonym and refusing any and all appearances or interviews. "Oh, the book. Yeah. It's not that big a deal," I said, brushing off years of journaling, posting, and then learning to navigate the social media fame that led to being discovered by my enthusiastic editor and the months of writing and revising that followed.

"I know, right? That whole category, aspirational lit or whatever—practically writes itself. I should do one. Hell, your mom even has. Have you seen it? *First, You Jump Through the Hoops* or something? Everyone I know with a graduating senior bought it, hoping their kids would go get a real job and not do the whole barista-with-a-screenplay thing."

Oh, I'd seen it. An hour ago on a display rack at the airport bookstore. My college president mother's scolding handbook sat right next to *The Modern Pioneer Girl's Guide to Life*, written not by plain old Margaret "Rhett" Smith, but by "Maggie Strong," aka the popular Instagrammer known as the Modern Pioneer Girl, aka the superhero alter ego Jasmine helped me create when I was a terrified fourteen-year-old, dumped at a fancy boarding school by the same absentee mother who now apparently believed herself qualified to give other people advice on raising successful kids. It had been an incredibly satisfying moment, and I'd taken a picture. My mother would never know it, but the book some people actually bought—as opposed to having their parents force it on them—was mine.

Jasmine had been the only person besides me who knew who the MPG, as I called her, really was. I would have preferred to keep it that way, but at least Zale wasn't a threat. He never talked about anything except himself.

"Yeah, I bet parents love it," I said, knowing he'd miss my scathing tone.

"What's not to love?" Zale turned to pick up the fitness magazine he'd been reading and return the pillows of his couch to pristine perfection. "She touched a nerve. Sells books, amiright? You too. Like mother, like daughter."

Nothing could have horrified me more.

He extended his fist to me and I returned the bump reluctantly. "Listen," he said, "I gotta go. Need to check in on the Houston Street branch. But great to see you. You and Jazzy have fun." He waved at Jasmine as she emerged from the kitchen with a plate of questionable-looking pastries in her hands, and was gone.

I collapsed onto the couch, to the detriment of Zale's careful cushion arrangement. "Why did you tell him?"

"I had to," Jasmine said, sitting next to me. "I wanted us to sell the books in the shops at the gyms, and it was the only way to convince him. Did you see Drew Barrymore shared it? She's one of his private clients." Jas held up a picture of Manhattan from the Brooklyn Bridge. "How about I post this, since you don't like our selfie?"

"Go ahead," I said. Jas had access to all the MPG's social media and sometimes took over when I was out of range, or when the ranch was crazy busy, especially in the three months since the book came out, thanking bookstagrammers or posting from our shared photo album.

"I'll add one with the book cover," she said, showing me an image of my book in the window at the Strand. "Can I say it's good to be back in the States?"

I shrugged. None of the reasons I was back were good ones, but the MPG made the best of things like that. "Sure."

There was nothing better than a friend who understood you well enough to know what wasn't worth arguing about. I never used pictures of myself on the MPG's Insta, only of her—my—adventures, at first because that wasn't what people did in those days—the app was for pictures you took, not pictures of you—and later because I never felt right presenting the real me as some kind of glossy icon of travel. I was the MPG and yet I wasn't. I'd written the book. I was the Maggie Strong who'd been alone and broke and running from a mother determined to crush me into her mold. My readers and my whole online community knew how I'd used my "superhero alter ego" to find a bigger, braver part of myself and escape into a more adventurous, less conventional life.

What they didn't know was how far short I still fell from being the confident woman I'd depicted in *The Modern Pioneer Girl's Guide to Life*—or how big a part my best friend had played in helping me create her.

Jas wasn't always the beach-waved blonde who sat across from me now, happily scrolling through her own social media. When we first met, she was deep in a goth phase that lasted all through high school, with a sharply angled, asymmetrical bob dyed black and carefully cultivated pale skin against dark scarlet lips. I was her terrified, nondescript assigned roommate. I unpacked my limited wardrobe and hid my boxed set of Little House books on my closet shelf, then kept my mouth shut through a freshman introductory dinner throughout which Jasmine dominated the conversation, comparing the lyrics of the Ramones to the work of Anaïs Nin. I'd never heard of either.

I was lost and overwhelmed by what I'd gotten myself into in letting my mother sweep me away from the farm where I grew up and create an entirely new life for me in the weeks after my father's death. The first exchange I remember clearly came that first night, when Jasmine found me huddled under the covers, comfort-reading *The Long Winter*. She stared at me and my book for a long minute without speaking, then pulled back my blanket and walked to our door, beckoning to me to follow.

We slipped down the hall and out into the slight chill of a September night, breaking at least half the rules that had been impressed upon us earlier in the day. Outside, Jas offered me a cigarette. Even then, I'd seen enough movies to know that if I accepted, the overture would end with me coughing and embarrassing myself, so I shook my head. I sat next to Jas in a silence that grew increasingly hard to break, plucking at the grass at our feet while she smoked, wishing for something cool or clever to say, or anything at all.

Jas finished her cigarette without a word, then led the way back to the building. She tugged on the door handle, then stopped and tugged harder.

"Shit," she whispered. "It's locked."

Jas was panicked, but to me it was a gift from some goddess of friendship who hadn't been a part of my limited homeschool curriculum. I knelt, examining the situation. It wasn't much of a lock, no different from the one on our door at home, and Dad had long ago shown me how easy that one was to defeat with anything small and pointy. An ice pick or screwdriver was ideal, but even a twig would do in a pinch.

"Hang on," I said, and pulled a small branch off the dogwood bush growing by the door. I stripped it of its leaves and slid it into the keyhole, feeling for the piece that, if pressured, would release the lock. The knob turned in my hand, and I wasn't just opening the side door of some obscure staircase at an elite girls' school that should really have had better locks. It was the door to a whole new world.

"Ta-da," I said happily, and Jasmine's grin lacked any of her earlier pretense of goth disdain.

"Cool. Can you teach me how to do that?"

Emboldened by my success, I shook my head, then laughed at Jasmine's expression. "If I teach you, you won't need me anymore."

Jasmine linked her arm through mine. "Oh," she said, "I think you'll be very useful." From that moment, we were a team, and nothing else mattered. Jas discovered my secret stash of Laura Ingalls fan fiction—stories I wrote and illustrated about who Laura Ingalls would be if she somehow found herself in, say, a New England prep school in 1993. I found Jas's photo album, which revealed quite clearly that there was a wholesome, perky blonde hidden underneath all that eyeliner.

Jas was totally unabashed. "Boarding school is a chance to become someone new," she said. "Don't you ever want to do that? Leave the old you behind?"

I did. It just hadn't occurred to me yet.

After defending her Beetlejuice style as "expressing the way I feel about the state of the world," Jas set about helping me find a new version of myself, one better equipped to handle the girls who made jokes about my long braids and said I was more at home in the school's stable than in the classroom. *You can do a ton of things the rest of us can't*, she reminded me. Start the school riding mower without a key, tame the Latin teacher's enormous beast of a Maine coon cat, climb to the roof of the library, light a fire without matches. Who cares if you've never been to Manhattan?

I'd never been anywhere, but Jas helped me see how far I could go. She even gave my new inner badass the name that stuck: the Modern Pioneer Girl, an homage to everything from the farm where I grew up—Pioneer Hill—to my ongoing obsession with the Little House books and the book my dad wrote about my childhood: *Raising Little Pioneers*. The day the other students found that one out was not a good day.

Jas's inner superheroes evolved over the years (no one stays goth forever). Along with her own inner MPG, she had an inner Meryl Streep to power her through years of postcollege auditions, an inner Julia Child when she put her acting plans on hold for culinary school, and even, during a short-lived stint as a stand-up comic after restaurant work proved too demanding and her acting career again failed to materialize, an inner Lucille Ball.

For me, the MPG was enough. I called on her through high school and in college and then when I left school before graduating. I was out of cash and alone in Barcelona when I saw a flyer seeking pedicab drivers and suddenly she was right there with me, my inner Laura Ingalls, firmly declaring that hells yeah we could do that. A Modern Pioneer Girl, I reminded myself as I fibbed my way into job after job, could figure out anything—and when Jasmine pushed me to start sharing it all on a brand-new app called Instagram, I used @modernpioneergirl as my handle.

It was fun being anonymous. On days when real life felt bleak, like this one, the MPG offered an escape. No one had to know that I wasn't sure how I was going to face heading home to the farm without my grandmother, or that I missed my life in Argentina, or that, the more I thought about it, the more clear it was that what I really missed wasn't my ex, Rafael, but his ranch and my work there. And my horse. I absolutely missed my horse.

So maybe I wasn't great at long-term human relationships, but connecting with the MPG's followers online? That I could do. I popped in the SIM card I kept for US visits and logged myself into Instagram, taking a moment to appreciate Jasmine's MPG post before drafting one of my own, with a stock image of a stalled car and the story of my latest adventure, a process that always served as the perfect antidote to everything that was going wrong outside the screen.

I liked a bunch of tagged posts, commented on the post of a young woman holding up the *Guide* at Machu Picchu— *awesome, wish I was there, totally try some chicharrones*—then started replying to messages from followers who mostly just wanted encouragement to travel, quit a dead-end job, or leave a relationship that had run its course. I answered them all, until I came to one that was different.

"Oh, hells no." I clicked the screen shut and set the phone facedown on my jeans.

Absolutely not.

3

Approval

MY HORRIFIED TONE caught Jasmine's attention immediately.

"What?"

"Someone thinks I would want to be on the *Today* show tomorrow morning."

Jasmine scooped up my phone from my lap, stretching out to put her pink-polished feet next to my athletic socks on the coffee table. "Well, most people would want to be on the *Today* show."

"Then I am not most people, because that has to be about the last thing I would ever want to do." I tried to pull the phone from Jasmine's hands, but she twisted away. She'd already swiped the screen open and was reading the DM. "And I knew I would regret giving you my password."

"If you get hit by a bus, everyone will be very glad I have your password. That's what we are. We're hit-by-bus password friends. In-case-of-emergency friends. And you turning down a chance to be on the *Today* show constitutes an emergency. Who is this, and how does she even know you're in the city?"

I raised my eyebrows at the person who had just moments ago masterminded the placement of multiple pics depicting the arrival of the Modern Pioneer Girl in New York.

Jasmine laughed. "Oh. Right. The student corrects the master. But see? This is exactly why you post things like that. Do what you love, share it, and opportunity follows."

"That's your advice, huh?" I leaned forward and took one of the heavy, chewy rings off the platter on the coffee table, dangling the sorry excuse for a donut from my finger. "Do what you love?"

Jas leaned away from me on the sofa. "Are you mocking my quest to make plant-based donuts the next big breakfast thing?"

Of course I was. I met her eyes and took an enormous bite—and instantly regretted it. Jasmine is an amazing baker. Seriously. Her oatmeal chocolate chunk cookies? I'd die for them. Her cinnamon buns? People weep. I used to wake up in the night in Argentina thinking about her flourless chocolate cake.

But some ingredients weren't meant to become donuts. I chewed, watching her carefully, then spoke around the heavy mass in my mouth. "Your quest?" I put a lot of emphasis on the word "your."

"My quest," she said, watching me. "What do you think?"

I wasn't sorry to have my mouth full. As I held the unappetizing pastry in front of my face, contemplating, I caught the faintest twitch at the edge of Jasmine's lips. I threw the donut at her. "You almost had me," I said. "They're awful. I can't even believe how awful they are."

"I know," Jasmine said, catching the donut and tossing it back on the plate. "But people in Zale's gyms like them. No, they love them. I think it's been so long since they've eaten a real donut that they don't even know what they're supposed to be like anymore."

"If I ever get like that, just shoot me."

"How about I shoot you if you start turning down amazing chances that any writer in her right mind would kill for?" She aimed a finger gun at me. "Bang."

If by "amazing chances," Jas meant "opportunities to screw up on live television," then I didn't want them. "Maggie Strong is faceless, and I like her that way."

"It's one appearance. You're not using your name. You're still anonymous—but now you're famous anonymous, and famous anonymous sells books, and selling books makes money, and money is good."

"I don't need money," I said. At least I was on firm ground here. Not needing money was where all this started. My brand-new Instagram profile had just a few scattered followers until someone swiped my bag at the ferry dock in Hong Kong eight years ago. I was between countries and bank accounts and should have been more careful—the bag had pretty much all the money I had in the world at that point.

There was no one I could call for help, which wasn't new but hit me hard in that moment. My whole situation suddenly sank in. I was thirty-two; I was exhausted; I was coming off a year of crewing a yacht for a billionaire jerk I never wanted to see again. I'd planned to use that cash to get myself a decent room, maybe teach English for a while. I was even thinking about buying a ticket home, if I could talk my grandmother into taking me. Now I'd be starting all over from scratch—again.

I cried, but you can't sit and sob in public without attracting the kind of attention nobody wants. I pulled myself together, hunched over my phone—which had been in my pocket, a travel-safety basic—and started writing. *I don't need money,* I wrote. *Modern Pioneer Girls know money is meaningless. The only thing that's important is to believe you can always make enough to get you to where you need to go next.*

I had to believe it. If I didn't, I had nothing.

I edited what I wrote into a full-on screed about the freeing energy of not needing cash, took a striking photo of the sun setting over the city skyline, and posted both. Then I got off the ferry and set about solving the immediate problems. I presented myself at the most fly-by-night English school I could find and secured the promise of at least a few weeks' teaching. I found an expat bar and traded cleaning and basic repair work for the use of a young woman banker's couch. I was educated, white, and able to speak the lingo of the American abroad. That meant I could make it work, and I always did.

I logged back in a few days later to find thousands of messages thanking me for the post, and suddenly—even though I'd never met a single one of them—I'd found my people, and I wanted more. I followed that missive up with other things a "modern pioneer" didn't need to make her way in the world—some things I might have liked to have but had to learn to live without. Permission. Approval. A man. Family. A degree, which was my favorite, given all that had happened between my mother, her university, and me. I added a couple of things nobody needs. Regrets. Debt.

Then there were the things you did need: A plan. Strong arms, which had been my only asset so many times. Pluck, which might have sounded classier if I'd called it audacity but I stuck with the word my father and grandmother had given me years ago. A passport if you could get one, a willingness to go where the work was closer to home if you couldn't.

Without ever meaning to, I became the biggest voice on solo women's travel on what was becoming the world's biggest photo-sharing platform. But what was more important was that writing the MPG manifestos helped me find my way again. I'd always enjoyed the challenge of moving around, finding a new job and new friends in a new place every time a visa—or my patience for the work I was doing—expired. But by the time my bag was swiped, I'd started to get tired without having any idea what I might do next. My new online community reinvigorated my love for my way of life and who I'd become. Before, I'd seen myself as kind of surfing from one thing to another. Now, I felt like I was making powerful choices.

It was a happier, stronger me who met Rafael while leading backpacking trips in Patagonia. He was the rancher who supplied the meat for our return-to-base final feasts; I was a farmer without a farm who loved hearing him describe his plans for his family's holdings. He was also a man and a charming one. I didn't need him but I wanted him and there was nothing wrong with that.

Still, I kept our romance strictly out of MPG, focusing on my periodic travels and older stories of adventure even after I moved out to the ranch three years ago. The distance between me and the "me" I was writing about grew. The MPG didn't do relationships; she did experiences. Smart girl, although I didn't see it then. I'd even started wondering if it was time to let her go when Emily Koh, editor extraordinaire, messaged me and suggested I turn it all into a book.

If I'd said no, I wouldn't have spent so much time holed up over the laptop she sent me in the tiny back room of Rafe's house. Maybe I'd have finally won over his mother, instead of just the rest of the ranch hands, if I hadn't put every minute I wasn't on horseback into typing. But then we wouldn't have had the advance, which I loaned Rafe to install a water-pipe system, or the acceptance payment, which went to cement feeders and another hundred head of cattle. But I might still have had Rafe.

Instead, he'd explained last month that he'd decided to make his parents happy by marrying the pregnant Argentinian girl he'd been cheating on me with. I left for a few weeks' solo backpacking, avoiding my thoughts by choosing the hardest and steepest routes, and emerged back into civilization to the news that my grandmother had died. All my plans, every step of that hike, had centered around going back home, not just for a visit but to live. I hoped it was time for Bee to stop stubbornly insisting she was fine on her own and let me take charge of the farm.

Instead, she was gone, and I was filled with those regrets I told my readers we should never, ever have. I was a mess. It was sort of cute that some *Today* show producer thought I—or rather, Maggie Strong—was morning show material, but they couldn't be more wrong.

I tried again to pry my phone from Jas's hands. "Give me that. I'll find you a job baking real food."

"We are not talking about me right now," Jasmine said. "We are talking about you, trying to let a golden opportunity slip away because you're too chicken to put on some decent clothes and go show the world who you really are. It's a segment on advice for graduates, for God's sake. For twenty-one-year-olds. You could do that in your sleep."

"I didn't even graduate," I argued. And not graduating was okay. I'd managed just fine without a degree and I always would—but that didn't mean I wanted to go on national television and talk about it.

Jas brushed that away with a wave of her hand. "They already know that. And besides, this is not about one missing line on your résumé. You've done all kinds of things people want to do, and you did it on your terms. That's inspirational whether you graduated or not."

"I am so not inspirational. The MPG is inspirational. I'm just me." Me, dumped and flattened and badly in need of inspiration myself.

"Rhett." Jasmine leaned over and looked intensely into my

eyes. "You are her. She is you. Your supposed alter ego merged with your real ego a long time ago."

I felt myself wavering. Maybe I could do it. Just once. Maybe it would even be fun. My thoughts must have shown on my face, because Jasmine didn't let up.

"You have to do it," she said. "I dare you."

"I don't have anything to wear." Nothing in my backpack was close to appropriate, or even clean.

"That," said Jasmine, getting up and extending a hand to pull me off the sofa, "is a problem we can solve." She took off up the brownstone stairs to her bedroom, and I followed reluctantly. Was I really doing this?

I found Jasmine digging through one of her closets, filled to the brim with the wardrobe of a would-be actress and now, as Zale's wife and part of his empire, sought-after party guest. She spun around, holding out a black denim blazer and a ridiculously impractical pair of shortie cowboy boots, and gestured to my phone.

"Speed it up, little buckaroo. I guarantee you're not the only person the *Today* show asked. If they're talking about tomorrow, it's because someone bailed and they're desperate. Respond to that DM, tell her you're in, and let me dress you for success."

I threw up one hand in surrender and started typing with the other. "Okay. I'm replying to her now. Hold your horses."

Jasmine waved the boots at me. "Giddyup."

4

De-plucked

THIS WAS A terrible idea. A resoundingly, unspeakably terrible mistake I was about to make, one that would probably destroy the Modern Pioneer Girl forever and leave me with nothing but boring old Rhett Smith. I stopped in front of the imposing gold-plated doors of Rockefeller Center, looking through the glass panes at the elaborate security desk beyond them, and grabbed Jasmine's hand.

"I can't do this," I said, pulling Jasmine around the corner and leaning against the building. I did not belong in there, no matter how Jasmine dressed me up, not even with my new hair (and it would be a long time before I forgave Jasmine for snipping off one of my waist-length braids and cheerfully saying, "I've been wanting to do that for years"). Anyone could see through the designer clothes to the ratty underwear and tattoos that clearly marked me as someone who should never, ever get past security into a place like this.

"You can," said Jasmine. "You can and you will. Hands

out." She laid one hand flat and said the first word of the familiar incantation we used whenever either of us needed a lift—calling on the women at the root of every female inner superhero. "Laura."

I put my right hand on top of Jasmine's. "Zora." ·

Jasmine's left hand. "Frida."

My left. "Gloria."

Then, together, lifting our pile of hands and dropping it at every word: "Ruth. Bader. Ginsburg. Go."

Without giving me a chance to think any further, Jasmine pulled me straight through the doors and up to the desk.

"Maggie Strong," Jasmine said confidently to the uniformed security guard. "The Modern Pioneer Girl. A guest this morning."

The guard's expression of disinterest didn't change as he consulted a list, then pointed us through a metal detector into a hallway. "Greenroom's just past hair and makeup, through there," he said. "Someone will be right out for you."

I would have waited, but Jas, of course, strode confidently forward, her blond hair caught up in the messy low bun she'd chosen as most appropriate to her assistant role. I put an awkward hand to my own head and ran my fingers through my altered hair, still feeling the shock as it ended just above my shoulders. Jasmine's arsenal of styling tools and the best hair color the local CVS had to offer had transformed my faded, chopped-off braids into glossy red waves reminiscent of the bright hair of my childhood. I didn't exactly hate it. I just didn't feel like I could live up to it.

Following the guard's directions, we passed the makeup

room, with bright lights and swiveling chairs. As Jasmine put a hand to the doorframe of what looked to be a lounge with a green sofa and a coffee maker, I heard a familiar voice and took an instinctive step backward.

"Now, who is this Maggie Strong? I don't think I've heard of her," the voice was saying. The accent was upper-class Brit, the tone sharp, confident, and piercing—as it had always been, commanding the attention of everyone within range.

I froze. It had been almost twenty years since I'd been in the same room as my mother, and that was not a record I intended to break now.

I shot out a hand and caught Jasmine just as she was about to cross the threshold, yanking her back. She spun around, clearly thinking I was having another crisis of confidence, and stepped back out into the hallway as a young woman dressed formally in a pencil skirt, pumps, and a sweater set that somehow still looked chic burst around the corner, moving fast, her smile wide and her arms outstretched.

"Ooh, I'm so excited to finally meet you! I loved your book. And I love, love, love your pictures and I'm so thrilled we caught you in between travels . . . Wait." She stopped, surveying us. "Which of you is Maggie Strong?"

I almost didn't take in what she was saying. All I could think was that my mother was in there. My mother, president of Yarmouth University, that tiniest and most exclusive of Ivies. Icon, scholar of economics and history, revered by women and men all over for breaking barriers while denying they even existed, a woman who wouldn't let a self-help book over her doorstep and considered any deviation from the most accepted standards of excellence to be a sign of weakness. Her thoughts on the economy were sought by leaders all over the world; her TED speeches got millions of views; her academic books were the subject of *New York Times* reviews and NPR segments.

Margaret Pearl Gallagher—never Smith; she'd always told my father she could never be a Smith—was about to discover that the *Today* show producers expected her to cross wits with the author of a competing book encouraging graduates to do exactly the opposite of what she advised and find themselves, not by seeking out their place in the world but by striking out to explore it. She would surely gnash her teeth with glee at the prospect. And once she found out that author was her black sheep, college dropout, and general disappointment of a daughter? She'd sharpen those fangs and sink them in.

I looked frantically for an escape route, but our greeter was between us and the door, waiting for an answer. We were trapped.

There was only one thing to do.

I pulled Jasmine forward, hard and fast.

"She is," I said, at the same time Jasmine said the same words.

"She is."

I laughed, panic inspiring me. "Very funny, Maggie," I said. Then, to the pencil-skirt woman: "She knows I'd be terrified to be on the *Today* show if I'd written a book." I started to laugh, but what if my mother heard me? I lowered my voice to almost a whisper, aware that I sounded like a maniac, but the important thing was to keep Jas from saying anything. "Maggie, though, she's great at this! She's going to rock it."

The young woman took Jas's hand eagerly. "Can I hug you? Let me hug you."

Jas accepted the embrace, turning her head as she did so to give me a look of confused disbelief.

The woman stepped back and put her hands together in a heart shape. "I loved the whole thing. And I've given it to everyone I know, so we're all so psyched you could come on today."

I cast an anguished glance toward the sofa room. If my mother came out now, it would be a disaster. I had to get us out of here, fast and without being seen. I dropped my voice to a real whisper this time. "Um, Maggie was telling me that she has to go to the bathroom—is there one?"

"Sure. Back this way," the woman said. I clutched Jas's hand hard, hoping she got my message to not say a word. The woman led us away from the greenroom, introducing herself as the producer who had sent that DM. As Jasmine had guessed, someone else had backed out at the last minute, and Maggie Strong's appearance in New York was a godsend.

"So we're thrilled this worked out. Don't you run away," she said, chuckling merrily at the thought. "I'll wait right here, and then we can go say hello to our other guest." She smiled. "She's a regular. Famous university presidents are pretty run-of-the-mill when it comes to advice for graduates. You're the new blood. Yours is the voice we're all excited to hear."

God, my mother would loathe that. I dragged Jasmine into the bathroom before we could hear another word.

"What the hell?" Jasmine asked, as soon as the door was closed.

I checked the stalls quickly to make sure we were alone. "The other guest. It's my mother. I heard her."

Jasmine clapped her hands together in delight. "That's perfect," she said. "You basically wrote this whole book to tell her to go fuck off, and now you get to tell her in person."

Jasmine had to know better than that. "Are you kidding me? I can't do this with her here. Isn't there, like, a back door?"

"To the bathroom?" Jasmine sighed. "Come on, Rhett. I know she freaks you out, but she can't touch you now, right? It's been twenty years. And look where you got, all on your own. Right where she already is. She's going to hate that."

She was. And oh, it would be awful. I could just hear her. *You wrote this . . . little book? How . . . interesting.* She would flick through the pages, and then she would tear it—and me— apart. The Modern Pioneer Girl would evaporate, and I'd be left alone, ready to sink through the floor.

"I can't," I said, and this time I really meant it. No chant of encouragement was going to get me past this. "You know I can't. She'll eat me alive."

Jas leaned against the bathroom counter. "Don't you think it will be different now? That you're different now?" She put a hand on my arm, her expression serious. "They asked you here. That producer is excited to meet you. To hear what you have to say. Not your mother. She's old news. They want *you.*"

"Not me," I said. "The Modern Pioneer Girl. And I can't do it, Jas. I can't do it in front of her." The Modern Pioneer Girl had helped me hold on to everything my father and grandmother taught me. Her voice pulled me together after my mother tore me apart and then carried me forward into a new life that Margaret had no place in. I wasn't going to risk the independence I'd gained by debating my mother about my life's worth on national television. That was a game I couldn't win.

"I've heard your mother's advice," Jas said. "She's years out of date. It's long past time somebody took her on and defended finding your own way instead of fitting yourself into someone else's."

I shook my head at Jasmine, already unable to speak. Damn it, I was going to cry. I had really believed, for a few minutes, that I would be able to take the MPG onto that stage and become her. I had almost thought I deserved a place at this table. The truth was I'd never been able to stand up to my mother. Doing it on the *Today* show would require a performance I didn't have in me.

But I knew who did. I grabbed Jasmine's arm. "Then you do it," I said. "Nobody knows who Maggie Strong is. You can go in there and say it. We don't need anyone's approval, or their permission, or their degrees or whatever, to be whole. We just need to believe that we are who we're meant to be." I glanced at the bathroom door. That producer could open it at any minute, looking for her fresh new guest. This was the perfect solution. It was the only solution.

Jasmine was gazing at me with pity in her eyes. She softly

chewed one perfect lip and tapped a finger against her chin. "I know she's a total witch," she said. "But that's exactly why you need to do this yourself."

"I can't, Jas. Twenty seconds in the bathroom can't make me into someone who can."

"I've been trying to make you see that you already are that person for twenty years."

The bathroom door swung open, and the producer's voice broke in between us. "Maggie—Ms. Strong—are you ready?"

We both jumped, still staring at each other. Jasmine narrowed her eyes, her face unreadable. If she didn't do this, we'd just have to apologize and make a run for it, and please God my mother wouldn't see us do it. I started getting my excuses ready—illness, mental breakdown, death—when Jasmine took a deep breath, and transformed. Her shoulders went back. Her hips relaxed into an easier stance. Her face seemed to open, and one eyebrow shot up. She turned to the producer and smiled, not the Jasmine sly grin but a full-wattage open and irresistible beam worthy of a Modern Pioneer Girl.

"I'm always ready," "Maggie Strong" said, and without so much as a look in my direction, she swept out the door.

5

A Superhero Alter Ego

ONCE I WAS sure the coast was clear, I scurried out of there as fast as I could to one of the coffee shops in Rockefeller Center, all tuned to the employer of many of their customers. I should have said no yesterday. I knew better. Or I should have grabbed Jas's hand and run all the way out the door. I probably wouldn't even have been the first person to chicken out at that point.

I might, however, have been the first-ever person to persuade her best friend to impersonate her instead.

I ordered the cheapest coffee available and perched on the edge of a chair with a good view of the screen and subtitles to make up for the moments when the barista's grinds drowned out the audio, waiting for my mother and Jasmine to appear onscreen, happy not to be facing off with the parent who'd never managed to live up to the role.

My mother had always been in motion, always pushing herself and everyone around her forward. I can't remember her ever relaxing. Even hunched over piles of books and papers, she projected intensity, and when she wasn't focused on her own work, she turned that same energy elsewhere. I learned early that it was better not to be its target. If Margaret appeared in the barn, that meant one of two things—either she was looking for my dad, which usually meant yelling and sometimes tears, or she was looking for me, which meant flash cards or counting beads, neither of which I was ever good enough at to satisfy my mother.

My grandmother was different, all hugs and affection and forgiveness, welcoming my help even when "help" was not an accurate way to put it. She'd tell me to put apples in a bowl, for pie or muffins or applesauce or who knew what, probably just to keep me busy, and then she'd take whatever I gave her.

Not Margaret. She'd look at my offering with disappointment. "You can't tell her 'good job' for that," I remembered her telling Bee once. "Rhett, your grandmother said six apples. You can count to six. How many apples are in here?"

I don't remember if there were too many apples or too few. I remember they were our apples, apples I'd picked from Dad's shoulders that morning. I remember the way they smelled, even before you bit into one, and the crunch when you did.

"How many apples, Rhett? You know this."

"Leave her alone, Margaret," Grandma Bee said.

I was going to count the apples. My mother was holding the bowl, waiting. But before I got past "two," Grandma swept down between us, taking the bowl and all the apples.

"Stop this foolishness," she said. "She's helping me in the

kitchen, not enrolling in graduate school, and she's more help than you are."

I don't remember what Margaret said next—something about not having to cook, or not wanting to. What I do remember is scrambling to pick the apples up after Bee flung the bowl to the floor. I remember wanting to go after my grandma, and my mother stopping me.

It was ironic that one of my earliest memories was of my grandmother leaving, because it was Margaret who finally left for good when I was nine. By then, my academic failures had grown to include adding when I was supposed to be subtracting, stumbling over words while reading aloud, and forgetting which was a noun and which a verb, and no amount of strict homeschooling seemed to shape me up. My skill in taking things apart and putting them back together had never, in Margaret's eyes, made up for any of my other shortcomings, which also included untidiness, a tendency to rip and soil anything I wore, and always being outside when I was supposed to be in.

I knew my mother was unhappy. Margaret seemed to hate the farm (endless, backbreaking, thankless work, and then you get up and do it all over again tomorrow), my father (you're capable of so much, why do you stay here?), my grandmother (controlling our lives, why can't we get a place of our own?), her teaching job (the students aren't interested in the work, only in their grades), her boss (I could do it better than he does), and the town (where there was nothing to do, nowhere to go, and no one to talk to). She'd earned her PhD from Yarmouth and walked across a stage in a cap and gown and then returned home immediately to more hissed arguments with my father that ended every time I walked into the room. Then one day I woke up to find Margaret loading her little Volkswagen with suitcases in the driveway. I sat on the steps and watched her pull away.

I had my dad and my grandmother, and after a while it didn't matter that my mother never came back and that our phone calls dwindled. I missed the idea of a mother—someone like Ma Ingalls from *Little House on the Prairie*, or my friend Carney's mom, who taught us to make change when we worked for her at the farmers' market. But I don't think I ever exactly missed Margaret.

Commercials rolled, and then there they were: the *Today* show hosts, my mother, and Jasmine, seated around a comically large table, coffee mugs in front of them as though they were ready for a pleasant chat. It was an impossible vision, the glowing blond adult Jasmine next to a woman who'd last seen her with purple-black hair sporting Doc Martens boots under her graduation gown, deep in a *Pulp Fiction* Uma Thurman phase that hadn't lasted ten minutes once Jas got to UCLA.

Jasmine's time in the makeup chair had left her with a mane of blond waves, intensely outlined eyes, and gloriously red-pink lips. Next to her, Margaret's severe, almost masculine style appeared faded and a little shopworn. She still looked dignified, yes. Commanding even. But behind her trademark stark, black-framed glasses there was no hiding how much my mother had aged, and I didn't know how to feel about it. She looked smaller, somehow. Until she started to talk, and became the same terrifying individual she had always been.

"Don't turn up your nose at a job that seems beneath your abilities," she said in response to the host's first question, as upright as if she'd been starched, her hands folded one over the other as she looked into the camera. The accent that she'd never lost, although as far as I knew she'd never gone back to England after marrying my father and moving to the US, made the platitudes she was uttering sound far more important than they were.

"I started out as a gofer in a college administration office—essentially the mailroom," she declared, a speech I'd heard many times—always leaving out the part where she was an Oxford graduate and a PhD candidate, and commonly regarded as brilliant as well. "I did everything that was asked of me, and then I thought of more things I could do. And even though I was at the bottom of the ladder, I dressed and behaved as though I belonged at the top."

I can only imagine how annoying she must have been. Maybe the host thought the same, because she turned to Jasmine, and I sat up straight, my hands clutched around my coffee. Jasmine looked amazing. She was confident, calm, comfortable—everything I would not have been—and the cameras ate her up. It would have been fantastic, except for one thing:

She didn't know what to say.

"You've had some unusual experiences at the bottom of the ladder," the beautiful host said. "You wrote that you learned 'ten years' worth of lessons' from work that was anything but a traditional starter job—in fact, it was a job many graduates would consider a real comedown." She paused, a clear invitation for "Maggie Strong" to step in, and I could see Jasmine spot the opening—and then come up totally dry, exactly like an actress who had forgotten her lines.

Uh-oh. I couldn't help it. I put my hands up over my eyes in horror. What had I done? I didn't care so much about the book, but I could feel Jasmine's panic from here, knew exactly how her stomach was turning over, how in a minute she would have to get up and run off the stage—

But she didn't. She sat there and smiled, and nobody but me would have known she was feeling any worry at all. The host jumped back in so smoothly that it was almost unnoticeable. "Most graduates wouldn't be thrilled to find themselves working in a fish cannery in Alaska," she said. "But you described it as one of the formative experiences of your life."

Jasmine, I told you about this, I thought frantically. The smell, my cold, raw hands every day, the way the men on the boats made so much more money than the women on the line. How some of us were starting out and some struggling to support families but the one thing everybody shared was that we were supporting ourselves in one of the wildest places left in the world. Jas knew how much Alaska meant to me. It was the first place after leaving the farm where I met people who worked to live, rather than living to work.

"Alaska," repeated Jas. "Alaska was . . . amazing." She put up a hand, holding everyone's attention. I could only hope she had thought of something else to say.

"And working so hard, side by side, every day with people who loved the place like I did"—good, good, that was good—"that was right for me at the time. And maybe the . . . mailroom . . . was right for you at the time." She said "mailroom" with just the right tone of disbelief at the antiquity of it all, and it was so perfect that I could hardly breathe as she went on.

"But where you're wrong is in assuming that the modern equivalent of a mailroom is right for everyone. Or even that it's available. The world has changed. You're setting people up to feel like they've failed before they've even begun."

Margaret, clearly outraged, shot a glare at the male host, who held up his hand. "There's no need to get personal," he said.

Jasmine nearly laughed in his face. "Of course there is," she said. "What's more personal than this?" She rose from her seat, hands on her hips, intent on my mother.

"Let me take you on a tour of the future, lady," she said. "There aren't any traditional starter jobs. There aren't any 'mailrooms.' And we shouldn't feel obligated to look for them. Today's graduates need to think for themselves, defy expectations, and find their own paths."

I wanted to get up and cheer. Margaret, with Jasmine looming over her, stood up suddenly, putting both her hands on the table that separated them as Jas stepped back, and that's when it happened. The huge, substantial-looking table must not have been the solid piece of furniture it played on TV, because when Margaret leaned on it, the table briefly tilted toward the floor. The hosts on her side leapt away as their coffee cups slid off, while Margaret, thrown off-balance, fell backward into her chair, her hands waving wildly as liquid from her own cup spilled into her lap, revealing itself—fortunately—as water rather than coffee.

Onscreen, there was a moment of chaos, but as it quickly became clear that everyone, including my mother, was fine, I started to laugh, not caring what the other coffee shop patrons thought. Jasmine, alone and untouched on the far side of the table, stood watching as assistants rushed onto the set, frantically wiping at the hosts and Margaret alike. The male host, who'd dodged the worst of the spills, was the first to recover himself and quickly walked to the front of the mess. Margaret, now standing, allowed herself to be pushed into position next to him as he smiled at the camera.

"Well, we certainly have a divergence of views here this morning, with lively results," he said. "President Gallagher, I'm sorry our set isn't as sturdy as the ladders to success you hope graduates can find."

My mother smiled thinly.

"Ms. Strong, you've spoken up, that's for sure. Wouldn't you like to also remind new graduates that forging a unique path is great, but sometimes you also need to tread carefully to get ahead?"

Jasmine paused, and for one moment I thought she had again drawn a blank, but then it became clear that the small silence was intentional. Jasmine—as Maggie Strong—put her hands on her hips and spoke emphatically into the camera.

"Hells no," said "Maggie Strong." "If you're somewhere where you can't be yourself, better to be somewhere else."

By now, everyone in the coffee shop, including the barista

and the woman waiting at the counter for her coffee, was staring up at the TV. I was almost crying with laughter while I texted Jas to tell her how amazing she was and where to find me. It was all worth it to watch Jasmine shut my mother down, and I couldn't help but think about how much my grandmother would have adored it. She would have understood—and savored every second.

"That was awesome," the barista said, laughing and turning back to her work.

"'Let me take you on a tour of the future, lady,'" said the waiting woman with a grin.

The cameras had turned off, and there, on the screen, was an image of my book, *The Modern Pioneer Girl's Guide to Life*.

I saw a woman writing it down.

I sat down, waiting. The door of the shop burst open sooner than I expected, and Jasmine came through it in a swirling energy of possibility that I remembered from a few triumphant school performances and auditions but hadn't seen in years. Every head in the place turned as Jasmine rushed over and hugged me, then pushed me out to arm's length and stared into my face.

"You are never doing that to me again, do you hear me? Never. Never." She couldn't really be that mad, not after how great that had gone, and when she gave me a jittery grin, I knew she wasn't.

The woman customer from earlier walked over to our table. "'Let me take you on a tour of the future, lady,'" she said and laughed. "Look." She held out her phone. "It's already on YouTube."

I looked at the screen in surprise, and sure enough, there was Jasmine, gesturing fiercely at Margaret. Apparently, Maggie Strong was a mystery woman no more.

Maybe I hadn't thought this through. But I'd had no other choice.

The woman took back her phone, smiling shyly. "I really loved it," she said. "I can't wait to get the book. Do you mind if I take a selfie?"

Jas shot me a look of wry panic, and I widened my eyes in response. I didn't know what to do either.

Jas shrugged and threw an arm around the woman's shoulder. "Do I mind?" She grinned. "Hells no."

Picture taken, Jasmine's new fan retreated. Jas plunked down in her chair with maximum drama and we leaned toward each other, both looking cautiously around the coffee shop until I couldn't take it anymore. "You did it," I hissed, grabbing Jasmine's arm across the table. "You did it!"

Jas grabbed back, and we began to giggle uncontrollably. "I cannot believe that worked," she said in an equally low voice, then blew any semblance of quiet by letting out a shriek of laughter. "It worked!"

I struggled to control myself, wiping my eyes. "I have never been so freaked," I said.

"Wait, when? When your mom showed up? When you pushed me in front of the bus? What do you mean, you? I'm the one who was freaked."

We laughed harder. Jas was the first to recover. "I mean it. Never again. The Modern Pioneer Girl is on her own now."

I smiled. "That's how she likes it."

6

A Man

ON THE BUS to New Hampshire and the farm that afternoon I watched in shock as the YouTube video appeared everywhere, my follower counts grew, and the book's Amazon ranking dropped. It was the bestseller in self-help within the hour, and I was staring at the m that replaced the k next to my follower count.

I was thrilled. Of course I was thrilled. I should be thrilled. Was I thrilled? I thought of the Modern Pioneer Girl's community as small and friendly, even when occasional evidence (usually in the form of an angry man who objected to the implication that his approval was unnecessary to a woman's happiness) suggested otherwise. Now unknown enthusiasts were sharing GIFs of Jasmine's best moments and posting pictures of the book splayed open, circling favorite phrases. Even protected by my pseudonym and now by my unexpected pseudo face, I felt exposed. This deluge of praise felt unearned and not entirely welcome. I wanted people to buy the book. Of course I did. Every writer did. I was proud of the book and the ways it seemed to help people who were also trying to figure out what they did and didn't need to build a happy life.

It was just . . . this was an awful lot of people.

I shut my phone down and shoved it in my pocket, turning my attention to the familiar view outside the bus window. Pine and hardwood forests alternated with cleared farmland in a landscape with more rivers and stretches of wetlands than billboards, which we'd left behind after passing through the last biggish city along the route. I loved the way towns and villages were rarely visible from the road, with only the occasional farmhouse marking settled territory amid the rich green mountains and hillsides. New Hampshire was not a state with fast food at every exit, and there were often twenty or thirty miles between gas stations, but that's how we did things there. You want something to eat? Get off the highway and get out of your car. I swear my dad had that on a T-shirt.

Dad had not believed in fast anything. When he was alive, our farm, Pioneer Hill, was a pioneer itself in organic growing methods, with the first CSA in the state, although we didn't call it that then. Neighbors paid at the beginning of the season, when we needed the money to get things growing, then got weekly seasonal produce and treats made by Grandma Bee all summer and into the fall.

My plan was to resurrect that glory. After Dad died, my grandmother let the fields and orchards go. She got a little strange for a while. She grew only what she wanted and only when she wanted and favored animals over people, even me, which I kind of understood. Grandma was broken when Dad died. We both were. Together, our grief felt even heavier. She turned me over to my mother, who had just returned to Yarmouth from a university in California to become the dean of arts and sciences. I could have hated Grandma for it, but I didn't. I hated Margaret instead, which was easier, as I had more practice.

My bus dropped me right in front of the college (which was the only reason it ran in the first place). I glanced across the college green to the tower of the library, the president's house out of sight behind it. I hadn't been near it in almost twenty years. When I came to Bowford, I visited the farm; I stayed with Bee and pretended my mother and I were still as far apart physically as we were otherwise. I presumed she did the same.

I turned my back on the green and thoughts of my mother. Backpack on my shoulders, I walked through town. Not much had changed. A bubble tea shop had replaced the drugstore. The bank's windows were still shaded, the hair salon's door was still propped open to reveal its two chairs set into the linoleum floor. Across the street, behind a sort of wooden porch/boardwalk, were the general store and the big town inn next to it, run by the college, both there since forever.

I wasn't all that likely to see anyone I knew. Sometime during my four years at boarding school and then becoming a student at Yarmouth, the people I'd grown up with stopped seeing me as a "townie." Even Carney, my best friend from the farm behind us, and the couple I used to scoop ice cream for at the general store started treating me like an outsider. So when I visited Bee, I tended to keep myself to myself. It was easier. It hurt less.

Still, I kept my head down when I passed the few people who were out, walking by the elementary school I'd never attended, then a line of houses, getting farther apart as you left town. After that, the road curved and a new street sign marked a change in name from Main Street to Pioneer Road, and there, around the bend and at the foot of the big hill that sat between the town and the river, was our driveway.

I stopped at the mailbox, but it was empty. I knew our old neighbors were looking after the animals. They must be getting the mail too. I hadn't sought Carney out for years, but I knew, because small towns don't need Facebook, that she'd moved home to her dad's place a few years ago with her two sons after she and her husband split. Their phone number hadn't changed and I'd let Carney know, in an awkward phone call, which bus I was coming in on, and that I would probably see her tonight.

From here, I could see the top of the big, beautiful hay barn over the trees, its faded red paint set off by the tall oaks that lined the road. In a moment, I'd see the old truck parked in the gravel drive, the front garden with its haphazard deer fencing, the pond, then the porch and the house behind it, both with peeling white paint that could have used a refresh even before I left. I let the familiar feeling of home wash over me, then set off up the driveway. I'd never come home to an empty farmhouse before. I knew even before I got there that it was going to hurt. A lot.

Except that it wasn't empty. There was a truck in the driveway, a big black diesel, and it wasn't Bee's.

The driver's-side door was already opening. Boots emerged, men's ropers. The guy wearing them turned and argued with someone in the cab before backing out quickly and trying to push the door shut—too late.

A dog, a big, sloping wolf-beast of a dog, leapt out and past the man, easily evading the hand that reached for its collar before heading straight toward the barn.

Damn!

Without another glance at the truck and its driver, I went after the dog, sliding out of my pack and dropping it to the ground behind me as I ran. An untrained beast could do more damage on a farm than a dog lover could imagine, and in far less time than it took the average idiot owner to get the dog back under control.

The man from the truck was running right in front of me, his broad plaid back obscuring my view of what was happening. "Grab your dog," I yelled. "Now! There are chickens and I don't know what else in there!"

"I'm trying—I'll get her—"

His voice sounded familiar, but I didn't have time to figure out why. He rounded the corner of the long side of the barn and came to a dead stop just as I heard Teddy, Grandma Bee's llama, utter his unearthly, piercing scream. I stopped too—if Teddy thought there was a threat, the dog might be in more trouble than the chickens—and consciously tried to manage my panic before coming into the animals' range. Calm farmer, calm flock. They were my grandmother's words, and I had drawn on them before. I took a deep breath and forced my shoulders down out of my ears before stepping within sight of the backyard.

The dog had, as I'd known it would, slipped through the split-rail fence and was romping in the mud from a rainy spring, black-and-white fringed tail wagging wildly. Teddy had the small flock of sheep and a mini pony herded in behind him along with the chickens and was facing the dog, one hoof in the air. I walked as quickly as I could to the gate, brushing past my unwanted guest. I didn't want the dog to hurt the animals, but I didn't want Teddy to hurt the dog either. I hoped Teddy would remember me. I was probably the dog's only chance.

"Shhh," I said to Teddy as I opened the gate. "Easy. I've got this."

The dog leapt merrily in the air and spun, barking wildly, and then dropped its chest down to the muck, stretching its legs out in front of it, tail still wagging as it gave one bark. A playful dog could do as much damage as a vicious one, and there was no telling what Teddy would think—

"Betsy!" The man behind me sounded desperate, and I glanced back to see him starting to slide through the fence, dropping his knees into the mud in the process. I gestured to him to stay back—I didn't need anyone else to get hurt here— but he paid no attention. Teddy looked ready to strike, but then the llama planted both feet firmly on the ground and feinted slightly to the right. What was Teddy doing? Was he . . . playing?

Teddy made a small, pouncing leap to the left before bowing his own head down to the dog, who sniffed him curiously before setting about wildly licking the llama's nostrils. Head down, Teddy waited and the man approached cautiously, then grabbed the dog's collar and pulled it away.

I rushed to the llama's side. "Good boy," I said, extending a fist to make sure Teddy was in a touching mood and then rubbing his neck affectionately. "What a good boy." As Teddy relaxed, the chickens and the sheep began to emerge from behind him, pressing against my pants and boots. I'd always wanted a dog as a kid, but Grandma Bee said they were more trouble than they were worth and then, after she got Teddy from a llama rescue, that a llama was worth a dozen dogs. Clearly, she was right.

I leaned on Teddy's brown fuzzy side, rubbing away, as the owner pulled the still excited dog to the fence, struggling to keep his grip on its collar as it wriggled and squirmed in an effort to get back to Teddy and the chickens. The boldest of the sheep, seeing an opportunity in the open gate, trotted after them, sending mud spattering into the air. The man twisted, trying to get the gate shut behind him without losing his grip on the dog, and I got a good look at him for the first time.

"Mike?" If I'd thought about it, I wouldn't have said his name. I would have pretended not to recognize him. I would have been cool, even though seeing him raised the hairs on my arms and set my heart pounding in my chest.

He was older, yes. Gray flecked through his dark curls, and his face was more tanned and worn, but even so, I didn't really have any doubt that this was him. Mike. My first love, until he suddenly wasn't. A guy who was convinced he was Yarmouth's finest from the moment I first saw him in our dorm's hallway until I left him staring after me in the wreckage of his room three years later. Mike taught me that a guy like him was the last thing I needed; it was the first step to figuring out that I didn't need a man at all. Really, my body should recoil at the sight of him. I should be shuddering in disgust.

Apparently, bodies don't work that way. "Mike? What are you doing here?" *What the hell are you doing here*? I should have said. Emphasis on "hell." Or "you." Because what the hell was he doing here?

Mike, struggling with the gate and the dog's collar and not enough hands to make it all happen, didn't answer. "Can you— I can't—"

If I didn't have the animals to worry about, I would have planted a foot on his expensively denimed butt and tipped him right over into the mud. Trying not to notice that the jeans were low-riders, and it was still a butt worthy of appreciation, I shooed the sheep back with big gestures and closed the gate behind the intruders. I turned to find Mike seated on the bench of the picnic table as though he belonged there, the dog held between his knees. He was, at least, breathing like someone who had just come out of a panic, and he should be. That had ended way better than he deserved. But I thought I detected a glint of pleasure in his eye that I'd recognized him, and I wasn't having that.

"What the hell were you doing anyway, letting your dog out of your truck? That dog's not trained. It could have had a chicken down before either of us got to it."

"That's how you're going to greet me, after twenty years?" I stared him down. Yes, it was, and he knew as well as I did that he didn't deserve anything different. "I didn't mean to let her out," he said. "She got past me. And I am sorry—and she is trained; at least, she knows not to chase the animals. She wasn't going to hurt anything."

Yeah, right. He was looking at me, appraising, and suddenly I was grateful that Jasmine had insisted I keep the outfit she'd created for my failed TV debut. I didn't look like I was coming home to the farm with my tail between my legs. I looked like a confident adult woman ready to take over a business. "That's what everybody says, right up until their dog gets in trouble," I said, staying on the offensive. "Teddy could have taken it—her—out with one kick. You can't go risking things like that. You get her back in the truck *now*."

Mike smiled infuriatingly. "Teddy—that's the llama?— didn't look too upset," he said. "I think he liked Betsy. And she certainly liked him. Look, I'm sorry. And I'll take her back to the truck, but I don't have a leash on me, and I'm afraid she'll slip my grip on her collar. Do you have— Did your grandmother use a lead rope or something on Teddy?"

I didn't want to lend him a rope, and I didn't want to have a conversation either. He was clearly waiting for me to ask him—again—what he was doing there, and I wasn't going to give him the satisfaction. I stood still, arms crossed and glaring. Let him drag the dog.

With a sigh, Mike got up and started pulling the dog by her collar. As he did, his jacket and shirt hiked up on one side and I could see a long triangle of skin, lightly tanned, a little hairy. I knew that skin pretty well, a long time ago. And look where that got me.

Teddy's rope was looped over the gate. Fine. I handed it to him. It would get him out of here faster, which was all I wanted.

Once the lead was clipped on, the dog's eyes went straight to her owner, and she sat obediently by his side, waiting for him to move. Border collie, I could see now. Well, no wonder. That was a lot of dog for someone who didn't know what he was doing. Mike started around the barn toward the driveway, and the dog trotted beside him in a perfect heel.

Maybe he kind of knew what he was doing. As I followed him around the side of the building, a familiar voice brought me to a standstill. "Mike? Is everything okay?"

For the second time that day, I took an inadvertent step backward at the sound of my mother's words.

7

Permission

THERE WAS NO Jasmine to shove in front of me this time, and no bathroom to hide in, only my mother, still in the same suit she'd worn that morning, standing next to Mike's truck.

She had the advantage—she obviously wasn't surprised to see me—but I thought I saw a moment of emotion cross Margaret's face before it regained its usual impassivity. She strode forward, like a politician greeting a dignitary, while I stood still. For the barest instant I thought she was going to hug me. I took another half step back, and she stopped an arm's length away.

"Rhett," she said in her clipped tones. My mouth opened, but nothing came out until I took a deep breath and tried again.

"Mom," I finally responded. "Margaret." I realized my hands were shaking, and I felt a surge of warmth through my face and a pounding in my ears. Why did feeling so angry also make me want to cry? I shook it off and concentrated on the fury. How could they blindside me like this? Who did she—who did Mike—who did they think they were, to drop themselves back into my life without any warning when I was already hurting for Bee? And to show up here, where I should have been safe?

Mike slammed the truck's door behind Betsy and returned, a manila folder in his hand. He gestured to Margaret with it. "You told her why we're here?"

Margaret shook her head. "Not yet," she said, and at this clear indication of teamwork between the two people who had caused me more heartache than even my father's death, I boiled over.

"No, she didn't tell me why you're here. I haven't talked to her in twenty years! And I can't even begin to— You should not be here. Neither of you. How did you even know when I'd get here?" But even as I asked, I knew the only possible answer. Carney and her father.

Margaret confirmed it. "I asked Carney to tell me if she heard from you," she said. "I have what I think will be good news, and I wanted to tell you before you had a chance to start worrying about"—she gestured around her, at the farmhouse flanked by the hay barn on one side and the gardens and hay fields on the other—"all of this."

I stared, and she sighed, as if I was letting her down by failing to comprehend what she was talking about. She held out a hand, and Mike put a page from his folder into it.

"This," she said, "is the new Yarmouth Welcome Center, which will double as a home for our admissions and financial aid staffs. The acquisition of the land has been approved by an independent committee, and the hope is to begin construction almost immediately following the sale. We've agreed to a price of 520,000 dollars for the land, which, after transaction expenses, will leave each of us with about 250,000 dollars."

I ignored the paper she was extending to me. "What are you talking about? I don't want to sell this place. And why would I give you half of the money?" With every question I grew angrier. I didn't understand what my mother was doing here, why Mike was with her, or why she thought Yarmouth would ever get its hands on this place that I loved. Everywhere I looked on the farm were memories of my father and grandmother and the life we'd had there. I couldn't get that back, but I had plans, and those plans—like my entire childhood, really—didn't involve my mother.

Mike looked from me to my mother and back again. "Is there somewhere we can sit down?"

"I don't want to sit down," I said. "I want you to leave, both of you. You have no right to be here."

"We're inheriting the farm," Margaret said, ignoring my words. "We need to make some decisions."

I couldn't keep the panic from my voice. "We?" *I* was inheriting the farm. And the only decision I needed to make was how to get my mother off it.

"According to your father's will—" she began, and I interrupted.

"Why are we talking about my father? He's been dead for years. Grandma left me the farm."

"Impossible," Margaret said briskly. "Bee didn't own the

farm. She had the right to live here for her lifetime, and that was all. Now that she has passed, you and I own Pioneer Hill, and it's our obligation to dispose of it responsibly."

Margaret's words rolled past me like boulders. My mother owned half of the farm? Dispose of it? None of this made any sense. Why wouldn't Bee have told me? The farm was meant to be mine and always had been.

I couldn't speak, and Margaret seemed to take my silence as permission to continue. "The place itself is obviously worthless," she said, with a glance around at the tarp anchoring the roof of the porch, the trash bags filled with recycling and old newspapers tumbling off the side, and a tractor with what had to be a load of manure from the barn in it, its front window cracked and the door hanging loosely open. "And with its position right as visitors arrive in Bowford, it's become a real eyesore—but fortunately for us, that also creates an opportunity. The location makes the land quite valuable. This is a very good offer."

I looked from one face to the other as my brain stumbled from one incendiary word to the next. "Worthless," "eyesore"—that was exactly why it was impossible that my father would have ever left Margaret half of Pioneer Hill. "I'm not looking to sell. I'll never sell."

"That isn't up to you," Margaret said.

Mike gave me a sympathetic look that was almost worse than my mother's brisk assumption of authority. I didn't need his pity, not when he was standing there taking my mother's side against me just like he had so many times before. But he spoke before I could say so.

"I'm afraid she's right," he said. "It sounds as if you didn't know the full situation, and I'm sure that's difficult."

I wanted to argue. No, I wanted to explode, to yank that folder from Mike's hands and shred it into a million tiny pieces. Instead, to my horror, I stomped a foot like a child and sputtered an incoherent objection. "But," I began, and found I couldn't go on.

"It's a very good offer," Mike said, his tone gentle. "I helped with the site evaluation for the building, and the land isn't suited for larger-scale farming. Its major appeal is its proximity to the town and college, which means most other potential buyers would be second-home owners, or even developers. We think this is a use that better serves both the town and the college."

"I don't want to sell the farm," I said, my voice sounding thin in my ears. I repeated myself, more fiercely, in the voice of the Modern Pioneer Girl, clinging to the one thing I couldn't lose. "I'm going to live here. Pioneer Hill is mine."

"It isn't," Margaret said. "It's ours jointly, with me as trustee, which means I make the decisions about what will benefit us both."

This couldn't be happening. I needed help—lawyers, bankers, something—to sort through this and explain that she was wrong. "I don't believe you," I said.

She crossed her arms over her chest, sighing and shaking her head. "Rhett. You have no idea what's been happening here."

"No. You have no idea," I said, struggling to keep my voice calm. "I've been back almost every year. Grandma and I always planned for me to take over. I'm going to build the farm back into what it was when I was a kid."

Margaret paused, a hand at her throat. "Every year?"

"Of course." If anything, her assumption that I hadn't was almost more infuriating than the rest. "I wouldn't leave Grandma that long." Did my mother think I'd inherited her willingness to throw people aside when they didn't turn out to be who she wanted? "She was basically the only family I had left."

I hurled the words at her, hoping they'd sting, and maybe they did. "This place can't support itself as a farm," she said, her words coming a little faster and a little higher. "You can't possibly imagine that you want to live here. It would take more than the house is worth just to replace the roof. This offer is the best thing for both of us."

"You're wrong," I said. "The work I've been doing—"

"The work you've been doing?" Something I'd said had hit home, because Margaret looked as angry as I felt now. "I heard all about that from the lawyers who found you after Bee died. Living with someone on his family ranch and throwing yourself into it only to have him dump you for a girl his parents approve of and—since you'd never bothered to formalize things—leave you with nothing? That's not work. That's embarrassing, is what it is."

How did she know about Rafe? "I helped build that place," I said. "And he's going to pay me back—" I didn't really believe that, and it showed in my voice. Damn it. I had nothing to be ashamed of, but I felt like I did. I didn't glance at Mike.

"At least you had the good sense not to have any children

under those circumstances. As it is, you've lost nothing but a few years. I'm trying to help you here—this money will give you a chance to start again. You could finish your degree—"

"I will never finish my degree," I shouted, then, a little embarrassed, brought my voice back down to a more normal volume. "I don't want your help. And that is not what happened. We were partners—and it doesn't matter. What matters is that I'm more than capable of running this place, and I intend to run it. I'll buy your half if I have to."

"That's not an option," Margaret said, aggravatingly calm. "Even if you could afford it, which—to be blunt—I know you can't. This land matters to the community, and your financial future matters to me. I will not watch you destroy one another."

"That's not your decision to make," I said.

"In this case, it is."

I took in a breath to respond, but before I could begin shouting, Mike spoke. "Margaret," he said, putting a hand on her arm. "It might be better to focus on the plans for Pioneer Hill." He turned to me, his voice mild and infuriating. "Try to see the positives. The college funds could restore the barn and the older buildings into something truly beautiful that preserves the landscape of the farm without expecting it to support itself." He took the page from Margaret's hand and held it out to me, but I barely glanced at it. Why would I want to see something he imagined could replace my home? "And a quarter of a million dollars is a lot of money, even after taxes. Most people would be thrilled with that."

"Why the hell do you care?" I couldn't even believe what I

was hearing. By the end of our relationship Mike had turned into a willing tool of my mother's, but he at least used to have a soul. Was this the guy who had once joined me in petitioning the university food service to source its products locally and enlisted the help of several business school friends to show how the choice could benefit Yarmouth as well as local businesses and the environment? Who'd listened to me talk about the farm for hours, stood with me in the fields while I described what it had once been and what it could someday be? Even Bee had been charmed by him, a thought that made me clench my fists even more tightly. I stared Mike down, hoping to make him look away. "Did you finally convince my mother to pay you to do her dirty work? Are you, like, her goon?"

"I'm an architect," he said, and I thought he looked a little abashed at my attack. "This building is my design, and my firm"—was he blushing?—"would build it."

"Not exactly a disinterested observer," I said.

"Maybe not. But that doesn't mean I don't understand where you're coming from." Another sympathetic look, and I felt my face tighten in response. "Sometimes it's not possible to carry out someone's wishes when they're gone, and that can be hard to accept."

The fact that his words were so reasonable only made me angrier. This wasn't "someone," it was my grandmother, and I didn't accept things, I did something about them. Mike didn't understand and I didn't want him to try. "It's more than possible," I said. "I'm going to make this place a farm again. My grandmother wanted me to do this. My father would have wanted me to do it. I intend to do it."

Margaret spoke over my words. "Don't be a fool. This is about you, not your father's crackpot rural fantasy."

I raised my voice, all pretense of keeping my temper abandoned. "My father," I began, but Margaret wasn't done.

"The farm is 120 acres of rocks and bad soil on the side of a mountain that barely supported anyone back in the days when there weren't other options, and you are an inexperienced idealist who wouldn't last a week here. This is what's best for both of us."

"I'm not." She knew one tiny part of my history, and I wanted to blurt out more, but as I fumbled through my brain for what to say next, I realized how incredibly lucky I was that her knowledge stopped where it did. If she knew what had happened this morning, she'd be even angrier, and even more determined to snatch the farm away from me.

The thought stopped my tongue, but it didn't soothe my temper. I threaded my fingers together, then yanked them apart. I didn't need to show how worried I was. The futility of my words against theirs made me feel frustrated and small, just as it always had.

Pioneer Hill was mine, and no one was taking that away. I wanted my mother and her pet architect to leave and leave now.

My eyes landed on my grandmother's John Deere with its loaded bucket and I knew exactly how to make that happen.

I turned and walked away from them both, my mother taking a step after me.

"You're being ridiculous," she said. "You need to calm down and listen to me."

I walked over to the tractor while they stared after me and swung one boot up onto the tall running board. The keys were in it, as they always were. I hoped I remembered how to run this thing.

"No," I said. "What I need is for both of you to get off my place now."

"It isn't your place," Mike said, walking toward me.

"It will be," I said. "And I'm going to clean it up and get it going the way my father and my grandmother meant me to, and neither of you is going to stop me." I sat down in the cab and started up the tractor. Just like riding a bike.

Margaret took several steps back as I reversed. Then I put it into gear and started, at slow tractor speed, toward the driveway. Mike walked along next to me, yelling up into the cab, "We really are trying to help you."

I let go of the steering wheel for an instant to put on the noise-canceling headgear that was looped over it. If nothing else, you can't argue with someone over the sound of a tractor.

"I can't hear you," I called. "I have a lot of work to do. If you won't go, I'm going to go ahead and get started." I stopped the tractor and put a hand to the controls, lifted the bucket with its full load high, then slowly started moving forward again as I opened the door and leaned out.

"I'm going to have to ask you to move your truck," I yelled. Mike said something back, and I made a big show of pulling an earpiece away from my head to listen.

"This is childish," he said. "Stop messing around."

I knew it was childish. But I couldn't face the two of them another second. My mother always brought out the worst in me, and in this moment—the shock of what they'd told me and the grief over my grandmother mixing together potently—I really didn't care. I shimmied the tractor up to the edge of the driveway, driving and reversing, until I lined up the bucket right where I wanted it.

Mike put his hands on his hips and glared at me.

"Tractor bucket's a little loose," I yelled. "I've got to dump this load. Move your truck." I pointed and then inched forward so that the bucket was right above the truck bed, which, I noticed, was downright pristine. City guys always bought too much truck for what they needed. Probably never held anything dirtier than a mountain bike, if that. "It's not going to hold much longer. Get in and go."

Mike didn't budge. Beyond him, I saw my mother's face, flat and expressionless. Our eyes met, and slowly, holding my gaze, Margaret shook her head.

When my mother gave me that familiar stop-that-this-instant look that had held me in such thrall as a child, the fire of decades of freedom lit my soul. I tilted the bucket of the tractor to allow an entire spring's worth of horse and chicken shit to slide, almost gracefully and with a satisfying *whomp*, into the back of Mike's truck. A little sprayed over the sides, but for the most part, my aim was true.

In the immortal words of Taylor Swift, there's nothing I do better than revenge.

8

A Plan

THE GLORY OF revenge fades fast. One minute, I was laughing while I watched my mother and Mike pull out of the driveway, but the next I was left with what I'd learned—and the heat of something like shame in my neck and chest over what I had done.

Even if it was pretty funny.

I stared out the tractor window at the farmhouse. The big hay barn was beside me. The horse barn sat behind both, the longer side of its rectangle snuggled up close to the backs of both of the other buildings, letting my great-great-however-many-times ancestors stay close to home and out of the wind while tending their animals. Out in front of me, behind the old farm stand, stretched the fields and pond and the hill beyond them, an idyllic view that I never thought I'd lose. My mother had to be wrong; that was all. This was Bowford. Someone would know the truth. I'd have to go find out.

The Baileys ran the farm behind ours, no distance at all

over the fields but a mile and a half or so on the road. I took my old bike, not wanting to show up unexpectedly behind their house the way I would have as a kid. I couldn't remember a time when I didn't know the Baileys. Carney and I grew up together, just like our dads did, playing and staying out from underfoot until we were old enough to help with the real work of the farms. I'd be the sixth generation of Smiths to run Pioneer Hill. Carney's grandpa bought their place in the sixties, a back-to-the-land success story. Her dad never left the farm, and it didn't seem to matter to their friendship that my dad chose Yarmouth and then Oxford over UNH. Earl Bailey welcomed Charlie Smith home when he returned with a very pregnant British wife, and even if Carney's mom could probably have done without her snooty new neighbor, I still grew up feeling as if the Baileys were family.

The Bailey kids and I were barn rats, riding bareback on the trails, scorning helmets, picking berries, and foraging for mushrooms we sold to the inn's chef. Carney went to the local school and while her brothers were loud in their intent to get out of Bowford, Carney—like me—loved everything about our life.

Carney and I mostly stopped talking after my dad died, then lost touch for real when she went to UNH and I got into Yarmouth. There was one moment, that last summer, when I was back from Miss Postan's School for Girls and she'd just graduated from the high school in the next town over. My mother had arranged for me to intern in our senator's office in DC, where I'd spend most of the summer walking her dog. I came home to find Carney and her dad and brothers cutting the hay in our field and throwing the bales up into their truck. I couldn't help, or I didn't think I could. Margaret was expecting me for dinner at the college, and I had barely had time to drop my suitcase and freshen up, as I knew she would expect me to do, but watching them do the work I'd grown up doing gave me a twist in my gut that made me pull over my mother's car and get out.

It was Carney who walked across the field to me, brown curls spiraling out of the back of her John Deere baseball cap. The sun had brought out the freckles she fought every summer, making her lighter brown skin look almost as dark as her dad's from a distance. Even dressed to stack hay, she'd had a newly-put-together, adult appearance that felt unfamiliar, and I hadn't known how to greet her. I'd stumbled over my words, saying something like *Hey, how's it going,* and she'd put a hand on her hip and stayed just too far away for comfortable conversation. "Good," she'd finally said. "Congrats on Yarmouth. Your mom must be proud."

I'd heard a world of meaning in that sentence then, and I heard it now. She was the girl who was sticking to the plan. I was the sellout. My appearance then—the skirt and ballet flats, sleeked-back hair and pale cheeks—said everything about who I'd become. I couldn't remember if we said anything else. In my mind, I slunk off without another word.

Now I was back, and so was she. Maybe we'd both learned that sometimes things don't work out like you planned. Maybe I'd ask her about it. Maybe we'd talk again.

Maybe.

Dropping my bike in their driveway was like traveling

back in time. If anyone knew what my dad and grandmother had been thinking, it would be Earl.

Carney welcomed my arrival with a smile as she came out of their greenhouse, wiping her hands on her shorts. She looked just the same, and as I said so, I felt a little self-conscious about my Jasmined-up look. At least I had on my own boots.

Carney didn't seem to notice what I was wearing. Instead, she looked a little surprised by the bike, so after we exchanged hugs, I tried to explain how I'd ended up riding over.

"The truck wouldn't start," I said. "I know I could have walked, but I was in a hurry." And I needed to burn off the adrenaline from my mother's appearance by pumping the bike up the hills between our houses, or I might explode.

I was about to ask for Earl, but Carney was laughing. "You going to have him trot along next to you?"

Now it was my turn to look surprised.

"You're here for Brownie, right? I've taken him home three times now, I think. You're going to have to fix his fence good."

I must have looked as confused as I felt, because Carney, turning toward the smaller of their barns, explained over her shoulder. "Brownie. The mini pony. He gets out, and when he does, he either comes here or he goes over to Preeda Walker's. Your grandmother always had him on a diet."

She gestured to the fat little beast with a shiny brown coat and a thick mane standing in a stall just inside the barn door. "I don't really mind—he's a funny little dude—except when he gets into the berries." She took a rope and began to open the stall door. "Bee kept saying she'd get someone in to help her out with the paddock, but she never did."

"I'm so sorry," I said. "You're right, I would have walked if I'd known he was here. I'll have to come back for him." In all the excitement, I hadn't even noticed that there should have been two minis. "I came to talk to your dad." Too late, I realized my mistake. "And to check in with you. About the farm. And say hi."

Carney shut the stall again on a clearly offended Brownie, shrugging. "What's up?"

I didn't know how much I wanted to explain. "Well, my mom came by—"

"Oh." Watching Carney's face, I realized that she knew. "She told you about selling the place, then? You must be pretty happy about that."

"I— No, not really."

"You should be. Your land's worth about twice as much as ours because it's so close to town. Not that we're selling, so really it's good, because the property taxes would kill us, but still. You get a nice chunk of change to head back out of town." She'd stopped looking at me and was walking back out of the barn. Her voice sounded hard and tired, and she looked tired too. Her legs were too thin between her cut-off jean shorts and boots, and her springy brown curls, tugged into a ponytail, were streaked with gray.

"I don't want to head back out of town," I said. It came out louder than I meant it to, and she turned to look back at me. "I was planning on staying. Starting up the farm stand, getting the orchard back into shape, maybe do the CSA again. But if my mom wants to sell the farm— I just can't believe my dad left it to her. I thought your dad might know if it was true."

Carney stopped and turned, and I couldn't read her expression. Mistrust that I wanted to stay? Scorn that I would pass up this chance to sell the land and be done? I knew the old Carney wanted nothing more than to be the one in her family who carried on at the farm. But people change. Maybe Carney didn't want to be judged by who she used to be any more than I did.

She turned away again. "Dad's cleaning the baler," Carney said, and I was about to ask her how long she'd been back when Earl came around the edge of the shed and I forgot everything else. He looked just the same, average height, balding, but striking because of his deeply tanned and wrinkled face. I'd never seen him in a hat—and rarely in a shirt—and his skin truly was the color and texture of a worn leather baseball glove. We didn't hug, but I could smell the mix of gasoline and grass that hung around him as he greeted me.

"Rhett was thinking she was going to take over Pioneer Hill," Carney said. "Get it running again."

"Ah," said Earl.

I waited for him to say something else—for either of them to say something—and when they didn't, I went right to the point. "My mother came over," I said. "I thought I was supposed to inherit the farm, but she says it's half hers." Suddenly, my rushing over here seemed foolish. What did I expect Earl to tell me? "I guess I should go to the lawyers," I said more slowly. "But I just can't believe it. I came over here to see if you knew what happened."

"Your grandma had it for life," he said. "It's how your grandfather left it. Then Charlie left it to you and Margaret."

Hearing the words declared so flatly, by someone whose word no one in Bowford would ever doubt, punched straight through any hope I had left that my mother was lying, or that there was some mistake. Now I knew. If I wanted Pioneer Hill, I would have to go around my mother to get it.

"Why?" The word burst out of me, and my anger came with it. "Why? Why would he do that? And why didn't Bee know about it? She's been telling me for years that the farm was going to be mine, and now— Do you know why? What was he thinking?"

Earl shifted his weight from one foot to the other. "Maybe if you'd been around more, you'd have had more time to figure that out. Your grandmother could have used help for a while now."

His accusation stung and I responded sharply, defending both of us. "Bee didn't need help, and she didn't want help. She liked living alone." I came home to Pioneer Hill for a few quiet weeks every year between jobs or, since I'd met Rafael, when things slowed down on the ranch. I'd do some of the bigger jobs that piled up in my absence. I always suggested staying. I would have given up everything, even the ranch, if she'd asked, but she always shook her head.

"You've got a whole world to be in. You don't want to be here with me, and I'm set in my ways." She would laugh and push me toward the nearest door. "See? I don't even want you here now. Get out of my kitchen." I got used to it after a while. It was just the way she was.

Earl crossed his arms. "That's what she said, maybe. Not what it looked like."

"Why is everyone so caught up in what the farm looks like? It looks fine. A little raggedy, maybe, but fine for a farm that's not really producing much, and once I get it running again, it will look great. A working farm's not a showplace." I looked around as I said it and had to admit to myself that, aside from the kids' toys everywhere, the Bailey farm very nearly was. But even here, there was evidence of work to be done and work in progress. "I mean, look. You've got a porta-potty over there, and I bet that old tractor bucket hasn't moved in years. And half of that field over there is practically a wilderness."

"That's the asparagus," Earl said. "Our season's over."

I realized, too late, that I didn't sound like I was defending Bee's farm. I sounded like I was attacking Earl's. "I didn't mean—"

"I know what you meant," Earl said. "You're going to come back for that pony, right?"

I nodded, biting back anything else I wanted to say. This wasn't doing me any good.

"Then we'll see you again later." He walked off in the direction of the house. Carney and I watched him go.

"Well, that went great," I said. Carney laughed a little. "I really didn't mean anything. About the asparagus."

Carney moved a plastic bucket full of toy tools out of her way and sat down on the bench outside their barn, patting the worn wood in invitation. "It's been hard for him," she said. "Your grandmother didn't want his help either, not with most things. And he can see what needs to be done, and he feels like he's letting your dad down somehow."

"It's letting my dad down to let my mother sell the property to the college," I said, sitting next to her. "Did you know too? That my grandmother couldn't leave me the farm? She must not have understood what was happening, and now . . . I don't know if there's anything I could have done, but now things are a real mess."

"I didn't know you thought she was leaving it to you," Carney said. "I know about the college's proposal. Your mom's been talking it up. They might need the town board's support to do it, but with the farm in the shape it's in—well, people are inclined to think anything would be better than letting it all just fall down."

I looked up sharply at this. "Why would they need the town board?"

"Because it's zoned for agriculture, and you can't sell land that's in agricultural use for other purposes without getting some kind of approval. I mean, really, it's not in use and it hasn't been for a long time, so it's basically a formality. That's what happened when they built those dorms a few years ago— a few people wanted to stop it, but because the Taylors hadn't grown anything in that field for, like, ten years, they couldn't."

"So if the land is being farmed—"

"Then it can't be sold to be anything but a farm without some kind of change in the zoning."

I stood back up quickly. "Then my mother can't sell it to the college," I said. "She can still sell it, but not for this."

"If it was being farmed." Carney looked up at me. "You know your grandmother hasn't done anything like that for a long time."

"Maybe not," I said, grabbing my bike. "But I will."

She looked doubtful. "I'm not sure it works that way."

"It has to. Because I'm not giving up Pioneer Hill. And the town never wants the college to expand, right? As long as I'm doing something, that should be enough," I said.

"It's not really like that anymore," Carney said. "Now—other towns around here, the main streets are dying. Some of them can't even keep their schools going. Yarmouth means businesses want to come here, people move in. Everybody gets that. Of course they'd rather have a farm than a dorm, but better a dorm than a dump. Not that I'm saying the farm is a dump."

I was pretty sure that was exactly what she was saying. "You can say it," I said. "Because it won't be. Not with what I'm planning." I was almost dizzy with the hope she'd lit under me. If there was anything I knew I could do, it was turn a run-down farm around. All I needed was a little time. It was graduation next weekend, and then college reunions—there was no way my mother could push this through during one of the busiest times of the Yarmouth year. "Remember what it used to be like?"

Carney and I would pick blueberries with families, showing them which of the many bushes were best for pie and which for eating out of hand. Take my grandmother buckets of them and then raspberries and then apples for pies to sell in the farm stand alongside whatever else was in season, from spring greens to pumpkins, with everything in between. Pioneer Hill's location was so perfect that other farms brought in some of their produce and a loose system of specialties had emerged—strawberries from Baileys', onions and garlic from another farm, flowers from somewhere else. Dad's thing was heirloom tomatoes, in colors no one had seen anywhere else in those days, and of course his book had been stacked behind the counter.

We'd been a team, me and my dad and Grandma Bee, and our Pioneer Hill had been glorious.

"I remember," Carney said. "I'm not sure anyone else does. You've been gone a long time."

"But now I'm back." I pumped my arms high. "So look out, Bowford. Things are going to start moving fast."

Carney got up more slowly than I had, but she was smiling. "Okay," she said. "Tell me how I can help." As she spoke, a boy who looked to be about eight appeared, followed by a smaller version.

"Mom," he said, his voice anxious, "*Frozen* is over. Can we watch *Brave*?"

"No," she said. He looked set to argue, and the younger one to possibly cry, but Carney was too fast for them. "You can take turns riding Brownie while I run him home. This is Rhett; she's going to live there."

"In Miss Bee's house?"

"In Miss Bee's house." She turned back to me. "This is Oscar," she said, pointing to the bigger boy. "And that's Martin. We'll come over and walk you through chores, anyway."

"Perfect." I'd need a refresher. I smiled at her warmly, and she smiled back, and I felt better than I had in hours, maybe better than I had since my plane landed. This was what I wanted to do. "Meet you there, Oscar and Martin."

I stood up on the pedals and swung hard out of their

driveway, aiming to beat Carney back. I couldn't do a lot to clean the place up in ten minutes, but I could show her that I was working on it. Because while I could run Pioneer Hill on my own, I would need a little help getting started. I'd already decided one thing. By Thursday, before Yarmouth graduation, the farm stand would be open for business.

9

Regrets

I DIDN'T EVEN go into the house. Instead, I started clearing the barnyard where Carney would see it, restacking fallen wood and cranking up the lawn mower to quickly mow a strip back to the path between our farms, because nothing looks better on a farm in spring than freshly mowed grass.

My phone rang the minute I turned off the mower, and with a quick glance toward the Baileys' to make sure they weren't coming yet, I slid my earbuds out of my pocket to answer.

"Hey, Rhett here," I said, and Jasmine's teasing voice returned the greeting.

"Jas here," she said. "Qué pasa, familia?" Jasmine's grandmother was from Puerto Rico, which meant her Spanish was almost as good as mine. But I had too much to tell her to play around.

"You will not believe what's happened." I poured out the

whole story, starting with Mike, then my mother, the farm, then Carney's good news, before I ran out of breath.

She let out a low whistle. "Okay, that's a lot," she said. "What are you going to do?"

"That's easy," I said. "This has to be a working farm? It's going to be a working farm. Starting right now."

"What does that even mean?"

"I don't know, but I'll figure it out. Meanwhile, what it means is I clean. Figure out what's growing and grow more of it. Plant some stuff. And I'm going to open up the farm stand. Anything we used to do, I'm doing again. Nobody's declaring Pioneer Hill dead on my watch."

"Got it. But I still don't get what Mike was doing there," Jas said.

"He's the architect. Or the builder. Or something." His parents had run an architectural firm in New York, but I thought they built skyscrapers, not piddly buildings for even the fanciest of colleges.

"So why would he be working for your mom?" Her voice took on a mischievous tone. "Maybe he was there to see you. All these years, he's been pining, and then he overheard your mom talking about this somewhere and he threw himself at her just because he knew you were coming back."

"Do not even joke about that," I said. "If there is anyone in the world I never want to see again, it's him."

A satisfied chuckle from Jas, who knew she'd hit a sore spot. "You two were intense," she said. "Didn't you feel anything?"

"Hatred. Loathing." I left out the part where I'd found myself contemplating his jeans.

"Do you think he's married?"

"No ring," I said, and she shrieked.

"I knew you'd look," she said.

"Stop it. He's a horrible person, and he probably has a girlfriend, and I have way bigger problems."

"He might have changed."

"He wants to tear down the farm and build a welcome center for Yarmouth," I said. "So maybe he's worse."

"Fine, I get it. No Mike. Just Rhett, farming away madly by herself like a true Modern Pioneer Girl. But how are you going to open a farm stand on a farm that doesn't grow anything?"

I'd been thinking about that. "We used to sell stuff from other farms, so I'll see what I can find. I'll buy it and resell it if I have to. And I can make some stuff."

At that, Jas snorted. "You can't," she said. "That is really not your forte."

"I make excellent Rice Krispies Treats," I said. "And iced coffee. I'm very good at iced coffee."

"That isn't baking, that's combining."

"Whatever," I said. "It doesn't have to be amazing. It just has to be open."

"But you want people to come, right? And impress your town fathers or whatever." She sounded a little excited. "What if I come help? Seriously. Clear out the spare bedroom. I'm practically in the car."

It was tempting, but I could do this on my own. "You don't have to do that," I said. "I can manage."

"No, really. It would be fun."

Having Jas here would be more than fun. It would be amazing. And if she baked things too—"But don't you have donuts to make?"

"Yeah," she said, drawing the word out. I wanted to laugh, but I heard something in her voice that made me hesitate.

"Jas? Everything okay?"

There was a pause. "I'll tell you when I get there," she said. "It's fine. Really. Everything's fine."

"Jas—"

"I'll see you tomorrow," she said, and hung up too quickly for me to ask anything else. Carney and her boys appeared, waving, and I was immediately caught up in the flurry of activity that was farm chores with two helpers who were too young to provide much in the way of real help. In between bringing in the horses and penning up the sheep, I told Carney what I had planned and was delighted when she actually seemed pleased. She threw out occasional ideas while reining in her kids with a practiced ease I had to admire, praising one for his gentle egg collection while catching the other just as he was about to pull the hose out of the water bucket without turning off the water first. When we finished, we sat down at the picnic table and watched the boys look for frogs at the edge of the pond while she gave me a list of farms that might be willing to sell enough produce to open the farm stand on such short notice.

"Including some Baileys' strawberries?"

Her lips twisted a little, just like they did when she was a kid and didn't know whether her dad would approve of some new plan. "I'll try," she said. "Let me see how we do this week."

I wanted to push her, but I stopped myself. The Carney I'd known wasn't much of a risk taker. But when it was important, she came through in the end. I'd have to wait and see. "Thank you," I said. "For all of this. And for"—I gestured to the farm—"all of this. I know it's been a lot of extra work."

"That's okay," she said, her eyes on the boys in the reeds. "Dad's not doing any animals right now, so the kids love coming over here."

There was something else I wanted to thank her for, but I didn't know how to put it. "I'm happy to have them," I said. "And I really appreciate— It's been so long." She didn't have to be so welcoming. She didn't have to help. I wouldn't have been surprised if she hadn't wanted anything to do with me.

"Yeah," she said. "It has. For both of us." As she spoke, excited shrieks came from the pond—the kids had caught a frog. She was gathering them to go, leaving the frog behind, when one of them—Martin, the smaller one—looked up at me.

"Do you have any kids we can play with?"

Carney looked appalled, but I laughed. "I don't," I said. "Just Brownie."

"I like Brownie."

His brother took his hand and pulled him toward the path. "Not all grown-ups have kids," he said firmly. "Like Uncle Darius." Carney caught my eye apologetically.

"I really don't mind," I said. "It's not a sore spot." It wasn't. Living like I had, surrounded by other expats and travelers, not having kids never felt like a big deal. A lot of people didn't.

And Rafe was a little younger than me and always willing to avoid the conversation, at least until it turned out he hadn't been avoiding it with everyone. Maybe I'd feel differently when I let myself think about it. Maybe I already did. But right now I had other things to worry about. "I can barely take care of myself."

"You seem like you're doing okay," Carney said. The boys caught her hands and tugged her along and she let them.

"Thank you again," I called, and she looked back at me.

"You're welcome," she said. "It's nice to have you back."

I found myself hoping she meant it.

The farm got a little quiet after they left. I sat at the picnic table until the light was gone, searching for a definition of "working farm" and reading websites about trust and estate law until my eyes ached and I had to face the truth: I was avoiding going into the house. I picked up my backpack from where I'd dropped it earlier and climbed the porch steps. Alistair, my grandmother's big coon cat, weaved in and out of my ankles as I opened the unlocked door. I dropped my pack and scooped him up, taking comfort from his fuzzy heft, but he twisted in my hands and I let him jump to the counter and back to the floor, where he led the way to his food dish. I looked around and found a stack of cat food cans on the counter, probably left by Carney, and opened one up.

At least I'd made somebody happy.

All day, I'd successfully managed to focus on the troubles ahead while avoiding the one that had brought me here, but there was no getting around it any longer. If I opened the cabinets, there would be food my grandmother had bought. In every drawer, hers were the last hands to touch the contents. I couldn't stop feeling like she'd come through the door any minute, pulling eggs from every pocket to fill the collection of cartons stacked on a shelf by the door. I leaned against the counter, surveying the room. An old picture of the two of us, stuck to the fridge, stared back at me.

I should have come back more. Should have spent more time with Grandma Bee. Now she was gone, and it was too late for that—but it wasn't too late for everything else. I was back, and I was here to stay. I hoped.

I looked at Alistair, now cleaning a paw disdainfully in the windowsill. I reached out and scooped him into my arms again before settling onto the old love seat next to the wood-stove, kicking my feet up on its cold hearth and settling the cat into my lap. This time he stayed, although he resumed his paw cleaning, just to show me, purring a little as I scratched his head hard and then nuzzled my face between his ears.

I had what passed for a plan. I was far from the first joint heir to face this problem, and as with most problems, there were solutions. First, I'd put a stop to my mother's plan of selling to the college. Then I'd take out an estate loan—sort of a mortgage on the farm—and use the money to buy her out. That would work, if I could persuade a bank I was a good risk for taking over the loan as the owner of the property. And if I could find the ten thousand or so dollars I'd need to get the process started.

And if I could persuade my mother to go along with it.

That last part didn't just sound hard. It sounded impossible. But my dad had been the kind of guy who mixed up Lewis

Carroll and the army, frequently announcing that we'd do six impossible things before breakfast, and I took after him. I wasn't going to let him, or my grandmother, down.

I shifted around and pulled my phone out of my pocket without disturbing Alistair. I needed a pep talk. What would the MPG say? What didn't she "need" that most people would want in this situation? I started to write, and Alistair pushed his head into my hands for a moment, demanding a return to petting, but gave up and curled up again, gently rumbling in the trademark Alistair purr.

You don't need a sure thing. Of course I'd like a sure thing. Who wouldn't? But maybe that wasn't even the way to look at it.

Sometimes sure things are great. Oreos. A peaceful walk on a sunny day, the third book in the Outlander series, your favorite episode of The Office: *sure things and we love them for it. But sometimes you need to take a flier. To run out and jump and fling yourself at the rope dangling from the tree and just hope you catch it. Maybe you miss and you have to try again. Maybe you miss and there's no second shot. But you gave it your all, and if life is all sure things, that's not really living.*

I hadn't posted anything to the MPG's account in days, besides the few travel shots that had caused so much trouble. I wasn't traveling, I was staying put, and I hadn't quite figured out how I wanted to play that online, but this would be easy and it would be fun to get something fresh up. I pulled out an image of a rope swing and then, after some thought, dislodged Alistair to add a second picture of the third Outlander book, pulled from Grandma Bee's shelf, splayed open, spine up next to an old cracked plate with a gold pattern on it that was similar to the book cover. I added a few Oreos, all arranged on a distinctive old cream-and-brown quilt that had been draped over the kitchen couch since I was a little girl. I was good at making pretty pictures out of nothing.

I popped the account open and hit the plus sign, adding pictures and words and the MPG's signature emoji string—heart, heart, muscle arm, smiley face cowboy hat, horse—and posted, feeling better. I didn't need a sure thing. I liked a challenge. And if I couldn't bear the thought of losing this one, that just meant I couldn't lose.

It was long past time to call it a day, but once you open Instagram, it somehow just sort of stays open. My hands slid into the usual social media dance, liking and commenting and re-sharing. I expected the bump from Jasmine's MPG appearance to have begun to die down by now, so the numbers that faced me came as a shock. I'd been tagged in . . . That had to be wrong.

The video of Jasmine schooling my mother, and Margaret's subsequent pratfall, had been shared hundreds of thousands of times, and the hearts and the cheers and the crying-laughing emojis all over the MPG's profile were the direct result. People all over were talking about, and to, the MPG.

Hands shaking, I opened my email. It, too, was full of new messages, although far fewer. Most were from Emily, my editor. Why didn't I tell her I was going on the *Today* show?! OMG!

I never even thought to tell Emily. I opened her most recent message.

WHERE ARE YOU?! Everyone wants to talk to you. I want to talk to you. Call me!!! Things are happening and we need to jump on it.

Call her? I was terrified of Emily. When she tracked me down through my Instagram three years ago, she changed everything. I thought I was happy with Rafe. My MPG posting had slowed down since we met. There were endless amounts of work to do to turn his family ranch around, and I never felt like it was mine to write about. I had started to feel like maybe I didn't need the MPG anymore.

But Emily lit a fire under me. Soon I had a book deal, and a lawyer who helped me set up an LLC and a business bank account for my new pseudonym. Emily knew my real name, but Margaret Smiths are a dime a dozen, and we both agreed: Maggie Strong was the perfect author for *The Modern Pioneer Girl's Guide to Life*. That decision to use a pseudonym freed me to write the book I would have wanted to have when I was younger, and once I started I didn't want to stop. I hid myself away every chance I could to finish the book, frustrating Rafael and probably contributing to our eventual end. Until Emily came along, I hadn't realized how much I needed an outlet for myself in a world where I would always be on the outside, no matter how fluent I was in Spanish or how much I was doing for the business. Emily and the MPG reminded me that there was at least a tiny world where I belonged.

Pretty soon, without ever meeting in person, Emily knew me better than anyone ever had. She pushed me hard on the book. It started as just expanded Instagram posts, but it became so much more—an entire narrative of evolution that felt like mine, but also separate from me. Over and over, she put a finger on the moment when something ultimately changed in me, and those moments became the story. The resulting book was as much her as me. I don't know what I did to get so lucky.

That didn't mean I wanted to call her. But it did mean I was afraid not to.

I'd resumed my seat on the couch, and Alistair, probably starved for human company, leapt up next to me again, rolling over and stretching out a white belly for stroking. I obliged, dropping my head back against the sofa and letting out a breath I hadn't even realized I was holding. It was after eleven. Too late to call anyone now. My eyes were drifting shut. Alistair woke me again, then again, and then I was asleep.

10

Approval Again

I TOOK MY time doing chores on my own the next morning, reacquainting myself with old friends and making new ones. I held out a closed fist to touch the noses of Bingley and Darcy in their stalls. I knew and loved those two already, along with Teddy, Brownie, and S'mores. Brownie really was adorable, but I had no illusions about the little escape artist. He'd been standing outside his stall when I showed up, butting his head into the door to the grain room. My first job after getting everyone fed, watered, and properly greeted would be to move the latch on his stall up and out of his reach. I knew Bee had been meaning to do it for ages, but I think she mostly thought Brownie was funny.

I lifted the heavy shock of his mane out of the little pony's face and looked into his eyes. "It's a new regime, little buddy," I said, tucking him back into his stall for now. "You'll get used to it."

I freed the chickens from their coop and rubbed a fuzzy head over the door of the big sheep stall before getting out the morning's grain, which Carney had helped me scoop the night before. In so many ways Bee was everywhere here too: the grain chart above the sink in her handwriting, the painted labels on the stalls, the "My Pets Poop Breakfast" cross-stitch on the wall. That one must have been a gift, because while the sentiment was perfect for Bee, her idea of a quiet indoor winter craft was retiling a bathroom, not stitching a seam.

But Bee clearly hadn't been on top of her usual DIY game for a long time. The animals were healthy, but shaggy and unkempt, and so was the rest of the place, inside and out, too much so to have really changed since my last visit. Earl's words wouldn't leave me. Bee had clearly needed help, had for a long time. She hadn't wanted that to be true, and neither had I, but I should have known. Maybe I even had known. Maybe I'd been so caught up in my life with Rafe that I'd refused to see it, because recognizing how much things were changing would have meant I'd have to do something about it.

After I fed the animals and walked them out to their various paddocks for the day, I took inventory. Two horses, two minis, one llama. Fences falling everywhere. Watering systems that didn't seem to have worked in years. Piles of recycling, rusting garden tools, grain bags, and baling twine everywhere. Seventeen chickens, all new since my last visit. As for the sheep, I had to admit I wasn't sure which I knew and which I didn't. You had to spend a lot of time with sheep to be able to tell them apart.

I was determined to have that time. The sunny spring morning, the prospect of Jasmine's arrival, and the discovery of a fridge full of eggs Carney had been collecting that represented my first stock for the farm stand fostered a sense of optimism. Pioneer Hill was practically working again already, and as anxious as I was about calling Emily, I was also hopeful. The advance from *Guide* was long gone, but if the book kept selling well, there would be more money from it eventually, money I could put toward the mortgage, or the massive repairs I could see were needed everywhere I turned. Maybe I didn't need money, but I could sure use some.

No shame in that.

Emily had put her mobile number on the email, and when I called, she picked up instantly.

"Maggie!" I'd never heard her sound so delighted. "I cannot believe you did that!"

"I'm sorry I didn't tell you," I started, then hesitated. Could she tell my voice wasn't Jasmine's? Did anyone listen to anything that closely?

"It doesn't matter. It's awesome. It's amazing. The book is sold out practically everywhere—we're going into a third printing. I'm so excited for you."

"Me too," I said cautiously, keeping my sentences short. Another printing sounded promising. I had to ask. "So it's selling well?"

Emily didn't seem to notice anything unusual. "Absolutely. We're delighted. And now that you're back, there's more we can do. I want to put you in touch with the publicity team here."

"Oh, no—I'm not really back." This was not where I hoped this conversation would go. Emily, clearly confused, didn't respond. "I mean, I am, but I've already left New York. And I don't have any plans to come back or anything. That was kind of a one-off."

"And it was an amazing one-off. But you don't have to be here to do more. We have requests for radio or you could do TV by satellite—where are you?"

"New Hampshire," I said, hoping that would dissuade her. "In a teeny-tiny town with, like, basically no reception for anything." That was mostly true. We dropped mobile calls constantly up here, with all the mountains and trees.

"New Hampshire? Where?"

I hesitated. People had heard of Yarmouth, of course. But they hardly ever knew the town. "Bowford."

"No way! I have family in Bowford. I went to Yarmouth."

I wanted to smack myself in the forehead. Why hadn't I made something up? I knew why. Because I never lied to Emily. There was stuff I kept to myself—she didn't know that the university I'd walked away from was Yarmouth, or any other telling details. She knew I liked staying anonymous, and she'd helped me make sure the book didn't take that away. And now I'd stuck a big fat boot right through it, because Bowford was simply not big. If she had family here, I knew them, and they knew me—the real me—or knew someone who did.

"I'm just passing through," I said quickly. "I don't know where I'll end up. I'm on the move. But not toward New York. Maybe Canada."

Emily talked right over me. "It would be great to meet up in person someday," she said. "But right now—you sure you can't hold still for an hour or so? Because"—she paused dramatically—"Terry Gross is interested."

Terry—*Fresh Air*, you mean? NPR?"

"Exactly," Emily said. "Now do you think you can find a cell phone tower in the wilderness?"

No. In fact, no, I did not. I didn't want to talk to Terry Gross, or maybe I did, but I didn't want to talk to Terry Gross if she was expecting Jasmine. I couldn't even be the audio version of Jasmine's MPG.

"I don't know," I said. "I'm not very good at that stuff."

"You were amazing," Emily started to say, but I cut her off.

"I didn't like it," I said. "I don't think I want to do it again."

"You don't say no to *Fresh Air*," Emily said, and it was pretty much exactly what Jasmine had said, and oh man did I ever wish I'd said no to the *Today* show. "I get that you're nervous. But you'd be great. And we could help you get ready."

"I just . . . the whole TV thing—"

"This isn't TV. It's radio. Look, I have to have the publicity team call you anyway. Don't decide anything. Don't even say anything. They'll be in touch."

She hung up before I could protest any further. I put my head down on the picnic table and started banging it gently against the wood.

What. Was. I. Thinking.

I had to say no, absolutely one hundred percent no.

And then I had to change my phone number. And share some pictures of some very rural, distant land. No MPG here in New Hampshire. Look somewhere else. My phone screen lit up with a text notification. From Jas, a picture. I sat up and opened it. It was a very flat tire, squashed against dirt and gravel.

Your road ate my tire. Help.

11

Strong Arms

I REPLIED TO Jas instantly.

On my way. On Pioneer Road?

> Yep never mind dude in black truck just
> pulled up, will flirt for help

Dude in black truck . . . it couldn't be. That would be too much. I ran to Grandma's truck and grabbed the tool kit from the floor behind the driver's seat, then threw it into the bike basket and set off, standing on the pedals to gain speed. It couldn't be Mike. But with my luck—

It was.

Mike was already jacking up Jasmine's tiny bright green Mini Cooper with a casual, jerky motion that managed to suggest that he could have just leaned over and picked the car up, if he'd wanted to bother. I hopped off the bike while it was still moving and leaned it against the closest tree. If there was anything I didn't need, it was Mike's help, and Jasmine didn't need it either.

"Hey," I said as soon as I thought Mike could hear me. "Hey, thanks, but we got this."

He straightened up. Yesterday's jeans had been replaced by athletic shorts and a T-shirt that stretched across his broad shoulders. Making him even more attractive was the capable way he held the lug wrench in his hand. I reminded myself that he didn't necessarily know what he was doing just because he could use a jack. I mean, he was wearing gym clothes. People who work on farms don't go to gyms. They have plenty of real work to keep them fit.

He was awfully fit. I pulled my eyes away from his legs and up to his face as he looked from me to Jasmine.

"Really?" Mike cast a doubting eye on Jasmine, then turned back to me. "She didn't seem to," he said. Jasmine, her white jeans immaculate under a flowy tank top and her blond hair wound into a perfect messy bun at her neck, shrugged. "And whenever I see half of New York in the back seat of a car"—he gestured to the Zabar's bags visible through the window—"I figure I better help. Boost the tourist economy and all that."

I dropped the tool kit on the ground, ignoring the small dig at Jasmine.

"Well, I'm here now," I said. "And you're decked out for the gym. We wouldn't want you to get all greasy."

"It's true that being around your friend here does seem a bit risky," Mike said. "I'd keep hold of my coffee cup if I had one, but since I don't, I think I can give you a hand."

I stared at him, dismayed. Had he really seen the video of the Modern Pioneer Girl driving the famously calm and collected Margaret Gallagher to apparent table-flipping rage? True, it was everywhere. (My favorite headline was YARMOUTH PREZ *TODAY* SHOW RAMPAGE.) And he'd been with my mother after—

"I drove your mom out from the city yesterday," Mike said. "She told me all about it." The faint amusement that had been on his face vanished as he looked at Jasmine again. "You made quite the scene," he said.

Jasmine glanced my way, clearly as uncertain about what to do with this as I was. I widened my eyes and gave her the tiniest of shrugs. She shifted her feet around to take a slightly different stance, one I recognized as belonging to her version of Maggie Strong, and gave Mike the wide, comfortable grin she'd worn yesterday, although it was a little at odds with the white jeans and show of mechanical ineptitude she'd been putting on just moments before.

"It's good to be memorable," she said lightly.

"I think most people would prefer to be remembered for something more meaningful," he said, turning back to the tire.

I saw a look of surprise on Jasmine's face, and I'm sure I shared it. His tone seemed unnecessarily snarky for the circumstances, even if he was solidly Team Margaret. Jas started to speak again, but I shook my head behind his back.

"Really, Mike," I said, putting a hard emphasis on the

"Mike" in case he'd introduced himself but Jas hadn't made the connection. "We've got this. Mike."

I saw comprehension cross Jas's face as Mike stepped back from the car, dropping his wrench to his side in a gesture of irritation.

"Well, Rhett," he replied, putting equal emphasis on my name, "I take it you're saying you'd prefer to do this yourself?" He extended his tool to me with a glance at the bike. "Seems to me if you're so anxious to get in some auto mechanics, you'd be using a different mode of transport," he said.

I snatched the lug wrench from his hand. "I can fix the truck," I said. "I just haven't had a chance yet." I knelt at the tire. He'd already loosened one lug nut, but the next stuck hard and I wrestled with it, aware that he was watching and torn between wanting to show him that of course this was no more a problem for me than it would be for him and wanting him to go away. I twisted harder, then stopped.

Why was I getting all worked up? And why was I messing with this stupid cheap wrench, which probably came with his truck? I knew better.

"Actually," I said, standing up and slapping the wrench hard into his extended hand, "I've got my own tools. There's no need for you to put yourself out."

He gestured to the Mini Cooper. "Sure you don't want me to loosen those before I go?"

"I said I've got it." I took a jack and a torque wrench out of my tool kit. "Let me send this home with you right now." I slid the new jack under the Mini Cooper and quickly freed up Mike's, tossing it to him and not caring a bit when he scrambled and only managed to catch it by dropping the wrench on the ground. I wasn't buying him as a guy who really knew his way around a garage for a hot second. "Here you go." I held up my more effective wrench with a smile before loosening the next lug nut easily. "All set."

Mike stared at me, holding the jack, and I met his eyes, aware that my annoyance was out of proportion to the situation, but then, so was his. Why be such a jerk to Jasmine? Why insist on helping? I held his gaze and thought I saw his skin redden a little beneath his tan and morning's stubble before he looked away.

"Great," he said. "Why don't you bring my wrench over to the truck, then. So I don't get greasy." He walked away, leaving the tool where he'd dropped it. I straightened, picking it up before I followed him, while Jasmine watched us both with a knowing look, and I shook my head at her fiercely. I knew what she was thinking, and she was flat-out wrong.

Mike set the jack in his truck and turned to me. I held out the wrench, expecting him to take it. Instead, he leaned against his open door as if ready for a nice chat. "About yesterday," he said. "I know things got pretty heated with your mom. But Pioneer Hill's a big project for anyone, and your grandmother did know this would happen eventually. It's a good offer. It's enough to buy something around here, even, if you want to stay." He smiled, as if he hadn't just said half a dozen infuriating things in one breath, and I seized on the worst of them.

"If my grandmother had known this would happen, she would have done something about it," I said. "Told me what was happening. Helped me save up. Maybe we could have even challenged it somehow. This is not what my father would have wanted either—maybe my mother made him do it when they were married. And then he didn't change it. He would never have wanted her to have the farm, or be any part of it. He definitely would never have wanted her to sell it out from under me."

Mike was looking at me thoughtfully, sympathetically, and it made me want to bite. I didn't need his sympathy.

"She did know," he said simply. "I'm sorry."

I stared, not wanting to believe him. Grandma couldn't have known. It wasn't possible.

He had to be wrong, that was all. I leaned past him to slam the tool down on the seat, aware that I smelled of barn and dirty horse but not caring. I'd dump another load of manure in that truck right now if I could.

He didn't move out of my way, and as I straightened up again, I found myself uncomfortably close. He must have been coming from his workout, not on the way there. He exuded heat, and I could see traces of sweat on his temples. Before I could move out of the way, he put an arm out and leaned on the truck, trapping me between him and the door.

"I'm not trying to make you angry," he said. His eyes met mine, and his face was serious. "I get wanting to come back here, if that is in fact what you want. I love this town too. But I think you're going to have to find another way to do it."

"You love this town?" Suddenly, the thought of Mike, rolling around in his fancy pickup as if he owned the place while I fought to convince people that I was back and wanted to stay, made me angry. "New York is your town," I said. "Always has been, even if you've managed to get some local plates for that truck of yours. Don't think I've forgotten that you're a born-and-bred city boy."

"Oh," he said, touching my arm lightly, "I don't think I'll ever forget that." He lifted his eyebrows slightly, and suddenly I knew exactly what he was thinking about.

Our second date. I still didn't believe Mike was really interested in me (and how right I had been in the end), but I couldn't resist his suggestion that we take swimsuits and walk down to the river at dusk. It was only the second week of class, and still hot enough for me to lead him away from the dock all the students used and along the worn dirt trail back to the illegal rope swing that got taken down every year and put back up just as quickly. This was a local haunt, and I climbed the tree like a local girl, feeling, for once, like I belonged here more than my dubious companion, who stood looking out at me as I unwound the rope and prepared to swing out into the water.

"Are you crazy? Is it deep enough?"

"Of course it's deep enough," I called back. "And it's the only way to get in." With a whoop, I sailed out and let go.

It wasn't, not really. There was a tiny little path down to the water you used to get back out and swing in again, and it was this path that Mike, slapping at bugs the whole way, finally made his way down.

"It's better if you jump," I said, treading water. "You don't have to deal with all the rocks and weeds."

Mike shook his head and hung our towels from a branch.

"I'll pass," he said, and picked his way into the water, throwing himself forward when it quickly grew deep. "In the city," he said, swimming out to me, "we don't swim in the river. Too much pollution."

"Around here," I said, "we don't swim in pools. Too much kid pee."

He laughed. I never did get him to jump off the rope swing, but he gamely stayed in the water while I swung out again and again. On my last jump he reached out to me, and I dodged, expecting a dunk, but instead he used one of his long arms to pull me in close, his face pale in the moonlight, his eyes serious.

Even then, I didn't do serious. "Sure you don't want to jump? It's easy."

He looked at the jump, then back at me. "Doesn't look easy," he said. "But it would be very easy to kiss you right now." A pause while we looked at each other. "Can I?"

I don't remember what I said, but it must have been yes, and the result was so much more than I'd expected, my legs wrapped around him, only our wet swimsuits between us as our lips met. I hadn't kissed many boys before. Fumbled around a little at dances or in the woods behind the school. This was different. I could feel every inch of him as our lips and hands grew more searching.

A splash nearby made us pull apart, startled. It was only a fish, but the sun was setting, the air getting colder. Mike took my hand and pulled me gently to the shore, and I knew that it wasn't over, that there would be more to come. The anticipation was bliss. Even more than anything that followed, good and bad, I remember the possibility of that moment. We made our way back to the road, Mike claiming he saw a bear at every turn and me telling him I wasn't worried, because while I couldn't outrun a bear, I thought I could outrun a city slicker. He'd grabbed my hand. "No way," he said. "If we're going to get eaten by a bear, we're going to get eaten together."

That wasn't at all the romantic sentiment it had seemed at the time, but I felt my face warm at the memory of the kiss we'd shared in the water, of threading my fingers through his dark curls, the hair on his chest tickling mine.

I pulled away from this older Mike's touch, my back up against the truck. I couldn't afford to be distracted by memories—not when Mike was so clearly on the wrong side of my present-day problems. Just like he'd been back then, I reminded myself. He was a city slicker in every way, and he hadn't changed. But I had. "Well, don't," I said, aware that my rejoinder was weak at best.

"I love this place," he said, still gazing at me intently. "I understand if you do too. I just don't want to see you get hurt if you can't save Pioneer Hill. I'm afraid you're hitching your wagon to the wrong star."

He was so smug. My nostalgia disappeared in an instant. Mike was tall, but so was I. I looked him straight in the eye and lifted his arm so that he was no longer blocking me in. "I'm my own star," I said, and I turned and walked back to Jasmine's car, glad that my voice had stayed steady.

Jasmine had picked up my wrench and was holding it as if she didn't know how it worked, and maybe she didn't. Irritated, I snatched it from her hand, then rolled my eyes back at Mike to show that it was him I was annoyed with, not Jas.

Jasmine winked and raised a hand as she called to Mike. "Thanks for helping!"

"I didn't help," Mike said. He looked directly at me. "But when you do need it, you know where to find me."

12

Someone Else's Plan

THE TOTE BAG with the second KitchenAid mixer in it finally broke me.

I'd started to freak out the minute Mike pulled away, but Jas was insistent that we wait and talk once she had unpacked at the farm. I helped her haul multiple suitcases and bags up to the only decent guest room, and bags of food and baking supplies into the kitchen, all the while uncomfortably aware that my best friend seemed to be planning to move in and might be going through a life crisis, when all I could think about was getting her Maggie Strong face out of here before my mother found out she was here.

"What is all this?" I asked as I hefted the second mixer out of the bag and up to the counter with a thud.

Jas was systematically lining up ten-pound bags of flour and sugar along the counter. She turned and spread her arms wide but avoided my eyes. "You are looking at the worldwide headquarters of Jasmine's Bake Shop on Pioneer Hill," she said. "A farm stand needs pies and things, but you don't bake pies and things, and I do. So. As previously discussed, you need a baker, and I am a baker, and here I am."

A baker who everyone thinks wrote my book, I wanted to say. The MPG did not cook or bake, and she didn't want to. But something else was happening here, something Jas wasn't telling me. "You," I said gently, "are a baker with a husband and a job in Manhattan, who I thought was going to come help me for a couple of days. Yet you just unpacked an entire kitchen and copious wardrobe from a teeny-tiny clown car and you don't look happy about it. What's up?"

Jas sat down at the kitchen table, where she'd piled a stack of stained notebooks and three-ring binders. She opened one, then shut it again, still not looking at me. "I'm a baker with a husband who wants me to be someone I'm not, with a job trying to mix all kinds of crazy ingredients into something they're not. I spend two hours a day exercising and the rest of it not eating, and if you don't think not eating is doing something, you should try it sometime. It's pretty much a full-time job in and of itself."

Okay. "And you're not happy," I said, encouraging.

"I'm not happy." She jiggled her leg, not speaking, and I waited. "Zale asked me while we were working out yesterday if I'd been sampling at the bakery. He wants me to write down every single thing I eat. He was like, 'Everything means something even if you break off part of a cookie.' I told him I knew what I was eating, and I was fine, and he said, 'I don't think that's what the scale will say.'"

"And then you picked up the scale, broke it over his head, and came here?"

Jas tried to laugh. "I probably should have," she said. "Then he started going on about how he's been reading about menopause, and how careful I have to be and—I'm forty. That's not menopause. It's not old at all. I think he wants me to be old. Because"—she inhaled through her nose and stared up at the ceiling, blinking fast—"I want to have a baby. And he doesn't."

"Oh."

Now that she'd started, it seemed easier for Jas to let it all come out. "I knew he didn't. He's always said he didn't. But I thought it was because he was working so hard, and that when things settled down a little, and got more secure, he'd change his mind. But he hasn't. You know why? Because he thinks parents get fat. Not women, all parents. He says there's research, that dads gain weight and it's not something you can avoid by being careful; it's lack of sleep and hormonal changes. 'Not good for the brand,' he said. Because his clients want him focused just on them. And I was like, 'What about me? What if I want you to focus on me?'"

"So what did he say?"

"He tried to make a joke. He told me to hire him, and then he pinched my butt like it was fat."

Oh man. "And then you decked him and left."

"I left, anyway." She put her hands on the table and looked at them. I wanted to take one, squeeze it, and tell her how wrong Zale was, how she was perfect and could have any man she wanted and all the babies she wanted too, but I didn't know how, or if she even wanted to hear it from me. Instead, I tried making a joke.

"The world is probably better off if Zale doesn't reproduce anyway," I said. I felt the wrongness of my words as soon as they left my mouth, and Jas didn't laugh or look up. "I'm sorry," I said. "I mean, really sorry. I can't believe you didn't tell me any of this. I just figured you didn't want kids."

Jas shook her head. "That's you," she said. "I do. Did. But I didn't want to do it alone."

"It's not exactly that I didn't want kids," I said. "I just didn't *want* want them. Enough to make it happen."

"And now you are forty," Jas said, "and according to Zale, your eggs are dried up and your vagina's a wasteland and the only thing that lies ahead of you is a future of stuffing your lonely face with cupcakes."

"You might be reading into it a little."

"Not much," Jas said. She leaned over and took a white bakery box out of the bag next to her. "I grabbed these on the way out of town," she said. Four beautiful pastel cupcakes with sprinkles.

I took one. Chocolate cake, buttercream frosting, so thick and tall that I had to wipe icing off my nose after my first bite. Jasmine had gone in with abandon and now wore a blue mustache. "It's not a bad future," I said.

"Parts of it I embrace fully," Jas said, licking her fingers as she polished off the cupcake and reached for her second. I didn't ask which parts, or what she was planning. She'd tell me when she was ready. She paused before taking a bite. "So, can I stay?"

I didn't hesitate. "Of course," I said, pushing thoughts of my mother, Mike, and Emily out of my mind. We'd cross the Jasmine / Maggie Strong bridge when we had to. Jasmine tipped her cupcake in my direction and I took my second and we toasted, yellow and pink frosting mingling together.

"To cupcakes," I said. "Are yours as good as these?"

"Better."

I showed Jas around the farm with pride, equal parts happy to get to share this with her and worrying about what would happen if someone who recognized her as Maggie Strong showed up. If I was going to keep the farm, I'd need my mother to at least grudgingly accept the inevitability of my plans. Having "Maggie" here wouldn't help. Plus, it was just weird. I'd wanted Jas to be me on the *Today* show. I'd needed her to do it. But I didn't want her to keep doing it. The MPG belonged in my book and online. And in my head. Not anywhere else. I kept looking over my shoulder. Jasmine either didn't notice or pretended not to.

I'd spent a couple of hours this morning on the beginnings of a cleanup, and the place looked a little better from the road already, with some of the piles cleared and the tractor neatly parked rather than left haphazardly by the driveway. Jas extended a tentative hand to pat all the animals except Teddy, who startled her by rolling back his lips and reaching out his long neck toward her face.

She jumped back, and I laughed. "He's just playing," I said, but Jas kept her distance.

"I think I'll stick to the smaller guys." She reached through the fence to Brownie, who accepted a pat cheerfully, clearly hoping for a cookie. "You are just so cute," she said. "I am going to put a bow on you and take your picture."

We went back inside, where Jas cooed appreciatively over the farmhouse and particularly the kitchen, with its woodstove and dark beams. "Can you really cook on this?" She put a hand on the burner on the woodstove top.

"Sometimes we do a teapot, but that's really just for show," I answered. "We mostly used the normal stove and oven." I knelt down in front of a cabinet to remove outdated cans and make space for some of Jasmine's supplies.

"Ahhh, counter space," said Jas. "I'm going to cook us the best dinner tonight. I brought everything we need."

"I saw. We have grocery stores here too, you know."

"And I will shop in them, but tonight we're all set."

There it was—that was the problem. Didn't she get it?

"You can't," I said, looking up at her. "My mom and Mike both think you're Maggie Strong. If they start seeing you around town, or hear you're around town—and they will—they're going to say something, and then everyone will think you're Maggie Strong."

"Oh." Jas, who had started chopping scallions, paused, knife in her hand. "Mike recognizing me was . . . unexpected."

"To say the least. But it's not like my mother wouldn't have been here anyway. We'd have the same issue."

"Can't you just tell them? Say we did it as a joke." She said it casually, as if suggesting we add some croutons to the salad.

"No!" I tossed a can into the trash can beside me with force. "Are you kidding? That's the last thing I can do. For one thing, my mother hates Maggie Strong."

"She hates me. Maybe that's different."

I shook my head and threw in another can. "No way. It's not just what you did; it's the whole thing. The whole idea of a book about being able to get on with your life even if you can't manage to climb the ladder of success. The Modern Pioneer Girl is, like, my mother's archnemesis."

Jasmine sighed. "Yes, I know that. Are you telling me you didn't?"

"I guess I never thought about it that way," I said. "But now—look. I can make Pioneer Hill a working farm, and that will stop her from selling to the college, only it's not just that. I have to convince her to sell her half to me, and I can't do that if in addition to being her disappointing disaster of a daughter, I'm also everything she hates most in the universe."

"But if you're Maggie Strong, you're not disappointing. You're a wildly successful author."

"Of a book she loathes. Seriously." I lay flat on my back on the wood floor. "That's only going to make it worse. Plus, I was too chicken to face her? And I was part of humiliating her in front of the whole world? Pioneer Hill will be some tech bro's hobby farm before you can say 'viral YouTube video.'" And I would be back where I'd been twenty years ago, unable to see myself except the way my mother saw me.

Jas came to join me on the floor. "Then we have to do it your way. But I can still help. I'll just stay behind the scenes, and we'll do it together. Make a website. Facebook, Instagram. Press releases—'College Goliath tries to ruin small-farm David.' We'll make such a stink that your mother doesn't have any choice except to give in, but it won't be about her. And we can use the Modern Pioneer Girl too."

I'd been gazing admiringly at my friend—that was brilliant—until she got to that part. "Yes and yes and yes but no. No MPG. The Modern Pioneer Girl is lying low for a while. I just told my editor so. Well, I started to."

Jas eyed me. "What do you mean? What did she want you to do?"

"*Fresh Air.* NPR. With Terry Gross."

"What?" Jasmine let out a shriek that nearly pierced my ear.

"But I'm not doing it," I said. "There's no way." I grinned, knowing she was going to try to persuade me, but I wasn't making that mistake twice. "Unless you want to do it."

"No and no and no," she said. "Fine. We concentrate on Pioneer Hill. You're the struggling farmer, I'm your secret baker weapon, and we just drop the Modern Pioneer Girl for a while. Send her on a silent retreat somewhere far away from here to meditate on her success until your mother forgets all about her."

My mother was an Olympic-level grudge holder, but this didn't seem like the time to say so. I sat up and grabbed the notebook where I kept all my ideas. "Website. Social media accounts. Press releases. We'll make Pioneer Hill the most famous working farm in the state and we'll make sure everyone within a hundred-mile radius knows it. Tourists, college parents, locals—they'll come taste your donuts and they'll be like, 'Hey, no, don't tear that down.'"

Jasmine stood up. "You had me at donuts," she said as she extended a hand and helped me up. "And scones. And pies." She rubbed her hands together in a parody of glee. "Just call me the Modern Pioneer Baker."

I brushed the dirt of the floor off her jeans. "No baking until we finish cleaning up, and not just the kitchen." I pointed out the window at an old building that stood in front of the barn, with its own little overgrown parking area off the road. "That's our project," I said. "Behold the once and future Pioneer Hill Farm Stand, home of Jasmine's brilliant baked goods and the season's finest produce. And we have exactly one week to pull it off."

Jas looked out the window, then held out her hands and surveyed her manicure. "Good-bye, French tips," she said. "Okay, Coach, put me in."

❧

13

A Degree in
Farm Life

THE *TODAY* SHOW'S "advice for graduates" segment ran early by Yarmouth standards. Yarmouth graduation was always the week after Memorial Day, and graduation weekend was, for Bowford businesses that depended on the tourist trade, like Black Friday and Christmas Eve combined. We'd have to bust our butts to make it, but it was just possible. Jas threw herself into cleaning and painting. I focused first on repair and second on figuring out what, besides Jasmine's treats, we could sell—in particular, things that came from the farm. If I wanted to show Pioneer Hill was a going concern, the faster some of the produce was "produced" here, the better.

Amid the overgrown gardens and fields, I found a few late fiddlehead ferns, spring greens and last year's onions, the very earliest leaves of kale, rhubarb, and the very last of the asparagus. Everyone's gardens vary. This was what we had, and it would have to be enough. After my conversation with Carney, I fixed up the truck and took it around to neighboring farms and talked several into selling me some of what they had: lettuces, peas, morel mushrooms. And after dodging the question for several days, Carney finally promised me some of the Baileys' strawberries, which were normally all sold at farmers' markets and a few local stores.

"Whatever you sell me, at whatever price, I'm going to mark it up a dollar a pint for the farm stand," I said. The farm's prime location and picturesque setting had always allowed my dad to charge a premium. "You can give them to me in the morning and I'll split the extra buck with you after I sell them, or I can buy them outright and keep the extra."

Carney, who'd had a hard enough time talking her dad out of the berries I wanted, had barely thought about it. "Buy outright, please," she said.

I'd hoped she'd be willing to wait to split the extra profit with me, and it must have shown, because Carney smiled ruefully. "A bird in the hand," she said.

"They're strawberries," I said. "And it's graduation weekend. I'll sell them." I had the money to front to Carney, but it would be a stretch.

"I'm sure you will, but I'll let you worry about that," Carney said. "Dad likes a good clean sale."

We ramped up the curb appeal of the farm, adding a little paddock right by the road where S'mores and Brownie would entice little kids to beg their parents to stop. Jasmine promised what sounded to me like an unlikely abundance from our single oven. I was as clumsy an assistant in her prepping and freezing things as she was in patching the farm stand roof.

The Modern Pioneer Girl took a brief social media hiatus

while I focused what little time I had left on creating a website and profiles for Pioneer Hill. I'd traded the promise of eggs all summer for a couple of advertising posts from a local woman who published a daily email that went out to half the valley, but first, we needed a site that looked good. I'd already written all the text and drawn logos, which Jasmine had insisted on turning into online "merch" to sell on our website. Thanks to the magic that is print to order, our so far totally imaginary fans could wear "Pioneer Hill" emblazoned on a hat or T-shirt, or drink their morning coffee from a Pioneer Hill mug, and we could be "in uniform" when the farm stand opened. Me up front, and Jas firmly tucked away in the house's kitchen.

"I wish you'd quit reminding me about that," she said as she selected a vibrant green and added two shirts to our cart.

"Well, you get to be front and center now." The new website was almost finished. All that remained was to take and add the photos, and we took off a glorious afternoon to do it, with Jasmine—her back to the camera, or face hidden—serving as the human model when an image needed to draw the viewer in with a personal touch. Jas with Clementine, the farm's only lamb, in her lap drinking happily from a bottle (even though Clem was well-fed by the ewe who'd birthed her)—but not Jas leaping up and shrieking after Clementine peed on her. Jas—in fresh clothes—leading Brownie and S'mores into the barn, the three of them silhouetted in the doorway. Jas, after some protesting, wrapping her arms around Teddy's neck, face hidden in his fur, standing in front of the red barn wall in the glow of the afternoon sun. Once the pictures were taken, Jas leaned away from the llama. "He's not my favorite," she said. "He's kind of smelly."

I couldn't blame Teddy for lifting up his tail and pooping in precisely the spot Jas was about to take a step backward into. In fact, I strongly suspected, based on the look on his face when Jasmine shrieked, that he had planned it.

"Just wipe it on the grass," I said, taking Teddy's lead rope and discreetly giving him a pat.

"I saw that!" Jasmine dragged her soiled boot through the yard. "It's not funny."

It was, though. Even Jas laughed. The whole thing was funny, once we got into it, posing cliché after cliché, vying with each other to see whose idea would be most over-the-top. Jas's cutest turquoise boots, bright against the tall grass. Her hands, cupped around a steaming mug of tea against the graying wood of the picnic table. Her legs up, face leaning back out of the camera, swooping through the air on the old tire swing in a gauzy skirt, bare toes pointed at the sky. When we were done, our Instagram would be populated for months.

"I'm not sure if we captured carefree farm life or a tampon advertisement," I said, swiping through the images on my phone as Jasmine let the swing twist to a stop. She leaned over my shoulder and laughed.

"We have also nailed hair conditioner, Wheat Thins, and butter substitutes," Jas said. "We done?"

"One more," I said. "Last one. No skirt for this; you're going to need jeans." Jasmine stripped the skirt off and waved it wildly around, making Teddy rush to the other side of his paddock.

"Rural living," said Jasmine, heading into the house to change. "I could be totally naked out here and no one would even know it."

"That's a very different website," I replied. I went into the barn to saddle the horses while Jasmine changed, mentally calculating the best way to get the shot I wanted: Jasmine's hands on the reins, with Bingley's head drinking from the pond, and one of her riding off, taken from the edge of the field where I could also capture the whole farm. I hadn't—exactly— filled Jas in on this plan. The one adventure she always re- fused to join me in was riding, not even when I promised her the very quietest mule to take her into Bryce Canyon, or the gentlest pony to ride along the edge of the surf in Uruguay.

Thank goodness Grandma Bee's horses were of the mature and docile sort. I had snuck out last night and saddled them both for a short ride, and they were still the same placid geld- ings they had always been. My grandmother took them to the Fourth of July parade every year, letting one lucky kid ride Bingley while she rode Darcy. That was my plan for Jasmine, a quick ride while I took the pictures. Barely a ride, even. Jas just had to sit on the horse.

But the minute Jasmine saw the two heading toward her, she started to back away. "No," she said. "Not happening. Never take a script that involves animals or small children."

"You already did Clementine."

"Who peed on me. Case in point."

"Bingley's beautiful, though. Look at him. He matches your hair." I stroked the gentle palomino. My grandmother could put a four-year-old on this horse in nothing but a halter.

Darcy was a tiny bit friskier, but I'd be on him to take the pictures. We might even get a ride in. Jas just needed to relax a little.

"That is the stupidest reason to get on a horse that I have ever heard." But Jasmine was coming closer. Bingley really was irresistible.

I handed her a carrot. "Hold it out on your palm," I said. In a moment, Bingley was crunching away, and Jasmine was climbing the mounting block and putting her left foot into the stirrup.

I handed her the reins. "Now, sit still," I said as she mounted Bingley. "Okay, you're just going to ask him to walk a little. Heels down. Squeeze him gently with your legs. Good."

Jasmine was not a natural. She sat stiff and tense on the big horse, but she seemed okay. We got the shot on the edge of the pond (Jas's manicure was actually holding up remarkably well) and made our way to the edge of the field, where I lined them up for the farm picture. "Got it," I said. "Now look back. Forget the website. I want a picture of you on a horse."

"Your first, and probably your last," Jas replied, but she seemed to be feeling much better as she let the reins lie over Bingley's neck and looked over her shoulder.

She started to smile, and then a look of panic crossed her face as we heard the sudden roar of a diesel engine and the sound of truck tires taking a turn way too fast into the driveway. Bingley, spooked by both his novice rider and the noise, shot forward faster than I had ever seen him move. Darcy, too, jumped, forcing me to take a handful of mane while I regained my balance and looked for Jas.

She was still on, at least, but Bingley was shooting across the field as though he had suddenly found the joy of speed, and the way she was bouncing around, Jas wouldn't last long. "Pull back on the reins," I called, and I heard another voice echoing mine from the truck behind me.

"Pull back! Sit deep!"

Words weren't going to help. I tossed my phone into the grass, dug my heels into Darcy, and took him off to the side in a circle, hoping to head Bingley off rather than chase him and scare him into further flight. As I came around the front of Jasmine and the horse, I could see that Jasmine would not be pulling back on the reins, because Jasmine no longer had hold of the reins. Instead, she was clutching Bingley around the neck, and any minute now she was going to get a horse's head thrown back into her face, unless Bingley caught a hoof in his reins first and they both went down.

Barely giving myself time to think about it, I urged Darcy on, right into Bingley's path. Bingley, who was beta to Darcy's alpha, would not run into Darcy—or at least, I sure as hell hoped he wouldn't, because Bingley didn't have time to get around us as he galloped up wildly, Jasmine still clinging on.

Bingley skidded to a stop with a foot to spare and stood, snorting, while Darcy gave him a reproving look. It was, after all, just a truck. Nothing to get so worked up about.

I sidestepped Darcy over to Bingley, leaned over and grabbed Jasmine's reins, then slid off Darcy's back to stand between the horses. Jasmine lay limply over Bingley's back.

"I hate you," she said. "I hate you and I told you I didn't want to ride the horse and my foot is stuck, and the only other picture we are taking today is of the giant margarita you are making me."

Jas's boot, which was not really meant for riding, had gone right through the stirrup.

"I told you to keep your heels down," I said, guilt and remorse coursing through me. Footsteps raced up to us, and the truck's driver appeared, panting, hand out as though ready to grab ahold of a wild steed.

Darcy and Bingley gazed at the girl placidly.

It wasn't him, of course. For one minute, at the sound of the truck, I had taken the intruder for Mike—it was exactly the kind of fool stunt Mike would pull, careening into the driveway like that. But the driver was a teenaged girl, dressed much like I was in cutoffs, a tank top, and boots, but with the addition of inked-on marker tattoos up and down both legs and one arm and a pierced eyebrow. "I'm so sorry," she said. "Really. I never thought— But I shouldn't have taken the turn so fast. I'm really, really sorry."

I freed Jasmine's foot, then held it to allow her to use the stirrup as a step. "Lean forward and swing your right leg behind you, then you can slide down," I said. Jasmine did, but she lost her balance as she dropped to the ground and sat back on her butt in the dirt while the teenager, oblivious to how little anyone would want attention in that moment, stared at her. "Wait," she said. "You're Maggie Strong."

I stopped in the middle of extending a hand to help Jas up, startled. The girl gushed on while Jas ignored my hand and scrambled up on her own.

"I loved your book. I mean, really, really loved it. My mom

gave it to me—I think she wishes she hadn't, I talk about it so much."

I could see that Jas wanted nothing more than to get out of here, but she stood, a little stiffly, and managed a smile for the girl while she brushed the dirt off her pants. "Thank you," she said. "Normally I'd want to hear about it, but I'd really like to go in and get cleaned up."

The teenager took a quick step back. "Oh, absolutely," she said. She stared after Jasmine and I rushed into speech.

"Those damn boots," I said. "I made her wear them, they're mine, they're not meant for riding, and when he spooked—"

"Her foot went through," finished the teenager. "I feel terrible."

"It wasn't your fault," I said, relieved that she didn't seem to be questioning why "Maggie," who'd written an entire chapter about working with a difficult horse, would need someone to rescue her from something as simple as a spooked Bingley. I turned the horses back toward the barn, and as I did, I saw the reason for the young woman's arrival. The bed of her truck, which was indeed the same kind Mike drove, was piled high with square bales of hay.

She dragged her gaze away from Jasmine as the screen door slammed behind my probably embarrassed friend. "Your grandmother got this every month," she said, pointing. "My dad figured you'd still want it."

I nodded, my mind still on Jasmine, who looked like she was trying not to limp. I shouldn't have pushed her to ride, and now here was this girl who was going to wonder what was up if she gave it any thought at all—

The truck's driver stared at me, waiting for an answer.

"Oh God," I said. "Yes. Totally. I'm sorry. I guess that just . . . shook me up more than I realized."

Her shoulders sagged, and she pushed her hands through short, straight black hair, the tips dyed an icy blue. "I know," she said. "I'm so sorry. If you hadn't been so fast—you're an amazing rider. Really. If even she couldn't control him, he must really have lost it."

"My dad taught me," I said. My dad, and many, many years of daily riding horses much more challenging than Darcy, but here, in this place, I only thought of my dad. "He thought every kid should be able to handle a horse."

"Mine too," the kid said, brightening. "That makes us lucky."

"Yep. Anyway—hay. Great." Now that I thought about it, I loved that someone was sending his daughter out to do the hay deliveries. I spared a respectful thought for that dad, whoever he was. "Let's get it unloaded."

"Oh, I usually just take care of it," she said.

"I'll give you a hand." Which reminded me of my manners. "I'm Rhett," I said.

"I know. Your grandmother talked about you sometimes. I'm Louisa."

"Just let me put the horses away, and I'll come help."

Together, we tossed down about twenty bales, then carried them into the barn to what I should have noticed was a dwindling stack. Louisa, I saw, knew her hay stacking—cut side up, alternating directions in every layer. I marked her down mentally as raised right.

When we were done, I rummaged hopelessly in my pocket. I didn't think there was any cash in there, and I was right. Louisa noticed what I was doing and stopped me. "No worries," she said. "It's paid for." She grinned. "Your grandmother used to tip me in cookies," she said.

"I don't even have those," I answered. "I will soon, though. We open the farm stand Thursday. Come over and I'll save you something."

Louisa fidgeted for a minute, as though she wanted to say something else, but I was in a hurry to get in to Jasmine. I left Louisa in the driveway and went into the farmhouse in the waning afternoon light, calling Jasmine's name.

There was no sign of her in the kitchen, but I could hear her moving about in the little guest bedroom as I climbed the stairs. I knocked, then opened the door and leaned in the doorframe. Jasmine was stretched out across the bed, facedown, her hair splayed around her. Her boots were kicked into a corner and the gauzy skirt she'd worn earlier hung on a bedpost.

"I'm really sorry," I said. Was Jas crying? She'd been amazing this week, throwing herself into rehabbing the farm stand and baking with gusto. I realized suddenly how little I had done to encourage her to unload more about her and Zale. Instead, I was acting just like him, expecting her to put all her energy into my dream. I stared anxiously at the floor, uncertain of what to say next. Jasmine was the only person besides Grandma Bee who had ever believed in me. I couldn't imagine my life without her, but instead of telling her that, I shoved her on a horse and scared her half to death.

I was a shit friend.

I looked around the little room, which I'd helped my grand-mother paint years ago. Bee made that quilt. Bee made this whole place, and she had made sure I knew it was my place too. She'd been the only steady part of my life, even after she sent me away with Margaret. What if I'd never left? Fought against boarding school, stuck my heels in, refused to leave unless they dragged me out? I could have stayed here, with Bee. No college, or at least not Yarmouth. No Mike. No de-cades of traveling. Carney instead of Jasmine, maybe. The Modern Pioneer Girl wouldn't even exist.

And then, in the end, the same thing would have happened. For some reason, my grandmother had kept the way the farm was left a secret, letting me believe it was mine when—without a miracle—it wasn't, and I just didn't get it. I had talked to her nearly every week. She must have known how much I cared.

But I wasn't here. Maybe she thought I didn't.

That idea hurt so much that I wanted to physically push it away. "I'm sorry," I said again to Jasmine. "I should have lis-tened to you."

Jasmine rolled over. Her eye makeup was only slightly smudged. "I told you I didn't want to ride the horse," she said. "I don't even like horses."

"I know," I said. "I was awful. I wouldn't blame you if you wanted to pack up and go home." Maybe my grandmother didn't really think I deserved the farm and had just never been able to bring herself to say it. And maybe she was right.

Jas sat up. "Of course I'm staying," she said. "I baked all that stuff in the freezer, right? If I leave it here, you'll just mess it up." She patted the bed and I came to sit beside her. If I were Jas, I wasn't sure I'd be so forgiving. Tentatively, I put an arm around my friend and repeated myself, because there wasn't anything else to say. "I'm really sorry."

Jasmine leaned her head against my shoulder. "I know you are. And I could have said no. Riding comes so naturally to you. I guess part of me wanted to be able to do it too." She straightened up. "Can you believe that girl knew me? Or you? Or whatever?"

I shook my head in disbelief. "Seriously. We never catch a break."

"You should have thought about that before you wrote such a good book. If no one read it, we wouldn't have this problem." She stared at me as though daring me to disagree.

"Maybe she just saw you on YouTube."

"That is not what she said, and you know it. She doesn't care about me. This is not about me."

It kind of was, and it kind of wasn't. I dropped my eyes, looking for a way to change the subject, and found it in my phone, which I had picked up out of the grass, undamaged, after the hay was stacked. I started scrolling through our pictures, and Jasmine shifted so that she could see too.

"Did you at least get anything?"

"What?"

"Me, on the horse. On stupid Bingley. Who named him, anyway?"

I laughed. "My grandmother and I read Jane Austen together," she said. "The horses before that were Bennet and Dashwood."

Jasmine shook her head as I tapped back through the images. We had captured a perfect outdoor life—one without peeing lambs, or llama poop, or horses that spooked and tore off through the beautiful sunny fields. In the last shot, Jasmine was leaning back toward the lens, laughing, hair backlit, confident and smiling.

"I guess I did get something, after all," I said, gazing at my friend's image. How could a photo be so totally misleading? "We can treasure it forever."

"We'd better," replied Jasmine. "Because from here on out, I stand on my own two feet." She pointed to my phone. "Get those pics up on the website, because my sacrifices better have been worth it. And that's not all I want." She crossed her arms over her chest and fixed her eyes on me. "I haven't forgotten, and I'm not going to. You are calling your editor, and you are saying yes to *Fresh Air.*"

"What? No."

"Yes." She pointed at me. "First of all, selling books is your livelihood now. Until you get this place running, you need that. But that's not all. You wrote it. People love it, and I want to hear you own it. You, not me. I'm not standing by while you pretend you're not the one who earned this."

"I'm not," I protested. But I did feel differently. Watching Jas walk on that set as Maggie Strong made "Maggie" feel even more like something I had dreamed but could never live up to. I wasn't the Modern Pioneer Girl. I just wanted to be, and sometimes I got close. Now didn't feel like one of those times.

"Then prove it," she said. "Call her, or I'm going home."

I looked hard at Jasmine's face—would she really pack up and go back to Zale if I didn't step up?

"Come on," Jasmine said. "This is what the MPG is for. You stay in your comfort zone, you get stuck. It happens to every-body. And then we shake it off and we do the thing. It's your turn to do the thing."

I didn't like it. But I didn't like the idea of Jasmine leaving either—or that she might stay but feel like I was letting her down. If she could pack up everything and come here, couldn't I talk to Terry Gross for an hour?

I held my phone, feeling like I'd gone down this road before and it hadn't ended well. "Really?" I tried to give Jas my most pitiful look.

"Really." She pointed at the phone. "Dial."

14

A Work Ethic

BY THURSDAY MORNING, we were ready to open. My hand-painted signs, made from old boards and hinges and bright with images of baked goods, strawberries, and asparagus, were propped up by the road as drivers came into town. The stand looked welcoming, with hanging plants around the open door and, once you came inside, Jasmine's cookies, scones, and other treats on one side and produce on the other. The big center table was entirely dedicated to Carney's strawberries, picked up by me in big flats at seven a.m. and set out for customers by nine.

It had been an extraordinary amount of work, but the result filled me with pride. Jasmine, too, to judge by her expression, which made it all the harder to say what I had to say as the first car pulled up in front.

"Okay," I said, pointing to the back door of the farm stand closest to the house. "You've got to get out of here."

Jasmine was looking out the door as a man lifted a toddler

out of the car's back seat while a woman pulled a stroller from the trunk. "Come on," she said. "We don't know them. Just let me stay for the first ones."

I shook my head firmly. "You know what happened with Louisa. We're not taking any chances."

Jasmine groaned. "I know," she said. "But I want to see what people think. It's not fair for you to have all the fun." She lingered, and I could tell that as much as she was trying to joke, she really cared. And she was right. It wasn't fair that she wouldn't see how much people were going to love the things she'd made, or admire the work we'd done.

But there wasn't anything to be done about that now. *Or ever*, whispered a little voice in my head that I determinedly ignored. I wasn't thinking beyond this weekend until I had to.

"You should have thought about that before you lured Margaret into practically breaking a table over your head on national television," I said, intentionally annoying in an attempt to lighten the suddenly heavy mood.

Jasmine made a face and played along. "I won't forget this," she said. "You owe me even bigger now."

"I owe you so much that we'll never get straight," I said. The people were approaching the door. "Now, go."

Jasmine, after straightening one last cookie tray, zipped out the back door just as the young family came in through the front.

The morning brought a steady stream of customers. Many asked for coffee, and I made a mental note to find my grandmother's big urn and fill it for tomorrow and the weekend. It wouldn't be the lattes the out-of-towners were hoping for, but it would be better than nothing. I was pleased to see people I recognized from Bowford, even when it led to awkward exchanges about where I'd been and how much I must miss Bee. And did I plan on staying? I did, I told more than one person. "I've always wanted to come back and do"—I gestured around—"this."

People seemed pleased and welcoming, but I didn't put too much stock in that. It would be what they said to one another, and what got back to the town zoning board and to my mother, that meant something. If they had doubts or criticisms, I'd hear about them, but not to my face.

Meanwhile, this bright June day was everything I'd hoped it would be. And Jas had been right—even though I was beyond nervous about it, calling Emily and telling her I'd do *Fresh Air* had brought the MPG back to me. I kept imagining how I'd write up this triumph if I could, and how many of my readers must also have long-held dreams they hadn't tackled yet. And I really, really wanted to share the beauty of this place. Spring comes late to my part of New Hampshire, but when it does, the greens are breathtaking, the views stretching out over the fields and ponds stunning. Add in a big red barn like ours—like mine—and it truly is like living in a postcard. For the moment, it was mine and I was grateful. I might have snuck a really good picture of the farm stand into my MPG feed. *I always, always, always pull into a farm stand when I pass one,* I wrote, *#shoplocal #supportfarmers #modernpioneerlife.*

Part of me kept expecting Margaret to show up, but she didn't, and after a while I stopped looking for her. That didn't mean I let Jasmine emerge. Instead, I updated her on how much people were loving her treats with constant texts and pictures. "You better push the turnovers," Jas said on one of her frequent calls to check in. "I'm making more."

That wouldn't be a problem. We'd found bags and bags of frozen blueberries and raspberries in the stand freezer, and people seemed thrilled by the out-of-season bounty—and Jasmine's pastry. One man bought one, ate it, then came back for a dozen more.

While my mother might not have been interested enough to come by, Mike was. He slipped in Sunday behind a group of customers that included Carney and her two little boys, and I didn't notice him until I'd loaded a couple of cookies into the toy truck Carney's youngest had zoomed across the counter and sent it zooming back. I was kneeling and trading high fives with his brother about selling "every single one" of the strawberries when I looked up and saw Mike looking around the little farm stand as if he were assessing it for the wrecking ball. I stood up quickly.

"Can I help you?" I spoke too loudly, and probably too angrily, because Carney turned away from collecting her strawberry flats to see what was happening.

"I just came by to see how things were going," he said.

"Great," I said, facing him down. "Really great."

"You should try a cookie," Carney said, and Mike smiled at her and pretended to be taking one from the toy truck, which caused little Martin to squeal. Obviously they knew each other.

"They're very, very good," said Oscar. "I don't think he wants to share."

Mike gave me an appraising look, and I immediately wanted to disown all responsibility for the cookies, but who would I say made them? Carney hadn't met Jas and wouldn't, and Mike didn't need to know she was still here.

"A cookie it is," said Mike, turning to survey the selection. Carney was looking from one of us to the other with curiosity.

"Do you two know each other? Mike just moved to town this year, although he's been coming in the summer for a while."

Did she maybe sound a little possessive? She could have him. "We've met."

I waited for Mike to make his choice, but instead he leaned suggestively across the counter and I had a sudden feeling he was about to say something that I did not need Carney—or her big-eared boys—to hear. I shoved a cookie into his open mouth, stopping whatever he was about to say before it started.

He reached up and grabbed it, then spoke around the bite he'd taken. "This is how you treat customers? Most people want to choose their own cookies."

"Not if it's the last oatmeal chocolate chunk," I said. "People knock each other over for those. I didn't want you to get hurt."

"I'd have fought you for it," said Carney.

Mike chewed thoughtfully. "Cookie accepted," he said. "At least you remembered that I do not eat raisins."

"Luck," I lied. Because he was right. I had.

After a few questions about what we'd sold that day and where it came from, which I answered proudly, Mike left, taking a few of the remaining turnovers "for the road," and

Carney and her boys went after him, although not before Carney turned around at the door and whispered loudly, "He's single."

"He's all yours," I said, and a funny look crossed Carney's face.

"I'm seeing someone," she said, ignoring the child tugging at her hand, and then she smiled. "And Mike's never been my type." Her look said plainly she thought he was mine.

"Well, my type is a lot more useful around a farm than a summer person," I said.

"He might surprise you," she replied, and then she was gone. Time to close up for the weekend. I followed her to the door, intending to flip the OPEN sign to CLOSED when I saw a familiar teenager trotting down the street, her blue-tipped hair bouncing, Brownie beside her, his halter attached to what was plainly a bungee cord rather than a lead rope. Louisa, no longer behind the wheel of a truck full of hay but still every inch a Bowford farm kid. I ran outside to greet them.

"What happened?"

"Found him eating Preeda Walker's rosebushes," Louisa said. "The woman who bought the general store. She wasn't very happy."

I turned to look at the round pen I'd set up outside the farm stand. S'mores and Teddy stood inside, calmly awaiting their evening meal. There was no sign of how Brownie got out. I shook the gate before opening it to let Louisa pop him inside. "It's shut," I said, mystified. "Maybe someone let him out?"

"I don't think so," Louisa said, then pointed, amused. I

turned around to see Brownie, all four legs bent up under him, crawling under the lower rail of the pen while S'mores and Teddy watched without surprise.

I burst out laughing and stood in front of him, ready to grab his halter when he stood up, although he tried to dodge me. "I have never seen any horse get out of a round pen," I said, and then, to Brownie, "What am I going to do with you?"

"Earl Bailey's brother has goats," Louisa said. "He had to wrap electric fence wire all along the bottom of his round pen to keep them in."

"Guess that's my plan for tomorrow," I said. "How do you know Earl?" Everybody knew everybody, of course, but it was always interesting to know why.

"I've been working with him for a couple of summers."

"That's great," I said. "I bet you're really good at it. I learned a lot from Earl."

"Carney says you're going to run Pioneer Hill by yourself," Louisa said. "And she's going to take over from her dad. With Amy. I think that's really cool. I might want to do something like that one day."

Carney—and Amy? That explained a lot. I contemplated my informant, wondering what else she knew about Bowford that I didn't. "How old are you?"

"Sixteen. I'll be a junior next year," she said. "Maybe I could help out here some too? If you need me. I mean, I'm pretty much full-time with Earl, and he's great, but I could do a little more." She looked around hopefully. "And maybe I could say hi to Maggie?"

That was the last thing we needed. "She's not here," I said. "And I'm not going to lie to you. I have, like, zero money. I'm going to be doing everything here myself for a long time."

"Oh, I didn't exactly mean that." She took in a deep breath, as if there were something she was having a hard time saying. "It's more—well, there's something I should probably show you. I've been working on this project," she said. "Your grandmother—Bee—she knew. And I think you should know, and Maggie might be interested."

I couldn't imagine what she was talking about.

"It's easier to show you than to explain," she said. "Do you have a few minutes? I mean, more like an hour, I guess. It's up Pioneer Hill."

Oh.

I hesitated. I hadn't been up the trail since I'd been home. Hadn't been up the trail in years, actually. Louisa shifted her weight from side to side, waiting for my answer, looking as though it mattered a lot, although I couldn't imagine why.

"Sure," I said. "I can close up here later." I went back to flip the sign to CLOSED, sent Jasmine a quick explanatory text, and grabbed my hat. "Ready," I said. Even though I wasn't.

15

Permission

THE TRAILHEAD FOR Pioneer Hill was just a few hundred yards away from the farm stand's parking lot. Once, it was a popular hike—not too difficult, and with a view across the river to the mountains of Vermont at the top—but it hadn't been used much in the past twenty-five years. I doubted many people even remembered it. Louisa stepped with practiced ease over the rusty chain that prevented snowmobiles and ATVs from entering. I followed, expecting to see the badly overgrown trail I'd occasionally looked at from the road when visiting Bee.

Instead, a path of fresh shavings stretched invitingly up into the woods. "We haven't shown anyone this yet," Louisa said, taking off at a fast pace.

"We?"

"The Valley Trail Alliance. But mostly Earl and me. We redid the whole trail, and at the top—well, you'll see." She kept moving, and I followed, taking a deep breath through my nose.

I could do it. I could go up there. As long as I didn't think too hard about it.

It looked different now, anyway. We dipped down into a gulley, then started to climb, leaving the road behind, until we came to a fork in the trail. Both ways looked equally inviting, but an arrow pointed to the left, and underneath it, on an elegantly simple wooden sign, was a quote. YOU CAN'T HAMMER A NAIL OVER THE INTERNET. —MATTHEW B. CRAWFORD

Louisa followed the sign. "So, to experience the trail, you go around this way," she said. We were surrounded by woods now, and the only sounds were the cardinals and the phoebes. Bushes that would be laden with blackberries later in the year lined the trail in any spot where the tree canopy was light enough to allow the sun to shine through.

"You did this yourself?" I wasn't doubting her, but I knew enough about trail restoration to know that what I was seeing represented hours of work. As we entered a boggy section of trail, boardwalks kept our feet out of most of the wet. Beyond it, a new culvert allowed the path to cross a stream.

Louisa glanced back at me, a little nervous. "Well, the alliance," she said. "At least, I—we—got a grant and a little help down here, and then at the top, to clear the view. But a lot of it is just me." As she spoke, we passed another sign. MEASURE YOUR WORTH BY YOUR DEDICATION TO YOUR PATH, NOT BY YOUR SUCCESSES OR FAILURES. —ELIZABETH GILBERT

We turned into a field of milkweed and goldenrod. Bowford residents had worn down this path for years, centuries even. I'd probably climbed it thousands of times as a child. At the top was a chimney, all that remained of a camp outpost built by a teacher in the 1940s who used to bring students here and set up tents to watch the stars.

"It's a meditation trail," Louisa explained. "At least, this part of it is." She slowed down again and kept speaking, as if she'd decided it was time to explain. "I designed it—I mean, these trails were here, but I wanted a way to bring them back to life and encourage people to use them. The quotes give you something to contemplate while you walk." She looked at me, as though checking to see what I thought of that, and I nodded encouragingly, trying not to think about the reason the trails had fallen out of use.

"At my high school, we can take the second half of our junior year to do a major project or internship. I want to work with the National Park Service. They have this preservation program, where you focus on learning historic land management and building techniques, but it's really small. This is basically my application."

"Got it."

The field ended, and we started up the steepest stretch of the trail, a section of rocky ledge surrounded by tall pines. I felt my shoulders and back tensing up. For me, it was hard to feel meditative here. *Breathe*, I told myself. *You'll be okay.*

I would have been too, if it hadn't been for the third sign.

WE NEED DIRT. DIRT NEEDS US. END OF STORY. —CHARLIE SMITH

I stopped without meaning to, and Louisa turned. "Oh," she said, and suddenly I could see that she hadn't really thought about my connection to this place, if she even knew.

"You quoted my dad," I said.

"That one was Earl's idea," she said, then added quickly, "But I like it. I really like it."

"I like it too," I said. I traced a letter on the sign, Louisa watching, worry in her eyes. "Did my grandmother know you quoted him?"

"Not the details. She said she'd come see it when we were done."

I wondered if she would have. As far as I knew, my grandmother had never come up the hill again since the day she told me to run up and see why my dad hadn't come home for supper.

Louisa was staring at me still. There was no comfortable way to do this. I spoke. "Did you know . . . that my dad died up here?"

The girl looked at the ground. "Earl said something," she said. "And I guess . . . people do know the story."

"He'd taken down some trees. He wanted to clear the view better, and we think there was another tree that must have been supported by one he was cutting. He was up here working, and it just . . . fell on him."

It didn't do that much damage. Didn't even pin him down. When I got there, I saw him lying across the ground and thought, *Oh, he fell*, and then, *Oh my God oh my God*, he wasn't breathing and the tree was on him—

There had been remarkably little blood. "He probably didn't even know what happened," I said, trying to shut down the image in my mind. "He died instantly. It was a total fluke. Just, really bad luck."

"I'm sorry," Louisa said, just like everyone always did.

"I know. It's okay." Not really okay, of course. But okay not to know how to talk about it. I never knew how to talk about it either. "I'm surprised my grandmother wasn't worried about you up here."

"She said as long as Earl knew what I was doing, it was fine."

I managed a half smile. Earl was who my grandmother had called when I stumbled back down the trail, crying and calling to her. He was the fire chief and head of the volunteer EMS then, and probably still was now. He was the one who had put his arms around me, helped me to tell him what I'd seen, then taken some of his crew and a four-wheeler up the trail. I didn't remember them coming back down.

"Yeah, if Earl said it was okay, she'd know it was okay." I turned away from the sign. "Let's keep going."

Another short climb and I could see the top of the chimney and then, as we came over the last rise, fully appreciate the work Louisa had been doing.

The clearing ahead was more visible and bright with sunshine, and as we reached the small summit, I paused, newly surprised by the beauty of something that was once so familiar.

They'd cleared a 360-degree view around the chimney, and you could see for miles. It hadn't been like this since I was very young, and seeing it again brought every hike up here back to me, with my father pointing out the church steeple, the pond, the river in the valley, the mountains of Vermont in one direction, and then looking down on our farm and the New Hampshire mountains beyond it in another. In the winter, when there was less work to do, we'd climb it every day—*Gotta get a hike in,* he would say. *There's no bad weather, just bad clothing choices.*

That would have made a good sign.

The view had gradually disappeared over the years. Dad would have been glad to see it back. Beyond the chimney were new benches, one on either side, set as far out as possible on the cleared area at the top of the hill, and in between them was a partially completed labyrinth, laid out in stones on the grass. More stones were piled next to it, probably the remains of the rock wall that I remembered running along just under the hilltop, where old apple trees suggested there had once been an orchard. Another sign marked the path's beginning.

THE LAND KNOWS YOU, EVEN WHEN YOU ARE LOST. —ROBIN WALL KIMMERER

"You think about that while you walk in," Louisa said. "Then there's another quote at the center, and one as you come out, and then that's all."

I started to step over the stones to read the words on the sign at the maze's center, then turned back to her. "Do you mind? If I don't walk it?" I didn't think I could handle a meditative walk at the moment.

"No, it's fine. You have to be in the right headspace. Plus, it's not even finished."

I walked over the lines of stone that created the usual path to read the centered quote.

DEFINITIONS BELONG TO THE DEFINERS, it read, NOT THE DEFINED.

"Toni Morrison," I said, even before reading the final line.

"I've always loved that one." But I hadn't thought about it in a long time.

The proper walker of the labyrinth would now wind her way out, but I stepped back over the stones to the beginning instead, and as I did, I read the final quote, the one that was meant to give you something to think about on the walk down.

IF YOU CAN'T BE WHO YOU ARE WHEN YOU GET THERE, DON'T GO.
—MAGGIE STRONG

"Oh," I said, unable to hold back my surprise.

"I told you I loved her book," Louisa said. "I made this weeks ago—not because I met her."

"I can tell," I said. "I'm sure she'd like it." She did like it. A lot. I almost wished I could tell Louisa so.

"I love what she says about living without things like money and fame or whatever and thriving. None of the things I want to do are really, like, conventional success stuff."

I looked at her, this teenager after my own heart, inviting her to say more.

"If I get to work with the National Park Service, I think I might want to go back after I graduate. Or I could find work designing trails, or making the parks more accessible. I really want to help people experience the outdoors."

"I love that," I said, and meant it. If I'd known myself as well as Louisa seemed to at her age, I could have done things a lot differently. "That's part of what I want to do at Pioneer Hill. Help more people know where their food comes from and what it's like to grow it."

Louisa smiled. "I meant it, about helping," she said. "You don't have to pay me."

I might be taking advantage of her affection for Maggie Strong—or "Maggie Strong"—but I'd be proud to work with this kid. And I might need the help. "Deal," I said, and we shook on it before I pulled out my phone and looked at the time.

"I should get back." Louisa nodded, and we turned to head down. "How much more do you have to do?"

"Just finishing the labyrinth," she said.

"Well, it's amazing. Your parents must be incredibly proud."

"Yeah." Louisa's open expression disappeared, and she ran a few steps, getting ahead of me. I hurried to catch up. Didn't want to talk about parents, then. I wouldn't push. Besides, I had another question.

"Why did you think I needed to see this, though?" I could understand wanting my grandmother to know what was happening—Grandma would have heard the noise and seen the cars or equipment it must have taken to clear the view—but now that all that was over, there would only be Louisa, finishing her creation. I probably never would have noticed.

"Well, you own it," she said. "Not the top, that's conservation land, but the trailhead, and part of the trail up, and maybe even part of that first field, I'm not sure. And because it's been unused for so long, Earl was worried the right-of-way would expire. That's why he made sure it was okay with your grandmother, but I didn't know how you'd feel about it."

"I love it," I said, making her smile again. "You don't have to worry about me. I can't wait until everyone can see it."

Her happiness seemed to fade a little. "When it's done," she said.

Okay. Not pushing that either.

We walked together in silence, moving faster going down than on the way up. The trail, instead of going back through the woods, now looped around through a second and third field, allowing the walker to appreciate one side of the view as she went. Again, the grass had been mowed to reveal the old path, once marked only by bikes, feet, and cross-country skis.

I did love it. I didn't even have to think about it to know that I would want everyone who could to enjoy Louisa's work. But it was possible that the college wouldn't feel the same way. They'd blocked the public from other places that were once used by locals, like a popular skating pond, citing insurance concerns. They might block this as well.

But I wouldn't give them the chance.

We reached the bottom of the trail, then walked along the short section of road back to the farm. Louisa pointed at the field behind it. "Are you going to let the sheep and horses out on that soon? It's getting pretty tall."

I could see what she meant. This had been a hayfield for years and arguably was still, but Grandma sold our haying equipment after Dad died. The Baileys worked it for a while, but she'd started using the field for pasture instead a few years ago, mowing it down in the fall if the animals hadn't taken care of it, which they usually had. Now the timothy heads were waving on the ends of their stalks and it was probably long past time to let the animals have their way with it. I'd have to get them out there gradually, so they wouldn't make themselves sick.

"Absolutely," I said. "I'd kind of forgotten. Thanks."

"That means you won't need hay for a while, usually," she said. She waved a hand at the field. "You could cut that first, before you turned them out on it. Then you'd have your own hay and you wouldn't have to buy it in."

"We used to," I replied. Maybe we would again someday. As pasture, it only fed our pet animals for a few months of the year. If I cut it as hay, it would save me whatever Grandma was paying for bales and still be good for grazing at least part of the time. I'd think about it.

Louisa was heading for home, wherever that was. I was too. Jas would be there, and we'd hash over the weekend and plan for the next. It was a good feeling, knowing what I'd be doing and who I'd be doing it with again. I could get used to this. If Louisa hadn't been there, I might have skipped down the road. I felt that cheerful.

Until I saw my mother in the driveway.

16

Permission Denied

I HOPED JAS had hidden upstairs. I knew she hadn't answered the door, because Margaret was seated outside in the old rocker, her hands resting in her lap as though she were avoiding the peeling white paint. There was no chance to straighten up or make myself look like anything other than what I was—sweaty, tired, and totally spent. That I liked this feeling, in fact sought it out, was not something my mother would ever understand.

What I considered "real work" was Margaret's "menial labor," and to Margaret, you didn't choose to spend your time that way unless you didn't have any other choices.

Margaret was all about choices. If I went to Miss Postan's for high school, then when I graduated I would have choices. She said the same when I was accepted—"accepted"—to Yarmouth. Not that I was arguing at that point. By then, I was totally caught up in my mother's world. It took me a long time to realize that the choices Margaret was touting were never the ones I would have made on my own.

She rose as I approached, getting out of the saggy cane seat with some difficulty, but by the time I came up the stairs she was standing, tall and stern. Her tailored pants and smooth, wide-collared cotton shirt could have been the same ones she'd been wearing when I stormed out of her office twenty years ago, but she was smaller at the edges, her neck and wrists bordering on delicate, her cheekbones even more pronounced under her short red hair, eyes boring into me from behind those heavy-rimmed glasses. In other words, she looked older, but still terrifying.

I had every right to be here, I reminded myself. I had every right to do what I was doing. Pioneer Hill was half mine and should be all mine, and would be too, if she would just give me a reasonable amount of time to figure things out.

I wavered between greeting her as Mom or Margaret and ended up not greeting her at all. I thought I detected a faint sigh as she spoke. "Can we talk for a few minutes?"

I gestured back to the rocking chair and leaned on the porch railing, but as I did a black fly landed on my arm and I swatted it away.

Margaret seemed to take in my bare arms and legs and compare them to her sensible June evening ensemble. "Inside, perhaps?"

I'd have to agree; I already had bites from the hike down from the chimney. I opened the door cautiously, giving Jas ample time to run if she needed to, but the kitchen was empty except for the mess and debris of the day, which was substantial.

My mother's eyes seemed to take in the whole place at once, sweeping over the mess on the counters and the table, the lamp with its burnt-out bulb by the sofa, lingering over the sink of dishes, before landing on me. I didn't invite her to sit down.

"I know what you're doing," she said. "I'm here to ask you to stop."

I wasn't sure what she meant, and I said so.

"Reopening the farm stand. Trying to re-create what you remember Pioneer Hill was like." She shook her head. "I know you're trying to do what you think your father and grandmother would have wanted. I'm hoping to make you see that you don't have to. You don't need to stay here. Your life can be so much more."

It sounded like a pre-rehearsed speech. If I didn't know better, I'd have thought she'd been coached by a therapist, but my mother did not do therapy. Or accept coaching. I imagined her searching "reasonable approaches to your estranged daughter" on the Internet. That I could see.

If she could try reasonable, I could try reasonable.

"You're wrong," I said, then tried to soften it a little. "I mean, mistaken. I can see why you might think that. But this is my dream. There's nothing I'd rather do than this."

She brushed my words off. "You need to look at this situation practically," she said. "What you don't remember is that running this place as a farm got harder and harder every year, and was probably never easy in the first place. Times have changed, and Pioneer Hill is worth more as land than it could ever be as a farm."

"I think we have different definitions of worth," I said, relieved to be able to keep my voice calm. I could be adult about this, see her perspective and show her mine. "But I do understand that to you, this is about money. I'm working on that. I'd like to buy you out."

She sighed. "It's not about collecting my share," she said. "It's about our financial futures—mine, yes, but also yours." She placed her bag on the kitchen table. "I know you don't understand why I'm doing this. And I know you have a dream, but you need to accept that it's just that. A dream."

This was not striking me as a conciliatory visit. "A dream you intend to squash."

"I hope to talk you out of it," she said. "But yes, if I have to, I'm prepared to go forward with the sale as trustee even over your objections."

Now that we'd turned Pioneer Hill back into a working farm, that wouldn't be as easy as she thought it would be. I felt a tiny, triumphant smile begin to creep across my face. "You can't," I began, but she was ahead of me, removing a paper from her bag and talking over my objection.

"You seem to be loosely familiar with the rules around land in agricultural use, but I think once you see the specifics, you'll recognize that I can." She held the page out to me. "After the disagreement over the Taylors' land a few years ago, the college encouraged the town to formally define the limits of agricultural use. I don't imagine they're available online, but if you consulted with the town hall, they would have provided you with this."

I took it and sat down, a page of dense print and numbered paragraphs with one highlighted.

Land in agricultural use refers to land used for the production of agricultural products such as horticultural, viticultural, floricultural, dairy, apiary, vegetable or animal products, berries, grain, hay, straw, seed or turf. To be considered as "in agricultural use," such activities must have been the primary use of the land for at least one of the preceding three years and must provide a greater than de minimis income or supply products used to support the maintenance of the farm or livestock.

"There's simply no way for you to meet the final requirement," she said.

I stared down at the page, reading it again and then again. All I could think was, *Mike.* Mike, with all his questions about what we were selling, and where it came from. I'd call him a traitor if I hadn't known whose side he was on all along.

As I read, my mother trailed a hand along the counter and walked past me, through the kitchen and into the living room just beyond it, as if she owned the place. I followed, trying to re-muster my arguments. This didn't have to change anything. Maybe she could still sell the land. But that didn't mean she should.

I didn't really expect her to listen to me. But I had to try.

Before I could say anything, she stopped short, staring at the coffee table, where the third Outlander book was still sitting on the quilt next to the plate I'd used in my post, although I'd eaten the Oreos. She stared for a moment, then swung around to face me.

"Is she here?"

I stared at her blankly for a moment.

"Maggie Strong," she said, her voice sharp and impatient. "Mike told me he saw you together, and I saw the farm stand on her Instagram, but I didn't realize she was staying here. She is, isn't she?"

No. This could not be happening. I shook my head in confusion, but my mother pointed to the table. "That quilt," she said. "I bought it at a craft fair when you were a baby. And the plate. It's cracked because the glaze was never meant to go in the dishwasher. Both of those were on her feed. She obviously took that picture here. Where is she?"

There could be other quilts or plates, I thought wildly. Couldn't there be another explanation? But one look at my mother's face told me how useless it would be to argue, so instead I let another dumb question roll out of my mouth, playing for time. "You have Instagram?"

"Of course I have Instagram. I am sixty-seven, not a hundred and two, and even if I were, that doesn't mean I wouldn't keep up with what my students were doing." She sat firmly down on the sofa. "Is she part of this? As much as I dislike her approach, she must be to some degree an intelligent person. And clearly you admire her. Perhaps she can help me convince you that I'm trying to help you."

I blinked rapidly, taking in the idea that my mother thought I—as in Maggie—must be intelligent enough to agree that I—plain old Rhett—was wrong. It was too hard, so I tackled the first part of her words.

"I don't exactly admire her. I agree with her. She values things like independence and self-reliance. And following your own intuition. And the kind of work that doesn't forget we're part of the earth, not its overlord."

Margaret raised her eyebrows. "That's quite a lot," she said. "Has your friend considered that without some of the things she says people don't need, society would have a hard time functioning at all?"

"She thinks society could use some shaking up," I responded, shaking a little myself. "And saying people don't need things isn't saying they can't have them if they want them. It's saying they should be able to choose what's right for them. Half of your students probably feel like they've been pushed into things their whole lives." *Like I did*, I thought but didn't say.

"Many of them like to think that, yes," Margaret said. "They rarely think about the disadvantages of the alternatives."

"There are disadvantages to not having someone else make all your decisions for you?"

"There are disadvantages to making the wrong choices. And to not having choices. People who have them, though, rarely recognize their privilege."

Was my white, British, overeducated ivory-tower mother actually privilege-checking me? "I know I'm lucky to have all this," I said. "That's exactly the luck—the privilege—that I want to take advantage of. To appreciate. But you think any choice that's not the one you would make is the wrong one. Isn't that what you're doing by trying to force me out of the farm? Making my choices for me—again?"

Margaret was facing me, her back to the stairs. A tiny movement behind her caught my eye, and I realized Jasmine was peeking down from upstairs. When she realized I was the only one who could see her, she bent down to nod fiercely at me and mouth something that was probably encouragement.

"I am being practical," Margaret responded. "You are not. And perhaps I'm giving your Maggie Strong too much credit. Possibly she's skipping around in the same cloudy-headed state as you seem to be, imagining that all it will take is a little elbow grease and whistling a happy tune to get this place profitable. But this is real life, not some photogenic fantasy, and we are not giving up the opportunity to dispose of this property responsibly just so the two of you can play Instagram farmer for a while."

Instagram farmer. The burn in my chest rose into my cheeks as I realized there was no way I could get her to listen to me. "This is not a fantasy," I said fiercely, knowing my words were pointless. "This is a solid business plan and I know exactly what I'm doing, and if you weren't so old and stuck in your own head, you could see that."

At the word "old," I could see my mother's hands tighten into fists. "Playing games with a tractor and taking a bunch of pretty pictures are not a solid business plan, and only a child would think they were," she said. "A child, or a vacuous influencer who's more interested in appearances than what lies underneath them."

"That's not fair," I said. "That's not who she is at all." I was flailing for words, and this was only getting worse. I needed to tell Margaret that she had it all wrong, about the farm and the Modern Pioneer Girl both, but nothing I said came out right.

Jas's upside-down head was still visible behind my mother. She grimaced.

Maybe if Margaret couldn't seem to hear me, she'd listen to someone else.

I gave Jas a quick frantic look as I spoke. "You want to talk to the Modern Pioneer Girl? You want to hear what she thinks? Fine," I said.

On the staircase Jasmine shot both thumbs into the air— she was clearly game. All right then, we were doing this. "She's right there."

17

Approval Can Be Won

I POINTED TO the stairs, while Jasmine looked shocked (how could she be shocked? she was listening), but after a moment of hesitation, she walked down with her confident stride and greeted Margaret.

"I don't want to get in the middle of a family discussion," she said.

My mother looked her up and down. Unlike me, Jas must have taken time to clean up. Her tank top was clean and tucked into wide-legged pants. She looked vibrant and unyielding.

"Possibly some interference is exactly what we need," Margaret said.

"I don't think you'll like what I have to say," Jasmine responded. "Although, first, I would like to apologize. It was my intention to enjoy a heated debate when we met on the *Today* show. It was not my intention for the merits of that debate to be drowned out by spectacle."

I stood frozen in between them, admiring the way Jas matched her style of speech to my mother's. Where I'd been pouring oil on flames, she was at least attempting to smother them with kindness instead.

There was a pause. "Thank you," Margaret said, her face impassive. "That's well put." Did she too see what Jas was doing? Even if she did, she seemed to welcome the shift of energy in the room. Jasmine pulled a chair over and sat across from her, while I remained standing and out of the way. "Can you apply those same skills to persuading my daughter to consider a perfectly reasonable offer?"

"I think I could," Jas said, and I stiffened—what did she mean?—before she went on. "If it was an offer. But I think at this point it feels more like a demand, and possibly you've known Rhett long enough to know how she feels about those."

Margaret's eyebrows lifted. Point to Jas—or "Maggie Strong."

"I think Rhett also has a reasonable offer." Margaret leaned forward as if to interrupt, but Jasmine kept going. "Calling her an Instagram farmer is unfair. She's not even on Instagram except in a professional way, and social media is key to promoting a business. She's told you she has a business plan. Have you considered that?"

"Reselling products from other farms at what amounts to a glorified bake sale isn't a business plan," Margaret said.

"It's not a—" I began, wanting to jump in and defend Jas, but she waved me down.

"No, it isn't," she said. "Fortunately that isn't what Rhett has planned. Instead, it's a way to get off to a quick start in order to—hopefully—preserve the family farm that's at the core of her ideas and demonstrate some of the possibilities."

"It's hard for me to believe that those ideas are worth as much as the offer we have on the table," Margaret said. "And I resent Rhett's assumption, which you seem to share, that I am focused on my own gain. The money from this sale, invested correctly, will provide the security Rhett will need as she discovers that a nomadic life of hopping from job to job and place to place gets more difficult as you get older." She looked up at me. "I understand that you don't view that as important yet," she said. "I truly believe you will."

Jas shifted, and I understood that this was the opening she'd made for me. Maybe my mother did think her plan was for the best, but then, she always did. Maybe her plan was safer. But money alone, without a way to invest my life in work I loved, wasn't ever going to be enough for me.

I wanted to offer her a calm, collected explanation of that. But all I could think about was how powerless I felt. "Money doesn't make you feel secure if what you sold to get it was everything you ever wanted," I said, unable to keep back tears. I spoke through them. "I have a business plan. I can take out a loan and buy out your half, and then I can build a Pioneer Hill that supports me and gives back to the community. I just need a chance. You think I'm a failure," I said. "I know you do. You think Grandma and Dad ruined me, the way they raised me. And if you do this, if you sell the farm out from under me, you prove you're right. And that's all you really want. To be right."

I knew I hadn't done what Jas hoped for. I couldn't match her impersonal approach, because for me, this wasn't impersonal. I got too worked up. I always did. I tried to take some breaths and come up with something better, to form some sentences about my real plans, the high-end restaurants I would supply, the farm education programs, the entire structure of which the farm stand was only a piece, but the words wouldn't come and I felt any hope slipping away.

"Then prove me wrong," Margaret said.

It was a window I wasn't expecting. I stumbled roughly into speech. "How?"

Margaret lifted her chin. "Convince me," she said. "Bring me that business plan. Line up your loan. Quit playing around and show me exactly what you plan to do with this land. The college acquisitions board meets in two weeks. I believe they will choose to pursue this, but if you have a better idea, I will consider taking the farm off the market."

Would she? With the light glinting off her glasses, I couldn't see her eyes. I didn't know whether to believe her, but I didn't have much choice.

She extended her hand to shake mine, as if on a deal. I took it and my eyes met hers. Her touch was cool and dry and somehow familiar, although if we'd touched at all in three decades, I couldn't remember when, or why. At my father's funeral, she'd stood stiffly by my side. When she dropped me off at school, or on her rare visits, she greeted me from a slight distance while other mothers embraced their daughters, sometimes with tears, sometimes with delighted laughter.

Her face unreadable, my mother dropped my hand and

bent to collect the car keys she'd placed on the coffee table. When she stood up again, she walked to the door quickly, without looking back.

"I know the way out," she said, and she was gone.

Jasmine stared after her until we heard the door shut, then collapsed dramatically on the couch. "Oh my God," she said. "You two are exactly alike. And you're awful. I couldn't have taken another minute."

I stared at her in astonishment, momentarily distracted. Alike?

"I thought you were going to tell her it was you, that you wrote it," she said. "It was the perfect moment! I didn't know you were going to throw me to the wolves again."

"You were waving. You gave me a thumbs-up—I thought you wanted to come down." I sat down hard beside her. "I thought you were okay with it."

"I was cheering you on," Jasmine said. "I thought you were going to be all dramatic. 'You want to meet the Modern Pioneer Girl? You want her to convince you? Well, you're looking at her!' Like that."

"There's no way that would have worked," I said. "The only chance was to get her to listen to someone who wasn't me—and you did. Or at least you got her to say she would."

"Maybe. But at least then the charade would have been done," Jas said. "And this would be done too. She wants you to prove yourself? You already proved yourself. And then you wrote a book about it. That's selling better than hers."

"Is it?" I started to grab my phone and check my Amazon rating, but Jas held me back.

"It is. Trust me. But you're all 'You won't listen to me!' and 'I won't listen to you!' until I thought my head would explode."

I sank back into the sofa. "Well, she wouldn't listen to me. And you're wrong. If she knew I'd written the book, it would just make things worse. She already hates me. Then she'd really want to destroy me."

"You think?" Jas was staring at me. "Because that's not really what I'm getting here."

"That's because you don't know her," I said, getting up and going into the kitchen.

Jas followed me. "You're going to have to tell her sooner or later."

"Nope," I said. "There is absolutely no reason she ever needs to know." I picked up the paper with the town ordinance printed on it that my mother had handed me and studied it again and sat down at the table, staring at the words. With her looming over me, all I could see was how bad it was. But if there was a way to make it work for me rather than against me, then I wouldn't have to rely on my mother's questionable promise to consider my plan.

Jasmine sighed. "You are seriously nuts," she said. "I just wish you hadn't dragged me back into it."

"But I needed you." I looked her in the eyes. "And she knew you were here. I can't lie to her face."

"I thought that was what we were doing," Jas said.

"This is different." I read the ordinance again, and again. *Primary use of the land ... at least one of the preceding three years ... a greater than de minimis income or supply products used to support the maintenance of the farm or livestock.*

Support the maintenance of the farm or livestock.

I sat up straight. Grandma hadn't made more than egg money off the farm for way more than three years.

But *products used to support the maintenance of the farm or livestock?* I set the paper down and patted it firmly with my hand, a surge of energy in my chest. That we could do.

Jas spoke before I could.

"Rhett," she said, "your mother thinks I'm Maggie Strong. Mike thinks I'm Maggie Strong. Louisa too. Pretty soon the whole town is going to think I'm Maggie Strong, or at least that she's here somewhere. I thought you didn't want that. What if someone asks? What are we doing here?"

"Finding a way to save Pioneer Hill," I said. "I have an idea too. I think we can do it."

"I'm happy for you," Jas said. "But what am *I* doing here?"

I sat back in my chair, the energy of my realization leaving me. "Helping me," I said. "Saving my butt." But the real reason she'd jumped in her Mini Cooper was to get away from Zale and all her problems in the city indefinitely. I should be helping her get through that—but instead, I'd just put a big expiration date on her ability to stay in Bowford, and we both knew it.

"And hiding, except when I'm pretending to be you."

Miserably, I nodded. She was right. So much for Jasmine's Bake Shop on Pioneer Hill. "You don't have to keep doing it," I said. I chewed one of my fingers, holding my eyes wide to keep them from tearing up. Jas needed to sort out her own life, not mine. "Forget the farm for a minute. Don't you want to get back to the city? Figure out what's next for you and Zale?"

"That's the thing," she said. "I don't." She picked up a

dishrag by the sink and then set it down again. "Do you want me to go?"

"No," I said quickly. Surprised at my own intensity, I tried to turn it into a joke. "I'd be more scared to face the people who wanted your cinnamon buns than I am to face my mother," I said.

Jas didn't laugh, and I saw by her face that I'd said the wrong thing.

"I want you here," I said. "Even if you never bake another thing." I meant it. I could do this alone and I would if I had to. But having Jas here made more of a difference than I wanted to admit, and not because of her scones.

She was still quiet, staring down at her hands, and as hard as I tried, I couldn't read her. The truth was, if she left, I'd be the only one who believed in me. And even though I'd come through that before, I didn't know if I could do it again. "Do you want to stay?"

"I don't know where else I would go," she said, and I realized that she was even closer to crying than I was. "I know it's weird, the whole situation. But I like being here. And the city"—she shrugged, avoiding my eyes—"Zale's probably changed the locks."

I got up and stood next to her at the sink, leaving the town ordinance on the table. "I know I'm not the only one with problems," I said. "Have you talked to him?"

She shook her head. "I told him I needed a break," she said. "I think he's probably . . . I don't know, relieved? Or pissed, maybe, but just his ego. I don't think he's cared about me, really me, for a while."

"It's so hard," I said, turning on the sink and taking up one of the dirty bowls. "Rafael and I just sort of stopped talking. And I almost didn't even realize it." Maybe I should have known, when I stopped having to struggle to say the things I wanted to say to him, that it wasn't that my Spanish had improved, but that we'd stopped having conversations about hard things.

"I feel like I wasted five years on a dude who was just interested in me for my donuts."

"Now you sound like my mother." I flicked some soap suds at her and she batted them away.

"Fine," she said. "Not wasted. Part of the journey."

I wanted to say something else, about the baby I knew she'd wanted, about it not being too late, but I didn't want to just lay out some platitudes. Instead, I put an arm around her and squeezed her tightly to my side. "Part of the journey."

She sighed and leaned her head on my shoulder before straightening and giving her shoulders a little shimmy, as if to shed the serious subject. "What's your idea for saving the farm? What have you got?"

I wanted to ask if that meant she was staying, but I wasn't sure if she was ready to answer me, or if I was ready to hear it. "A way to make sure Pioneer Hill is really a working farm—to meet the whole 'agricultural land in use cannot be sold for other purposes without approval' thing," I said. "We have to have produced something in the last three years, and I thought we hadn't, but we have." I shut the sink off and turned to her. At least I had this, and it was brilliant. Without Louisa, I never would have thought of it.

"Hay," I said. "There's a huge hayfield. My grandmother's been using it for pasture, but it's still hay. If we cut it and bale it and put it in the barn, then that's it. We're producing a product that sustains our livestock."

"Really? Like, that's enough?" Jas looked confused but willing to believe.

"I really think it is. That, plus everything we're already doing—I can't see how you say it's not a farm then. It's not a sure thing," I said, remembering my MPG words from earlier. "But it makes it harder for the town to just roll over and approve a change."

"So you double down." "You," I noticed. Not "we."

"And figure out how to bale a field of hay with no equipment," I said. "We're going to need help." And I still needed her help, or at least, I really wanted it.

"You'll still talk to your mother, though, right? Show her your business plan? It can't hurt."

I thought it could. "I guess so," I said. "I don't think she'll really listen."

"I'm not sure either of you is capable of really listening to the other. But I think you have to try."

We'd started washing dishes again, and I handed her a bowl to dry. And then, scrubbing another bowl hard, I asked the question we'd been avoiding.

"And what are you going to do?"

"Bake a hella lotta cookies," she said. I looked at her, hopeful, and she laughed. It was a little grim, and not really like she thought anything was that funny, but it was a laugh just the same. "I'm going to bake cookies. And—if anyone asks, apparently I'm Maggie Strong."

I scrubbed harder, happier now. At least we would be together. "They won't ask," I said.

"And at least it will mean I can come out of the kitchen. I mean, what difference does it make now?"

I hesitated, thinking. "I guess." Jas looked irritated, and I backed down immediately. She was probably right, and as weird as it would be, I at least owed her that. I wasn't even sure why it would bother me. I didn't want anyone—especially my mother—to know I was Maggie Strong. For me, the Modern Pioneer Girl was a secret identity. Having her on the inside made me stronger on the outside, while trying to be her on the outside would just make me more aware of how far from her I really was. But Jas was different. "What will you do, introduce yourself as Maggie?"

"Maybe Maggie is my pen name," Jas said. "A pseudonym. Like yours."

"And you're my pseudo face. Every introverted author would have one if they'd only thought of it."

"But would we even know?" Jasmine wiggled her eyebrows, then sighed and rubbed the back of her neck. "I don't know how I'll introduce myself. I'll just be Maggie, I guess. Why not?" She struck a pose. "I make a good Maggie, don't I?"

"The very best," I said, and it was true. She did, I didn't. I'd just have to live with it.

But that wasn't the only thing that was worrying me. Jas put, what, a year into the stupid plant-bakery thing? And however many years before that helping Zale with all his paleo-keto cookbook craziness? And now here I was, basically getting her to do the same thing.

"But what happens when you want to do something else?"

"Like what?"

"Do your own thing. Open a bakery, write a cookbook. Meet someone. Start over."

She snorted. "Slow down, pardner. I have no idea what I want to do next. And this is fun. Really. I mean, you can keep Bingley, but other than that it's great."

"Except for pretending to be someone else."

She paused, wet dish and towel still in her hand, and looked thoughtful. "Honestly? Pretending to be you is kind of a relief. I've kind of messed up these past few years. I don't really want to be me right now. And you're a badass."

"Some badass," I said. "I'm just doing my best not to give up."

"Isn't that what badasses do?"

Maybe. It was probably what the Modern Pioneer Girl would say. But being that MPG-style badass, solo and unwavering, was starting to feel harder to live up to than it ever had before. "I can't say I'm really feeling it at the moment."

"Nobody could possibly feel it all the time," Jas said. "But thank you for sharing her. I'm in need of an inner badass at the moment."

"No problem." I turned off the sink again. "So for now, you're the badass."

"And you're the farmer. And we cut all that grass and wrap it up or whatever and the town loves us and you convince your mom you've got your future retirement in the bag and make all your dreams come true. And then I . . . I don't know. Ride off into the sunset."

I didn't imagine it would be that easy. But with Jasmine on my side, it would definitely be easier. "And you're okay with that?"

"Up to a point, yes." She stopped drying dishes and turned to look at me, hard, shaking her towel at me. "I will wear the Maggie Strong hat on the farm and I will fly the MPG flag high when I need to. But you're doing your *Fresh Air* interview."

I saw a chance to object. "But my voice is different from yours," I said. "Won't people notice?" Talking to Emily on the phone was one thing. This had so much more potential to go wrong.

"On the radio? Versus in person?"

"Or on TV," I argued.

"You are giving people way too much credit. We're about the same age, we have the same education, we sound basically the same. Heck, we're both tall, fair-skinned forty-year-old white women. To half the world we're basically indistinguishable."

I eyed her, my city-loving, fast-talking friend, trying to speak my language. "Heck?"

"Heck," she said firmly. "Hells yeah. Practically the same person. But more importantly, no one else is paying that much attention to either of us. They never are."

She was probably right. And she sure wasn't backing down.

"Okay," I said. I stuck out a soapy hand. "Deal."

Jas took it. "We're not doing anything really wrong," she said. "Just a little innocent impersonation among friends."

Of course we weren't doing anything really wrong.

We stood there, hand in hand, for a moment, looking at each other. "This is probably dumb," I said.

"I know it is. I'm pretty sure I've told you that."

"But we're doing it anyway."

Jasmine nodded, grinning, and it was like we were back in our dorm room. "Sometimes," she said, "that's what we do."

18

A Man with
a Work Ethic

SETTING UP THE haying wasn't easy. Grandma had sold all our equipment to Earl and his brother decades ago, and although they'd cut and baled the field a few times during the intervening years, it wasn't on their schedule. Earl's first reaction—especially after we stood together looking at the weather on our phones—was that it was impossible. It takes two or three really dry days to get good hay, and with the forecast suggesting rain later in the week and the fields he already had on his schedule, he didn't have time to get to me and couldn't spare the woman who worked with him and Louisa in the fields, Amy Renfield, also known to me now, thanks to Louisa, as Carney's girlfriend.

Amy knew me. We'd worked for UPS together over a long holiday season once, when I was staying with Grandma between other gigs and Amy was saving up for a bout of her own preferred traveling, which involved mountains and snowboards. Even with her on my side, I couldn't quite over-come Earl's reluctance to lend me a 35,000-dollar mower—but I did get him to agree that if I could talk Louisa's dad into doing the mowing, we could use the machine.

"Louisa's a good kid," he said, "but she's never run the mower. Her dad could take care of it, though. You get the two of them over there, you'll be all right." Amy nodded at me be-hind him, and I knew it was the best I could hope to do. I took Louisa's number and called her.

Louisa sounded dubious about her dad. "He's working. He said he had calls all day tomorrow."

That really didn't fit in with my mental picture of a sort of younger version of Earl Bailey, but I didn't have time to think about it. I felt a frantic knot tightening in my stomach. With the forecast like it was, I couldn't let this wait. If I let it go until the next block of sunshine, it would almost certainly be too late to get hay my animals could eat, and any local would know it. I needed to have a barnful of hay to show our bona fides, and I needed it pretty much yesterday.

"Could you ask him? Maybe if he came for a little while, Earl wouldn't care if I took over? And it's not that big a field. It will take a few hours to mow, maybe three—"

"I'll ask," Louisa said. "I'll text you."

I had to be content with that. I left my phone faceup as I drove back to the farm, desperately racking my brain for al-ternatives and finding nothing. Her reply finally popped up as I was pulling into Pioneer Hill.

He says he's happy to do it, I read. We'll be there in the morning.

I ran into the house, calling to Jas, and showed her the text while I explained.

"See," she said, almost as delighted as I was. "You've got the town on your side already."

I almost felt like she was right.

I did chores early the next day, wanting to be ready when Louisa and her dad appeared. I already felt like I'd improved the place and was pleased at the idea of showing it off to another farmer. I was back inside for a refill of my coffee when I heard a truck in the drive.

"They're here," I hollered up the stairs, and as I heard the sounds of Jasmine—who was distinctly less excited about the actual haying than I was—getting ready to come down, I opened the door to greet the father and daughter who were going to help me get everything on track to establish Pioneer Hill as unassailably in agricultural use.

The driver's- and passenger's-side doors of the truck opened at the same time, and as I waved to Louisa, I was staring at the man accompanying her, uncomfortably aware that my mouth was open.

Mike.

"My dad says he already knows you," Louisa called. "That's why he said he would help."

Her . . . dad? I opened my mouth to speak, then closed it when I found I had nothing to say. Mike took a step toward the porch, his expression the friendliest I'd seen yet, Betsy leashed and tight at his side, tail wagging. "I was surprised you asked for my help," he said, and in spite of myself I enjoyed the warmth in his voice, "but I'm glad you did."

His face shifted as he saw my blank stare, but before I could try to recover myself, I heard Jasmine's voice from inside. Jasmine, who Mike and Louisa thought was Maggie Strong—and whose lack of knowledge about haying really didn't need to be aired right now.

"I'll be right back," I called, then backed up into the kitchen and slammed the door behind me.

"What's happening?"

I spoke softly, aware that the windows were open. "You have to stay in here. Louisa is out there with her dad and her dad is Mike."

Jasmine's eyes grew wide. "Mike," she repeated, and I could tell she was trying not to laugh. "Mike is the guy who is happy to help you."

"It isn't funny! Mike, who is second only to my mother in thinking I'm not capable of running this place. Mike, as in the one who told my mother Pioneer Hill wasn't selling enough of our own stuff to be a farm."

Jasmine nodded, still biting back a smirk. "What are you going to do?"

"I don't know," I wailed softly, getting as far from the windows as I could. "He's the only one Earl will let use the baler. But—"

But I didn't want his help. And I didn't want him to think I needed his help.

"But you're stuck with him," Jasmine said. "And you need him. You'd better be nice." A wicked look spread across her face. "And if he hates you," she said very, very softly, "then why is he here?"

I groaned and went back outside.

I had no idea why Mike was here. If I got this hay cut and baled, he wasn't building his welcome center—or at least, the odds were significantly less. We couldn't both end up happy, so he had to be here to mess with me, or mess things up for me. But I had to let him help.

I was so screwed.

My expression must have reflected that thought, because as I stepped back out onto the porch, Louisa's smile faded, and Mike's unusually friendly expression was replaced by one of slight disappointment and then his usual supercilious half smile, as if he was waiting to see what I would do now. Only Betsy looked the same, seated back on her haunches, panting, totally at home in the world. I glared at her owner.

"You're . . . Louisa's dad," I said.

Mike nodded. "I thought you knew," he said.

I waited for the snarky words that were sure to come. When they didn't, I tilted back on my heels and leaned against the closed door. My words were probably poorly chosen. "What the hell?"

"Louisa told me you needed me," said Mike. He matched my physical shift and leaned against the porch railing, and I had the feeling he might be enjoying himself. "So here I am."

So sweet, and so totally crap. Because if I knew anything at all about Mike, it was that coming through when you needed him was not his thing at all.

"I had no idea," I said slowly, making the most of it. "None."

He nodded. "I see," he said.

Louisa stared from one of us to the other. "What didn't she know?"

"That when you said your dad, you meant me," Mike replied. "I thought she was rising above it in the name of what's better for Pioneer Hill, but it looks like I was wrong." He turned back toward the truck. "We'll just go," he said.

Could he say anything more infuriating?

He was so smug. So condescending.

And so my only hope of getting this hay cut in time.

Louisa looked after her father, then back to me. "I thought you needed the hay cut," she said, and I swallowed. She really was a nice kid—who looked nothing at all like her father. She did look like someone who had just got caught in the middle of something she didn't understand, and I could relate to that.

I forced a smile. "I do," I said. "Mike, wait." Oh, those words cost me. But I wasn't going to show it. "I didn't know. And I guess I don't see why you'd help me, since baling this hay shows that Pioneer Hill is a working farm and makes the sale to the college that much harder. So I think I'm a little . . . dubious."

I didn't want to say right out in front of his kid that I didn't trust him. But I didn't, and he should know it.

Instead, he looked confused. "Why would that matter?"

"Because of the town ordinance. About not selling ag land for other uses." I crossed my arms. "Don't pretend you didn't know. You were in here asking all those questions for my mother."

Louisa still looked confused. "Why would my dad want you to sell Pioneer Hill?"

"Because he wants to build something for Yarmouth," I said.

Now it was Louisa's turn to cross her arms at her father. "You can't build here," she said. "This is Rhett's farm."

"I've gathered that," he said. He looked straight at me, all traces of snark gone. "I wasn't asking questions for your mother," he said. "I don't know what you're talking about with the ordinance. But if it's something that helps you keep the farm, and that's what you want to do, then I'm happy for you."

I narrowed my eyes. "You're not," I said. "You have plans. You've probably lined up the bulldozers."

Louisa stared her father down, and for the first time I noticed that although she was wearing boots and jeans suited to a day in the field, she was also heavily made up and wearing more earrings than I'd noticed before, and the Sharpie tattoos on her left arm appeared freshly inked. She looked like she was sending a message to someone, and I didn't think it was me. "You can't do that," she said again.

"I can't," Mike agreed, and where Louisa's tone had been challenging, his was aggressively mild. "It's possible Margaret can. She's the one who's pretty set on this."

"And you're not?" I asked.

"I'm really not," he said. "I can see why you might think I was. But here I am, and I promise you I am not here to sabotage whatever plan you have. Earl would kill me if I messed up his mower."

This was true. I bit at my lip, uncertain.

"But if you don't want us here, we'll go." The little spark of amusement was back in his eye, and I could see that he'd realized my dilemma.

Maybe he wasn't the one who told my mother. Maybe she figured out for herself that we weren't growing anything much to sell. It was pretty obvious.

Maybe I should—gah—trust him.

I stared at him again. He looked good, with the gray in his hair and a much broader chest than the college boy I'd known. I suspected he knew it.

He also looked weirdly right, dressed to run a tractor, happy dog panting beside him. Even with a surly teenaged daughter (daughter! I still hadn't absorbed that) ready to pout at him at any moment, he looked ready to get the job done.

There really wasn't any way around it. I was going to have to put my pride, and my doubts, aside and let him. I swallowed—dang, who knew that phrase was literal?—and consciously backed my body out of the tense fighting stance it had taken up. I could do this.

"I want you here," I said, and then I wondered why I'd put it that way, when I could have just said yes. But it was too late. "To hay. I do."

"You sure?"

Damn him, was he going to make me beg? I shot him a look, and he grinned.

"All right, all right, all right," he said. "Let's do this."

19

Approval Can Be Won (Again)

I SENT LOUISA to grab the four-wheeler and go drop the fence at the road while I followed Mike to his truck to get the tractor and bailer, trying not to feel awkward about being alone with him. "So," I said as I dropped into the passenger seat, "how are you Yarmouth's architect, and also the dude Earl Bailey trusts to run his tractor and mower?"

"I'm not Yarmouth's architect," Mike said. With Louisa gone, his ostentatious pose of reason had also disappeared, and he shifted the truck into reverse more violently than necessary. "I was an architect, in New York. Now I'm trying to start up a design-and-build firm here, and your mother was giving me a shot with the welcome center, which would be a pretty big deal for me. Would have been. Might be."

I appreciated the parsing of his words. "Must be working out okay," I said, looking around the truck's cab. "This is a nice truck." Nice, and new, and expensive.

He followed my gaze. "Louisa totaled our old truck last year. Got hit by a plow over winter break when she didn't slow down in time at an intersection. She walked away without a scratch, but the truck didn't make it. Insurance bought this one."

In a quick glance at his face, I could see it all, the plow, the old truck, Louisa shaking, Mike getting the phone call no parent wants. I went back to a safer subject.

"Your parents were architects, right?"

"Still are. I was at their firm until I left."

Was that another sign of disharmony in Mr. Perfect's world? I'd like to dig into that, but even though I knew Jasmine would tease me relentlessly, there was something else I wanted to ask. Carney said he was single, but "single" could mean separated. Or she could have been kidding. I was finding handling Mike-as-dad confusing enough. If he was married, I just wanted to know.

"Where's her mother?" Oops. That didn't come out right.

Mike swung the steering wheel around with what seemed to be unnecessary vigor. "I take it you've been talking to the neighbors. She's not here, she lives in New York, and, no, we're not married anymore. You want my whole life story in the two-tenths of a mile we've got here?"

Of course I did, but there was a limit to how willing I was to ask for it. I sat silently until Mike continued. "We got married right out of grad school. It lasted six years. Louisa is my only kid."

Well, if your mother was going to take off on you, New York was better than California, Margaret's first stop. It had taken her years to make her way back to the East Coast. I felt a moment's kinship with Louisa, and more than a little curiosity about their situation. Might as well be hung for a sheep as for a lamb. "And she lives with you?" We were already at the pull-in for the Baileys' field, the tractor and mower sitting there waiting.

"Did you head for journalism school when you left Yarmouth?" He shifted quickly into park. "So many questions."

"Just wondering." I slid out of the truck and walked around to the driver's side.

"She mostly lives with me. We've both been mainly in the city until this year. I'm transitioning to being here full-time, and the hope is Louisa will go to Yarmouth, but either way, she's doing a program here second semester this year. This fall she'll live with Emily—her mom. Not ideal, but it's worked out okay."

"It doesn't sound so bad," I said, wondering if Mike remembered that I, too, had lived with my dad after Margaret left. Mike was wrong, actually. It was ideal. But maybe not if your dad was Mike.

Mike gestured to the tractor, and I realized I was just standing and staring. "Key's in it," he said.

"I know," I responded, irritated with myself. "I was . . . waiting to see if you can start that thing."

"That thing" was an old green John Deere, the kind with a steering wheel the size of a car tire. It looked like an illustration out of a children's book, but if Earl said it ran, it ran.

Mike grinned as he climbed up. The tractor coughed once,

then started up. "He told me not to turn it off until I'm done, and park it on a downhill."

In the end, cutting the field went quickly. Mike pulled the mower, with Louisa zipping ahead in the four-wheeler to clear the branches that had fallen over the winter and spring, while I followed along in my tractor, pulling the tedder, its tines spinning the fresh hay up and flipping it over to speed the drying. It was bumpy work and took enough concentration to keep my mind busy. It was pleasant, driving along, and I was grateful for the protection of the cab every time I passed Mike, who was totally exposed to the hay chaff and the sun on the old John Deere. Louisa waved good-bye at some point, and it was me and Mike, going around each other in circles except when something went wrong and we bent together over the equipment, me ready to reach in and make a quick adjustment, Mike always insisting that we turn everything off first even if it took more time.

"It's better to wait for this than to wait for them to sew your hand back on," he pointed out, and I knew he was right. There's a reason workers' comp for farming is among the most expensive there is. It's deceptively dangerous, especially if you get a little cocky, and I have to admit that there was a lot of satisfaction in being able to replace a mower blade or pin before Mike had even figured out what was wrong.

Mike and the mower finished first, but the tedder was faster, so I wasn't far behind. I parked my tractor back at the barn, then jumped into his truck to pick him up after he'd returned Earl's tractor. The windows were down, and Betsy was waiting in the shady back seat, thumping her tail as I climbed into the car. I didn't know much about dogs, but this one, in spite of her first impression, seemed okay. Driving Mike's much newer version of my grandmother's old Ford felt both familiar and distinct in the way of picking up someone else's phone and realizing that although it's exactly the same as yours, it's also totally different. There was a glasses case in the console, an empty seltzer can, a rolled-up leash.

The Mike who climbed into the passenger side after I pulled into the Baileys' farm was not the clean-cut professional who had started up the tractor a few hours before. As he pulled off his baseball cap to wipe his forehead, I could see a clear line of dirt where the hat had been, and I laughed and grabbed his hand to stop him without thinking. A small shock of recognition passed between us as I quickly released it, making me stumble over my next words. "Wait. Don't mess it up."

"What?"

"You've got a stripe." I pulled out my phone and took a quick picture of him, hair standing straight up and multi-toned face, then showed him. "If your city friends could only see you now. They wouldn't recognize you."

Mike smiled, a little ruefully. "This is the real me, I'm afraid." He took a towel from the dashboard and wiped his face as I started the truck.

I pointed to the towel. "The Boy Scout, always prepared?"

"Always," he said. "But for the wrong things. Prepared to get dirty working, every time. Prepared to woo a new client away from a competitor on the golf course? Not so much."

"That sounds like pretty dirty work."

"I'm better at the tractor."

It wasn't the conversation I would have imagined having with Mike, but it was better than arguing, or at least, better than the kind of arguing we'd been doing in the driveway earlier. A weird ease had returned between us after the day in the field, and it was enough to carry us through the short drive back to Pioneer Hill. "Well, you were great today. Dirty work and all. Thank you. Again. I appreciate it."

He smiled, and it was a different smile from the ones I had seen before. Calm. Real. "You're welcome," he said. "I enjoyed it."

"More than office politics?" The question came out before I could stop it. Okay, he was right. I was nosey all of a sudden. But he was both so familiar and so strange, and I couldn't stop the part of me that wanted to know what had taken him from the college student whose face smiled next to mine in the pile of pictures shoved into the bed-table drawer of my room at the farm to Louisa's dad, worrying about clients and car insurance and SAT scores.

Mike didn't seem to mind. "Always," he said again. My eyes met his. That wasn't something the Mike I'd met on my first day at Yarmouth would have said. That Mike had loved nothing more than sparring and maneuvering even within our small college circle, and he was always willing to take the opposing side in an argument. I'd opened the bag lunch Yarmouth gave us for student orientation, taken out my apple, and seen the words "Washington State" on the sticker. My exclamation of disgust caught his attention, and maybe it was meant to. I'd already noticed him—he was the only guy in the group who was as tall as I was—but I didn't know how to just say hello.

"What's wrong, you don't like apples?"

"I like apples," I'd said. "I love apples. My family used to grow apples. Right here, less than a mile away, like tons of other families. So why are we eating an apple that had to go across the whole country to get here?"

Most of the kids I'd met that day would probably have shrugged that off. But not Mike. He'd turned the apple over thoughtfully in his hands and started to quiz me. Did I know how many apples were grown locally as opposed to in other places? As it happened, I did—New England only grew like two percent of the apples in the country. "But still," I argued, "they're right here. And it's apple season."

But how were they marketed? Where were they sold? Did I know where Yarmouth got its produce? Had I ever considered the economics of the commercial food system? Before I knew it, we were caught up in a heated discussion of global policy that lasted throughout that lunch break and resumed in our dorm's common room later. I thought Mike shared my interest in farming, and he kind of did, but mostly it just turned out that he was interested in everything. And he liked arguing. And debating. And—it had to be said—hearing himself talk. I would have thought whatever maneuvering was involved in getting people or places to hire you as their architect would have been his favorite part of the job, and nothing about the Mike I thought I had met again in the past few days argued against that. But this grubby, relaxed Mike was someone different.

"Me too," I said. "Not that I know anything about offices. But this work—things you can see you've accomplished at the end of the day—that's what I like."

"It's a hard way to build a life, though," he said. "Especially if you have a family."

"Yeah." I could tell he was talking about himself, and Emily and Louisa, but I had poked around enough there. "That's why my mom and dad split. I mean, you know that. But she wanted him to . . . find a more golf course kind of job."

"And he preferred the honest dirty work?"

"At any cost," I said as I pulled in at the farm and turned off the engine.

"Mmm." Mike stared out the windshield at the farmhouse. "I guess I'd like to think you can do both," he said. "Find a way to make a secure life for your family and do the work you want to do."

"Maybe," I said. "It's easier not to have a family to worry about, probably." I grinned, trying to lighten the mood. "I win! I get to screw up all by myself and I don't have to worry about anyone but me."

Mike reached into the back seat to rub Betsy's head, his arm uncomfortably close to my shoulder as he leaned toward the dog, and incidentally toward me. "There's no one coming to help with all of this? No husband or partner or whatever?"

"Nope. You heard my mom—I was with someone, in Argentina, but it ended a few months ago." Of course, there was Jas—but Mike wasn't a fan of Jas, or rather, of whoever he thought Jas was, and I didn't want to bring her up. Mike had no such hesitations.

"Shouldn't your guest be out here? Maggie? Louisa insists she's quite the farmer."

With no idea where Jas would be when we got back to the farm, I couldn't pretend she wasn't around, so I shrugged his words off instead. "No need," I said. "Everybody deserves a break sometimes."

"She looks like she's better at taking breaks than taking on a job," he said, and while part of me was a tiny bit pleased that at least one man didn't think Jas represented his womanly ideal, I was mostly irritated.

"What, because she's well-dressed? Because she's pretty?"

"Mostly because she didn't seem to know which end of a lug wrench was up," he said. "But maybe a little of that too. She's not what I expected. Or what Louisa expected, I gather, although she's still as enamored as ever." He paused, and Betsy pressed her head into his hand for more petting. "Even you have to understand that it's tough for a parent to be thrilled when his kid goes all in for a role model who thinks college is an unnecessary frill."

I wasn't sure how to take his words. "Even me, huh?"

"You didn't graduate, unless you went back somewhere else." I shook my head in response to his questioning look, and he went on. "And you're fine. I mean, look at you." He gestured around. "It's a lot, what you're ready to take on."

"And you don't think I can do it." I wasn't challenging him, just stating a fact.

"I wouldn't say that."

I shifted my weight in the seat, putting some distance between us. "I think you're misjudging Maggie Strong," I said.

"She'd want Louisa to do what was best for her." Louisa seemed fine to me, even if she was clearly pushing Mike's buttons. She had goals and she was going to crush them—and I happened to know you didn't work for the park service without some kind of degree. Mike didn't have anything to worry about.

I opened the truck door, but I had one more question. "So, if you're so happy to be a part-time farmhand, why are you on board with helping my mother and Yarmouth shut this place down?"

He leaned back, watching me. "She hired me," he said. "Like I said earlier, I want to do design and build, and while I've got a couple of houses for clients, the commercial work tends to be where the money is. This would be a big project and would probably bring in other clients."

"No golf necessary." I started to get out of the truck.

"No golf. But"—his words stopped me—"I didn't know you wanted to come back," he said. "When I started. Your mom told me you were gone, and I figured she'd know."

Oh. "Well, she wouldn't."

"I probably should have guessed that," he said.

I shrugged. "Not really," I said, my voice intentionally brusque. "It's been a long time."

"That it has." He was silent a moment, and our eyes met over the gear shift. "So, you going to call for help when you're ready to bale?"

"Probably," I said, and in the close quarters of the truck, it seemed to mean more than I intended it to.

20

Regrets

THE GREAT THING about a radio interview, in theory, should be that you don't have to dress for it. But the next morning, after chores, Jasmine took over, insisting I needed to look the part by noon. "I'm not turning on my video," I argued. "Obviously."

"Obviously," she said, rifling through my closet. "But if you look good, you will sound good." She turned. "There is literally nothing in here."

"I came from South America with a backpack, remember? Have you seen me go shopping?"

"No, but I should have." She took out my least-worn pair of jeans. "Start here," she said. "Be right back."

I pulled them on, listening to her rustle around in the guest room, and she reappeared with a gingham-checked shirt in bright pink, a belt, and the boots I'd worn on our ill-fated *Today* show adventure. "Redheads don't—" I started.

"Redheads look great in pink," she said. "This is not *Anne of Green Gables.* This will brighten you up and make you feel happy and good about yourself."

She was right, of course—and being belted and booted did make me feel more ready for whatever came next than my T-shirt and socks. I accepted the powder and lip gloss Jas was offering and ran my fingers through my hair until she pronounced me ready.

"Okay," she said, clearing my old desk of everything but my laptop and a reusable water bottle, with the headphones she'd lent me at the ready and my mobile phone by its side. "I am leaving you now. You will be great. And you will not pull any last-minute craziness."

I eyed the setup nervously. "If I could think of any, I would," I said.

"That's why I won't even be in the house. You're on your own. You will have fun, Terry Gross will love you, and your editor will instantly call and offer you a new book deal that solves all of your financial problems."

I laughed. "Maybe that shouldn't be our standard for success," I said. "How about no table flipping."

"No table flipping," said Jas. "Unless there's wrestling. Then you flip tables." She extended a hand. "Laura."

"Wrestling's always so great on the radio," I said, putting my right hand on top of Jasmine's. "Zora."

Jasmine's left hand. "Frida."

My left. "Gloria."

Then, together, lifting our pile of hands and dropping it at every word: "Ruth. Bader. Ginsburg. Go."

"Maybe we should add Xena, Warrior Princess," I suggested. "You know, for hand-to-hand combat."

"Use your words, Modern Pioneer Girl," Jas said. "Use your words."

I'd already done a call with the *Fresh Air* producer. This would be the real deal, the interview itself via my laptop, running live on some stations and taped for others. As Jas left, my phone rang—that would be Emily, calling to make sure I was ready and to wish me luck.

As I answered, something inside my brain clicked. Emily. Someone else had mentioned an Emily recently. The niggling feeling unnerved me until an answer quickly followed: Mike. Louisa's mom was named Emily.

Louisa's mom, who gave her *The Modern Pioneer Girl's Guide to Life* and might regret it.

Who lived in New York. Like the editor greeting me excitedly while I stared in horror at an old *Fresh Prince* poster above my desk, who—I suddenly remembered—had "family in Bowford."

Not. Possible.

Either I'd responded to her automatically, or she hadn't noticed my silence, because her voice carried on happily in my ear. "Are you ready? This is going to be great."

"Totally ready," I said. It came out in a squeak, and she laughed.

"Nervous is fine," she said. "It's not nerves, right? It's excitement. Adrenaline. Because you're going to have so much fun and be amazing."

"I hope you're right." I was scrambling around in my head, trying to find some way to get her to confirm that she couldn't possibly be the same Emily without risking the mad clashing of worlds that would result if she was. Maybe her bio on the publisher's website? I typed her name into the search bar while she repeated the same advice I'd been given earlier about the show—breathe, stop at the end of sentences to let Terry respond or ask another question, try to enjoy it.

Emily Koh. Executive editor, books such as blah-blah . . . *Lives in New York City with her teenaged daughter Louisa May and her cat, Cliché.*

Boom. I grabbed for the water bottle and sent it careening off the desk, spraying liquid everywhere as the top popped open. I shrieked, and Emily's voice took on a note of panic.

"What?

"Oh gosh . . . shoot—" I swabbed at my keyboard with my sleeve and realized the water had missed it, at least, and also that this was the perfect opportunity to get off this call and deal with the ramifications of Emily-as-Mike's-ex later, much later, and possibly never. "It's okay, I just spilled some water. But I need to get a towel before they call."

"Go. And get more water too; you'll need it. And have fun!"

I really felt like people were insisting too hard that this was going to be fun. I picked up the water bottle and closed it firmly, wiped up the damage with my T-shirt from earlier, and threw it out of sight before remembering that I'd very firmly insisted this not be a video call.

Breathe. That was good advice. Terry Gross seemed very nice in the interviews I'd heard. Insightful, yes. And maybe a little probing, sure, but I didn't have anything to hide. Well, not anything you'd hear over the radio, anyway.

I clicked the link I'd been given and almost immediately, there was a voice in my ear. "Ms. Strong? Are you ready?"

"As I'll ever be."

"Terry will be with you in a moment."

Mostly, the interview was like a trip back in time. I talked about leaving college without a degree—let's leave the college name out of it, to protect the innocent, I said—and the wild ride that followed, in which I said yes to anything and everything legal and lucrative, and a few things that were on the shady side (you're kidding yourself if you think the pedicabs in Barcelona are really regulated). And I talked, very happily, about the Modern Pioneer Girl—herself, or myself, or however you put it.

"Creating a superhero alter ego is a big part of your *Guide*," she said. "Can you talk to me about how that started for you?"

"I grew up obsessed with Laura Ingalls Wilder," I said. "Like a million other kids, I know. And when I was a teenager, my family life fell apart in a big way, and I got sent to live somewhere else. I was new, I was this hick kid who didn't know anything, I didn't have the right clothes or say the right things, and I pretty much wanted to crawl into the Little House books and not come out."

Terry laughed. "I think a lot of girls can relate to that."

"Exactly. And I know, we all know now, that the government that encouraged the Ingalls family has a lot to answer for. But Laura herself just really spoke to me. Especially if you read her memoir, and biographies, which of course I did—she was brave, which doesn't mean fearless, it means doing things that scared you. She struck out on her own when she had to. I wanted to be like that, not like this scrawny scared kid who sort of scuttled around the school hallways hoping no one would talk to her."

I took that breath I'd been advised to take, but Terry seemed inclined to let me go on, so I did. "I made one friend, and she was impossibly smart and confident, and all the things I wasn't, and she was like, 'I'll let you in on my secret. Everyone is scared. Everyone worries they're the biggest dork in the room. The difference is, they're all pretending they don't.' I didn't really believe her, but she convinced me to pretend to be someone else—someone tougher than me, someone who didn't care what anyone thinks of them—for just one day. Of course I picked Laura. It really helped." I laughed at the memory. "Also, she cut my braids off. Apparently, it's cool to channel your inner Laura Ingalls Wilder but not to go around looking like Melissa Gilbert."

"That's become your signature advice to young women. There are the things you don't need, and the things you do."

"Exactly. And the 'thing you need' is really confidence or at least the willingness to fake it. I say it's your passport, your superhero alter ego, pluck, and strong arms in the book, but those are all part of the same thing. Creating an alter ego gives you a place to find that confidence when you're not feeling it, and a way to talk to yourself about who you are and what you can do."

"And coming up with a name is fun."

"It's fun, but it serves a purpose too. It tells your brain,

'This is our moment to be a hero.' Maybe other people don't talk to themselves in the plural?" For a moment, I felt exactly like the hesitant kid I'd just described. My voice got high and questioning before I reined myself back in. "And maybe they do. It doesn't matter. Any way you call on your alter ego that works is right."

"I get the feeling you called on yours right now."

I smiled. Okay, everyone won. I was having fun. "You are absolutely talking to her," I said.

"But you've been criticized for setting a bad example for other young women. Maybe it worked for you to leave college and become estranged from your family. That's not going to work for most people. What do you say to critics who accuse you of encouraging people to make those choices?"

Had I been criticized for that? It was one of those moments where you see yourself through someone else's eyes and it's like putting on clean glasses. There was Rhett, the dropout screwup with the alter ego that allowed her to pretend otherwise, and then there was this version of me, successful enough in my unconventional choices that others might emulate me.

"I don't think of my book as a guidebook," I said slowly, thinking my way through my answer. "The name is just for fun, because there's no such thing as a guide to life."

I paused, thinking, and Terry waited. I created the MPG at a moment in my life when I felt like I had nothing, and returned to her when it seemed as if I had even less. Taking on her persona helped me realize that I never had nothing, because most of what I had—and what I needed—wasn't physical. I had an education, I had freedom, I had the privilege that comes with being a white American and the savviness to avoid most of the problems of being a woman traveling alone, and I had the courage to reject a life that wasn't right for me in search of one that was.

I didn't feel enviable back then, but I was.

"You don't need to drop out of college, or even leave town," I said. "The passport is metaphorical. What you need is a willingness to try things that speak to you but you've been told won't work. To figure out who's in you trying to get out. Don't do what I did. But question what I questioned."

"It's time for a short break," Terry said, and I reached for the water with relief and even pleasure.

To my amazement, the rest of the interview continued in the same vein. Terry didn't ambush me with questions about my book's literary value, or produce my mother or some other bogeyman from a closet. She asked me questions about my work, and I answered them. It only got a little dicey toward the end, when she asked me what I was doing now. "More of the same," I said, aware that what had qualified as finding myself and my voice in my twenties might sound flaky now that I was forty. "I admit I'm probably ready to find a place to land for good," I said.

"Well, when you do, we hope you'll write about it."

And that was it. I'd been interviewed. I'd survived.

Hell, I'd nailed it.

I opened the window and stretched out on the bed. In the distance, I could hear the satisfying sound of Louisa, who'd volunteered to ted the hayfield with my tractor. It was a very productive feeling, like being in two places at once. Jas was still out and I was alone in the house except for Alistair, who was rarely seen during the daytime. There were piles of work to do, but it was good work, on my terms. And I never, ever had to produce my inner Modern Pioneer Girl for public consumption again. I felt benevolent toward the entire universe.

The phone rang. The rest of the world had moved to mobile, but here in Bowford, where service is still spotty, landlines remain.

"It's Margaret Gallagher," said the voice on the other end of the line. "I'd like to speak to Maggie Strong, please."

So formal. As though there were half a dozen employees trotting around here who might have answered the phone, instead of just me and Jas, and at the moment, just me, which was a problem. Because I'd just told Terry Gross on live radio that I—meaning Maggie Strong—was speaking from a friend's farm in New Hampshire.

Margaret couldn't have been listening. Could she? Aw, hell. It was NPR and she was an Ivy League college president. Of course she would have been listening. She was probably listening while drinking coffee from an NPR mug before going shopping with an NPR tote bag.

My tongue, which had readied itself to say that Maggie Strong wasn't here right now, instead stumbled over my response. "Speaking," I said. I hadn't talked to my mother on the phone in more than twenty years, at least. It wasn't as if she would recognize my voice, especially if she thought she was talking to Maggie. Just like Jasmine told me all those years ago, she would be thinking more about herself than about me, especially if I said as little as possible.

"Ah." If I hadn't known better, I would have thought my mother was nervous. "I'm calling to congratulate you on your *Fresh Air* interview. I happened to be in the car, and I found myself enjoying it so much I turned it on in the kitchen when I got home, which was unexpected."

Whoa. "That is unexpected," I said. Almost as unexpected as this phone call. "I'm surprised you didn't change the station."

"I came close. But in spite of our rather loudly aired differences, I wanted to hear what you had to say. If nothing else, your message holds great appeal for many Yarmouth students. I admit that concerned me. But the way you expressed yourself in this interview answered a lot of my questions."

"Thank you," I said carefully.

"While I believe Yarmouth students have much to offer the world in following what you call conventional paths, it would do most of them good to ask more questions, and question more answers."

I sat down on the bed, a huge smile stretched across my face that I had to work hard to keep from creeping into my voice. I thanked her again, grinning the whole time. I had no idea why she'd decided to say all this now, but I would take it. Her next words answered that question.

"Given that, I was calling to ask if you would consider addressing the Yarmouth summer class while you're in town. I think you have a lot to offer them, and I admit I would enjoy introducing you. I'd like to have the chance to remedy our last encounter."

I didn't think my smile could get wider, but it did. "I'm sorry," I said, still carefully keeping my voice neutral and, hopefully, nondescript. "I'm not really a public speaker, and certainly not the kind that gets up behind a podium. I'm not doing any more appearances."

She tried to talk me out of it, and I held firm in as few words as possible while enjoying the process. This wasn't my mother validating my book, or the Modern Pioneer Girl, and I didn't pretend that it was—if she knew it was me behind it, and not the confident woman she'd encountered on the *Today* show, her attitude would be completely different.

That didn't mean I wouldn't take what I could get here.

"Sleep on it," Margaret finally said. "Give it some thought. It just seems like a shame—you're here, and you have so many fans on campus." And, I was realizing, presenting "Maggie Strong" to her students would be my mother's way of erasing what had happened on the *Today* show and replacing it with something better, something in which she became more mag- nanimous mentor than hidebound combatant. It was possible that even my mother wasn't entirely immune to worrying about how others saw her.

I could agree to pretend to think about it if it meant ending this conversation. "Fine," I said. Then, because why not: "Or what if we arrange a trade? I speak to your students, and you sell Rhett your half of Pioneer Hill?"

There was the faintest pause, in which I almost allowed

myself to consider the possibility that she would say yes, and then what would I do, before she laughed. "I do intend to listen to her plans," my mother finally said. "But I come at this from a different perspective. I hope you don't think I'm unreasonable. I know Rhett does."

True that. I didn't say anything.

"I watched my husband throw away a promising academic career to burn himself out trying to make that farm into something—for his dad, his mother, his ancestors, who knows? He shut out everyone who tried to help him. By the end, he was reckless, trying every scheme he could think of, taking risks by doing work he shouldn't have been doing alone, and it cost him his life. I don't want that for Rhett. I care too much about her to let that happen."

This time the silence was mine. I'd never heard my mother say anything like this before, never heard her express regret over my dad's death, never even considered that she might, on some weird level, have actual concern about my taking over the farm. It was the same condescending conviction that she knew best that had infuriated me before, many times, the same smothering, demanding Margaret, but with a layer of emotion I didn't want to open myself up to. I responded quickly, bringing it back to more familiar ground.

"What if it's what she wants for herself?"

"Now you sound like Rhett," Margaret said, and although I knew what she meant, I shut my mouth firmly, determined to end this call before I said much more. "I told her I'll hear her out. I can't do more, but I meant that. I listened to you, didn't I?"

Somehow I didn't believe that marked the beginning of a new, improved Margaret. I offered as brief a good-bye as manners permitted.

"Congratulations again on *Fresh Air*," she said. "I've never been on it myself. That's quite an accomplishment." She hung up, and I collapsed back onto the bed again, feeling as if I'd just chased an entire herd of runaway cattle into the branding pen. There had never been anything, ever, as mentally challenging as going even a single round with my mother. And she'd said plenty that I did not want to think about.

But still. "Quite an accomplishment."

21

Permission

WHILE I BROUGHT my inner Modern Pioneer Girl to radio, Jasmine, apparently not noticing that it might be weird if someone saw "Maggie" out wandering Bowford while simultaneously being interviewed by Terry Gross, had done a supply run and in the process seemed to have charmed half the town. When she returned from what she called her "scouting expedition," she unloaded a gorgeous, shiny Italian espresso machine from the back of the Mini Cooper. I boggled while helping her carry it inside.

"It's on loan, maybe to buy, from the woman who runs the Bowford Inn," Jasmine said. "She said she hates it and she's putting the Nespresso back out at breakfast there. She wishes her nephew had never convinced her to get it."

"There's no way we can afford it," I said.

"You never know. We could pay in kind—baking for their guests, or free lattes for guests and staff ... we'll come up with something. Meantime, she's very happy to have it off her hands. And she also happens to be on the zoning committee you need to get on your side before you make your case to your mom."

"It's so awkward," I said as we hefted the machine up onto the counter in the farm stand. "I hate that it's so conditional. *If* I can buy my mom out. *If* the college isn't taking over. It makes me sound weak and needy. I hate that."

"Everything is *if*," Jasmine said. "*If* I don't get hit by a bus. *If* I don't meet the wrong guy and lose five years of my life to doing his thing not mine. *If* the store has marzipan."

"Please. I prefer to live with the illusion that I am totally in control at all times."

"That would be admirably self-aware if I didn't know that you actually believe it."

I didn't want Jas to dwell on the question of Zale, so I moved on. "Did the store have marzipan?"

"No, but surprisingly the general store did. The owner said she loves baking, so she sometimes stocks things she herself wants to have. She offered to get us stuff wholesale too—we settled on just a little markup—and she gave me an idea for a Thai iced latte special. You didn't tell me people up here were so cool."

I scooped ice cream at that general store as a kid, but I hadn't met the new owner. "I didn't know they were that cool." Jasmine looked delighted to have connected with someone, and I was happy for her too. Except—"What did you tell her your name was?"

"Maggie, of course." She stuck her chest out and took up the loose cowboy stance I recognized as her Modern Pioneer

Girl. "I told everyone I was Maggie. I waved the Pioneer Girl flag high and talked to everyone about how excited I was to be here, and working with you to save Pioneer Hill from college development. And I asked everyone what their favorite coffees and desserts were, now and from when they were little." She took out her phone. "I have a whole list of new things to try. Do you know what a pandowdy is?"

"My grandmother used to make that. It's like a deep-dish pie with no bottom crust, and biscuits or something easy on top." I tried to imagine Jasmine greeting people on the Bowford green, in her trendy denim miniskirt with the ruffle on the bottom and the boots that were her concession to Modern Pioneer Girl style, and found that I couldn't. No one walked around on the green talking to people they didn't know. A nod, a faint lift of the chin—that was a Bowford greeting. "Good morning" was just about acceptable. "Hello" and "What did your grandmother make you for breakfast?"—she might make the local police report.

"Maybe I'll make that a special. Like, if it was all fruit and oat topping, it could be breakfast. It's even healthy." She stopped and shook her head. "I'm trying not to think about food like that anymore, though. It's real food, is what it is."

"Real food is good." I looked more closely at Jasmine. I'd swear her face looked a little less bony. She looked happier at least. I put aside my irritation at the Modern Pioneer Girl bopping around town like Reese Witherspoon in *Legally Blonde* and remembered that I was happy too. "Did you listen to me? It went great."

Jasmine stopped fussing with the espresso machine and

threw her arms around me. "I did and it was amazing. I told you you could do it! I even took notes."

Because my advice was that good? Wow.

"That way when I'm being you, I can sound like you," Jasmine continued. So not that. But still good, I guess. "I like the idea of talking to people about who their inner alter ego is," she said. "That might be the best cure for small talk I've ever heard."

In person?

She giggled. "You should have asked Terry Gross if she had one."

Right. When it was all I could manage to get through the interview. Jasmine's Modern Pioneer Girl would have, though. Her Modern Pioneer Girl would probably have emerged with a coffee date with Terry the next time she was in town and her address to send her a basket of her favorite cookies.

I walked around the counter and surveyed the setup. "I think we should put the machine on the back counter," I said. "Then there's more room here."

"But then I have to turn my back on people while I make their drinks," Jas said. "This way I can chat."

"But there's more room for cups and things back here. Come on, let's move it." We hefted the machine to the other side. "Look, the plug is easier here too. We'd need an extension cord if we left it over there."

Jas nodded, looking a little dissatisfied. I was about to argue my point—people weren't coming in to chat, anyway—when a shadow fell across the door we'd left open as we carried the espresso machine in and we both looked up. It was

Mike, with Betsy on a leash beside him, saying he thought he'd heard us in here, and stepping aside to let the person behind him come fully into the small space. The slender, dark-haired woman burst in quickly, her face excited.

"I have been dying to do this," she said, her eyes on Jasmine. "Maggie. I'm Emily Koh, and I'm so happy to finally meet you."

There wasn't time for Jas and me to even trade a glance. All I could do was hope Jas was quick on the uptake, as I was pretty sure I'd told her my editor's name but I definitely had not told her yet about my discovery that Emily-my-editor was also Emily-Mike's-ex.

Jasmine came around the counter and took Emily's extended hand. "I'm so excited to meet you too," she said, and it at least sounded entirely sincere. I was trying to figure out how to fill her in subtly on anything she hadn't figured out, but Emily took care of it for me.

"I'm so excited that you turned out to be right here. For once I'm happy that my ex can never stay away from a farm, especially not one that needs work—not that I'm saying this one needs work," she said quickly. "Just that Mike can never keep his fingers out of farm work. It used to make me crazy— but now that it's led to us finally having an editor-writer meetup, I can't complain."

"Emily would have preferred I kept my white collar clean," Mike said. He was speaking to Jasmine as Maggie, but his eyes sought me out with a smile that told me he was remembering our conversation in his truck yesterday. I tried to smile back, but I was more worried about Jasmine—and fascinated by Emily, who turned to me.

"And you must be Rhett," she said. "I've heard so much about you. Louisa's been talking about nothing except coming over here." She laughed. "She's pretty annoyed with her dad for even thinking about helping tear the place down. I hope you and Margaret work it out." She turned back to Jasmine and started to congratulate her on *Fresh Air*, which she'd apparently listened to in her car on the way up here. I had to admire the smoothness with which I'd been handled.

"Louisa managed to put aside her belief that I'm a traitor to everything she stands for long enough to send me a message," Mike said, looking at me. "She's worried about the forecast. Apparently, it's changing and she wants to know if you think we can bale the hay today."

I grabbed for my phone. "Changing? How?" I tapped on the weather app and saw it—clouds gathering for tomorrow. Rain late in the day, and that could easily change to earlier. Plus, with no sun to burn off the dew, baling on a cloudy day was risky. I groaned. "Noooo," I said. Jas could deal with Emily. She would have to. This was bad. I went outside, as though staring up at the still-clear sky would help, and Mike and the others followed.

"I know," he said, his tone sympathetic. For once I didn't resent it. Betsy had been sitting quietly beside him in the farm stand, but outside, she strained at the leash in the direction of the barn and paddocks and we let her lead the way. "I talked to Earl. He's at a funeral service this afternoon, but he'll let us run the baler. As long as it stays light, we'd be able to bale it all and get it in the barn. Or we can wait until tomorrow. Your choice."

"Is he loaning us his rake?"

"Louisa's out in the field, but she's ready to go get it."

Emily looked from one of us to the other. "Why does it have to be dry?"

"Wet hay catches fire easily," I said. "Plus, it molds."

"So if it's not dry, we should wait," Jasmine said, and I turned to her, not even caring that I was telling her something that "Maggie" should know.

"If we wait and it rains, the hay is useless. I can't feed it out." And then it's not supporting livestock. And the land's not in agricultural use. And boom—Mike's building his welcome center. I looked at him hard, but I could see no sign that he was gloating at the prospect.

Jas was still sorting through what I'd said. "Then we . . . bale it now?"

"And it rots because it's wet and maybe burns the place down." I shoved both hands into my hair.

Betsy sniffed at Teddy, who'd stuck his neck through the fence to greet her, while Mike looked again at his weather app. "I hate to say it, but the rain is looking pretty likely," he said. "And it might not be just a little."

Or it might be. "I'll go find Louisa and check the hay myself," I said, suddenly anxious to get away from all this advice. "If it's dry, we'll bale."

22

A New Plan

I WALKED THE field, scrunching bundles of cut hay in my hands and trying to detect any lingering damp while Louisa watched anxiously, then told her to text Mike that we were ready to bale.

The words sounded more confident than I felt. I thought it was ready. I was pretty sure it was ready.

Pretty sure was going to have to be good enough.

When I got back to the barn, Emily was still there, talking to Jas and Mike and pulling her hair back into a ponytail. "Louisa's staying, right? I'll help."

I tried to look grateful. Any help was help when you were stacking four hundred bales. Emily made the whole Maggie/Jasmine thing that much more complicated, but how could I say no? We clearly needed her.

Emily seemed to take my hesitation for doubt. "I grew up riding. I've stacked hay. I've never done the field part, but it got delivered, we stacked."

I looked over at Mike, and he shrugged, then gestured to Jasmine as if to say they'd be about the same amount of help. Oh God, he was right. Even knowing I was supposed to be protecting Jasmine in her Maggie role, I couldn't help but give him a conspiratorial grin. They were just a couple of levels better than nothing, and we both knew it.

But stacking hay isn't brain surgery. Anyone can do it, and we did fine. Mike drove the baler while I made good use of my helpers to ready the barn, and by the time he returned with the first full hay wagon, we were ready. He dumped the bales and returned to the field, and we had just enough time to stack the first load before he was back with more. The hardest part was listening in to Louisa and Emily's conversation with Jasmine for any questions she couldn't answer and leaping in to rescue her or change the subject.

After a little while I realized Emily was doing her own version of the same thing. Louisa wanted to talk to Jasmine— or "Maggie"—about what she'd done instead of finishing college. Emily wanted to show off her author—but she also didn't want Jasmine/Maggie to make anything that wasn't heading straight to university sound too good.

"Louisa's going to spend next semester at Yarmouth," Emily told "Maggie" when we paused for Popsicles while waiting for what should be the final load, interrupting Louisa's questions about backpacking and a discussion of whether or not it would be fun to hike the Appalachian or the Pacific Crest Trail. (I found out later that Jas was relying heavily on having read Cheryl Strayed's *Wild*.) "I think once she gets there, she's never going to want to leave." I had a feeling Emily was talking more to Louisa than to either of us, and her next words confirmed it. "She'll have plenty of time for adventures over the summers."

I'd liked Emily a lot until that moment. Louisa hadn't said anything about Yarmouth that I remembered. I thought she was planning to do something with the park service. "But what about—"

Before I could finish, Louisa leaned over and pulled my Popsicle from my hand.

"Here," she said, handing me her treat instead. "Didn't you say you wanted cherry? I'll take lime." Her back was to her mother and her eyes were huge and pleading. "I really like lime," she said.

"Louisa!" Her mother sounded embarrassed. "Maybe Rhett wanted lime."

Louisa extended the lime Popsicle back to me, eyes still wide. "I just thought Rhett might be about to say she wanted cherry," she said. "I'm sure she's not interested in my summer plans."

Suddenly, I understood. "You're right," I said. "I did wish I'd taken cherry. Thanks." A look of relief crossed Louisa's face, and as soon as I was certain Emily wasn't paying attention, I gave the teenager the faintest of nods. Emily wanted Louisa to spend a semester at Yarmouth, and probably to go to Yarmouth in the end. Mike wanted the same. Louisa might want . . . something else.

And I wanted nothing to do with any of it. I took everyone's wrappers and went into the house to throw them away, Louisa rushing after me. "Please don't say anything to my mom or dad about the park service," she said as soon as the door closed behind her. "I'm deciding between them. I'm applying to both."

I didn't entirely believe her—but I also didn't understand why this was an issue. "What's wrong with the park service, if that's what you want to do?"

"My mom and dad think doing the Yarmouth semester will help me get in there later. And I'm not even sure—" She stopped. "It's a great school," she said. "I might do the semester there. But I might do the other thing, so I still need to finish the project." Her Popsicle started to drip down her arm, and I handed her a paper towel. "I'd ask Maggie what she thinks, but I think I know what she'd say."

What "Maggie" would suggest wasn't as clear as Louisa thought. An internship with the park service would obviously be much cooler than a semester at the college you were probably going to end up at anyway, but dancing around things this way with her parents wasn't going to help. "Why don't you just tell your parents what you want to do? A semester at the park service would probably help you get into Yarmouth anyway. You'd be so much more interesting. I'm sure they'd understand."

Louisa gave me a look that almost rivaled the one she'd given her father earlier, then took a lick of her Popsicle and managed a smile. "You're probably right," she said. "I will. But it would be much better coming from me, right? So if you could just not say anything . . ."

I was being manipulated. I knew it. But I also couldn't imagine taking Emily or Mike aside and trying to explain how I came to know all this, let alone what I thought of it. I'd almost certainly just make things worse for Louisa, and even if she thought she was putting one over on me now, I liked the kid. She reminded me of who I wished I'd been when I was her age. She was making a little mess of things, but I wasn't exactly in a position to judge that.

"I won't," I said.

"Promise?" She sounded about ten years old, and I laughed. This really wasn't any of my business.

"Sure," I said, and then, when she fixed me with another look: "Promise."

23

A Man's Approval

BY THE TIME we finished the last load, Emily was like one of the gang and she and Jasmine clearly felt like hay-stacking pros. I could see the three of us sitting down with beers—except that every time Emily called Jasmine "Maggie," I was reminded of the many reasons that would never happen. The uncomfortable feeling that accompanied those moments made me wrap our day up faster than I normally would, skipping the usual sweeping out of the barn and the traditional post-haying pizza.

I thanked Emily and Louisa profusely. Jasmine, as Maggie, promised to talk to her later—by email, she said after catching my eye—and they were gone, Louisa practically pushing her mother into Mike's truck and seeming as anxious to rush Emily away from me as I was to have her go.

I liked Emily. And I hoped she'd leave town. Soon.

I found Mike in the barn dragging the second hay elevator

back into its place along the barn wall, Betsy poised and watching him, leash on the ground beside her, and realized he should have gone with them. "Oops," I said. "Your ride just left."

Mike made a gesture to Betsy, who appeared to be about to get up, and she settled back onto her haunches. "They're taking the truck to get dinner," he said. "I told them you'd give me a ride home." A pause. "You will, won't you?"

"Oh—of course." He'd just helped me put up four hundred bales of hay. A ride was the least I owed him. "Let's go. Keys are in the truck."

He glanced around the barn, still in disarray, the four-wheeler with loose hay sticking out everywhere. "You sure you don't want help cleaning up?"

"No, that's okay," I said, heading for the truck. I felt kind of done with help. I took a quick picture of the freshly stacked hay for the farm's Instagram with the last of the evening light. I had the caption planned out in my head: *Livestock: sustained. Enough to feed the entire Pioneer Hill crew this winter!* And the unspoken hashtag, for my mother's eyes only: *#Iwin.* No one could say we weren't agricultural land now. "I'll manage."

Mike didn't argue. Betsy hopped into the back seat of the truck and he climbed in beside me while I started it up, shifting it into reverse with the jerk necessary to get the old gears moving. Mike had seemed almost nervous as he had climbed in, until a look of wonder crossed his face.

"Wait a minute," he said. "Is this the same truck?"

Oh my God. I felt a deep flush start in my cheeks until it

must have covered my entire face and neck, and I looked into the side mirror for longer than I had to as I backed to the end of the driveway, hoping to hide my reaction.

It was the same truck. The truck I borrowed from my grandmother the fall of our freshman year, the one we drove out to the back end of the lake two towns over, the part where nobody ever went, with a boat dock that was no longer sturdy enough for real boats and a parking area guaranteed to stay empty. I remembered the feeling of lying on the pile of bedding we'd thrown in the truck's bed and staring up at the stars, knowing my hand was close enough to Mike's that he could take it, and how quickly we'd gone from pinkies touching to clasped hands to staring into each other's eyes.

Back then Mike was still just Mike, not the frat boy he would shortly become. He'd whispered into the darkness, repeating his words from the river, words he would say often that first year, and even the second, and then less and less as things got more complicated between us. *It would be very easy to kiss you right now*, and I'd turned to him and made it even easier, waiting until he did.

We'd brought this truck out to that same spot at least once every fall and spring that we were together, exploring each other fully. We would argue as we got older. Mike grew into Yarmouth student life, with his frat and student government, sports clubs, and the not-so-secret honors society that culminated a truly successful student experience, while I struggled more and more with why I was there in the first place and with my mother's expectations, so different from my own, about what I would do after graduation. But we never argued at the lake. Never in the truck. There, we somehow always became our old selves.

"Yep," I said. "Driving it into the ground. Not like some people." I risked a glance at him to be sure he knew I was joking, and saw a faint smile on his face as he looked around like someone who'd just opened the door to the TARDIS.

"I can't believe it's the same truck," he said. He turned to look into the back seat, and I felt my flush deepening. The bugs are bad in New Hampshire. We spent a lot of time in that back seat.

"So where am I going?" Time to bring us back to the present.

"I forgot you wouldn't know," he said. "I bought the Harrisons' old place."

I knew exactly where he meant. "Must have needed some work?"

"Great bones, though."

It was one of the older houses in Bowford, off a quiet road, badly in need of a paint job at a minimum and probably a total overhaul. We talked for a few moments about the work he'd done, but Bowford is small, and very quickly I was turning into what was now Mike's driveway. "Thanks again for today," I said. "I'm sure you had other things to do." I'd thought a lot about that. How he dropped everything on a random Tuesday afternoon to help me out.

"Sure," he said, still looking around the truck and then focusing on me as if he, too, was shaking off memories. I'd stopped, but Mike didn't get out. "Come in for a drink?" His voice was even, but he was staring at the glove box, and I had the sense he'd been planning those words for the entire short ride.

I don't know what I would have said ten minutes ago. I had every reason to avoid getting embroiled any further into anything that involved Louisa or Emily, and it was hard to see how spending time with him wouldn't end up complicating everything.

But alone in the truck with Mike, I felt a pull I hadn't felt in a long time. Once, he was the person I told everything to. Then that person changed—but sitting in that truck next to this older version of Mike, I wanted to believe he was still in there, and that there could be a way to get that back. "Sure," I finally said, aware that I'd taken too long to reply, and that Mike had let me.

I was so focused on Mike that I hadn't looked up as we pulled into the driveway. When I did, I saw that the once simple Cape-style house was now transformed into what can only be described as the Cape idealized, with floor-to-ceiling windows, a covered porch, and a newly attached barn garage. I stopped short and stared while Mike let Betsy out of the truck.

"This is amazing," I said. "Did you do this?"

"Took a few years, and not all with my own two hands, but yes."

"It's gorgeous." The thought of Mike lifting window frames into place made me smile. "You taught Louisa to build here, didn't you?"

He nodded. "Did she tell you?"

Not exactly. It was more that I knew what she could do, and

that my father taught me to build like that, as we put up the farm stand and did house repairs over the years, first *Here, hold this*, then *Try hammering this nail*, then drills and saws and nail guns and all of it as I got older. "She said something," I replied. "And I can imagine."

He led the way inside, through a blue-and-white mudroom full of cubbies and baskets and then into a big open kitchen with white cabinets that matched the mudroom, a wagon-wheel-style chandelier hanging over an island, a blue gas stove with huge burners and neatly organized open shelves over the counters. "Seriously," I said. "This could be in a magazine."

"It is kind of my calling card," Mike pointed out. "I haven't done that many projects up here yet, so this is how I show people what I can do. Beer?"

I nodded, and instead of going to the refrigerator as I'd expected, he opened a drawer under the island. "I've got a Switchback Ale, Green State Lager, Heady Topper . . ."

He really had gone local. In college he would have had a fridge full of Sam Adams and thought he was pretty cool for that. "Has anyone ever chosen anything other than Heady Topper? You must have connections." Heady Topper had a cult following in a place where people take their craft beers seriously.

"I did some work for one of the guys at the Alchemist," he said as he handed me a bottle. "There's an opener under the counter there."

"A little bit of a man cave, then." I sat down on a barstool just slightly reminiscent of a saddle.

"A little. I tell my clients to build the kitchen they want, because the next people will change it anyway."

Not many guys would even know what they wanted in a kitchen. Jas would love him. If she could ever really meet him. "If there are next people. I live in my grandparents' house. Maybe Louisa will live here someday, and then her kids. Sometimes things last longer than you think they will."

"And sometimes they don't last as long as you hoped." Mike turned away quickly, as though aware he'd said too much, and busied himself pouring a can of nuts into a bowl, which he slid across the counter before coming to take the barstool next to mine. "Now that I've got you cornered, give me some highlights. I feel like you've got mine. Emily, grad school, Louisa, the city, my parents' firm, the divorce. My nutshell. But what's yours?"

His real grown-up life. And now he wanted to hear what was up with me—but the truth was, if he'd looked at *The Modern Pioneer Girl's Guide* or even just heard Louisa talk about it, he already knew most things. He just didn't know it, and I could never tell him.

I felt more alone than I had since learning of Grandma Bee's death, and I really didn't want to parse out why, or make small talk about parts of the story I could safely reveal—Rafael, the ranch, all the failures my mother had already dragged out into the open. I turned the question back on him. "There's more to you than that," I said. "Was this a summer place? When did you move here full-time?"

"I bought it a few years ago," Mike said. "We basically camped here in the summers while I worked on it. I planned to make it permanent when Louisa graduated from high school, but now that she's got this semester-at-Yarmouth thing coming up, it felt like I could do it sooner and not miss so much time with her, so I moved up this spring."

The Yarmouth thing. I realized my leg was jiggling under the counter and consciously stilled it. Both Mike and Emily seemed to talk about Louisa's Yarmouth plans a lot. It was hard to avoid getting the idea that Louisa might have sworn me to secrecy over something that was a bigger deal than I thought. "Cool," I said for lack of a better response. "Your mom and dad—still together?" I never felt like Mike's parents thought I was good enough for him, but I'd loved them anyway. I'd spent some of my happiest Christmases helping them build ridiculously complicated Lego sets while watching whatever old holiday movie they could find on cable.

"Still together. They got the fairy tale." Mike stared down at his hands and took a breath, as if he were getting ready to say something. He picked up his beer but didn't drink. Instead, he looked at me and put the beer back down. "Like I thought we were going to get," he said.

That was why I should have just turned around and gone home. The flush that had warmed my face in the truck returned, and I took a long sip of my drink.

"Sorry," he said, although I suspected he was not. "I've been not asking about this for days now. Just, you know, seeing you, hanging out, talking about the weather and the farm and my kid like nothing ever happened. But I like being with you, and I think you like being with me. So we can't just gloss over it. If we want to . . . see if there's anything here still . . . we have to talk about this. I guess I'm hoping for some kind of explanation."

"Explanation?" What was there to explain? "You were there. I can't imagine you've forgotten."

If anyone should want to forget about the last time we saw each other, it was him. I would love to forget. The humiliation of discovering that after almost four years, Mike didn't feel about me the way I did about him was not something I'd ever been able to spin into a Modern Pioneer Girl moment, even if it did lie at the bottom of my determination not to "need" a man, ever. Even then, I didn't "need" Mike. Obviously, I'd come through it fine.

But the things he'd said about me stuck in my head for years, reminding me at the worst possible moments that even the people you think love you for who you are will betray you in the end. And it wasn't only that, I reminded myself. It wasn't about that last moment; it was about the way he treated me like I didn't know how to act at parties, the way he backed my mother up whenever she started nagging about studying, or grades, the way he'd cancel on me at the last minute if something better—as in, more exclusive, more prestigious, more whatever—came up and always insisted that we go to every event my mother hosted, or attended, or even mentioned.

Plus, it wasn't really about him at all, and it was just like him to think it was.

"You walked in on me after I said one thoughtless thing to one idiot fraternity brother," Mike said. "And then you walked out of the room, and I literally never saw you again. You were just gone. Your mother said you were fine, and that's all I got for twenty years."

"One thoughtless thing," I said. I shouldn't be able to remember it so clearly after all that time, but oh, I did. First, my senior seminar literature professor, shaking his head while I tried to argue that my take on Virginia Woolf deserved more credit than the C he'd returned it with. I might not have known what the hell I was going to do when I graduated, and I was beginning to understand that I lacked a love for academics that many of my classmates had, but I did not get Cs. At least on paper, I believed I was among the best Yarmouth had to offer—until he chose that moment to set me straight.

Simplistic, he'd said. *Puerile, like all of your work, but who cares? We all know why you're here*, he'd said, holding his hand out for the essay I held in my suddenly shaking hands. *I'm sure your mother will fix it for you.* He stood up and snatched the paper, slamming it down on his desk and grabbing a pen. *What grade do you want, an A? A-plus? There you go. It doesn't matter anyway. Nothing matters.*

Maybe I could have written him off, if his words hadn't fit so well with everything else that had been happening to me that year, and that I probably should have been noticing all along. My friends getting accepted to internships and graduate programs while I'd done nothing about my own future. The opportunities to work for her colleagues and friends that my mother kept presenting. The student-run honors society that took only a few students each year and selected Mike—but not me. I couldn't believe how naïve I'd been, and when I burst into the office of the dean of arts and sciences, weeping,

Margaret apparently couldn't either. She ushered a curious French instructor out and stood over me as I sat on her couch.

Show me the essay, she'd demanded, but I'd left it on the professor's desk, and Margaret had sighed at this continuing evidence of her daughter's ineptness. *I'm sure it's worth a better grade than he gave you.* Then, when I asked directly—*Are you really why I'm here?*—Margaret hadn't even bothered to pretend. *You're an excellent student,* she'd said, throwing me a bone, *but there's no point in pretending the world doesn't work the way it does.*

I didn't give her a chance to say anything else. But—because of what came next—Mike didn't know any of that.

"Do you know why I was looking for you that day? I was coming to tell you that I'd just found out my mom got me into Yarmouth. Pulled all the strings, and was still pulling them. Nothing I'd ever done mattered. It was all about her."

We both knew what happened then.

I ran from my mother, looking for the only person on campus I could count on—Mike. Climbed the stairs of that run-down frat house I never understood why he'd joined, with the smell of kegs and overturned cups that never went away, and found Mike, his back to the door, taking a drag of a joint. I could still picture the bro with him on the broken-down plaid couch, arms and legs spread out, pyramid of beer cans on the coffee table, beer bottles scattered around it. I could still hear his words.

What's the deal with her, man? There are so many more tasty morsels here. Why do you keep her around? Mike, passing the joint on: *Come on, her mom's a dean.* The bro, his eyes on me: *Dude, you'd be better off with the mom. She's smokin'. Here's to Mrs. Robinson.*

Mike laughed and the guy with him lifted his beer to me, like he was toasting me somehow, before I stormed in and snatched it from his hand, then whirled to face Mike and threw the bottle straight over his head into the mirror behind him. That was the most satisfying crash of my entire life.

Even now, the memory made my stomach churn.

But still. That wasn't why I left. It was my mother who had ruined everything—by not trusting me enough to make my own way. Taking away any sense of pride and self-worth that I had. Even if Mike had been who I thought he was, I still couldn't have stuck around.

Mike was turning his beer bottle slowly in his hands. I'd never told anyone this story except Jasmine. It should have felt huge, but instead I felt empty. The illusion that there might be something between me and Mike again was gone, and I was left wishing I'd never imagined otherwise.

Mike looked at me as though he was waiting for me to say something else, and it burned through me that my words were not a surprise to him. Of course he, like everyone around me, had known all along that my mother was behind my Yarmouth career.

"So. There's your explanation. But as far as needing to talk about it, we don't. It's in the past and it stays there, and if you've been thinking anything else, I'm sorry. Whatever we had is long gone and not coming back." It felt good, hurling those words at him, like pulling off a scab and letting the wound underneath bleed freely.

Mike crossed his arms tightly over his chest and leaned away from me before he spoke, carefully. "That's not how it felt to me, the past couple of days," he said, and as he did he unwrapped his arms as though trying to force his body to relax. "And I've learned to trust those feelings more than what people say, because we say things to people for a lot of reasons. I know I screwed up. But don't you wish you'd stuck around and let me explain?"

"Hells no," I said. "And you're not the reason I left. Not even close. She was. I got what I needed, which was my own life, far away from her—and you. And you got what you needed, which was the opportunity to go tasting all those morsels. You even found your way back into my mom's orbit with this building stuff. Nice work."

He blinked. "Whoa," he said. "That was . . . uncalled for."

Maybe. But like that bottle crashing into the mirror, it was momentarily satisfying. The knowledge that I had stung him soothed me, and I took another sip, more calmly. It had been twenty years. And I meant it about getting what I needed—if I'd gone down the road my mother had paved for me, my life would be unrecognizable now. Things were a little messy as they were, yes, but at least I wasn't divorced with a kid I was trying to push into making the same mistakes I'd made. I looked up and found Mike watching me.

"There was nobody else," he said. "There was never anybody else. And if you'd asked me, I would have told you that. Emily came later. A lot later." His eyes held mine, and I couldn't bring myself to look away. "You could have given me a chance."

"After your roommate suggested you bonk my mother instead of me, and you laughed?" But that wasn't the part that hurt, and I shouldn't pretend it was. "After you said we were only together because of who she was? You couldn't have come up with anything that would have hurt me more if you'd thought about it for a week."

Mike stared straight ahead, over the counter. "But I didn't know the rest of it. And . . . you knew it wasn't true. I wanted him to think I was cool. It was meaningless, something to say."

I knew exactly how true it had been. "What, to a guy who didn't think I was hot enough for you? There is no way to shake this out that doesn't involve you being a douche, okay? There just isn't."

"Yeah," Mike said. "And you being a coward."

"What?"

"You heard me. You ran away. You turned it into this big drama, and you didn't give anyone, including yourself, a chance to try again."

He was making it my fault. Of all the ways I had imagined this conversation going—and, yes, I had imagined it more than once over the intervening years—I never imagined Mike trying to drop the hot potato of blame squarely in my lap. So this was the story he had told himself all these years. That he was the good guy, and I was the hysterical female, overreacting. I felt the heat of anger spreading down through my shoulders and out into my fingertips. I didn't run away. Leaving was my only chance to become my own person.

"I didn't give you another chance because you didn't

deserve another chance. Neither of you. And it wasn't just that one day. I was trying to figure out who I was, and my mother was trying to turn me into someone I didn't want to be, someone who makes practical choices and does what everyone expects, and you were totally on board with that. Every minute," I said. "Part of you probably still is, even if you did help me today. Both of you would be totally happy if I gave up right now, let her sell the farm to Yarmouth, and, I don't know, got a job as an admin or something. That's not who I am."

Mike set his beer down on the counter, hard. "Fine, let's talk about your mother," he said. "It never really stopped being about your mother to you, did it? Because you can only see things one way. Maybe that's all she wanted, for you to see that it isn't all black-and-white, good guys–bad guys. She helped you get into Yarmouth, but they wouldn't have taken you if you weren't qualified. Same with high school. With everything. You're right. The farm is great, and I hope you can keep it, but it's not like the college's plan is East German cinder-block housing."

"I'm keeping it," I said firmly. "Putting that hay in the barn today means the end of your welcome center, or at least, it helps. She's finally going to have to listen to what I want."

"She's not that bad. She's trying to help."

"I don't need help. When is she going to admit that I do all right on my own?"

"I don't know," Mike said. "When are you going to admit that she didn't ruin your life?"

That was exactly as much understanding as I should have

expected. "You're right," I said, getting up. "She didn't. I like my life exactly the way it is."

I shouldn't have come inside. I could see a snapshot of Mike and what must have been a very young Louisa propped up against a windowsill—a reminder that he'd had a whole life without me, and I'd had one without him. There was no way I could tell him who I was now. And even if I could, there was no way he'd understand. Or want to.

"I really should get going," I said, unable to bother with niceties. I set my bottle on his counter. Mike stood too, but instead of heading for the door, he leaned around the counter and opened his fancy drawer of beers.

"Really? Because I'm having another," he said with a challenge in his eyes. "How about you stick around this time and have this out?"

"There's nothing to stick around for," I said. "Sometimes it's just time to let go."

I walked out of the house, telling myself not to look back and meaning it in every sense of the phrase. The past was past, and I'd keep it there.

24

A Sure Thing

IT DIDN'T RAIN after all.

It didn't exactly not rain either. I woke up to heavy clouds and the oppressive feeling of change coming. The air was hot but damp, uncomfortable and undefinable, as though even the weather couldn't give me the satisfaction of knowing for certain that I'd made the right call.

My mother, too, insisted on staying firmly in the realm of the uncertain. I'd sent her an email the previous night, not wanting to risk a phone conversation. The farm was in use now, I wrote. And I had a mortgage broker lined up—a slight exaggeration, but I'd left one a message. So could we make a decision about how I was going to buy her half of Pioneer Hill?

All I wanted was a yes. Instead, she was coming over Saturday to "discuss the matter," and thinking about it made me feel as unpleasant as the weather. Chores and the animals— and the sight of the barn full of hay stacked high—would at least give me something else to think about.

I expected Jas to sleep in after our haying extravaganza, so I was surprised to find her brewing coffee even before I came downstairs, and dressed to help. "If I'm going to be Maggie, I'm going to make it look good," she said as she followed me out. "No riding, though."

"No riding," I promised. "Maggie's exploring her relationship to horses from the ground right now."

Some barn time would absolutely help me feel better. If Jas was a little more comfortable around my horses, sheep, and chickens, I knew she would feel the same way, and I wanted that for her. I didn't care about the Maggie part of it. I'd overheard her on the phone with Zale last night, and I wanted her to know that the farm was a refuge for her no matter what.

After we fed the entire crew—which would make any human popular—I gave Jas Brownie's currycomb and showed her the places where he loved to be scratched, and together we groomed the little pony to a sheen, Jas brushing while I pulled his mane and tail. Jas ran inside and emerged with a bandana that we tied in his forelock, giving him a rakish look suited to his personality, and at the same time we both pulled out our phones.

"Instagram will love him," Jas said cheerfully. "We can call him *hashtag rogue pony*." She started typing away, and I left her to it. I spent the next few hours weeding and staking the tomato garden. Grandma Bee had planted too many for herself, as she did every year, and I was grateful. There were also plenty of volunteers popping up in the unexpected places where fruits had fallen and seeded the year before, and pumpkin vines that probably sprang from the remains of last year's jack-o'-lanterns. We had a tradition of rolling them into the garden after Halloween and hoping for the best.

Jasmine gave S'mores a turn being groomed while I worked. When she was finished, I dragged out Grandma's old harness and cart. Who knew how long it had been since the little ponies had pulled anything, but we started slowly and before long I had them driving down the road with a delighted Jasmine holding the reins. I walked alongside happily, taking pictures and making sure nothing happened to endanger Jas's newfound equine love affair.

We got as far as the corner and I was guiding Jas through turning her tiny team around to head back down the road toward the driveway when Mike's truck appeared. I stopped the smile my traitorous brain started up before it had a chance to reach my face—I didn't want to see Mike or talk to him. And then, as I glared at the driver's-side door, I realized he wasn't in the truck at all. Emily hopped out and gave me a slightly startled look before she pointed her phone at Jasmine. "This is perfect," she said cheerfully. "You couldn't be more Modern Pioneer Girl unless you were wearing a bonnet."

I scrambled for something to say, but Jasmine spoke first. "I'm having the best time," she said. "But these little guys are all Rhett's."

At my direction, she piloted the ponies toward the farm, Emily trailing them slowly in the truck. Jasmine handed me the reins and ran inside, promising to return with snacks, and Emily gave me a very competent hand untacking.

She helped hang the harness, then looked around with

interest as we emerged from the barn, and clapped her hands together when she saw Teddy, Darcy, and Bingley in their paddock with the sheep grazing a little in the distance. "Oh—I didn't really get to see these guys yesterday. Can I say hi?"

I nodded, but before Emily could approach the paddock, Jasmine came out and set a tray of iced coffee and scones on the picnic table, and Emily turned to her. "Those look amazing," she said.

"All Rhett, like the ponies," said Jas agreeably. "You know I'm not a baker."

"You've pretty much created heaven on earth," Emily said to me, making appreciative noises while she bit into a scone and I tried not to glare at Jas. "This place is wonderful. What are the horses' names? Who's the— Is that a llama or an alpaca?"

"That's Teddy. He's a llama," said Jasmine.

"It must be great having someone who really knows what they're doing stay with you," Emily said to me as I struggled to hold my neutral expression. I hoped she would go soon. I liked Emily, and the longer we deceived her, the worse I felt about it.

As Emily turned the conversation back toward the scones, I was willing to bet Jasmine felt the same. Emily stayed just a few minutes, but it was long enough that after she left I went alone to the barn to do evening chores while Jas went back to the house, saying something about getting things ready for the farm stand tomorrow.

I don't think either of us liked being reminded that we were doing more than just having fun together.

Even so, when the farm stand opened the next morning, I could see that Jas was over any hesitation she'd had about her role. She certainly wasn't hiding anymore. With her barista station set up, she became the chatty face of Pioneer Hill, quickly learning people's names and favorites—by Saturday morning she was asking everyone she remembered if they wanted their "usual." She insisted on continuing to attribute the baking to me, and I hated it, especially when someone tried to talk recipes or technique. But if I even hinted at protest, Jasmine waved one of the copies of *The Modern Pioneer Girl's Guide* that she kept by her counter, replacing them any time I tried to sneak them inside. "Maggie Strong loves your baking," she'd say, and I would have to go along.

Jasmine, even when people called her Maggie, really did seem to be in her element. I was starting to feel a little penned in by having to interact with people all day long, especially the few who came in looking for Maggie Strong. Emily put the picture of Jasmine driving S'mores and Brownie up on the publisher's feed, which we should have known she would do, and after going back and forth a little, we reposted it.

At the time, it felt small—the video of the *Today* show was in there, after all—but somehow that image of Jasmine with her head tossed back, blond waves pouring around her shoulders, reins in one hand and the other holding one of my old cowboy hats on her head with the ponies prancing along in front of her, became my mental image of the Modern Pioneer Girl. It was as if I'd released her out into the world, and now she wasn't mine anymore.

Cooped up in the farm stand, I kept staring outside. There

was so much to do: fences to repair, more planting to be done, the small orchard to tend, the pick-your-own bushes to weed and maintain. I itched to get at it all, fidgeting and counting the hours until Jas finally called me on it.

"You," she said, bringing over an iced mocha at a quiet moment Saturday morning while I filled out bank paperwork at intervals between customers. "You need to chill. What's up with you? Everything's going great."

"I don't know," I said. "I'm sorry."

"Don't be sorry," Jas said. "We're in charge of our own destiny here. What do you want, right now?"

"I want to nail down this mortgage and restore the farm. I want the town to be glad I'm here. I want to pay off some bills, and get somebody to repair the fencing, and—"

"No, I mean, what do you want right now? Ice cream? A massage? A cookie?"

I looked around the dim farm stand, with its neat piles of produce and baked goods. "Sunshine," I said. "I want to listen to loud music and get dirty."

"Then go outside. I've got this. It doesn't take both of us."

"My mother's coming." That might partly explain how antsy I felt. "I want her to see me working."

"You'll be working. Go work somewhere else. You're making me crazy."

But even outside, earbuds in and music playing, I felt disgruntled and anxious. No matter how hard and fast I worked, I couldn't outrun the feeling. Jasmine was inside, happily running the farm stand and charming everyone who came near, and while I didn't want that—had been chafing against it—a part of me wanted to want it. Or maybe wanted Jasmine not to be so good at it. I knew she was a better MPG than I could ever be, and somehow this was just rubbing it in. I'd feel better after my mother and I talked. After we agreed, finally, that as soon as I got the mortgage set up, Pioneer Hill was mine.

I repaired the sliding door on the big hay barn, the oldest structure on the farm and the thing that made it a landmark for Bowford travelers. Its classic red paint needed a refresh, and the cupola with the weather vane on top leaked, but that spinning pioneer wagon, chosen and installed by my father so many years ago, made me proud. The inside of the barn was still a mess from haying. I needed to sweep it out, set up the temperature sensors that monitored the hay, move the four-wheeler, put away the gas cans and the work gloves and the loose baling twine that littered the floor, but there wasn't time right now. I headed for the house, planning to clean myself up before my mother arrived, when I heard someone calling my name from the porch.

It was Margaret, looking freshly pressed, one of Jasmine's coffees in her hand, fifteen minutes early and putting me in the wrong by her mere presence. I wished she could just, for once, do things the way I'd asked her to and give me half a chance to feel some control over the situation. But that was not her way. And while I probably looked as irritated as I felt, Margaret was smiling.

That was a little disturbing. I greeted her and led the way into the kitchen, refusing to apologize for my appearance.

"I still can't believe how little this place has changed," she

said, looking around. "Other than all of your baking equipment, your grandmother could walk in here at any minute."

At the reference to "my" baking equipment, I felt my shoulders drop a little. "Well, she won't," I said, aware of the blunt-
ness of my words but unable to moderate myself. My mother
shouldn't have been early. She threw everything off.

Margaret set her drink and bag on the table and tapped the
tips of her fingers together, looking at me. "I'm sorry about
Bee's death. It must be hard for you. I hadn't realized you were
still close."

"We were," I said with a little difficulty. I didn't think I
could talk about Grandma Bee with Margaret.

"So this place is going to stay in the family," she said, turning around and taking it all in. "You know, I might be glad."

As relieved as I was to hear her acknowledge my plans, I let
my disbelief at her words show in my face. "You hated it here,"
I said.

She shook her head. "I didn't hate it, exactly. I hated the
never-ending work. I hated how no matter how many times I
came out and helped fix the fencing, or hauled water, or moved
this pen or that trough, it was never done. And I hated how
your father and grandmother took every minute I spent on
other things as some sort of personal affront."

I was interested in spite of myself. This was more than I
had ever heard my mother say about the days before she
"packed her bags and walked out the door without looking
back," as Grandma Bee always described it. Margaret sat
down at the table, and after a moment's hesitation I sat across
from her.

"Dad didn't like you studying? Wasn't he studying too?"

Margaret folded her hands in front of her and addressed the mason jar of daisies Jas had placed in the middle of the table. "We were going to both get our graduate degrees, but your father got so caught up in his projects here that he never finished, and he never finished any of those projects either. One year it was cows. Another year, he was learning to make goat cheese. Then it was wool and yarn. He'd get everything he needed, and then just— He always had another idea." She shrugged. "When you got old enough, you were another one. *Raising Little Pioneers.* To his credit, he stuck with that long enough to write a book about it, at least."

I remembered the sheep, and the shearing. And the goats. And the efforts that had come after Margaret left: the pumpkin patch, the corn maze, the awful year of the Thanksgiving turkeys. Even the timber he was cutting up by the chimney when he was killed was part of one of Dad's plans. I never thought about why there were so many, and why they never lasted very long.

Margaret went on. "'Serial entrepreneur,' that's what they'd call him now, except that none of his ventures ever came to anything. But they always seemed so plausible, the way he talked about them. He was the most charming man I've ever known, and the least capable of sticking with anything. The minute a plan stopped going his way, he was on to the next thing." She gave me a look, and I knew what she was thinking.

"You haven't been around me for twenty years," I said. "Longer, really. I'm not like that." It was just like my mother to judge me by a childhood of varied enthusiasms. If anything, I stuck with things too long now. Margaret just didn't know it.

Was it possible that she looked a little hurt? "I was not, actually, thinking that," she said. "I'm sure you could be charming if you tried. Do people tell you that you look like your grandmother? You do, you know. It's quite disconcerting. She used to sit there and glare at me too. She never liked me."

I took a moment to process that accusation. "I'm not glaring," I said. If I was, I didn't mean to be. "And . . . I liked you." It was true. I had. When I was little.

Margaret laughed, a short bark with no real humor in it. "You, like everyone else, liked your father. Your grandmother thought the sun shone out of his arse." She looked intently at me, as if deciding something. "Did Bee ever talk to you about me, after I left?"

I shook my head. "Not really," I said. "And not since I left, probably." Not since I'd blown through the farm to grab my backpack and passport and told Bee I was quitting college and taking off. I'd expected an argument—didn't all grownups think college was practically mandatory?—but I didn't get one. My grandmother helped me pack, listening to my complaints about Margaret and nodding, then hugged me fiercely when I said good-bye. "I'm sorry," she said, and I pulled back, knowing what she was apologizing for, refusing to accept it.

"It's okay," I said, but Bee brushed off my words.

"I never should have let you go with her." She'd held me by my shoulders, stared at me. "I should have kept you here with me."

I couldn't argue. In that moment, I'd wished so much that

she had. "Just help me get away now." She did too. Maybe too well.

Margaret gazed off into the distance, beyond my shoulder. "Of course she didn't," she said. "From the minute your father and I moved in with Bee, she was always competing for your love. For both of you. She encouraged every one of those plans. Every time I wanted to wait, be cautious, finish one thing before we started another, she told him I was destroying his dreams. If I suggested that maybe four-year-olds couldn't milk cows, or shouldn't drink raw milk, or that it might be safer not to let you drive the team, she told him I didn't believe in his vision. She never wanted to face reality. Neither did he."

Margaret took a sip of her drink, her face far more impassive than her words would suggest. "She loved making me the bad guy. I wondered if she kept it up after I left."

"I was here," I said, trying to argue and pleasantly surprised at my ability to match my mother's almost casual tone, as if we were discussing the merits of Jasmine's coffee. "It wasn't like that. Grandma knew what was real. Dad too. All this." I gestured around at the farm. "Papers, degrees, even books come and go. This stays."

"A matter of opinion," Margaret said, then, when I started to object, "and a valid one, I suppose. Your father could never just out and out say that. Instead, he was always spinning it. How he'd do the farm and academics. Or make a lot of money, start a big business. Anything. He could never just be who he was, Charlie the farm boy, who liked school pretty well but when it came right down to it would always like getting his hands dirty more."

Her voice was so dismissive. Like she'd categorized him and now didn't need to give him any more thought—and like she hadn't considered her own role in that equation. "But there's no way you would have stayed with Charlie the farm boy," I said, my heart hurting for my dad. "You wanted him to finish his degree. You wanted him to do something else." Old, half-overheard arguments came back to me. Margaret and Dad, in the kitchen, yelling until my grandmother and I came in. Dad's voice, big and self-assured, Margaret questioning, her hands shaking while she filled a cup of water for me, so that the sides were wet when I took it.

Margaret didn't deny it. "Maybe I did," my mother said. "But only because he seemed to want so much. I wanted him to be good at something. To feel proud of himself."

"He had plenty to be proud of," I said, angry. This conversation was going way off the rails. We were supposed to be talking about the farm, and my triumph, and how she would back down and agree I could take over, not about my father's failures and especially not about the ways I might echo them. I stood up and walked away from the table, unable to maintain the charade of calm without some movement. "He had the farm. And he was a great dad, which is way more than you could say. He was trying. And you left anyway." I yanked open the fridge to pour an iced coffee, desperate for something to do with my hands. "You left him. You left *me.*"

In all these years, I'd never called her on it, first because I was too busy trying to please her and then because it was clear that once I'd failed at that, she wanted nothing more to do with me, a wish I'd been happy to grant. But if she was going to try to change the past, I wouldn't allow it. "You packed up and left. There's nothing you can say to change that."

Margaret sat quietly, knitting her fingers together. I couldn't tell if she was bothered by the accusation. Of course. Why would she care that when I watched her little Volkswagen drive away, I hadn't realized she wasn't coming back?

Finally, after a few seconds that felt much longer, Margaret looked up. "Your father wanted me to go," she said. "Every bit as much as I wanted to leave. I planned to take you with me. That's how things were done then. But your father thought we should give you a choice. At nine years old, for God's sake. California and me, or him and the farm."

She put the cup to her lips again but put it down too quickly to have taken a sip. Her eyes met mine, and I turned away. I never knew that.

"I couldn't do that to you. So I said you could stay. You were supposed to visit me, but your father and Bee always said it was a bad time. We never formally divorced, or made custody arrangements. My immigration status depended on our marriage at that point, and it all felt complicated. The longer I was away, the less we talked, and the less I could feel you wanting to come."

I hunched over my glass, bit at one of my hangnails, caught myself, yanked my hand down. I couldn't imagine getting that choice at nine. Margaret, to me then, was distant, yes, but glamorous. Difficult to please, but that only made me try harder. I'd loved the farm, my father, Bee, but I was also an adventurous kid. Would the new have tempted me over the familiar? I had no idea. It was as if an alternative life had just appeared beside the one I'd had.

I was lucky they didn't ask. Lucky to get to stay at Pioneer Hill. But as I thought it, I realized those were my grandmother's words. *You're such a lucky girl to have a place like this and a father like yours. No matter what happens.* Grandma Bee, wrapping her arms around me and telling me it was fine that Margaret hadn't called, that I didn't need to write her. *You're fine, she's fine. You have everything you need right here.*

Margaret spoke into my silence. "You said I hated it here. I don't think that's the word I would choose, but it was difficult. Being here now, with you, feels like laying ghosts to rest."

Her words—"with you"—touched something deep inside me that I very much did not want disturbed. I didn't believe her. She did not want to be here with me and never had.

"I'm glad it feels like laying ghosts to rest to you," I said, putting ice in my drink and finally turning back to her, proud to be keeping any emotion out of my face. "It seems to me like you've been trying to sweep them away. Make it all disappear. Make me disappear. No farm, no memories, and poof—it will be like I never existed at all."

I didn't even know that was what I thought until I said it, but there it was. Margaret didn't just want to sell the farm. She wanted to erase it—and me—from her sight.

To my surprise, Margaret shook her head hard. "No," she said. "Never. I know you don't believe it, but I thought I was arranging something that was right for both of us. I know you objected, but you're stubborn. I could see you imagining you'd be doing what your father and Bee wanted and getting in over your head. I wanted to protect you."

It was the same thing she'd said over the phone, when she didn't know she was talking to me. That she was doing this for me. But that didn't change anything. She still wasn't listening to me. She still wasn't interested in who I was, or what I wanted, any more than she'd wanted my father to be who he was, all those years ago. I wasn't sure why she wanted me to believe in this new possibility of a mother with good intentions, no matter that those intentions had had their usual result.

And I wasn't sure I should. I'd won this on my own terms. It was Margaret who needed things to be different. If this was about her magnanimously giving her wayward daughter a chance, then it couldn't be about me proving that I was a successful independent adult.

My grip around my glass tightened, and the condensation dripped down my hand. "I've been telling you all along that the Yarmouth offer is not what I want," I said. "It's very convenient that you only decide to listen to me when you don't really have any choice. The land is in agricultural use now. You can't sell it to the college so you might as well sell it to me. Done, great, thank you very much. But please don't pretend you ever thought you were doing this for me."

I saw a flicker of emotion in Margaret's face, and her voice hardened. "Of course I thought you would want to sell," she said. "You've had twenty years when you could have come back to stay. Why would I imagine you wanted to do that now?

After all, I'm here. Can you blame me for believing this was the last place you wanted to be?"

"All you had to do was ask," I said.

"In one of our many visits, perhaps? One of our mother-daughter chats?"

"You could have called," I said. "You could have written. You could have waited until someone told you I was in town because I know people did. You could have tried." I wanted it to sound flip, but I knew I'd failed. Some of the real bitterness I felt around her willingness to let me go so easily came through in my words, and Margaret, still seated, reached out a hand toward me as if to draw me back to the table.

So could you. I could see the thought cross my mother's face as clearly as if she'd said the words, but she didn't. Maybe because she didn't want to hear why.

I took a step backward, and Margaret dropped her hand. "I've grown accustomed to guessing when it comes to you," she said. "I don't think it's entirely my fault that I got it wrong."

I wanted this conversation to be over, now, before it went any further. "Now you know." I set my glass, still mostly full, in the sink. "I'm arranging a mortgage," I said. "I should be able to get you your money by the end of next week." I crossed the room to open the door. "I'll sort it out and let you know the details, but right now I should get back to work."

"Of course." She rose, polite as always, trying to catch my eye, but I stared down at the doormat, the one that read HELLO as you came in and GOOD-BYE when you left. *Good-bye,* I thought. *Good-bye, good-bye, please go now,* but she was still talking. "Perhaps we can talk again then."

Not if I could find an envelope and a stamp.

She swept out the door in front of me as though there had been nothing unusual in our conversation, and I walked slowly after her. This should feel like a moment of victory. Instead, I felt the uncertainty she always brought to the surface, and I took in a deep breath. Just a little more time, and she wouldn't have any hold over me.

I expected her to walk to her car in the driveway, but instead she turned toward the farm stand. "I'm going to get another coffee," she said over her shoulder, as though she could feel my confused gaze. "Your barista is grossly overqualified, but very good."

I sighed at the snark. Weren't we done? I followed her to the door of the farm stand, and as I did, I realized an awful and completely obvious truth about my return to Bowford.

My mother lived here. And she was never going away.

I went inside after her, listening to her call out her order to Jasmine as though she expected to be doing this every weekend for years to come, Jasmine, with that "Maggie" lilt to her voice, greeting her with a friendliness I couldn't help but resent. It took a moment for my eyes to adjust from the bright sunshine outside and register that someone else was already in there, sipping a drink while smiling knowingly in my direction, ignoring my mother.

Zale.

❧

25

A Different Man

ZALE WAVED GAILY to me as he was about to walk out the door. "Good to see you," he called. "Be sure to have one of . . . Maggie's . . . donuts. They're the real thing!" Before I had time to respond, he was gone, and I turned to Jas, almost forgetting my mother was there in my panic. She gave me a warning look.

"You have donuts?" Margaret looked around with interest. "And—wait. I thought Rhett was doing the cooking."

"Donuts are my specialty," Jas said, "but they're all gone. Next time."

What was Zale doing here? I wanted answers, but Margaret wanted another latte. And, apparently, I realized with a sinking feeling as she settled onto a stool in front of Jasmine's counter, a chat. Jas started up her coffee preparations, but I was still frozen in place.

Margaret sighed and shook her head at me. "Rhett and I

have just agreed that she will purchase my half of Pioneer Hill," she said to Jasmine. "She should be quite pleased."

I should be. I was. Jas looked at me, her face excited, and I nodded. To me, this had been a done deal since the moment we stacked the hay in the barn, but apparently my mother considered it news worth celebrating. Maybe I would have given her the reaction she wanted if it hadn't been for Zale.

But also, my mother wasn't giving me a present. I deserved this. I yanked out the other stool and sat down, grateful that it was late enough in the day that we might not see any other customers. "I am," I said, aware that I wasn't getting the right enthusiasm into my words. "It's great."

Jas made up for my lack. "That is great," she said. "Extra whipped cream, then. Chocolate syrup. Sprinkles." She flourished up my mother's coffee with abandon, and I expected Margaret to resist, but she looked pleased. "Tell me all about it."

I couldn't resist trying to ask about Zale. "I would, but what about—" Jas shook her head.

"I have had a very good uneventful day," she said firmly, with a glance at my mother. "My last customer just needed some directions as well as his drink, and I knew just what to tell him."

Jasmine held our gaze, and I nodded a little. I got it. She was trying to tell me that whatever he wanted, she'd settled it. That would have to do for now.

Jas went on. "But this is big." She set my mother's drink down in front of her. "I'm excited for Rhett. For you both, really. I wish I had family to settle near." I glowered at that, but Jas was fully in character and focused on my mother. "Tell me how it happened."

"Well," I said, "once we got the hay in—"

Jas interrupted me with a wave. "I know all that. But I'd love to hear what Margaret has to say about it."

She could stop buttering my mother up now, she really could. Unsurprisingly, Margaret seemed pleased to be asked.

"The hay was certainly part of it. That took impressive effort, and it does establish the farm as being in agricultural use. That wasn't entirely dispositive, however. The board could have been petitioned. Or another sale could be arranged, and I briefly considered that."

She hadn't told me that.

"But I also kept thinking about what you said," my mother said to Jasmine—to "Maggie." "Both in your *Fresh Air* interview, and in our conversation afterward."

Jasmine's eyes flicked toward me. Another thing I hadn't told her.

Margaret continued. "You said something about questioning assumptions—other people's, and your own. About asking questions about what we really want. And I realized that while selling Pioneer Hill is a practical choice, whether it's the right choice depends on what we—Rhett and I—want from it. Rhett says she wants to stay here. And if she wants that, I want her to be able to stay."

Margaret's eyes stayed firmly on Jasmine as she spoke, and I was grateful, because I'm sure my mouth dropped open. "In fact," she went on, "if I'd thought it was an option, that's what I would have wanted from the beginning. I never imagined

Rhett would want to settle down here, and so I never thought about it. But I'm glad she does."

Jasmine looked hard at me. "Because of something I said? The Modern Pioneer Girl?"

"You were certainly part of it."

Margaret took a sip of her drink, and over her head Jas mouthed an emphatic message. *Tell her.* I shook my head hard, still absorbing my mother's last words. If she wanted me here, she had a strange way of showing it. And even if it were true, it didn't change how she felt about me, or the way she made me feel. She was still her domineering self, and I was still her disappointing daughter.

We sure weren't rocking this boat now. Jas was still glaring at me, and I gave my head one last definitive shake and mouthed a response to her for good measure. *No way.*

"We are each other's only family," Margaret said, as if determined to surprise me further. "This might be our last chance to act like it."

Jasmine apparently saw that I was incapable of speech. She leaned on the counter. "I think that's wonderful," she said warmly. I crossed my arms over my chest, even knowing that I looked childish and probably hostile, but my mother's words on top of everything else she'd just told me were too much. I couldn't just throw open my arms and play family with her, and I still wasn't convinced she even wanted me to. There had to be a reason she was saying all this to "Maggie" and not to me.

"We'll see," said Margaret briskly, reaching for a napkin to wipe the whipped cream from her nose and upper lip. She set the cup down firmly and sat up on the stool, as if aware that she'd let her guard down for a moment, and her demeanor shifted. "The opportunity is there. And while I'm here, I'd like to extend a different opportunity to you," she said, looking at Jasmine. "There are students here for the summer term—I mentioned them to you before—and I'm still hoping you'll agree to speak to them while you're here. Get them excited about finding their own paths."

Jasmine looked at her thoughtfully, and I appreciated her pretense of considering the idea.

Margaret went on. "You're very right about some things. There aren't many internships left out there, and not as many ladders to climb. Many of our graduates are finding that discouraging. Hearing from you would give them a different vision of success that might be more useful to them in the current climate." She smiled. "Of course, they'll still need to compromise and fit themselves into society. But I trust we've taught them that. I'd like them to hear more from someone with a trajectory like yours."

I looked at Jasmine, waiting for her firm no, but as she opened her mouth Margaret spoke over her. "It will be very informal," she said. "I hear you when you say you don't consider yourself a podium-and-audience speaker. They'll be gathered at our annual picnic next week, I will welcome them as I always do, and then I'll invite you to talk while they sit down with their food. At the same time, the college will purchase enough copies of your book not just for the summer students, but for our entering class."

My first thought was that telling my mother no really made

her double down. My second was regret that I wouldn't get to watch one of the country's most exclusive universities give their entering class a book declaring that you didn't need their degree to succeed.

My third thought—because now Jasmine was answering—was flat-out horror.

"Sure," Jasmine said. "I'll do it."

26

Approval

I TRIED TO protest, but it was impossible. As far as my mother was concerned, Jasmine's yes was Maggie's yes. Margaret left clearly feeling like she'd pulled off a major coup, and I just barely managed to refrain from grabbing Jasmine by the shoulders and shaking her.

"But we're done," I wailed. "We won, I get the farm—it's all over! You can't give a speech to the Yarmouth summer students. You're supposed to be riding into the sunset." I stopped, because that wasn't right. I didn't want Jas to have to go anywhere. "Or just, staying chill. Not drawing attention to yourself."

"I decided I wanted to do one more thing." Jasmine's voice was firm as she began cleaning out the espresso machine, which she tended like an orphaned lamb.

"But something could go wrong. Why risk it? All we have to do is get through one more week."

"For you," Jas said.

I barely heard her. I was still trying to figure out why she'd do this. Unless—"Do you not believe she's going to let me buy the farm? Is it so we can have something to hold over her?"

That made Jas stop what she was doing and put her hands on the counter. "That is not it," she said. "I absolutely believe her, and there isn't any reason not to. You've said yourself that your mother always does what she says she'll do. She says she'll do this, and she wants another chance with you."

I ignored that last part. If my mother wanted anything from me, it was only another chance to change me. "Then why do this? Especially with Zale coming around?"

Jas went back to cleaning. "I took care of him," she said.

I walked closer to her so I could look up into her face as she bent intently over some small espresso-making part. "If you told me that and I hadn't seen him leave, I'd be looking for his body in the compost pile. What did he want? What did he say?"

"He's not going to tell anyone," Jas said, waving the brush she was using at me so that I had to back off. "He just wants his donut recipes. He's not interested in what I'm doing."

"He sure sounded interested. He wanted me to worry too—did you hear him? 'Maggie's donuts are the real thing'?" Every time I'd mocked Zale's fake food was coming back to haunt me.

"I know. And yeah, he thinks this is funny. He'd love to mess with you. But he doesn't want to get on my bad side, I promise."

I did not want Zale out there thinking of ways to mess with me. "Should I talk to him? Maybe I could explain—"

"It's okay," she said. Then she put her work down and looked at me again. "I have a plan. You'll see. You just have to trust me. And trust me on this thing with your mother too. She's coming through for you. So we're coming through for her. End of story."

None of that sounded like a good idea to me. But I did trust Jas.

Everything was coming together. I should have a mortgage lined up and set to sign at the end of next week, and my mother, as unlikely as it had once seemed, seemed ready to accept payment and leave me as sole owner of Pioneer Hill. The farm stand was a winner—we weren't exactly turning a profit yet, because I was still bringing in produce from other farms at their retail prices, but I'd already started to talk to them about doing things differently next year. I'd sketched out plans in my notebook to work with everyone from the inn to the elementary school in various ways, and some of them were bound to work. I could see a five-year plan, heck, a ten-year plan, and it felt good.

What I couldn't see was the same for Jasmine, and that's what stopped me from putting my foot down about speaking to the summer students. I didn't understand why she wanted to do it, but she wanted it, and that had to be enough for me. Zale's appearance reminded me that whatever was waiting for her back in New York wasn't going away. She'd put aside her own problems to help me with mine, and even if she'd welcomed the escape, I owed her. I wanted to give her the kind of support she'd given me and more.

But as long as Jas was here, Maggie Strong was here too,

and I was starting to hate her a little. I wanted Maggie Strong to go away and leave my friend here, and I couldn't see how that was possible, and rather ridiculously I felt like it was all "Maggie's" fault.

I wouldn't be who I was without the Modern Pioneer Girl. I couldn't exactly wish I'd never created her, or never shared her. But I did wish I'd said no when the *Today* show came calling. I almost had. If that message had just come later, when I was on the bus or even after I got back to the farm, everything would have been different. The Modern Pioneer Girl would still be hidden away inside me, mine, instead of walking around reminding me that I wasn't at all what anyone expected a proper MPG to be. The bigger Jas made Maggie, the smaller and less Maggie-like I felt.

Emily had emailed asking for more from Maggie Strong—if not a whole second book, then additional essays to reissue the original with. Or maybe a cookbook. I had put my head on the table and groaned when I saw that one—and then I quickly sat up and deleted it.

Jas would love to write a cookbook.

But not as Maggie Strong. She wouldn't want that. Would she? I didn't know what Jasmine wanted anymore, and I was beginning to suspect she didn't either.

Jas steadfastly refused to discuss her future. "Let's just get through this next week," she said whenever I tried to bring it up. She'd gesture around at the happy farm-stand crowds and push another scone on me. "Enjoy this! We're locking things down for you. Then we'll deal with me."

I tried to believe her.

After we wrapped up the weekend of the farm stand, I threw myself into outside work while Jas baked and prepped for the next one. I found myself trying to stay as busy and as far away from the house and barn as possible, focusing on the few things I could still get into the ground and expect to harvest before it grew cold: lettuce, more kale and radishes, spinach, broccoli and cauliflower, carrots, some squash. Those weren't moneymakers like strawberries, and it was too late to put in a pumpkin patch, but along with Grandma's tomatoes, they'd support me in September.

September. And then October, and November, and the days would shorten and the snow would come. Jas would be—where? What would it be like here without her? I thought of myself as a loner, but now that I'd lost the enforced camaraderie that comes from working together on a ranch or a boat or leading camping trips, I was starting to wonder if I'd been more dependent on those temporary families than I'd thought. Who would I hang out with when it started getting dark at four thirty? Carney and Earl would have me. And Amy. Mike? Not Mike. Of course not Mike.

Maybe I should get a dog.

For now, I tried to join Jasmine in ignoring the future in favor of the present, although I also desperately wanted to ignore the upcoming Yarmouth picnic on Wednesday. I never stopped trying to talk her out of it. Something about Jas taking my creation back to Yarmouth—exactly the place where I'd needed the MPG most and somehow lost her—bothered me more than I could explain. It was one thing to shove Jas out on the *Today* show on impulse. Another, even, to have her playing Maggie around the farm. But once she got up on the green and informed the assembled crowd that she was what a Modern Pioneer Girl ought to be, I knew I'd never feel like the MPG was mine again.

Which would be fine, I kept telling myself. I was settling in here. That savvy, bartering traveler wasn't me anymore, and maybe never had been. As soon as I put words to the thought, I realized I'd been thinking it for a long time. I needed to let the MPG, and most especially Maggie Strong, go.

Instead, I had to cheer her on. Jas seemed oddly excited, and I tried not to let my misery show. "I want to feel like this has come full circle," Jas said. "Like I left Maggie Strong at least as good as I found her. Better. I want to feel like I did more than come along for the ride."

"You did. You have," I said. "You've been everything I needed."

"Not yet," she insisted. "But I will be."

Together we wrote a speech that combined the determination of *The Modern Pioneer Girl's Guide* with what Jasmine insisted was the underlying message and the thing people really responded to—the idea that while all you need is you, you get to decide who that is again and again, forever evolving along with your inner superhero to meet new challenges.

"It's still hard for me to stand up and be who I want to be sometimes," said Jasmine as Maggie, standing in the kitchen. "I still make mistakes. And then I try again. Because if I don't accept myself, no one else will."

Watching her, I hoped she meant what she was saying.

Maybe we really did both need the MPG. Because all I wanted for Jas was for her to find a place to really be herself, and I wished more than anything that I hadn't made it impossible for her to find that with me.

After Jasmine delivered the whole speech, which was only about ten minutes—short enough to not need to go get another sausage, as she put it—she reached out and pulled me up off the sofa, handing me the words we'd written, which she'd printed out in a huge font.

"Now you do it," she said. I tried to beg off, but she wasn't having it. "I know you," she said. "I want this to be your speech too. Unless you hear the words coming out of your own mouth, you're going to let me say whatever just to get this over with."

She wouldn't let me off the hook, so I stood there and read, my hands shaking even in front of an audience of one. When I finished, Jas applauded.

"Perfect," she said.

"Perfectly awful." I expected her to laugh, but she shook her head vigorously.

"No, really perfect," she said. "I don't know why you think all people want is to hear some polished speaker tossing off platitudes. Sometimes they want the real thing."

I tossed the pages on the couch next to her. "They get what they get and they don't get upset," I said. "You're as real as they come."

Jas smiled as she gathered up the papers and turned off the light next to her. "We're good together," she said. "Like that stuffed bunny in the book. Maybe we make each other real."

I reached for her, and we hugged. It felt like good-bye.

THE YARMOUTH PICNIC was in the evening, so I did chores early. We spent Wednesday mostly apart, with me putting the finishing touches on new outdoor shelving for the farm stand and Jas making jam, seeing each other only in passing. As I finished bringing the animals in for the night, I found Jasmine beside me, handing me the last buckets of grain for S'mores and Brownie.

"Need anything else?"

I was filling a water bucket for the minis' stall, so I gestured to the four-wheeler, which I'd used to bring over a couple of bales of hay. "Want to put that away?"

Jasmine's face lit up. "Sure," she said. "I love driving that. Makes me feel like a real farmer."

I laughed. "Just park it in the usual spot," I said. "No joyriding."

"Sure thing, boss."

Jasmine zoomed off in the direction of the carport where I kept the ATV and other equipment when the barn was full of hay, and I finished filling the rest of the buckets. I gathered the eggs from the laying boxes and left the door open—the chickens would put themselves to bed at sunset as they always did, and I would come shut them in later.

Later. When it was all over. Just a few more hours, and we'd be done. I hadn't told Jas, but my plan was that after tonight, we'd retire Maggie Strong for good. Close the social media accounts, tell Emily there would be no more books, no more anything. Jasmine would go home sooner or later, and when she did, the rest would all fade away.

It was the only way I could see out of this mess.

An hour later, we were ready for Jasmine's last performance as Maggie Strong. Jasmine was wearing an outfit very similar to what she had worn on the *Today* show. I was dressed up too, at Jasmine's insistence, and she was right—it did feel better walking across the Yarmouth campus "dressed like a successful adult" in stylish colored denim, clean, shiny boots, and a shirt that hadn't seen its best days two continents ago, hair smooth and lip gloss on. My plan of wearing the clothes I'd done chores in might have been my middle finger to Yarmouth, but as long as it would've bothered me—and it would have, I thought, looking around at the polished and well-groomed students and staff—then I would only be hurting myself.

I was forty years old. You'd think I'd have known stuff like that.

Margaret might have described this as a "picnic," but it was a production, with a big tent and tables set up on the grass, and I saw plenty of people who weren't students, including Emily and Mike with an uncomfortable-looking Louisa between them. The familiar scene catapulted me back to a dozen similar events, some I'd attended with my mother when I was younger, smiling nervously at the adults around me, some I'd come to as a student, where I was still, even though I didn't realize it, nothing more than my mother's daughter. I hadn't been back on campus in years, and nothing about this experience was making me want to repeat it.

True to Margaret's promise, there was no podium, but there was a microphone on a small raised stage that I was grateful I would never stand on. At her invitation, we followed her through the food line, accepting plates from the caterers and whatever they piled onto them. I was too nervous to do more than pick at the food. Jas, though, chatted with my mother easily, although she turned her back on a few students who clearly hoped to talk to "Maggie" in a way that surprised me. I sat in nervous silence until Jas finished eating, then got up to compost both of our plates.

The compost bins were tucked off to the side of the party, and it took me a minute to make my way to them and return. As I reentered the tent, some trick of acoustics carried Jasmine's voice clearly back to me. "I think approval is the hardest thing," she was saying. "I wrote about not needing it. I know I don't need it. But sometimes, especially when it comes to people close to me, I want it so badly. Is there anyone who isn't terrified of finding out what other people see when they look at us?"

I couldn't hear Margaret's response, but I heard Jasmine as clearly as if she were sitting next to me. "I think that's why we make mistakes. You. Me. Rhett. I know she doesn't let it show, but she cares a great deal about what you think."

Margaret said something else, and they both laughed, a little moment of conspiring together. About me.

If Jasmine hadn't turned around and seen me at that moment, I would have backed away, disappeared, gone anywhere but here where they could both see my hot cheeks and wobbly legs. Hearing what Jas really thought of me was humiliating. Hearing her throw me under the speeding bus that was my mother was worse. Probably she was right. Probably I did care what Margaret thought of me, far too much. If I didn't, I wouldn't care what Jas said, and I did.

I definitely did.

But the only thing worse than knowing they were talking about me would be having them see that I knew. I pulled my shoulders back, resisted the urge to wrap my arms around my chest, and met Jasmine's eyes with what I hoped was a cheerful blank gaze as Margaret spoke.

"Well then, let's get started."

She led the way and we followed, with me scouting out a place to sit down away from the students. As we crossed the sidewalk, Jas leaned over and pressed the folder she'd brought with the written-out speech into my hands. "Hold this for a second," she whispered. "I'll be right back."

I glanced back and saw her walking quickly toward the side of the building, maybe to pull her lipstick out and do a quick refresh out of sight. My mother walked up the steps, took the microphone, and greeted the students, waving and asking if they were enjoying themselves as though instead of introducing a speaker, she might be handed a guitar, and while she asked a few of the closest what they were enjoying about the Yarmouth summer, I glanced down at the papers Jas had put in my hands.

I knew what was in there. The whole speech, written out, from the very first words to the final thank-you.

This is not so much an easy path as it is one that's easily followed. I don't make light of how hard it is to get to a place like this. Not at all. But unless—no, until—you've looked hard at that path and made sure it's the one you want to be on, not your parents or your teachers or that nice lady who saw your Yarmouth bumper sticker and congratulated you at the grocery store, then you don't know if it's your path. And if you think maybe it's not, then suddenly you don't know who you are.

That's where your version of the Modern Pioneer Girl comes in. You can't be me. You have to be you. And then you have to be you in front of everybody else.

She would say it so well too. Calmly and confidently, and while secretly thinking about how much I sucked at living up to my own words.

What was Jas doing? She should be back by now. There was a note taped to the cover of the folder in Jas's handwriting, and I looked at it more closely. The first thing I saw was my name, and then—

Start with "a funny thing happened on the way to the Today show," it read.

What? No. Oh no. No, Jas, not now—

Then just keep going. Tell them what happened. They will understand, and they will love you for being honest about how hard it always is to be true to yourself when you're afraid that self is not what other people you care about want you to be.

You can do this. Read it if you have to. No one cares. They're all thinking more about themselves than you. That is the way it has always been and the way it will always be.

This is what I should have told you the first time. This is your rodeo. The only person who can ride this bull is you. Just be you—in front of everybody else.

I looked down the sidewalk where Jasmine had gone. There was no sign of her. Glanced back at the note, as if looking at it again would change what it said, but all that was left to read was the signature—*I love you, Jas.*

Margaret, at the microphone, was beginning to talk about *The Modern Pioneer Girl's Guide.* At any moment, she would turn to introduce "Maggie Strong," and "Maggie" would not be standing there.

Jas wasn't coming back. This was why she wanted to drive her own car, not so she could stop at the store on her way home.

Jasmine had been planning this all along.

The vision of Margaret and her microphone blurred in front of me as a buzz that had nothing to do with the assembled students filled my ears. Did Jas really imagine that I would walk up those steps and take that microphone when my mother finished the introduction she'd just begun? Tear off my ordinary Rhett Smith costume to reveal the Modern Pioneer Girl within? It was impossible. Because ordinary was all I had. My mother, this whole crowd—they were waiting to hear from Jasmine's version of Maggie Strong, charming, self-deprecating, comfortable in whatever role life threw at her.

And instead, they would see me, palms sweaty, legs shaking, a folder in one hand and a note from someone I thought was my friend in the other. I couldn't do this, and Jasmine—who'd just stripped me bare in front of my mother—knew it.

I pulled out my phone, but I knew Jasmine wouldn't answer, and she didn't. This was the same Jasmine who once locked me in a supply closet with a boy I had a crush on. The stakes were different now, but Jasmine was not. I was on my own, and Margaret was turning around, pausing in surprise, then turning back to her audience and making a small joke about losing her guest.

A drop of sweat ran down into my eye, salty, and the sting brought a tear that I brushed quickly away. There was only one possible thing to do, and the lightness in my head and the tingling in my limbs told me I was ready to do it.

27

A Plan Gone Wrong

I WALKED AWAY. Quickly. Refusing to process anything I might hear Margaret saying as I went. I rounded the corner where Jasmine had disappeared and—as soon as I was out of sight—broke into a run, heading straight into the Yarmouth campus, my only goal to end up somewhere no one would look for me. I tore down the sidewalk as fast as possible and then slowed to a casual walk. Just a Yarmouth tourist, out for a stroll, then back in my truck and—taking the back roads— home.

My hands were clutched around the steering wheel so tightly that they made a sound like sweaty thighs coming off a leather seat when I released it. I dropped them in my lap and stared at the farmhouse. Jasmine's car was parked in the driveway, the lights in the kitchen on. I didn't want to see her. I didn't want to see anyone. If I had a choice, I'd just keep driving, but the old Rhett who used to put her money and passport into a wallet around her waist daily had gone soft, and there was no escape.

Jasmine, who must have been watching for me, was out of the front door and down the porch steps almost before I turned the truck off. "That was fast. What happened? How did it go?" I climbed down to face her, and she stopped as soon as she saw me. "No. You didn't."

"How could you do that to me?" I didn't care that we were in the driveway. I didn't care that I was shouting loud enough to be heard from the road, or by whoever was outside enjoying the fire I could smell in the distance.

Jasmine apparently didn't care either. "How could *you* do that to *me*? What did you even say? Any minute now your mother is going to show up here and she's going to think I humiliated her—again."

"Why would you care what my mother thinks? If you cared so much about her, you should have just done what she wanted." I slammed the truck door as hard as I could. "She wanted you anyway, not me. Can you imagine her face if I'd walked up and taken that mic? She would have laughed me out of there."

"She would not. I care what she thinks because she's your mother and she's trying to reconnect with you and you're too blind to see it. She's at least making the first move, but no, you can't budge one inch, and I am just. Trying. To. Help." She punctuated her last words with pounds on the hood of her Mini Cooper.

I strode forward, tripping over my boots and righting myself almost without noticing. "You want us to reconnect? Great, so that's why you told her I'm so scared of everything, and that I care what everyone thinks about me. That's totally going to help." I pushed past Jasmine and went inside the house, trying and failing to slam the door on Jasmine, who caught it and slammed it herself as she came into the kitchen.

"At the picnic? Holy shit, Rhett, why does everything have to be about you all of the time? I wasn't talking about you. I meant me. I want people's approval. I'm afraid to hear what they think of me. Hell, I want your approval even though I *know* what you think of me. Spineless, chicken, dependent—I hear it every time you mention Zale or anything I've done since I met him. And then your mother said she does the same thing, because everyone does. She wants your approval, you want hers. Damn it, why couldn't you just do it? Rip off the stupid Band-Aid. How much longer do you think we can keep this going?"

I'd backed into the counter while she stood in the center of the kitchen, and I had to swat away Alistair, who was butting his head into me from behind. "Because I can't! I can't just 'go out there.' If I could, I would have done it a long time ago. Did you really think all it would take was a little push? Like I was some little kid who just needed to have the ladder on the high dive taken away?"

Jasmine sat down on the kitchen couch and put her face in her hands. "Oh my God. This is such a mess. What did you do, then? What did you tell them?"

"Nothing. I just left." Jas looked up and stared at me for a moment before bursting into horrified laughter.

"You just left? A couple hundred people, or whatever, sitting there waiting for you, and you just left?"

"They weren't waiting for me. They were waiting for you." Jasmine's laugh deflated my fury. I knew I'd screwed up. I also knew there was nothing else I could possibly have done.

I walked to the refrigerator, opened it with no real idea of what I was doing, closed it again, then began angrily washing the dishes from breakfast. Jasmine got up and leaned around me to turn the water off, then handed me a towel to dry my hands before walking me back to the sofa. I was too exhausted and upset to resist.

"They were waiting for you," she said. "There's no one in the world who wouldn't rather hear the true story you have to tell them than listen to me lie."

"You wouldn't have been lying," I said sadly. "You were playing a part."

"I was lying. I was pretending to be someone—someone strong, who takes risks, who takes charge, who doesn't take no for an answer—someone I'm not. And you are."

"Not here I'm not," I said. "Here I'm still a fourteen-year-old who runs away from her problems." I stared at my hands, my clothes—everything looked so normal, and everything was still so wrong. "What are we going to do now?"

Jas was sitting on the sofa, bent over, arms around her knees and staring at the floor. "We? I don't know," she said, her voice sounding terrifyingly distant.

"I should have said you were sick."

"No, you should have told the truth." Jasmine got up and turned to look down at me. Her shoulders sagged and her face looked defeated rather than angry. "For you. For me. Because what am I supposed to do now? How am I supposed to be here?

In ten minutes everyone in this town will know that I didn't show up for your mother, and what am I supposed to say about that when it wasn't even me?"

I put my hands over my face. I didn't have an answer. I didn't want the one I knew she was about to give.

Any patience that had remained in Jasmine's voice disappeared. "I'm going to have to leave, aren't I? Is that what you want?" Jasmine spoke quietly. "Is that what you've been waiting for? For me to go?"

I sniffled mightily, wiping tears away without looking at her. It wasn't what I wanted. But I couldn't see any other choice.

Before Jasmine could say anything else, I heard a knock at the door and looked up to see Emily. At the sight of us, she let herself into the kitchen, and as she did I caught a glimpse of Mike's truck and another car outside.

I should have run without my passport and wallet. I could have snuck back for them later. Wasn't it obvious to everyone that we were a train wreck here? Why couldn't people just leave things alone?

Jasmine glanced at the stairs as Emily came in, possibly thinking the same thing, and Emily stared at us both.

"What," she finally asked quietly, "is going on here? Why did you leave—was it because of that guy who kept asking people questions about you?"

"Guy?" Jas asked, eyes sharp. "Super built, bald, probably wearing a muscle tank?"

"Yes."

Zale had been there?

"He asked how long I'd known you," said Emily slowly. "And he asked a couple of students if they thought you really looked like someone who could gut a fish, or fix a truck. One of them called him a misogynist." She waited, as if for us to laugh, and when we didn't, she looked worried. "Is this a problem? Is there something I need to know?" She waited, and neither of us spoke. "Please just tell me that I don't have a James Frey situation on my hands here."

At that, Jasmine laughed, a little hysterically. I stood up quickly, intending to rush Emily out of the kitchen with frantic words about how Jasmine hadn't been feeling well, needed a break, something—but a sudden pounding on the door behind her made us all jump. I looked over, expecting to see Margaret, but the face in the window was Mike's, and he was hitting the glass so hard I thought he might break it.

"Smoke!" He banged and pointed. "Come on!"

Suddenly, I realized that my tears weren't just from emotion, but from smoke as well. Something was wrong, something big. Jas stood frozen in the middle of the kitchen while I ran out the door, pushing Mike aside, and stopped dead next to him on the porch.

The hay barn was on fire.

28

A Superhero Alter Ego

I STOOD STILL for a moment, taking it in. Jasmine, Emily, Zale—none of that mattered now. It was my worst fear, every farmer with hay's worst fear, and it was happening. Smoke, clearly visible against the outside lights in the night sky, was curling out of the hay barn on the south side of the house, and in the sudden dead silence I heard the faint crackle of flame— and then I moved, starting toward the horse barn out back at a run that was interrupted when Mike grabbed my arm and yanked me back.

"You can't go in there," he shouted.

I shook him off. "I'm not," I said, but he was right, I'd been going to, until his words jump-started my brain. Emily and Jasmine burst out the door behind me. Louisa stood by her father's truck, looking as ready to run to the barn as I felt, and beyond her, in the driveway, were both Zale and Margaret, each climbing out of their cars. In that moment, I saw them all as hands, not problems. I had help. I was going to need it.

I turned. "Emily: 911. Now." Emily didn't move, and I raised my voice. "Now! The rest of you, we're going to get the animals out of the other barn, but this is dangerous. Nobody does anything I haven't told them to."

Emily blinked and I pushed her back into the kitchen. "Call 911. Phone's on the wall."

"Should we try to put out the fire?" Louisa was looking from her father to Jasmine, her face frantic. "Fire extinguishers . . . water . . . Maggie? What do we do?"

Jasmine looked as terrified as I felt.

"No," I said, and everyone turned to me. "The animals are the top priority, and there's too much chance of something going wrong. No one goes in the hay barn. Hay fires spread fast and they spread weird." The one I'd seen in Argentina, roaring up again in a different spot every time we thought we had it out. That one I'd heard about in Wyoming, where someone climbed up the pile to look for the flames and fell through into them.

Mike argued. "If we put it out, we save the animals," he said.

I shook my head fiercely. "Not worth the risk," I said. What were they waiting for? I realized, to my horror, that Mike's eyes were on Jasmine and Margaret's were as well. Louisa, though, was staring at me. And so was Jas.

"What should we do?" Jasmine grabbed my arm, her voice panicked. "Rhett?"

Louisa let out a wail of frustration and started toward the horse barn, and I dove off the porch to grab her, but Mike did the same, faster than I had ever seen anyone move, until we each had Louisa by an arm.

"No," Mike shouted. "We need a plan—"

"That's what I said," I yelled over him. "Louisa. He's right. Wait." We needed to do this together. "We need everyone's help. We're letting the hay go and getting the animals out to the field before it spreads."

Emily reappeared. "They're on the way," she said, but it would take time; the volunteers had to get to the station—we'd have to get the animals out and hope the trucks arrived in time to save the house.

I took a determined breath. "The animals will be panicked, but we have time." We were losing it fast, but as long as they couldn't see the flames— I glanced at the big hay barn as a curl of fire licked through the window closest to the other barn, the one that held the animals. The wind was coming from that direction too.

"That doesn't seem safe," said Margaret, walking toward me as if to stop me from moving.

"I'm not sure—" said Mike, still gripping his daughter's arm.

"I don't want Louisa—" said Emily.

Louisa shook us both off. "We have to get to them! Come on!"

"Wait," I said firmly, ignoring them all. At my tone Louisa stopped. They were going to listen to me, or I was doing this myself. "We'll go in together. Emily, can you bring out as many chickens as you can carry? They'll be roosted; it will be easy.

Just carry them out to the yard for now. Mom. Help her or wait here."

Zale moved away from his car to join Emily. "I'll help," he said. I didn't argue.

"Louisa, Mike—we'll get Teddy and the horses." I started for the barn. "Stay calm, everyone. No running. The animals are going to take their cues from us, and we are safe as long as that fire isn't spreading. And if it does—get yourself out. People first."

Jasmine caught up to me. "I'm helping too," she said, and I grabbed her hand. "Grab chickens," I said. "There are so many of them—thank you."

We'd come to the open aisle door. In their stalls, Teddy and the horses were frantic, rushing from side to side, snorting. This wasn't going to be easy. I pointed to the chicken coop. "Chickens are in there. Louisa—"

But I didn't need to say anything to Louisa or Mike. They'd each already gone to a stall, Louisa haltering Brownie, Mike working on Darcy. "One at a time," I said. "We've got time. We do." There were five big animals. Two of us would have to make a second trip. And there were the sheep—but we had time. We had to have time. I haltered Teddy and led him out, holding the rope right up under his chin, trying to calm him with my voice, hearing Louisa and Mike doing the same.

As we emerged from the horse barn, I could see that the flames in the barn that held the hay were visible now, not only at the windows but coming out around the metal roof, gobbling the old wood of the structure and lighting the night sky.

At the sight, Brownie and Darcy tried to pull free, but father and daughter held on as I opened the gate to the big field and let Teddy go. "Get out of the way and let them run," I shouted. Released, horse and pony took off for the other side of the field, but Teddy stayed at the gate, frantic and pacing.

"He's waiting for the others," Louisa said.

"Let's get them," I said. Mike nodded, and we plunged back toward the horse barn, the only light coming from the flames, illuminating mostly the smoke in the air. My mother and Jas passed us with more chickens, and at any other time, the sight of Jasmine with an arm full of roosted chickens would have made me laugh, but not now. My mind was on getting the rest of the animals out. We needed a plan for the sheep—

A sudden noise of hooves made me look up. Bingley was tearing toward us, nostrils flared, at the frantic speed of a terrified horse trying to escape a fire. Behind him, I saw Zale on the ground, Emily running to him. They must have tried to take Bingley out instead, but of course he'd be losing his mind—damn it—

And Bingley was heading straight for—

"Jasmine!" I shouted her name, and Jas looked up and froze as I raced toward her in front of Bingley, feeling his force coming at me as I seized Jasmine and knocked us both to the grass, chickens flying out of Jasmine's arms, just out of the horse's way. He tore by us and took the fence at a jump, heading off to join the other animals.

Jasmine sat up, rubbing her shoulder. The two chickens she had been holding ruffled their feathers and hunched back down in the manner of heavy sleepers disturbed from their rest. I got to my knees and felt the cold grass through the new tear in my jeans.

Margaret ran up to me, moving faster than I thought her capable of, only to stop short and stare. "Jasmine," Margaret repeated, her eyes narrowing. "Jasmine." She took in a breath, and an expression of almost wonder came over her face. "You're not Maggie Strong. I knew you looked familiar. You're Jasmine Venice. Rhett's high school roommate."

Jasmine, still on the ground, looked up at me while Louisa's eyes grew huge.

"She's not Maggie Strong?" Louisa turned to me, face full of confusion, while my mother went on.

"Did you— Is this all a lie?" Margaret stared down at Jasmine. "You made the whole thing up."

"She...made it up?" Emily's tone was disbelieving. No one moved. The sound of the flames grew louder, roaring in my ears until I could hear nothing else except Louisa's voice, barely audible above the noise as she spoke only to me.

"She's not Maggie Strong," Louisa repeated. "You are."

With a crash, the front wall of the hay barn fell in.

I leapt to my feet, but everyone else stood frozen. Emily ran to Louisa. "You're not going in there," she said, staring at Jasmine.

Louisa shook her mother off. "We don't have time for this," she said, grabbing Mike's arm. "Dad. Rhett. Let's go." Mike looked at her, his expression remarkably like Margaret's, and Louisa turned to me. "Rhett," she started, and I knew what she was going to say and this wasn't the time to say it. I yelled over her.

"Mike. Please. S'mores is still in there," I said. "And the sheep, sheep are dumb, I won't be able to move them myself, they'll want to stay in the barn—"

Mike was staring at me as if he'd never seen me before, not moving. Then, just as I was about to give up and run for the barn myself, he grabbed Louisa and pushed her toward me. "Help her," he called as he ran toward the driveway. "Get the pony. I'll get the sheep!"

Now it was my turn to freeze and stare after him. Where was he—

"I'm getting Betsy!" yelled Mike.

Emily got in front of Louisa. "Stay right here," she said. "No one knows what's safe right now."

"Mom!" Louisa's look of outrage would have been funny if things weren't so serious. "Don't you see? It's Rhett—"

I put my hand on Louisa's shoulder, stopping her words, shaking my head hard. This wasn't the time.

"I'll get them," I said, pushing Louisa toward her mother. "Don't worry."

I turned and ran into the barn, not sure what I would do first, when I heard Louisa beside me, shouting.

"Dad and Betsy will get the sheep. Help me get S'mores."

Betsy shot past me into the aisle, Mike running after her, the dog barking short, businesslike barks at the sheep, whose door Louisa opened. The barn was full of smoke, and Louisa and I coughed desperately as we tried to restrain and reassure the frightened mini pony. If we had to, we could let her go and run for it—but we had her now. She was haltered. Louisa was leading her out. I gathered the last of the chickens in my arms and hurried after her, dropping them in the yard.

"Wait there, hold the gate," I shouted to Louisa, and ran back toward the barn. Sparks were flying toward the horse barn and the house, flames licking out onto the grass between them. Where was the fire department? Then suddenly there they were. I could hear them, see their flashing lights cutting through the darkness and illuminating more smoke—

Mike was still in the barn. I ran in. Betsy was in with the sheep, circling, nipping, and the sheep were moving, but only from one side of their big stall to the other, little Clementine running frantically behind the older ewes.

"They won't come out," shouted Mike, and I plunged into the stall, catching Betsy's eye through the smoke as if she were another person and feeling, clear as anything, the dog's frustration. As if I'd been cued myself, I went to the other corner of the stall. I could feel the heat of the flames more strongly here, and I cast a worried glance at the back wall of the stall, closest to the hay barn, as I waved my arms at the flock.

"Go!" I shouted. "Git!"

Driven forward from both sides, the sheep moved, into the aisle and out into the yard, where Betsy circled them and we pushed them along from the rear toward the gate, which Louisa slammed behind them.

Everything in me collapsed in relief. "We did it," I said softly, then more loudly, to Louisa and Mike. "We did it."

They stared at each other, and I wanted to reach for their hands. "You were amazing," I said. "Betsy was amazing."

But Mike's face, which had been open and as relieved as mine must have been, was hardening. He walked away, calling Betsy to him. I looked at Louisa, who was watching him go. "He's angry," she said.

"Everyone is," I said.

"Why was she pretending? Why would you do that? I don't understand."

"I had to," I said.

The fire trucks were in the driveway. Men and women in their big flameproof coats were everywhere, dragging hoses to the pond, calling out. Emily and Margaret were pointing to me. Jas was nowhere to be seen. I needed to tell the crew what was happening—

"You have to tell them," Louisa said, and her words pierced through my spinning thoughts as I realized what that would mean.

"Not now," I said, catching at her hand. Jas had disappeared; Zale had other things to worry about. I still had a little time. "I'll tell you the whole story. I promise. But not now." I'd ruined everything, burned it all down. Everything was over and that was enough for one night. I couldn't deal with anything else. "Please. Don't tell anyone. Not tonight."

She pulled her hand out of mine and took a step away, and Emily was walking quickly toward us, Margaret following, and for a minute I thought for sure she would say no. "I didn't tell," I said. "About the trail. Or Yarmouth. That's your secret. This is mine."

Just as the others reached us, she nodded, and while Emily threw her arms around her daughter I ran to the fire crew, leaving Margaret staring after me.

"The animals are out," I shouted, pointing to the horse barn. Flames were creeping up the back wall of the horse barn where we'd been standing a moment before.

"I think we can save most of it," the man closest to me yelled, and I saw that it was Earl Bailey. "Other town trucks are on the way." I backed up as two men and a woman rushed by me, pulling a hose toward the hay barn. Two others targeted the horse barn. Water sprayed back at us, and when I wiped my face, the grime of the smoke got in my eyes, drawing out tears that I could not let come.

While the firefighters worked and the others watched, I moved, and I could see Mike doing the same. I made sure Teddy had followed his flock out to the farthest reaches of the big field. Started up the tractor and parked it away from the fire. Moved the chickens into the farm stand, shutting them in, passing Emily, sitting at the picnic table with her arms around Louisa, sobbing, and Mike, as he moved cars and trucks out of the way. An ambulance pulled up and paramedics rushed to everyone, checking them over, Jasmine with Zale, Zale still clutching his arm. I didn't need to be checked. I needed to keep going.

The firefighters finally slowed, turning their hoses away, first from the horse barn, still standing but minus the rear wall, the one behind the sheep and chicken stalls at the end of the open aisle, then from the ruin of the hay barn. Sheets of the hay barn's metal roof were strewn across piles of rubble, a few posts still pointing up at the stars that were beginning to appear as the smoke cleared. When they finally shut down the spray, I realized how loud it had been. Now, as the firefighters around me began to clean up their equipment, I could hear the horses still running back and forth in their paddock and someone's engine as they pulled out of the driveway.

Earl Bailey, a clipboard in one hand, came over to me, pulling off his hat and wiping his face with the other. He replaced the hat and pulled a pen from his pocket.

"I think I've got the story," he said. "We found a utility vehicle parked by the hay pile, and you can see it started there. Probably smoldered for a while, but with all the hay on the floor it had a lot to grab on to."

"The ATV shouldn't have been in there," I said, trying to think. "I park it outside when there's hay."

"Well, somebody didn't." Earl lifted a hand to wave to Louisa, who was pulling her bike out of the back of her dad's truck. "It was right next to the gas cans. Bunch of paint in there too. Went up fast. You have to be careful with that stuff."

Gas cans. I couldn't believe how dumb I'd been. And paint? I hadn't seen any paint in there. I was careful, I wanted to argue, but what would it mean when I clearly wasn't careful enough? The four-wheeler. I'd noticed hay starting to collect up under the mud covers and meant to clean it out, and I'd told Jas to put it away, but she must not have known I didn't mean in the barn. I should have told her. I should have checked.

I didn't sweep the barn. I didn't pay attention, not to the four-wheeler or anything else that was in there with all that hay.

I stared at the ground, shaking my head. Earl patted my shoulder.

"Rest of the hay must have been wet to go up like that," he said. "It happens."

"Only to me," I wailed. "It was dry, or I thought it was, and it wasn't even me who put the ATV in there and I don't know where the paint came from—"

Earl kept patting, but I could tell from his expression that he was waiting for me to say something else, and it all burst out.

"I know, it's my farm, I'm responsible for everything. Or it should be my farm, but it isn't even yet and now it never will be and I'm still responsible." I broke into sobs and Earl pulled me into the rough shoulder of his fire jacket, which smelled of smoke and sweat. I stayed there for a few seconds, wishing I never had to step back and see everything, the ruined barn, Earl's face, Jasmine, Emily, Mike, Margaret, anyone. I'd ruined everything.

"You'll be okay," said Earl, and while I didn't believe him, I pulled back, drawing a hand across my face and smearing the grime again, gulping and nodding. I couldn't cling to Earl forever. I stepped back and watched him walk away, holding everything in as tightly as I possibly could.

Mike's truck was gone and Emily and Louisa with it. The fire crew was winding up the last of their hoses and loading into the fire engine and the various vehicles the all-volunteer team showed up in, which lined the road. The house was safe, the animals safe, the little farm stand still standing.

I was still standing, but it was as if there were a wall

between me and what was going on around me. I couldn't take any of it in. The tears dried on my cheeks and there weren't any more. I watched everyone drive away and I didn't feel anything at all, and that was good, I wanted to hold on to that, but as I turned and walked toward the porch, I saw that the front door was open, and Jasmine standing in it. She wasn't looking out at me, but back into the house, and something about her posture stopped me from rushing to her the way I wanted to, to let everything that had happened today pour over us both while we huddled and figured out what to do. I paused, and waited, and as I watched, another figure appeared.

Margaret.

❧

29

Regrets

"I DON'T KNOW what you were doing," my mother was saying. Jasmine's back was to me, but I could see Margaret's stony face under the porch light. "I don't even know what you thought you were doing." She turned, and although I tried to shrink back into the shadows, she saw me and spoke even more loudly. "Either of you. I'm . . . appalled."

I didn't move or speak.

Margaret stood on the porch, her gaze sweeping from one of us to the other, but when she didn't get a response, she made her way down the steps. She stumbled a little and had to grab the railing, and I caught just a glimpse of the frailty that I'd seen my Grandma Bee fight for years. Then Margaret straightened and marched to her car, her back stiff and straight. I'd started toward her as she slipped, but I stopped, knowing she wouldn't thank me for my concern, and pushed my treacherous emotions back where they'd come from. Maybe—a few hours or a few days ago—I could have offered her a hand, and maybe she would have taken it. But at this point there was nothing to do but watch her get into her car and drive away.

Jas, too, stood looking after her. I expected her to turn my way, to meet my eye, but she went back into the kitchen, letting the door slam behind her.

When I came in, she wasn't in sight. I found her upstairs, shoving clothes into a bag she'd thrown on the bed. She spoke without turning around. "Was it really my fault? Because of where I parked the four-wheeler?"

"Who told you that?"

"Zale. One of the firefighters recognized him, which he loved."

I leaned against the doorway. "No," I said, trying to make it sound as definitive as possible. "No, it was my fault. Is Zale okay?"

"He'll be fine. Probably a sprain. He's supposed to see his own doctor tomorrow."

"What was he even doing here?"

"I have something he wants," Jas said. "But it doesn't matter now." She had her head down, not looking at me.

I crossed the room and stood in front of her as she carried clothes from a drawer to her bag. "This is all my fault."

"Excellent," she said, going around me and continuing to pack. "That would show extreme growth and maturity if you told anyone but me."

"I told Earl—" I started, and she interrupted.

"That you wrote the book?"

"No. Of course not. But the fire—"

"Yeah, great." She shoved another shirt into her bag, one I

knew was one of her favorites, and I wanted to take it from her and fold it gently. No, I wanted to put it back into the drawer and convince her to stay.

"Zale will tell people, anyway," I said. The thought of it made the muscles of my chest clench around my heart. Once Margaret knew what had happened, she would change her mind about selling me her half of Pioneer Hill, and it didn't even matter, because who would give me a mortgage on a farm I'd just half burned down? And what town would want someone like me sitting at their doorstep like a time bomb?

I'd ruined everything, and it really was all my fault.

"No, he won't," she said. "I took care of Zale. And I let your mother believe that I made the whole book up, or whatever she thinks happened. Fate's not going to drag you out of this, and I'm not going to either. Probably someone will figure it out eventually, but it won't be because of me, and don't think I took care of Zale for your sake. If he blows you up, he'll use my name, and I don't want to be part of it. Somehow I don't think your mother will bother about me." She shoved another shirt in the bag. "And Emily is calling in the morning. I don't know what the hell you're going to tell her, but you better keep me out of it."

I couldn't stop watching, horrified, as Jas packed a bag to walk out of my life. I couldn't let her go. "Jas," I said, searching for words, "I'm sorry. I wish I'd never started this."

She turned and crossed her arms over her chest. "Started what? Which part?"

"All of it. I wish I'd never written the book in the first

place." The more I thought about it, the more that seemed like the turning point. I wasn't Maggie Strong or the Modern Pioneer Girl. I was only ever pretending.

Jas sighed. "Seriously? That? Why?"

"Because I'm not her. I'll never be her. You are, maybe. Not me. I'll tell Emily tomorrow that we should shut it all down. Take the book back. Do whatever it takes."

"You're kidding, right?"

I felt the sharp edge of the guest room dresser pressing into me as I leaned back. Wasn't that what she wanted, for me to tell people this was all my fault? "I already meant to do that. Before the picnic. You've been amazing, you kept coming through for me—" Until the picnic. But I understood what she was doing. "I can never thank you enough for trying to make this work out for me. It's time for me to make it stop."

"No, it's time for you to be who you are."

"I'm not," I said. "I never could have invented her if it weren't for you. Every time she says something positive, it's you. Every time she tries to be encouraging, it's you encouraging me. The rest of it is just me making stuff up to justify all the ways I kept failing." Just like my mother said. The one thing I wasn't going to do was see her face when she found out how right she'd been. At least I could clear out of here before that happened.

"Are you nuts? I didn't get myself a job in a stupid fish cannery, or end up helping to crew some billionaire's yacht. I didn't work on a dude ranch, or talk a tourist out of a canyon before it flooded, or help start a new guide company. Every word of that book is your life, while I sat in New York and went to auditions and yoga classes. I can't even do a push-up."

"I did it," I said, trying to make her understand, "but I didn't do it like the Modern Pioneer Girl says. I didn't feel great all the time. I didn't feel tough and invincible, or qualified, or like I was going to make it half the time. I was terrified."

"Of course you were," said Jas, "but you still did it." She stared at me. "You're so frustrating, you know? You do all these amazing things, and you write a book that people love exactly because every time a little voice in your head says maybe you can't do something you turn around and do it, apparently just to spite yourself, and then you try to insist that it's that first little voice that matters. Everyone has the little voice. What's incredible about you is that you don't listen."

"That's not what you said to Margaret," I said. "You told her I'm only pretending not to need approval and all those other things. Underneath it all, I'm just as scared as everyone else." She might be the one who'd said it, but we both knew it was true.

"I told you," Jas said, dropping her arms and turning away as if there were no point in even talking to me anymore. "That wasn't about you."

I made a sound of disbelief, and she dropped the clothes she'd picked up and put both hands on the bed, looking down.

"I've been in New York for almost twenty years. I've been with Zale for five. We're not going to have a baby, because Zale doesn't want a baby; he wants his gym and his supplements and his acolytes and I knew that but I pretended I thought he would change, because I wanted him. Or at least, I wanted someone. What I said, about being terrified? About not knowing who I am if I'm not seeing myself through someone else's eyes? That's me, it's not you, it's me." She looked up, not at me, but at the wall in front of her, and I could see she had tears on her cheeks. "I loved being here. I loved being Maggie Strong. What does that say about me, that I feel more alive pretending to be you than I have ever felt as myself?"

I was stunned, and I took a step toward her. "But you're fine," I said almost without thinking. "You can start over."

"Right. Like the great Maggie Strong. Not everyone wants to start over again and again. Some of us want to try to get it right with what we have. But I don't have that choice, do I? Not this time. Zale doesn't want me, not really, and you're only interested in me when I fit into your plans. Maybe you've always been like that, and just like with Zale, I didn't want to see it."

She lifted the rest of the clothes, stuffed them in her bag, and heaved it over her shoulder. "I wanted to help you. I thought I was helping. I had this fantasy that you would tell everyone the truth," she said. "And then I could stay here, and we could work together, and everything would be great, you know? But you don't let people help you. You don't let anyone get near you, not really. You're too caught up in your own shit to even see how it could be, and you always will be. You showed me who you were a long time ago," she said. "I should have believed you."

She walked out of the room, and I chased after her down

the stairs. "I'm sorry," I said. "It just got out of hand—but I'll tell. I'll tell everyone if that's what you want. Please."

She stopped at the front door, and I thought I'd done it, that she would come back and we could take this all down and somehow come out of it together, but she didn't turn around.

"That is not the point," she said to the door before turning the handle and walking out. "That is not the fucking point."

She closed the door behind her. Headlights flashed through the kitchen window and then disappeared. Jas was gone.

30

A Passport

I WOKE TO the smell of smoke and wet wood, a burnt-toast mustiness that sank into my nostrils and that I wasn't sure would ever wash away, along with the sound of a hard driving rain outside. The animals would be crowding the gates of their paddocks, asking to go into a barn that could no longer shelter them and waiting for hay I didn't have. I was alone in the house except for Alistair. Worse, I really was alone. I'd driven Jasmine away, and there wasn't anyone else. There was nothing to get up for, but I got up anyway, chased out of bed by a feeling of doom that was completely appropriate and a sense of guilt that I badly wanted to ignore.

I was dragging on my Carhartts when I heard someone outside.

I opened the door to find Mike's truck sitting in the driveway, and Mike himself standing in the back, rain dripping down around him, dropping four bales of hay over the side.

The kindness of the gesture took my voice away for a

moment. I hesitated, my hand still on the door, when Betsy, in the driver's seat, barked once in friendly greeting. Mike looked up and saw me as he dropped the last bale, then vaulted gracefully down from the truck bed and walked up to the porch. His expression hardened as he approached, and I realized that his kindness was meant for Brownie and Teddy and the other animals, not for me.

He looked behind me, into the house. "You alone?"

"Yep." I tried for a smile. "I'm not very popular anymore."

He didn't smile back. I waited for him to turn and go, but Mike stood at the foot of the porch stairs in the rain, his hand scratching the back of his neck, staring down at his boots. When I'd walked out of his house last week and away from exploring whatever there might still be between us, I was sure I was doing the right thing, but now that the door I'd closed was slammed and locked, I wondered if I'd been wrong not to stay. I wanted that to be why he was here. I knew it wasn't.

"Louisa snuck out last night," he finally said. "Which . . . maybe I shouldn't worry, she's sixteen, but I don't think it's a teenager thing. I haven't told Emily—she has enough problems."

Which I'd caused, although Mike and Emily didn't know it yet. I started to say something, but he didn't let me speak.

"I don't care about any of that right now. I need to find Louisa." He wiped the rain off his face, looking around. "I thought maybe she was here."

I shook my head. "I'm sorry," I said.

Mike looked intently at me, and I met his eyes, because I

was done running away. He was still angry with me—and he'd be even angrier soon enough—but behind his anger was something else. Fear, and a kind of reflection of the hopelessness I was feeling. The look of someone on the precipice of losing everything and trying to find a way to claw it back.

"I found her application for the Yarmouth semester," he said. "She didn't mail it."

Oh, Louisa. My eyes dropped to his shoes, and he caught it immediately. "You knew," he said.

"I told her to send it," I said. "She told me she had."

"What the hell is going on, and why didn't you tell me?"

"She told me she wanted to do something else," I said. "She didn't even mention the Yarmouth thing, you did, and by then she'd made me promise not to tell—"

Suddenly, I knew exactly where she was. "Oh," I said without thinking, and again he practically read my thoughts.

"What? Where do you think she is?"

This wasn't a secret I wanted to keep anymore, but I still hesitated. If I took Mike up to the chimney, Louisa was going to tell him the truth, and I didn't feel ready. I'd never felt less like a Modern Pioneer Girl than I did in this moment. I knew my lies would come out. I just didn't think I could stand to be around when they did. Last night, before I'd crawled into bed, I'd pulled my backpack down from the top of the chest of drawers and cleaned it out, not letting myself think too hard about what I was considering.

Mike was getting impatient. "I don't care what promises you made to her. She's a child. I need to be able to find her."

"I'll show you," I said, and leaned inside to grab a hat and my rain slicker from the rack by the door. "It will be faster."

I set out down the driveway, heading for the trailhead, and Mike opened up his truck door and gestured to Betsy, who hopped out. "We're walking?"

"There's an old trail here that goes to the top of Pioneer Hill. She's been working on something up there—but if I'm right and she's there, I'll let her tell you. I swear that's the only secret I meant to keep for her, and you'll see, it's harmless."

I was walking fast, but Mike easily matched my pace. Betsy romped ahead, plumy tail wagging like a show pony, unbothered by the mud and wet. I turned my head away from the remains of the hay barn.

There was no sign of Louisa at the trailhead, but a few hundred feet in, we found her bicycle stashed in the trees and Mike visibly relaxed.

We pushed on in silence for a few minutes until Mike spoke. "I know you promised Louisa to keep this place a secret, but you're taking me up there—maybe I'd better be prepared." We were side by side on the trail, and he glanced over at my face. "Keeping secrets isn't working out very well for you."

He didn't know the half of it. "This used to be a popular hiking trail. She's helped the trail alliance redo it," I said, gesturing to the plank bridge keeping us out of what would be a boggy spot in drier weather and was now almost a stream. "They cleared a bunch of trees, and there's a view at the top. And an old chimney." I'd almost brought Mike up here more than once when we were in school, but by then, it had been years since I'd climbed it and I'd never been able to make myself come back. He knew the story, though. If he remembered. His next words told me he did.

"It must be hard for you to come up here," he said. "I'll find her, if you want to go back."

I didn't let myself stop. "No," I said, pulling my hood farther over my head against the rain. "I'll take you."

The rain finally began to let up as we kept climbing, and I found myself talking about Louisa.

"She's built a resting place at the top," I said. "Benches, a place to picnic, and a stone labyrinth, you know, one of those meditation trails. She must have been working on it for months."

"It sounds amazing."

"It is." I couldn't keep from smiling. "She's amazing, you know?"

"I do," he said. "I don't understand why she kept this secret, though."

"She has something she wants to do next summer," I said. "Something more like this. I know it isn't any of my business. I didn't mean to get involved. But I don't think she's sold on Yarmouth."

Mike shook his head. "She's done plenty of outside work. The Yarmouth program will set her up for college applications." He sped up even more. "It's not you; it's your so-called friend. And that book, which Emily should have known was a great big fraud," he said. "Ever since Emily gave it to her, she's been pushing back at us. Why do we care so much about where she goes to college, maybe Yarmouth was right for us but not her, maybe she wants to take a gap year, travel or something.

She used to be excited about college. Now it's like she's turned into someone else."

I wasn't trying to defend my book, or myself, but I didn't think he was giving his daughter enough credit. From what I'd seen of her, she wasn't a person who'd be easily swayed by a single book, or even by a natural urge to question whatever her parents said. "Do you think maybe it's because it's getting closer? Because she'll really have to decide soon? Maybe she's just thinking more about it. It really is a hard choice. Maybe she just wants to explore other options."

"This isn't the time to explore other options. I know you don't value college. That stuff about not needing a degree— you could practically have written it. But most people do."

We'd reached the steep uphill before the trail flattened into the old orchard right below the chimney, and as he finished speaking I sped up almost to a run, Betsy happily tearing along in front of me. At the top, I saw what I'd hoped to see: Louisa, kneeling over the far side of the labyrinth, trowel in her hand and stones and a shovel beside her.

I turned back to Mike, knowing I only had a few seconds before Betsy reached Louisa. I wanted to do this now. On my terms.

"I did write it."

Mike, about to take off toward his daughter, stopped short, a foot slipping on the wet ledge beneath us. I caught his arm, but he shook me off. "What?"

"I wrote it," I said. I saw Betsy reach Louisa and nearly knock her over with joy, and Louisa standing up to see who was with the dog. "I wrote the book. Jasmine was pretending to be me. I'm Maggie Strong—I changed it because Smith was too common. And because . . . it felt easier, to write it but not have to live it all the time." I searched his face, trying to decipher his reaction. "Emily even helped."

Why was I babbling on about the name? Because I didn't know what else to say to the blank expression on Mike's face, which was quickly replaced by confusion. "Wait, Emily knew? Knows?"

"No. She knows Maggie Strong is really Maggie—Margaret—Smith. But she doesn't know I'm that Margaret. She thought Jasmine was." Confusion, anger, disappointment. I thought I could see them all. "It's kind of a long story."

Mike looked from me to Louisa, who was slightly above us and watching, her hands on her hips, her expression as unreadable as her father's. The ledge was slippery under my feet, but in every other way I was finally beginning to feel like I was standing on solid ground.

Mike strode toward his daughter and I walked after him, more slowly, uncertain. Louisa waited, her eyes on me rather than on Mike, and as we got closer I realized she wasn't angry, but worried, as she rushed into speech.

"I'm sorry," she said quickly. "I put the paint in the barn. I was done up here, and I was in a hurry. I didn't think about it being flammable—I'm so sorry."

It took me an instant to understand what Louisa was saying, and then I couldn't get my words out fast enough. "It wasn't your fault," I said. Above everything else, I didn't want Louisa blaming herself.

"But Earl—the paint—"

That was where the paint had come from. But it didn't matter. "It wasn't the paint," I said. "It was the four-wheeler, and it's on me for not cleaning it, or cleaning the barn. And the hay was probably wet, and that's on me too."

Now Mike was looking worried too. "No," he said. "Damn it, I'm sorry—we shouldn't have baled it then."

I'd thought about this all night. "I got unlucky," I said. "I screwed up and left room for things to go wrong, and they did. Maybe I should have been able to tell, and maybe anybody would have baled it, and maybe it would have burned anyway. No one is to blame except me, and fortunately no one was hurt." I took a deep breath and looked at Louisa. "You are not responsible. Not for the fire. And not for anything else that happened last night. I shouldn't have asked you not to tell, and I'm sorry."

Louisa's eyes flicked to her father, then back to me, her disappointment with me showing. "Looks like you decided we were both done with secrets."

"I found your Yarmouth application," Mike said. "Rhett didn't tell me much I didn't already know, or wouldn't have figured out." His voice was far calmer than I would have expected as he turned and surveyed the entirety of the work Louisa had done—work I found impressive but that he might see as replacing hours of SAT prep and academics, or, not unreasonably, as representing hours of deception. I had no idea what it would feel like to have a child who was capable of this kind of single-minded devotion, or of hiding it.

"Wow," Mike said. "This is amazing. Did you do all of this?"

Wow. *Wow.* Of all the things Mike could have said, that had to be the best. Louisa looked almost pleased before she bent to pick up her trowel. "Earl Bailey and the trails alliance helped with the trees and the bridges," she said. "I did the rest."

Louisa turned her attention back to her work, or pretended to, putting one of the final stones into the spiral base of gravel she'd dug for her labyrinth. Up here, I could see that the morning's rains were clearing. The neighboring Vermont mountains were already drying in the summer sunshine, and the sun behind the clouds made shadows against the green forests. Louisa reached for a brick, apparently ignoring us both, but I could sense her awareness of her father standing beside her.

"You didn't answer your phone," Mike said. "I was worried."

"Battery's dead," Louisa said. "I used the flashlight too much last night."

"Oh." There was a long pause. "Do you want to show me what you've been doing?"

Louisa shrugged. "Not really," she said. "I know you and Mom won't think it's worth anything. I wish I'd never started it."

She hit at a paving stone with her trowel, knocking it out of place, and as she spoke I heard my own words from last night—*I wish I'd never written the book*—and knew that Louisa wasn't telling the truth any more than I was.

It was hard to be proud of your work when it meant hiding a part of yourself from people who were important to you. It might feel safer. Nobody knew that better than I did. But no matter how hard you tried to convince yourself that it was better for everyone if you just pretended to fit their expectations, all it really did was turn the roles we were playing into walls that became harder and harder to tear down. Because it wasn't just that Louisa wasn't letting Mike see what she really wanted, or who she was. She wasn't giving Mike a chance to accept her either.

I watched them, Mike with his hands in his pockets again, Louisa turning away from him, and I couldn't stand it. Mike wasn't Margaret. He was standing here, his heart open, and I could see his ache to connect with his kid in a way Margaret had never been interested in connecting with me. They could have something my mother and I never could, because underneath whatever was happening here, they believed in the same things. And they believed in each other.

"Don't say that," I said to Louisa. "This is wonderful, and you know it. Don't sell yourself short."

Louisa looked up from her work. "Don't sell myself short?" She glanced at her father. "That's pretty funny coming from you."

I deserved every bit of her anger. "Yeah, well, I screwed up," I replied.

"So now you just tell the truth and it all goes away," Louisa said.

"Not hardly. I made a huge mess because I didn't have the guts to be real with people, and I'm going to pay for that for a long time." With Jasmine. With the farm. With Mike, Emily, even my mother, but none of that was Louisa's problem. "You have a chance to tell your dad what you really want," I said. "I hope you take it."

I didn't hear what either of them said next, because they'd

be better off without an audience and because, if I was honest, as much as I wanted things to work out for them, it was hard to watch something I would never have.

I ran down the trail, watching my footing carefully, concentrating on landing each step in a solid spot to avoid thinking about anything else, leaping over sticks and puddles the way we used to leap over the lines on the single sidewalk that ran along one side of Main Street. Step on a crack, break your mother's back.

My mother and I had broken apart a long time ago.

I slowed down to a jog and came panting into the parking lot at the trailhead, then walked, tugging off the raincoat that it was too hot for now and regretting my coverall. The sun was out, the road steamy in a way that was rare in New England, and ahead of me, outside the farm stand, there were . . . cars? And people getting into them, coffee cups in their hands? I sped up again, avoiding getting caught by anyone who might want to sympathize about the fire or chat, and burst through the door of the stand to see what was happening.

31

Permission

IT WASN'T HER, of course. Amy, Carney's girlfriend, was standing behind the counter, steaming milk in a professional style for the woman waiting in front of her. She looked over her shoulder as I came in, and then her face took on a guilty expression, which I waved off immediately.

"Earl and I came up first thing this morning," she said. "He says if you want to get rebuilt before winter you'd better start now, so he's trying to see how fast he can get you a report for insurance—and then he wanted a mocha," she said with a grin. Two weeks ago, Earl might well have not known what a mocha latte was.

I was disappointed, but I tried to match her amused tone. "Good thing you were here," I said.

"I work shifts at the Starbucks in Lebanon in winter," she said. "So I came in to make him one, and people started showing up at the door, and, well, I hope you don't mind."

"Not at all," I said.

"I'll let you take over," she said, starting to duck under the counter.

"I really can't," I said, looking back at the doorway, which was empty now but might bring in more caffeine seekers any minute. "I had to run out to help Mike and Louisa with something, and I still have to do chores, and I should talk to Earl—" Earl, who thought an insurance estimate might help solve the problems I'd created for myself. "My friend who was doing all this, Jasmine, had to go home."

If Amy thought Jasmine's name was Maggie, or knew anything about the Modern Pioneer Girl's failure to appear at Yarmouth yesterday, she didn't show it. "Tell you what," she said. "You talk to Earl and I'll take over here for a while. It's a lot more fun doing it here than at Starbucks, and I'm just getting in Earl's way. I can run a tractor, but I know shit-all about fire insurance. Or building."

A young couple had come in behind me and were looking around at the empty shelves. "I'm sorry," I said to them. "We had a fire here yesterday, and I didn't stock this morning."

"I heard," said one of the two men. "Saw the barn too. We're so sorry." His partner nodded.

"I can get you a coffee, though," Amy said.

I looked at her gratefully and pulled Jasmine's COWS DON'T LIKE BEING TIPPED, BUT BARISTAS DO jar forward. "Thank you," I said. "You're working for tips and the coffee is all on the house, is that okay?"

"Done," she said. "But people keep asking for turnovers."

"They're in the freezer with instructions, if you have time—"

Louisa walked through the door as I spoke. "I'll help," she said. I glanced behind her, and she saw me look. "Dad went home," she said.

I wanted to know a lot more than that, but she shrugged and dodged past me. I tried to ask. "Everything okay?"

"I don't know," she told me. "I'll go in and find some scones and things," she said to Amy. "I can figure it out."

At least she was here helping. She couldn't be that mad. Mike must know she was here too. That was all I was going to know for now.

The animals would be long past anxious for their morning grain, and stressed from the night before and the changes in routine. I rushed to get to them. The hay wasn't in the driveway anymore, and I walked back to the barn in confusion before I saw Carney sweeping the aisle.

"Morning," she called. "I figured you could use a hand, so I got everyone fed."

"Thank you," I said in surprise, a little embarrassed and hurrying to grab a second broom. "Mike brought the hay, but he needed help with something—" I stopped. I didn't know how much of what was going on with Louisa they'd want out there.

Carney, very obviously getting the entirely wrong idea, was smiling broadly. "Mike, huh?"

It wasn't worth trying to argue. I started to say again that I was about to get to the animals, that I was fine and didn't need help, and realized two things. First, that would be rude, and second, it was wrong. I was very grateful for her help. "I'm glad you were here, thank you," I said, meaning it. "What's left to do? Anything? You sure it's okay to be in here?" The aisle, now open in back, was much brighter than usual.

"Dad said it was fine." She swept at my feet with her broom. "I'm almost done. Go talk to him, will you? He's worried about you."

"He's in the hay barn?" What was left of it.

Carney smiled back in sympathy at my tone. "Yeah," she said.

I walked slowly. I hadn't seen the barn in daylight yet, and it was every bit as crushing as I knew it would be. Big charred pieces of the red walls lay over the ruins of what had been inside. Wet hay was crushed under the fallen metal roof, and on top of it lay my father's wagon weather vane, blackened and bent. The sight of it made it even harder to hold back my tears.

Earl was kneeling next to the shell of the four-wheeler, but at the sight of me he stood and picked his way over one of the beams to stand beside me in the still-damp grass.

"Pretty bad," he said. "But in some ways maybe it's better if it's a total loss." He took an old-school carbon paper form from the legal pad he carried and pulled off the top page to hand it to me. "Fire report," he said. "You'll need it for the insurance."

"I don't even know if I have insurance."

"This place has been held in trust for you and your mother, right? And your mother is the trustee? You have insurance."

He was probably right about that. I took the paper from his hand without looking at it and stared at the ruins in front of us. "It's not mine anymore," I said. "My mother's going to want to sell it to the college, and now I don't blame her." I kicked at a piece of charred board. The humid air only amplified the smell around us of smoke and burn and defeat. "I really screwed up," I said. "Can you imagine what my dad would say?"

The hay barn was his pride and joy, the way he described the farm and told people how to find us. He mentioned the hand-hewn beams that held it up nearly every time he walked through its doors, and when he did repairs, he carefully pulled out the handmade nails from the wood and saved them all in a jar he'd kept on a shelf near his toolbox.

Some of the beams could probably be salvaged for some decorative purpose. The jar wouldn't have survived, but the nails and the toolbox, which was steel, were probably under there somewhere.

Earl put a hand on my shoulder. "Your dad screwed up plenty," he said. "You're building something here that people like, and last night you saved what mattered. This old place was something, it's true, but maybe it outlived its usefulness. Don't beat yourself up. You'll figure it out."

I didn't understand his optimism. "I don't think I'm going to have the chance," I said. "Who'd give me a mortgage now? And you already said it. My mother is the trustee. She's never wanted to sell it to me, and now I can't imagine she will." Margaret's face, in that moment when she recognized Jas, had been as angry as I'd ever seen her. I'd helped humiliate her. And as much as I wanted to pretend otherwise, she was bound to find out exactly how many lies I'd told that led us to this place.

Earl picked up the paper coffee cup he'd set down on the ground while writing up his notes. "Have you talked to her?"

"No." And it wouldn't help.

"You're giving up without even trying? Now that, Charlie would have had something to say about."

I'd been trying not to cry from the moment I walked in sight of what was left of the barn, but Earl's words thwarted my best efforts. I sniffled and wiped my face with my sleeve. "It doesn't matter what Dad would say. It's what my mother says that counts."

"And you have no idea what that will be," Earl said, adding, before I could argue, "until you ask. I know you see your mother one way. And you're right. She's a tough one. But Charlie married her. And she married him. And that's where you came from. You can quit without talking to her, and then you'll be right about what comes next. But that won't be on her. That will be on you." He tucked his legal pad under his arm and then stilled, as if to emphasize his next words. "This is a piece of advice your dad probably wouldn't have given you, but I will. There are no shortcuts."

He turned and walked away.

No shortcuts. No hiding. Well, there was pretty much my entire strategy gone.

I tried to laugh, but it wasn't funny, because it was true. My dad loved shortcuts. There has to be an easier way, he'd say, and sometimes there was, like installing a heated automatic waterer in the paddock instead of hauling water, and sometimes there wasn't, like standing with a horse and soaking its leg when it was hurt.

Sometimes the hard way was the only way. And Earl was right. Dad always made sure he wasn't the one holding the horse.

I turned and walked around the back of what was left of the hay barn. The back wall of the horse barn was gone, but it still seemed structurally sound. In front of it, looking out at the farm stand and with the house blocking the absence of the big barn, I could almost pretend everything was normal if it weren't for the smell.

When I got to the front of the farm stand, I saw Teddy and S'mores standing in the shade while Brownie knelt down as low as he could, sticking his head out under the lowest rail of the round pen as far as he could to get at the grass that was just out of reach, avoiding the electric wire I'd strung along it. "Dude," I said to him, shaking my head and plucking up a handful to feed him. "You have got to learn to be thankful for what you have."

That sounded like some kind of life lesson. I *was* thankful for what I had, and I wanted to stay. I wanted Carney and Amy and Earl next door and Carney's kids getting paid a pittance to pick tomatoes and spending it all at the country store under the new owner's stern eye. I wanted Jas calling out people's latte orders as though they were nicknames. I wanted Louisa leading people up to see her labyrinth. And—as long as I was fantasizing—I wanted Mike driving the tractor, and Margaret, what? Smiling benevolently over it all?

What was harder than admitting to what I really wanted was owning how much I'd done to get in my own way. I didn't wish I'd never written *The Modern Pioneer Girl's Guide*. But I wanted to grab the Rhett who got off that plane and came straggling into the sunshine at JFK and shake her. Why did I shy away when Zale wanted to congratulate me on the book's success? Why couldn't I just say thank you? Turn down the *Today* show if I wanted to, but not turn away from what I'd done?

The worst part was that in retrospect it all seemed so incredibly stupid. Probably nothing would really be different. Margaret would have hated the Modern Pioneer Girl and the book no matter where she encountered them. I would still have found out that Bee couldn't leave me the farm, and had never been able to bring herself to say so. My mother would still have wanted to sell the farm to the college. Mike would still have been on her side. But at least I'd have gone into that fight at full strength instead of with a gag on my tongue and one hand tied behind my back.

It would have been hard. I would have felt shamed and small when Margaret said all the things she would have had to say about the book and what it said about me. I might have needed to crawl into a hole for a while. But I would have picked myself up, swatted away my doubts, and used everything I'd learned, and I would have been okay. And I would have had Jasmine to talk to about it and to buck me up.

I needed to face Margaret and own who I was and what I'd done, not apologize for it. I might not talk Margaret into letting me buy Pioneer Hill, but if I was going to try, I couldn't hide so much of who I was any longer.

I handed Brownie a last handful of grass before sticking my head in the farm stand door.

"You good for a while?" Amy nodded, and Louisa looked up from where she was sorting snap peas she must have pulled from the garden. "Thanks." I hesitated. I wasn't usually someone who announced my business everywhere I went. But if I wanted to be someone who got what she wanted, maybe that needed to change. "I'm going to talk to my mother."

I waved. "Wish me luck," I called as I headed for the truck.

32

Your Middle Finger

IT WAS STILL only ten thirty in the morning. I backed the truck out confidently, but when I got to the road, I pulled off. I was going to find Margaret, and I wasn't going to put it off any longer. But there was one call I should make first. Emily, whose phone surely popped up my number as "Maggie Strong," answered on the first ring, and I told her everything before she could do much more than get a word out. Mike and Louisa hadn't said as much, but I could picture her panic and didn't want it to go on for another minute. The book was true. She'd done nothing wrong. I had.

After I talked to her and agreed to her plan to "sit tight unless we need to comment, and then we will," I restarted the truck and drove through town, past the Yarmouth library and toward the administration offices. I parked and hopped out, realizing as I did that I was far from the well-dressed version of myself who'd been on campus yesterday. A lifetime ago. My boots were muddy from the walk on the trail, and I was wearing my work overalls over my shorts, so even taking off the Carhartts wouldn't have improved things much.

It should have made me feel out of place. But this was how I dressed. I was comfortable in these pants. I felt confident in these boots. Like Maggie Strong? Like the Modern Pioneer Girl? It didn't really matter. I felt like me.

That thought carried me past my mother's assistant before she could stop me and right through my mother's closed office door, expecting to find my mother typing, or taking notes, or possibly on the phone.

She was doing a crossword puzzle with a cup of tea at her elbow. I caught the scent of bergamot and an unexpected memory: my mother, persuading me that Earl Grey was sweeter without sugar. I still took it that way.

She looked up as I came in and pushed her newspaper to the side. I didn't give her a chance to speak.

"I wrote the book," I said. *"The Modern Pioneer Girl's Guide to Life.* I wrote it, and I used a pseudonym, and then I pretended I didn't because I was afraid of what you would think, but you know what? I don't care anymore. You can say whatever you want about it, but I wrote it. Me. And it's all true."

I put my hands on my hips and waited defiantly to see what happened when she realized that as much as had gone wrong since then, the daughter Margaret thought would never amount to anything without her guidance had managed to do plenty on her own.

But Margaret's expression didn't change. "I know," she said.

I rocked back on the heels of my boots. "You know?"

"I suspected something after you both ran away from the event yesterday. I read the book to prepare, and something felt off to me the whole time. The Maggie Strong I'd met wasn't just confident; she was almost casual about it. She didn't feel like a person who'd gone through a lot to know herself. I figured maybe she'd grown up. Or exaggerated her struggles, a common thing in memoir, although that didn't explain a reluctance to address our summer class. But when you took charge last night, and then when I realized who Jasmine actually was, it was fairly obvious."

She took a sip of tea, like Miss Marple explaining away the mystery. "And once I could see it, I can't imagine how I didn't guess sooner. You and she were trouble together from the minute they put you in the same room. If there was a bad idea to be had, one of you had it and the other acted on it."

This was not what I had expected. "Why didn't you say anything?"

"When? Last night, watching Charlie's barn burn? It didn't seem appropriate." She set her cup down. "You even used his title. Pioneer. I don't know how I could have missed it."

"Then now you know I was right all along," I said. "I've been working toward inheriting Pioneer Hill my whole life. I'm more than capable of running it."

An expression of faint derision crossed my mother's face. "Yes, last night was certainly demonstrative of your skills."

"I made some mistakes," I said. Why weren't there any chairs in front of my mother's desk? Did she do that on purpose?

"You did."

We stared at each other for a moment, and then Margaret got up. I almost expected her to show me to the door, but instead, she took a chair from the corner behind the desk, walked it out to me, and returned to her seat. I accepted it uncertainly.

"It is easier if I choose who gets to come in and sit down," she said. "A certain number of people will wear out their welcome."

The chair was at least something. I put it in front of her and sat down, and she put her hands on her desk and leaned forward. "Why are you here?"

I shifted a little. "I wanted to tell you the truth."

"And now you have." She paused. "Is that all?"

It wasn't all. I wanted her to admit that she'd been wrong about me. I wanted her to talk to me the way she'd talked to Jasmine, when she thought she was talking to someone closer to an equal. And I knew that to get there, I had to try to make her understand why I'd done what I'd done.

"It started when I saw you at the *Today* show," I said, even though for me, it started long before that. "I was afraid to face you. I felt like I'd done so much, but in your eyes it would never be enough. Sending Jasmine out to pretend seemed easier." It sounded so foolish now.

"I can't imagine what it would have been like to see you walk into that room," Margaret said. "I think I would have been glad. But you couldn't even give me that. Instead, you enlisted your friend to humiliate me, and she was very successful. I should never have given her a second chance—but then, it was never her, was it? It was you."

"You've never given me any reason to believe you would be glad to see me," I said before I remembered that I hadn't come here to argue. If I wanted to tell Jas I'd finally faced Margaret, I needed to finish what I'd started. "I didn't believe it then. I was nervous, and I was scared of how you would react, and I did something dumb. You have to understand that I wish I hadn't."

"Do I?" My mother's voice was cool, almost thoughtful. "I have to understand you? It's my job to listen to you and allow this to all be okay? You lied. Not just to me, but to everyone who wanted to hear from you. You cheated them, and me, out of seeing a genuine version of success that wasn't conventional or glamorous. And you cheated your own book by hiding how hard that road can be."

"That's not what I meant to do," I said.

"It doesn't matter. You claimed to be proud of who you were and what you'd done. And then you proved you weren't."

I sat back in the chair she'd given me. "Don't you think that's a little harsh? I told you. I was surprised to see you. I felt . . . intimidated by you. I made a stupid mistake, and I'm sorry." I'd said it. I was sorry. Couldn't she at least accept it?

"It's a harsh world," she said. "What are your plans?"

I paused, confused. "Plans?"

"For your alter ego, your 'Modern Pioneer Girl.'"

I'd always known I wouldn't like the sound of that coming from Margaret's mouth, and I didn't.

"Emily said she'd find someone in publicity for me to talk to, but that we might be able to just let it go. No one needs to know what Maggie Strong looks like."

"But don't you think they deserve to know who she really is?"

"They do," I said. "It's right there in the book."

"Is it." Her words weren't a question, and in that moment I knew that while she might believe in the literal truth of what I'd written, she'd never believe in me. "Maybe the person you became is in there," she said. "But what about everything you burned in the process?"

I thought I knew what she meant. My degree, the opportunities that came with it. Maybe even Mike, or some alternative life I could have made under her watchful eye, one that would have meant we weren't sitting here, completely at odds over Pioneer Hill and its future. My future.

But I could make a future without Pioneer Hill if I had to. I'd learned that much. And even if I could somehow go back and undo everything, I wouldn't. I'd made some god-awful mistakes, but I'd been free to make them.

"I didn't burn anything I wanted to keep," I said.

She nodded, as if that made perfect sense, although I don't think we'd ever been further from understanding each other. "In that case, I think we're done here." She reached for her puzzle. The audience was over, but I couldn't just get up and go. I had to ask.

"What about the farm? Will you still sell me your half?"

She filled in a clue without looking up.

"Certainly," she said. "The college land acquisition board

meets Friday. They'll have an offer prepared then. If your offer precedes theirs, I'll accept it."

"Next Friday?" Today was Thursday. There was no way I could make that work.

"Next Friday."

"Couldn't you— That's too fast. I have to deal with the insurance, get a new valuation—"

"I'm sorry," she said, still concentrating on the page in front of her. She didn't sound sorry. "You have to understand. I've given you long enough."

❧

33

Regrets

I WALKED OUT of Margaret's office and I kept walking, leaving Grandma's truck behind. The rhythm of my steps helped keep my thoughts from spinning out of control. I walked across the green out to Main Street, lifting a hand to the new owner of the general store across the street, noticing that someone had weeded out the garden beds around the gazebo, deadheading the day lilies so that the later summer asters and salvia could pop. The rain was completely gone, leaving behind a day fresh with all the possible shades of green against the lightest of blue skies, and tiny Bowford was at its most charming. This time of year was glorious, but I loved this place in every season. Even the bubble tea shop took on a homey glow. I should have taken time to try some. Whoever started it was just trying to find somewhere to live and do her thing. Just like me.

I stopped twice, once to call the estate loan mortgage broker I'd been talking to, who didn't exactly laugh at the idea that I could get a mortgage within a week on a property I'd burned half down the night before, but might as well have. Then I gave in to my urge to call Jasmine, but she didn't answer.

I passed the farm stand, head down. When I reached the trailhead, I turned and headed up it.

The farm was a lost cause, and when I left it behind, I'd leave Mike and Louisa as well, along with my unforgiving mother. I'd had my chance to be part of this community again. It was my own fault I'd lost it.

I still had one community left—the one I'd built around the Modern Pioneer Girl, my travels, and my writing. No one but me knew that when I pushed Jasmine into playing Maggie Strong, I lost that part of myself, at least for a while. Maybe I could get it back. But I wanted Jasmine back even more.

I took out my phone and tried to call her again, with no more luck than I'd had earlier. I paused my steps, our text string open, a last message about cinnamon rolls mocking me. I didn't know what to say. This didn't seem like the way to say it.

I quickened my steps to the top of the trail, rereading Louisa's chosen quotes for musing as I walked and thinking about what I'd tell Jas if I could. That I was sorry I hadn't seen what was happening to her. That I was sorry I'd refused to be me. That maybe now we both had a chance to define ourselves. That I didn't want to lose her.

The top of the hill was empty, and I walked Louisa's labyrinth for the first time, reading my own words as I came out.

If you can't be who you are when you get there, don't go.

I'd done the worst possible job of living up to that. But I could do better, and now I knew how I could reach Jas. I pulled out my phone, framed the labyrinth and chimney for a beautiful shot against the Vermont mountains, and started to tap out the words I'd been thinking of. *There are things you don't need to conquer any world,* I wrote. *Those are important. But so are the things you do need. Hard work. A willingness to take risks. Your middle finger, for people who don't believe those things are what matters.*

The courage to be yourself.

Friends.

Instagram being Instagram, I could probably have written anything I wanted after that. But I wasn't writing this for Instagram. I was writing for the one person I knew would read it, and she was the only one who mattered. I thought for a moment and then began exactly where I thought she would want me to.

A funny thing happened on the way to the Today show . . .

Instagram only gives you so many words, and I used every one. Scared. Ashamed. Afraid. Grateful. Disappointed. Trying. Ready.

I told the whole story, and this time I didn't let the justifications speak more loudly than the truth: that I'd chosen to hide when I most needed to be exactly who I was.

I knew now that this was what Jasmine had wanted me to see all along—that even if I lost the farm and everything else, as long as I was still that person who could get up and start again, I had everything I needed.

And I had a feeling she needed to see that in herself too.

I finished and looked over my work and realized the image, while beautiful, was all wrong. I pulled off my hat, loosened the pigtails that held my too-short-to-braid hair, and turned into the wind with the view behind me. I tried a few expressions—apologetic, smiling, tough—and settled on just staring into the camera.

It was not a great selfie. But it was me. I hit post before I could think too hard and put the phone in my pocket, running down the trail for the second time that day, hoping I hadn't worn out Amy and Louisa's goodwill yet. I was going to spend the rest of the day welcoming everyone I could to Pioneer Hill in the finest Jasmine style, a fitting end to what we'd begun to create. And then I'd start packing. And, when I was ready, planning. Leaning into the substantial upside—I might be losing my home, but when it sold, I'd have more money than I'd ever had in my entire life. Enough to decide what came next. I didn't get what I wanted, but I could get what I needed—once I knew what that was—and that made me luckier than ninety-nine percent of the other people on the planet.

I didn't exactly feel lucky yet. But I would.

❧

34

Money

LOUISA AND AMY had a few things out on the counter and seemed to be doing a steady stream of business—but I wanted Pioneer Hill's last day to be big, and they were easily persuaded. Louisa produced a small speaker from her bike bag and started playing music while Amy went to see what more we could bake and I put up our two-sided chalkboard sign. PIONEER HILL, LAST CALL, I wrote on one side and LAST CHANCE TO TRY OUR "SMOKED" LATTE on the other. I added FREE SCONES, COOKIES, AND TREATS AS LONG AS THEY LAST and propped it outside, then took pictures of it to share on both the farm and the MPG's social media. My accounts. *I'll tell y'all how this feels later*, I wrote, *but for now, if you're nearby, come enjoy.*

Louisa biked into town to ask at the general store if she could commandeer their sign to point even more people our way. I sent a message to Carney and asked her to bring the boys and all their friends. The farm stand started to fill up and took on a party feeling.

Still no word from Jas.

I started playing a game with the people who came in for coffee, telling them I was a coffee reader and could guess what they wanted. I did pretty well too. Amy tried to teach us to make latte-art ponies. I remained stubbornly stuck at the blob stage while Louisa caught on quickly. "Maybe a heart," Amy suggested kindly.

"Sounds about her speed," said a cheerful voice, and Jasmine, carrying the LAST CALL sign, walked through the door. "Or a cloud. Or you ask people what they see in whatever you made. Latte Rorschach test."

I ran around the counter and hugged her, hard. "You're back! Wait—how did you get here so fast? Did you see my post?"

Jas took my hand and dragged me out the back door of the farm stand, waving to Louisa as we passed her.

"I just saw it," she said. "But I've been seeing your text bubbles since last night. I knew you'd do something. I knew I would too." She gave my hand a squeeze. "I already knew I was coming back." She walked us all the way back to the paddock, away from everyone else, and set the sign down firmly on the grass between us. The ground was dry again after the rain. The animals, seemingly unbothered by their ruined home, grazed on the other side of the fence.

As soon as Jasmine stopped moving I launched into my apology. "I'm sorry. Not just about the Modern Pioneer Girl. About everything. Not seeing what was happening with you, shoving you into this whole fiasco. I have been a horrible friend, and I am really, really sorry, and all I want to do now is make it up to you. Whatever you're doing next, I'm your dishwasher, or Sherpa, or lady's maid. Whatever. Anything." This wasn't just about the Modern Pioneer Girl. This was us, and our friendship was one of the most important things I had in my life. I wanted to make sure she knew it.

"Apology accepted," Jas said, "on one condition. No, two conditions." She held up a finger. "First, you never, ever again deny being Maggie Strong. Not even if, like, someone is calling her and trying to sell her a vacation property. You're done. Agreed?"

"Agreed. I will be Maggie Strong no matter how Smith-like I'm feeling. I will be proud when I can and fake it when I can't."

"That's all anyone manages," Jas said.

"I know." I leaned against the split rail fence and Bingley came over for a head scratch. "I just wish I'd been able to live up to my own advice from the beginning."

"That's how we know it's good advice," said Jasmine. "Good advice always sucks to follow. Bad advice is so much better. It's way easier to do dumb things than hard ones."

She was so, so right. I began to laugh and Jasmine joined in, and what started small became the kind of hysterical, relieved laughter that comes with exhaustion, after narrowly avoiding disaster and finding yourself still standing on the other side. We laughed until my sides ached and Jasmine was making tiny, hiccupy noises while she gasped for breath until I insisted—my words still interrupted by bursts of laughter—"It's not that funny."

"But it is," said Jasmine, wiping tears from her eyes and gulping. "You were a total dope."

I reached out a booted foot and nudged Jas's ankles, noticing that she still had on a pair of my boots as well. "You were dumb too."

"Not dumb enough to write a book about it," Jasmine said, laughing more. I had to smile, but I wasn't starting up again; I couldn't. If I laughed any harder, I'd cry, and once I started down that road I didn't think there would be any stopping.

Jas finally subsided, sighing and breathing heavily, and when she did, she knelt beside the sign. "So, about this last-call business," she said.

"I didn't want to waste anything you'd made," I said. "And I wanted people to really remember us. So we've been handing out free coffee and stuff all day. I let Amy and Louisa take tips, but that's it. We're going out with a bang." I winced at my own choice of words. I could see the ruins of the hay barn beyond the house. No tears, I reminded myself determinedly. I could cry over this later. Right now, I was standing strong. "My mother gave me until next Friday, and I've called the lenders, and there's no way. I have, like, five thousand dollars in my checking account. I'm going to be fine—the book is still selling, and eventually I'll have the money from Pioneer Hill too—but I'm going to have to be fine somewhere else."

Somehow it was easier to lay it out like that. She knew how much I cared. I didn't have to tell her.

"Would you buy it? If you could?"

"You know I would." I reached out to give a curious horse a pat.

Jas rose and wrapped her arms around herself, rocking a

little onto her toes before she spoke again, and when she did, her words came out in a rush. "Would you let me buy it?"

I stopped petting Bingley. My arm brushed the electric fence as it fell and I barely noticed. "What do you mean?"

In answer, Jasmine reached into her pocket and pulled out a check. She stared down at it, her hands gripping the edges tightly. "You might not want to," she said. "I know it's not what you planned on. But I thought"—she looked up at me, her eyes wide—"what if I bought your mother's half of the farm?"

Oh. Oh. Crazy, chaotic words were bubbling up inside me so fast I couldn't say any of them. Jas couldn't do that—could she?

"I thought we could run it together. You could teach me the farm stuff. I could teach you to bake. If you wanted to."

I couldn't move. I wanted to throw my arms around Jas, to scream and dance and shout because I could not think of one thing, not one single thing, that I wanted more. "If I want to— That would be amazing! But . . . how? Would you really want to? I know you're done with Zale. But coming here—"

I wanted this so bad. But I wanted it to be right for Jas too.

"I want to do something real. Being with Zale, helping him build his dream—I know you and I couldn't get excited about turning a donut into a superfood. But he did. He knew what he wanted when I didn't, and he went for it; that's what I liked about him. And now I know what I want. I want this."

I reached out and took the check from her hands. Made out to my mother, for 250,000 dollars. I'd never seen a check that big. "But where did you get the money? And can you even write a check this big? There aren't rules or something?"

"Zale and I are splitting up. I'm done with being treated like I don't measure up unless I measure down. We'll have to figure out who gets what, but I helped him build his empire, and some of it is mine. In the meantime"—she grinned—"I sold him the recipes. That's what he came back for. I'd been telling one of his bakers how to make everything, but she quit on him and she didn't give me up. He needed them fast, I needed this fast, and we made a deal."

I was impressed. More than impressed. "Nice," I said. "How could I turn down a partner that wily? But are you sure? You could open a bakery anywhere. You really could." I didn't even have to think about it. "I could come help you. My turn."

"I don't want a bakery somewhere else. I want this. I want Carney telling me Earl can only have a skim latte and Earl telling me he wants a mocha. I want the general store calling to make sure we're not going to cut into their business. I want to stand over your grandmother's old stove and melt while I make jam. Well, probably I want a better stove. And ovens. Maybe we expand or something. But for now, I want to wake up in the morning and do something I love. And I do not want to make any more gluten-free vegan kale donuts, ever." Jasmine leaned over and tapped the check in my hands. "I want to blow everything up," she said. "Help me light the match."

I snorted. "I think I need you to find another way to put that," I said. "But yes. Absolutely yes. If you're sure you want to trade New York for my grandmother's back bedroom, I am there for that."

"I'm sure. I might not want to live in that bedroom forever,"

Jas said. "But it's fine for now. And the work is fine for always. That's not the question. You've always thought this was your place. Can it be our place? Is it what the Modern Pioneer Girl would do?"

I felt a huge smile stretch my cheeks almost to bursting, and held a hand out low. "It's what both the Modern Pioneer Girls would do," I said. "Laura."

"Zora."

My other hand. "Frida."

"Gloria."

Then, together, lifting our pile of hands and dropping it at every word: "Ruth. Bader. Ginsburg. Go."

But instead of going anywhere, we threw our arms around each other and laughed, not the hysterical laughter of earlier but a shared burst of joy and relief. There would be a lot to work out. It wouldn't be what I had imagined.

It would be so much better.

35

Permission

HOW TO TELL my mother that—with Jasmine's help—I was going to be able to pull this off after all?

I will admit that my first impulse was to gloat. To blow Jasmine's check up to the size you see on televised lottery drawings or conduct a ticker tape parade down Main Street. I threw out ideas for the rest of the afternoon, while we continued what we now dubbed a "Rising from the Ashes" party.

Jas rained on every one of my outrageous ideas. "Just call her," was all she would say. "She was okay with you taking over before; she'll be okay with it again."

I stopped in the middle of sketching a new version of the farm, with a rebuilt barn towering over the other structures. My mother's cold declaration that she'd given me long enough rang in my ears. "I don't think so."

"Give her a little time," Jas replied.

I would have kept arguing, but Louisa turned up the music, and Amy started dancing with the broom, and we kept up that

party atmosphere until we shut the door at four, offering pro-
found thanks to our helpers and a promise that they'd be first
on our list of possible employees when we got that far along.
Louisa stuck her chin out proudly. "I might not be here next
summer," she said. "My dad's taking me up to Acadia tomorrow to deliver my application for the national parks program
in person."

"That's great," I said. "You convinced him? Them?"

"We're dropping off the Yarmouth program application
first," she said, looking a little less excited. "And then we're
going to see what happens, and I think they really mean it."

"You'll get to choose," I said confidently. "When you get
back, we'll have a big grand opening for your trail, and everyone will see what you've done."

She looked pleased. "That would be cool," she said, then to
Amy and Jasmine: "Don't peek. I want to show you myself."

"I won't let them," I promised. "I'm putting up a 'No Tres-
passing' sign. Nobody goes up there until you're back."

"Next weekend," she said. "We'll only be gone a week." She
ran her hands through her black hair, the ends now tinged in
bright violet. "Can I maybe take my dad a cookie?"

"Of course." I rushed to grab a bag. "He liked the oatmeal
chocolate chunk, right?"

"He says raisins are an abomination of nature and their
presence in baked goods should be punishable by law, so yes."

"I wholeheartedly agree," I said, putting a few cookies in
the bag and handing it to her.

"I'll tell him you said so," she replied, and I realized that
she, Jasmine, and Amy all had matching grins. I'd been a little

fast off the draw with that cookie, and it was true—part of me had been hoping Mike might come in all day. Earlier I was just hoping for a chance to say good-bye. Now that we were staying I didn't know what I was hoping for. Or maybe I knew and just didn't want to admit it.

No more hiding.

"Sure," I said. "Tell him his law has my vote."

Jas and I cleaned up and took care of the evening's chores. Over a scrounged-up dinner of flatbread and tomato and white bean soup, because Jasmine's ability to scrounge far exceeded mine, I brought up the question of telling Margaret again.

"Maybe you want to do it," I suggested.

"Oh, no. If you think she's mad at you, I can't even imagine what she thinks of me. I can absolutely wait until she cools off."

"I don't think that's going to happen." I dipped a piece of bread in my soup.

"I do," Jas said with what I felt to be misplaced confidence.

"You didn't hear her. I know she was angry before. But this was different."

"And you, of course, were just completely calm and apologized profusely and suggested all kinds of ways that the two of you could start over again."

I wiped a little soup off my chin. "Um, no."

Jasmine waited, eyebrows raised.

"I apologized," I insisted. "I took responsibility. And she wouldn't even listen."

"What did you say, exactly?"

"I said I made a stupid mistake. That I did something dumb because I was intimidated by her and that I wished I hadn't. But all she could talk about was how if I really was who I wrote that I was, I wouldn't have done it. She wanted me to believe it wouldn't have been so awful. That she would have been glad to see me."

"Maybe she would have."

"Why would you think that?"

I meant it as a rhetorical question, but Jas answered it, holding up a finger. "One: because she was practically standing here waiting for you when you got off the plane from South America." Another finger. "Two: because she had everything all arranged to sell this place—for you. I know that's not what you wanted, but she didn't and she planned that even though it meant you would leave again. Which I don't think is what she wanted."

I sank down in my chair, trying to put myself in my mother's shoes, possibly for the first time ever. "Okay, maybe."

Jas held up a third. "Three: she kept coming back here, no matter what you said. You don't believe she really wanted to see me again—or rather Maggie Strong—do you? That was all for you."

I pulled my lip in and pressed my teeth against it, thinking. I wanted to swat what Jasmine said away. It didn't fit what I thought was happening. But it didn't not fit either.

"Then why would she yank it all back?"

"Because we made her feel stupid," Jas said. "And because you suck at apologizing."

She wasn't the first person to tell me that.

Jas said she was tired, and that we had plenty of time to talk, so I cleaned up the kitchen before I followed her upstairs. Her door was closed, but I could tell she'd been in my room. The light was on, and a card my mother sent me for my tenth birthday, which for some reason I'd kept stabbed to my bulletin board for years, was in the center of my pillow. I picked it up, and a sprinkling of glitter fell off the giant number ten on the outside. Inside was what my mother had written: *Many happy returns of the day, darling. That's what my parents used to say to me. I love you and miss you and I've enclosed some money for you to buy yourself a treat. I know it's hard being so far away right now, but that just means we'll have to try harder.* It was signed *Love, Mum,* which I hadn't called Margaret, even in my head, for years.

Jasmine had stuck her own Post-it note inside. *She was trying,* it read. *Are you?*

Sometimes Jasmine was really annoying. Sometimes she was right. And sometimes she was both. I could see, looking back on the past few weeks, the moments Jas was talking about. Times when Margaret might have been extending her own stiff-upper-lip version of an olive branch.

Sitting there on my bed, with that card in my hand, I let myself feel the disappointment and confusion I'd felt as a child when I realized she wasn't coming back. It was just a few weeks before she would have sent this card, marking my worst birthday ever, one I'd refused to celebrate. Because she was gone.

She couldn't hurt me any worse than she already had, I reasoned, as I took the card to my desk and propped it up next to me while I tried to figure out what to say. I took a piece of lined paper from the drawer and stopped and started a dozen times. *Dear Margaret, Dear Mum*—none of it felt right. Finally, I settled for starting with something simple, took a new sheet, and began to write. *I've found a buyer for your half of Pioneer Hill. A check is enclosed.*

That was the easy part. But there was more.

Once upon a time there was a girl who thought her mother was pretty scary.

She thought she could never get anything right.

She thought her mother wished for a different daughter, a better one. And sometimes she wished for a different mother. A better one.

But she would have settled for feeling loved by the mother she had. And maybe—it took her a long time to figure this out— her mother would have settled for feeling loved by the daughter she had too.

Maybe they both just needed to start over. And try harder.

I folded the note up, put it inside the birthday card with the check, and found an envelope to fit. I'd drop it off in the morning.

❧

36

Approval

JASMINE, PERPETUALLY OPTIMISTIC, put out a call around town for old patio tables and chairs before I was even back from Yarmouth, where I'd handed my missive to my mother's assistant. This time she'd apparently been primed for my possible arrival—she stood up when I came in and assured me that "Margaret isn't in" before I had time to open my mouth. She looked relieved that all I wanted was to leave my envelope behind.

By the time I came back Jas had an excellent start on a better outdoor seating area and was deep in a conversation with Amy over whether we could winterize the farm stand to make it possible for her to serve coffee and baked goods year-round.

All day and into the weekend, she told everyone our plans. Everyone. In the time it took for her to make you a latte, you got the whole story; if you wanted a mocha, you got the whole Modern Pioneer Girl saga too.

She made it a lot funnier than it felt.

It took a little getting used to, but it turned out to be a relief. Once everyone knew—this was Bowford; everyone knew fast—not dancing around topics or avoiding conversations was freeing. Most people didn't care a whit one way or the other, but the few that asked I just answered. Simply. Honestly.

Online wasn't nearly so easy. I was mocked in an extremely snarky piece on BuzzFeed (THE AUTHENTIC INFLUENCER'S FAKE SELF, AND WHY YOU SHOULDN'T CARE). My Instagram post was screenshotted and shared and made into collages with pictures of Jas from the *Today* show and highly unfavorable comparisons. There were some supportive comments. There were more mean ones. Jas found me reading them Saturday, took the phone from my hands, and told me I could have it back next week.

I howled. "I need my phone," I said, but she shoved it into her pocket.

"You don't. The only person you need to hear from is me, and I'm right here. If Mike calls, I will give the phone back."

"That's not what I meant," I said, although maybe it was.

Jasmine put a cookie in my outstretched hand. "Here," she said. "Eat your feelings. Anything's better than reading all that."

I missed the phone for about an hour. After that, not so much. Turns out that if you live in a tiny town in rural New England, and if you have a busy life that takes place entirely offline, you can weather a burst of Internet infamy pretty comfortably. Nobody was mean, or even critical, in person. Jasmine, with her cinnamon buns and turnovers, was far more of a local celebrity, but I was getting used to being asked about the *Guide*. When that meant conversations about travel and adventure, I even liked it. I loved being home, in Bowford, on the farm. But when I got to talking about a mountain trek or my friends in South America, I was happy to realize that with Jas as a full partner, Pioneer Hill would never tie me down the way it had my father and grandmother. Once it was fully ours, we could make it into a place that supported all our dreams.

Once it was ours. On Monday, I opened an unstamped, unaddressed envelope I found in the mailbox to find a piece of paper with a single word on it in my mother's unmistakable copperplate handwriting.

Fine.

That was it.

I filed an insurance claim. Piled up debris and got it hauled away. Caught Brownie sneaking under the fence three times, electric wire be damned, and finally just let him loose in the yard. I attached a short lead rope to his halter so that I could grab him if I needed to, and realized that as long as he wasn't in a fence, he didn't try to get out of a fence. He just kind of hung out, and he was good company. S'mores preferred to stay with Bingley and Darcy, but I wound up letting Teddy roam free too. It's possible that all the scones he begged off toddlers weren't good for him, but he seemed happy.

I felt bright and optimistic. Mostly. Jasmine and I cleaned out the farmhouse because Jas thought I should move out of my childhood bedroom and I thought she might like a different room. I sat up late one night gathering all the cards and notes from my mother that I'd tucked away in a variety of places, then putting them all in a single pile. I didn't read them, but I knew how they went, getting more and more awkward and distant with every passing year.

I'd always held Margaret responsible for that. I knew now that it was a two-way street, sometimes made harder for me to cross by my grandmother, who had her own challenges. I could see the ways I could have done things differently too. Just in time for it to be too late.

If I hadn't sent that note with the check, I could still keep a tiny, secret illusion that if I reached out, my mother would respond and we would forge a new way forward. But I had, and she didn't, and after a couple of days went by I gave up on thinking she would. This being-vulnerable business was kind of crap.

When my thoughts got to be too much, I would saddle up Darcy. Tuesday afternoon turned out to be spectacularly beautiful, so I rode up Louisa's trail to the chimney, going around the plank bridges that weren't designed for horses and avoiding the steeper bits in favor of looping around and heading home.

As we came out of the trees and turned onto the road, a flash of light reflecting from a car's mirror blinded me for an instant. I blinked and saw my mother's sleek silver sedan pulled over to the side of the road. Perched uncomfortably atop the hood, looking as though she would rather be anywhere else, was my mother.

I rode closer, lifting my hand in the same greeting I would give anyone.

"I am having car trouble," she said as I approached, the words sounding almost rehearsed. "Can you help?"

"Sure," I said, stopping Darcy. I slid out of the saddle and threw the reins over Darcy's head, securing them around one stirrup leather, then led him to a patch of grass to graze. "What happened?"

"It won't start," Margaret said.

"Can I try?"

"I think I know when a car won't start," Margaret began, and then let the words trail off as though they weren't the ones she was looking for. She got down off the hood and gestured to the driver's seat, starting again in a calmer tone. "Be my guest."

One quick press of the starter button confirmed what my mother had said. "Your battery's likely dead." I got out of the driver's seat. "It will be easy to jump. I'll just go get the truck."

Margaret nodded, and I retrieved Darcy, thinking. I turned back to my mother. "But why would you turn your car off here? It's not like the battery just suddenly gives out and the car stops. How did you end up out here?" I didn't want to admit to myself how much I was hoping she'd been on her way to see me.

"I don't know," Margaret said, looking uncomfortable. "I just stopped for a moment. To send a text."

"And turned the car off?"

"It's better for the environment," said Margaret in more confident tones.

I felt crinkles of skepticism on my face. I didn't want to

disturb this fragile peace we seemed to have established, but something wasn't right about this story.

"And no one's come by?" This was a busy road, which was why the farm stand was so successful. I touched the car hood. "Engine's cold. You've been here for a while. Where were you going?"

"I was— To the— Oh, all right. Fine." She looked down the road determinedly. "It didn't die here. I brought it here. So you would fix it."

I stood, holding Darcy, and felt a tiny spark of satisfaction light deep within me. If that was true, it was even better than her being on the way to the farm, and I felt a smile warm my face.

Margaret stood silently, eyebrows knotted, as if unsure how much she wanted to admit. "The tow-truck driver was very confused," she said.

I laughed, disbelieving, and my mother cracked a teeny, tiny smile. We stood for a moment, staring at each other, Darcy shifting restlessly, until another car pulled up and slowed, its driver leaning a head out the window.

"Need a hand?"

"No, thanks," Margaret responded, and I had a feeling she might have turned down more than one offer of assistance before I arrived. "My daughter can fix it."

At that, the spark of satisfaction lit into a full-on flame.

I turned Darcy toward the farm. "Come on," I said to my mother, and then, after a second's quick glance at her clothes, "Want to ride him?"

"No."

Margaret shook her head quickly, but I couldn't stop smiling. "You used to ride, though. I remember. Dad used to kid you about your helmet."

"Brains are important," Margaret said, and I took off my helmet and extended it to her. After a moment's hesitation, she put it on, and I held out my hands to make a step for her, which she scorned, instead taking Darcy's reins and neatly mounting from the bumper of her car.

I didn't mind letting my admiration show. "I guess some things you don't forget," I said.

She steered Darcy down the road, and I walked beside her. "How many people stopped to help?"

"Six," said Margaret, concentrating on Darcy.

We walked a few more steps.

"I got your card," she said. "My card."

"I don't think the kid version of me could see how hard you were trying," I said.

"Your grandmother and your father didn't help."

I nodded, able to hear the truth of the criticism for the first time. "I know," I said.

We'd walked through the driveway—I could only imagine Jasmine's face if she happened to look out the window—and Margaret leaned forward and dropped down out of the saddle as though she'd done it daily for years.

"I have to put Darcy away," I said. "Then we'll take care of your car." I paused, uncertain. It seemed wrong to just throw this out there, walking along, as though it didn't come after years of silence. But here we were—and there was no pretending my mother didn't want to be here. I wasn't going to pretend either. There were things I wanted to say, even if they might make my mom turn around and walk away.

At least she wouldn't get far on foot.

"Grandma screwed up some things. She should have told me how the farm was left. Given us time to work it out." It would have been hard for her to admit, I could see that. To tell me she couldn't give me the one thing she knew I most wanted. "But she did give you a chance."

I wasn't going to let my father and grandmother become the only bad guys. "You said she asked you to take me when Dad died, but then you didn't. Not really. You dumped me at boarding school, and even if you had good reasons, well, Dad had just died. When you dropped me off, it was like I'd lost everything again."

I pulled Darcy's saddle off and put it on the rack I'd set up outside the barn, since I was still unsure how safe the tack room was. Margaret looked off at the other horses, gathered at the gate waiting for Darcy's return, and I wondered if she was going to respond. "I know," she finally said. "There's a little more to the story."

I curried the saddle marks off Darcy's side with more vigor than was strictly necessary. Of course there was. There had to be more to the story. And I'd asked for it. It was time for me to hear it.

"I told you that I left you with your father and Bee the first time because I didn't want you to have to make a choice. Because I thought it was wrong to force you to choose, that you were too young. But the truth is—" I could see my mother squeezing her hands together more tightly as she went on. "I didn't want you to choose, because I knew what you would want. We all knew. Your father, your grandmother, Pioneer Hill—those were the only things that mattered to you. I was never going to win. So I didn't even try. I didn't even really argue."

Margaret looked straight at me. "I let you go, and while it would be an exaggeration to say I've regretted it every day since, I have regretted it. I wrote. I sent you things, I called, but it wasn't enough. Maybe if I had tried harder, or been able to forgive myself, things might have been different."

I felt much of my anger slipping away at the sight of Margaret's eyes, shiny with unshed tears. But there was something Margaret wasn't saying. I straightened, holding Darcy's halter.

"Then why didn't you try when Dad died? I needed you then. I needed someone, and you were so . . . we didn't talk. We drove four hours to school and hardly said a word except about the radio, do you remember? And whether I had enough clothes. Nothing about Dad, or how I might feel, or anything. I thought you'd made me come with you, and then it felt like you hated me." I had hated my mother at that moment. But I didn't want to hate her. I would have taken any opening Margaret had offered. There hadn't been one—and in that moment, looking at Margaret's face, I knew why.

"It wasn't just yourself you never forgave," I said. "You never forgave me, did you?"

Margaret didn't answer. She turned away, and I walked Darcy to his paddock and released him to his friends before returning to her. I knew I was right. We'd both been waiting for a sign from the other that we were wanted, and we were both too stubborn, or too young or too old or too grieved or too something to make the first move.

But we were both here now.

"I loved you," I said. "You were glamorous and beautiful and smart and maybe a little scary and I wanted to please you, but it was hard, and Dad and Grandma were so easy." On purpose, maybe. Because it's easier to be the good cop when someone else is the bad cop. My grandmother loved me like crazy. I knew that. But that didn't mean she was entirely above using me to get to my mother, and that explained a lot. "I think I knew you were unhappy, but I always thought you were unhappy with me."

"I was never unhappy about you. I know I wasn't the warmest parent. My parents weren't demonstrative, and I thought I needed to be firm, and it made me so angry when Charlie and your grandmother weren't. And the older you got, the more I felt shut out. It was so easy for you to hurt me. I had never learned to be vulnerable, the way you are. I needed to protect myself, and I did. I'm not saying I'm proud of it. I wish I had done things differently. And I am trying to do them differently now."

I looked at my mother. Even for a clandestine roadside mission, she was fully, neatly dressed, pants pressed, pearls at her throat, her trademark glasses masking much of her face as they always did. She'd set my helmet on the picnic table and straightened her hair, and she appeared about as vulnerable as a tank. But maybe inside she felt like I did. Raw and sensitive and easily wounded.

You two are exactly alike, Jasmine told me once. *And you're awful.* At the time, I'd resented the suggestion that my mother and I had anything in common, but now I could see all the ways Jas was right.

"Me too," I said.

"I was very angry about the ways you deceived me. I was angry that it was possible for you to fool me like that, and hurt that you would go to such lengths to avoid me, because in the end that's what you were doing. You were pushing me away, and I pushed back. Because that's what I've always done. When I got your note, I was still angry at you, and I wasn't ready to stop."

I nodded. I could understand that. Being angry was at least familiar.

"But then I realized if your friend buys my half of Pioneer Hill," she said, and then when I looked up, startled, corrected herself, "when she buys my half, then that's that. All these years, I was counting on the farm to be the one thing that would bring us back together in the end, and when that's gone, there's nothing left. You can walk away; I can walk away. And I was afraid that if I didn't say anything now, I never would, but I still didn't know how."

"And then your car wouldn't start."

"I thought it would give us a chance to talk."

"It did," I said. "But after I fix it? What then? Do I have to have some kind of college-president-only emergency outside your office so we can talk again?"

Margaret laughed. "You could slip on the sidewalk outside my house this winter," she said. "I'm terrible about keeping it shoveled."

"Or you could come buy a coffee and spill it on yourself, and I could rush you to the emergency room. Unless I was still in a cast from slipping on your ice."

"Or we could just have dinner." Margaret took a deep breath. "Because I would like us to start over and try again. That's what I should have said. When I got your card. Or when I first saw you, at the farm, weeks ago. That I have missed you, and I am happy to see you, and I never want to not know where you are or what's going on in your life again."

Wow. Talk my mother into showing her feelings, and she really went for it. "That's what I want too," I said.

Any other family might have hugged, but we were who we were, my mother and I. I gestured to the truck. "Should we go get your car started? So it's not blocking the road?"

"Do we need a new battery or something?"

I smiled. "Or something, yes," I said. "I have jumper cables. We'll get it started and running, but once this happens it sometimes happens again, so we should get you some."

"I'd prefer to call you," Margaret said.

"That works too."

37

Permission

ON WEDNESDAY MORNING I got a text from Louisa, and Jas, with a stern look on her face, handed me back my phone while I sat at the kitchen table eating Cheerios. "No Instagram yet," she said. "No Internet. But you can text."

"Do you want to put some training wheels on it?"

Jas made a face at me. "I set limits," she said. "At least you have to think about it before you do it."

I read Louisa's message—We got back late last night, can we come over and talk about opening the trail—then tried to hand my phone back to Jasmine. "Actually, you answer this. Tell her you have my phone. I don't know what to say."

Jas took it and pretended to type. "Dear Louisa, yes, of course, be sure to bring your dad because I have mentioned him twenty-seven times since you left and Jasmine is tired of me pretending I'm not interested."

"I have not." Had I? "I mean, he is the logical person to ask about rebuilding the barn. And if we should winterize the stand. And to look at the roof on the farmhouse."

"All of that is true and so is what I said," she said, and then she looked out the window as we both heard the sound of a truck in the driveway. "It's also true that you don't need to answer that, because he's here."

I got up quickly, bumping the table and spilling my bowl a little. Jas grabbed a towel and waved me away. "Go," she said.

Mike was already standing in the back of the truck, unloading the bales of hay he'd brought. They'd got back late, Louisa said. And here he was already.

I hoped it wasn't just the animals he'd been thinking about.

I forced myself to pause on the porch, even though I felt a little as if he might disappear if I didn't run up and hold him in place while I tried to find a way to show him that this time, I wasn't going anywhere.

"Hey," I said, brilliantly.

"Hey," he said, then pointed. "Hay."

"Country people have so many rich opportunities for humor," I said.

"I thought you took me for a city slicker."

"Not you," I said. "Your dog's too well trained." Betsy sat in the truck, waiting to be released, and I walked up and put a hand on the door. "Can I?"

"She's been jonesing for some llama time." Mike jumped out of the truck bed to stand beside me as I opened the door and Betsy tore off around the side of the house.

I picked up a bale of hay in each hand. "Thank you," I said, like we did this all the time. "We were getting low."

Mike grabbed the other three bales by the strings and followed me around to the paddocks, where we stacked them next to the open bale already on a pallet in the grass.

Mike stood looking at the burnt side of the horse barn and the gaping hole in the back, where we'd herded the sheep out just a remarkably long week ago. "You could reframe this out pretty easy," he said. "Pull off the bad wood—everything holding up the roof looks fine still."

"Is that your professional opinion?"

He put a hand on one of the posts and shook it hard, looking up to see what happened. "This is an official stress test," he said. "Seriously. I think you're okay." He looked over at the hay barn. "You need to think hard about whether to rebuild that, though," he said. "I'm not sure it's worth it. That is—are you staying? What's happening with your mother?"

I'd assumed he knew. "Jasmine's buying her half," I said, and then I hesitated. Mike wasn't a fan of what he knew of Jas, and that was on me. "She's not who you think she is," I said, and then, when he looked at me wonderingly, because of course he knew that: "I don't mean— Of course she's not Maggie Strong. But she's my best friend, and she's smart and fun and funny, and she doesn't care any more about social media than anybody does. And she thinks she knows how to change a tire but honestly she probably doesn't. And . . . Mike . . . I'm sorry. Again. For lying. And pretending, but not just that. I'm sorry I didn't give you a chance. Ever. I'm sorry I unilaterally decided that I was the only one who got to screw up."

"That's very thorough."

"Well, I had some time to think about it."

"So did I," he said slowly, and turned toward the hay barn, away from me, and I just knew what he was going to say. I was not someone he wanted to be around, or have around his kid, and—

Mike swung back to face me. "I'm sorry too," he said. "I'm sorry I wasn't the guy you thought I was in college. I'm sorry I didn't chase after you and make you listen to me, or beg your grandmother for an address, or something—did she ever tell you that I tried? She wouldn't tell me where you went. Said you wanted a fresh start and you were getting one."

I shook my head. "There was a lot of that going on," I said. "You, my mother—" All my grandmother had done was exactly what I asked her to do, and if, in retrospect, I might not have known what was best for me, there wasn't anything to be done about that now. "I don't think you have as much to apologize for as I do."

"I'm sorry anyway," he said. "I let you down. I don't want to let you down again."

"You were there for me when everything was literally going up in flames," I said, stepping closer to him. "I think I'll risk it."

He took a step toward me too. I could see a tiny bit of sweat on his jawline from the sun and feel the energy that had always been between us. "I could help," he said, gesturing around us at the farm, his arm not even brushing mine but so close I could feel the air as he moved. "We could hit the lumber store, start on the wall."

"I can do it," I started, automatically, before I shut my mouth tight and wished I could pull the words back in, but

Mike didn't look hurt, just amused. "I only meant, I could. Do it. Myself."

"I know you can," he said. "I hope you don't want to." He moved his arm again, slowly, and this time he took my hand. His touch sent a welcome feeling of warmth straight through me.

"I don't, exactly," I said. "I just like knowing I can."

"I get it. I don't want you to lose that. But if I help you get it done faster, you'll maybe have more time for the next thing. And the next thing. Because I know you have plenty of next things in mind."

I grinned. I had a whole notebook full of next things. "I have big plans," I said.

"I know you do. It's one of the things I like about you. And you will make them happen with or without help. But maybe I could make this a little easier?"

One of the things he liked about me. One of the things. He liked. "I think," I said carefully, "that the way you make some things easier could possibly be one of the things I like about you."

He pulled me a little closer, and I didn't resist. "It would be very easy to kiss you right now," he said. "If that's okay?"

I felt an unaccustomed sense of mischief and leaned back just a little. "Hells no," I said.

Then, without giving Mike even the tiniest chance to feel disappointed, I kissed him instead.

Epilogue:
One Year (and a Bit) Later

"TRICK OR TREAT!"

The bright voices called their greeting into an empty door-way, and as they peered into the spookily lit interior of the farm stand, my mother, dressed by Jas in a witch's black cape and hat, sprang out at them, her fingers crooked and beckoning.

"The better to eat you with, my dearies!"

Carney's son Martin, dressed as a tiny Spider-Man, screamed and ran out the door into his mother's arms. Oscar took a step back but staunchly refused to flee.

"That's wrong," he said, trying and failing to put his hands on his hips, which were encased in his costume, a foil-covered box that read CANDY-TESTING MACHINE. "That's the wolf. In 'Red Riding Hood.'"

My mother took off her hat and looked after Martin. "Yes," she said, "I'm well versed in the classics. What should a witch say?"

"Maybe cackle? And maybe not so jumpy with the little kids. But big kids like it."

Margaret gave a *Wicked*-style cackle and Oscar took another step back. "Not quite so loud," he said.

Jas extended a tray to him. "We're not doing candy," she said. "You can take a wrapped cookie or ghost for later, or one to eat now. Or both." Her cookies were works of art, witches' hats and spiderwebs with designs swirled into their glossy icing. The ghosts were meringues with chocolate chip eyes. We were going to be the most popular stop on the Bowford Halloween circuit.

Oscar extended both hands and Carney stepped in, Martin behind her. "Just one," she said firmly. Looking a little disappointed, Oscar carefully chose a cookie while Martin grabbed a meringue and bit into it, then both stepped back from the tray.

"Man, mothers are powerful," Jas said. "I'm not sure I can do it." When Carney looked away, she slid a wrapped meringue into Oscar's pumpkin-shaped bucket and a cookie into Martin's.

"You'll be great," I said. Jas was doing the training to become a foster parent, and maybe—if things came together—eventually adopt on her own. "Honestly. The bar for maternal success around here is really quite low."

"And yet oddly high," Jas said, looking at Margaret, who had set her peaked hat on the coffee bar and was filling in the last squares of the Sunday *Times* crossword.

"You'll have the kid at donuts," I said.

Amy stuck her head in. "Did I hear a rumor about grown-up treats?"

I had hot mocha-spiced lattes prepped and waiting. "Spiked, or not spiked?"

"Not for me, spiked for Carney," Amy said. "I have a feeling that by the end of the night she'll need it."

I handed her two cups, one with a skull-and-crossbones sticker. She toasted me and took a quick sip from the other before disappearing into the darkening evening. A crowd of kids appeared and Jas busied herself handing out treats, while I took Margaret's hat away to plonk it on Jasmine's head.

"I think Jas might be better suited for this than you are," I said.

My mother looked up. "You're probably right," she said. "I'll take a cookie, though."

Bowford Halloween ran a strict five-to-eight schedule (and always took place on Halloween itself, due to a firm feeling among the older residents that attempting to move Halloween to a Saturday because you were worried about waking the kids early for school after the festivities amounted to blasphemy). More than one customer said how much they'd miss us over the next couple of months, while Mike's team continued the renovation they'd already started in the farmhouse and turned the stand into a year-round structure, complete with a small commercial kitchen. Thanks to a bank loan and the continued income from *The Modern Pioneer Girl's Guide to Life* on my side, and Jasmine's hard-earned chunk of Zale's Powerhouse Fitness on hers, we were both investing in Pioneer Hill and we couldn't have been happier about it.

"I'll still be baking," Jasmine kept promising. "Preeda's going to give me some space at the general store. And I'm already taking Thanksgiving pie orders."

After half an hour of complimenting costumes, my mother had had enough. She removed her cape and draped it over Jasmine's shoulders. "I'll see you back at the house, then." Jas was staying in Margaret's guest room during the renovations and consulting on a plan to add a small café serving only local foods to Yarmouth's library.

Margaret looked at me. "You're sure you still don't need a place to stay?" Her face was serious, but the glint in her eye told me she knew what I was going to say.

"Thanks," I replied as Mike came through the door, followed, much to my delight, by Louisa, who'd insisted on coming to Bowford for the Halloween fun. One of us—probably both of us—would have to get up at the crack of dawn tomorrow to get her back to New York in time for her afternoon classes. "I'm all set."

"Come see Brownie," said Louisa, staying in the doorway and beckoning. Mike took my hand to pull me outside, and I felt a combination of ease and excitement at his touch. I squeezed, and he glanced down at me quickly with the smile I wanted. "You are absolutely all set," he whispered. "Unless you'd like to do a little cosplay with me climbing the tree to get into your bedroom at your mother's house?"

I nudged him with my hip, laughing, then laughed even harder at the sight of Brownie. Louisa had refused to tell me her plan for him, and now I could see why. He was wearing a classic striped prisoner costume over his front legs, with a pillbox of a hat attached to his halter and a foam ball and chain on one hoof. "I put a sheriff's hat on Teddy," she said. "But I think he ate it. So I made one for Betsy instead."

"I bet you get all the candy," I said.

Louisa held out a coffee can and shook it so we could hear the change jingling inside. "Donations for Home at Last," she said. "Mini horse rescue."

I caught Mike beaming proudly, and he should be. He had a great kid, and a semester spent helping to restore a historic building at Fort Yellowstone had only increased her well-deserved confidence in herself. As much as I wanted to have her around, I had a feeling Yarmouth might not be her first-choice college—but she would figure it out, and Mike would handle it.

They disappeared in the direction of the trick-or-treating route and Margaret took herself home. Jas and I gave away treats and lattes until we ran out, then settled into clearing the farm stand for the last time in this incarnation. We made two last drinks for ourselves before cleaning up and loading the espresso machine into the back of her car and the last of the cookies into mine, then turned to look back at the little building where we'd done so much.

I reached out and took Jasmine's hand. "You sure about this? It's not too late to change your mind. Open up a place in Manhattan, replace Magnolia Bakery as the darling of the *Sex and the City* remake."

She dropped my hand and put an arm around my shoulders instead. "Not for me," she said. "I'm going for more of a *Gilmore Girls* thing these days." She was still wearing the witch's hat, and she reached up and transferred it from her head to mine. "Or maybe *Hocus Pocus.*"

"Anything but that," I said. "Which reminds me." I'd left Alistair in the farmhouse, but it was time for him to make the move to Mike's with me. I found him prowling the kitchen, waiting for dinner, and by carefully pretending to be planning no such thing, was able to scoop him up and press him into the cat carrier, carefully avoiding his claws as I closed the door. He yowled in protest.

"Change is hard," Jas said.

"Sometimes. I think we're doing pretty well, though."

"We," Jas said firmly, "are killing it." She wound her hair, which was still long and blond but darker and with more of her natural curl, up into a bun on top of her head and secured it with a scrunchy from her wrist, then tilted her head to look over at me. "You sure you're okay with me moving in here? When it's done?"

"I'm sure." We both knew, although we hadn't really said as much, that once I moved all the way in with Mike, I wasn't coming back. "It's still mine. It's ours. And it's still Pioneer Hill."

Jasmine handed me the drink she'd been holding while I captured Alistair, then tilted hers to toast mine. "To Pioneer Hill."

"And Modern Pioneers. Who—it may be time to face this— might not be girls anymore."

"To being grown-ups," Jas said. "Except when we aren't."

I tapped her mug again. "To calling the shots," I said. "All by ourselves. But together."

Acknowledgments

I WAS LUCKY enough to be able to work on *In Her Boots* with not just one but two amazing editors. Margo Lipschultz, thank you for believing in Rhett from the beginning, and Tara Singh Carlson, thank you for seeing that Rhett and Jas were stronger together.

And thank you again to the team at G. P. Putnam's Sons for helping to get the whole Pioneer Hill crew out into the world, and to everyone at Hello Sunshine for continuing to support me! Sally Kim, Ivan Held, Emily Mlynek, Ashley Hewlett, Nishtha Patel, Ashley Di Dio, I feel so fortunate to get to work with you all again. Dominic Riley, Gretchen Schreiber, Jane Lee, Melissa Seymour, Sarah Harden, Cynthia Rupeka, Megan Butterworth—I know you think you know how much your authors appreciate you, but you need to multiply that by hundreds. Thank you for continually making me feel like I deserve a place at your table. Caryn Karmatz Rudy and the team at DeFiore, thank you for helping me earn that spot.

Reese Witherspoon, just, wow. We have never met, but thank you for letting me get to know you through the books you choose to share, and thank you for making *The Chicken Sisters* one of them.

Jennie Nash, I do not write books without you. Jessica Lahey and Sarina Bowen, I do not do anything without you. Mary Laura Philpott, Christine Koh, Lisa Belkin, Susan Ellingsworth, Laurie White, Laura Vanderkam, Gretchen Rubin, Liz McGuire, Mimi Lichtenstein, Amy Wilson, Margaret Ables, Nancy Davis Kho, Wendi Aarons, Kimberley Moran, Judi Fusco, I can't imagine what I would do without you! Kendall, Jen, Sarah, Teddy, Zion, Sella, thank you for that thing we do: all the walks in all the weather. Suzanne Dunlop pulled me through one draft, Virginia Sole-Smith and Lisa Christie checked my privilege in another. Kristin Roth Nappier made sure no character spontaneously aged a year or teleported from one location to another mid-scene. I only hope my screams of frustration at my dopey errors didn't pierce her ears for a fourth time.

On the home front, I couldn't do anything without Heather Dunnett. And without Kristyn and Greg, there would be no farm and no horses and no S'mores and Brownie. Kristyn would not miss Brownie, who may be the only fictional character I ever base entirely on a real being and who is, at this moment, double-bolted into a stall while we rebuild his fence.

Mom and Dad, thank you for putting up with and supporting my "eclectic" career. Mom, thanks for knowing that I am never writing about you. Dad, I don't know why dads get short shrift in my books so far. Maybe you're just too hard to live up to.

Rob, thank you for being the kind of partner who hears "buy a little chocolate for the ride home" and comes back with two pounds of the good stuff. You make me feel seen.

Sam, Lily, Rory, Wyatt, you're everything I ever wanted. Thank you for understanding that the people in my laptop are never more important than you are, but sometimes they demand my attention anyway. And Marco, thanks for joining our craziness and inspiring us all to take chances and go big instead of going home.

In
Her
Boots

KJ Dell'Antonia

––––––

A Conversation with KJ Dell'Antonia

––––––

Discussion Guide

––––––

PUTNAM
—EST. 1838—

A Conversation with KJ Dell'Antonia

What inspired you to write this story?

I'm hampered in answering this by knowing that my mother's book club will surely read it! I was inspired by two things: First, I love reading memoir, and I love following certain authors on social media because they at least appear to be so willing to share their vulnerability—but I always wonder about the reaction they get from their friends and family, and how it might sometimes feel easier to share something sensitive with strangers, who aren't going to come knocking on your door with soup or call you up in a panic just when you're starting to feel better. Second, I do have a little farm—and my parents think I'm nuts. So the idea that Margaret would want Rhett to do something different probably came from that.

How was writing *In Her Boots* similar to or different from writing your first novel, *The Chicken Sisters*? Do you have a favorite part of the writing process?

Well, both times I wrote way too much and then had to figure out what the real story was, so that seems to be a thing I do, although I'm trying to learn to do it a little differently. And both times I came to "what the story was really about" at the end, not the beginning. I think it would be easier to do it the other way around but I'm not sure I can.

My favorite part of the process seems to be whichever part I'm in—except maybe the deciding-on-an-idea part. I find that stressful, landing on something that I'm going to spend a year-plus working with. There's always this period when I'm like, no, wait! Here's a better idea! But once I'm in it I like the constancy of the demand to write or revise pretty much daily. It gives me a sense of routine that I really like. As long as no one else is making me do it.

How did you craft Rhett's character? Are any of the characters inspired by real people?

Rhett came from the question, Who would write a book like *Eat, Pray, Love* and then really, really wish she hadn't? I just kept writing her and writing her and writing her until I understood why she would do that—and then I had to switch the point of view in the book from third person to first, because it was really hard without that to let the reader in on her thought process. She's not based on anyone real—no one in this book is, although Earl Bailey talks with a very local accent and is kind of a blend of several pillars of my community in New Hampshire, in what I hope is a very loving and respectful way.

The farm setting is very atmospheric, and the many hilarious animals add such fun color to the read. Do you have a personal connection to farm life? Do you have any animals of your own, such as a temperamental llama named Teddy?

I have an escape-artist mini pony named Brownie, and he has a buddy named S'mores. We have a largish horse farm on our property that is entirely run by someone else who lives there now, but at different moments in my life I've done morning and night chores and I'm very, very aware of how hard it is for any agricultural endeavor to be self-supporting. (You do not want to get me started on insurance.) I've thought about a llama, but I have the only kids in the world who start screaming in protest when I suggest another animal. They know it will just end in my forcing them to go out in the dark on a miserable February night to figure out whether there's a hole in the fence.

In Her Boots is such a thought-provoking read about the different relationships one juggles in life—from friendships and romantic relationships to the complexities of mothers and daughters. Why did you choose to write about these dynamics in particular? Are any of them derived from personal experience?

Probably all writing about relationships comes from personal experience to some extent, but I have a great relationship with my mother, and most of my core of people at the moment is family oriented and so pretty different from Rhett, who's really finding her way and figuring out where she fits in with other people still. But I think we can all identify with that—no matter how solid our relationships appear, there's always this background sense of. *But who does she think I am? Am I that person? Or am I someone else?*

Who was your favorite character to write, and why?
Probably Louisa. She's so nice and willing to just burn it all down, mostly because she doesn't know how hard it is to build it back up.

What do you think lies at the heart of Jasmine and Rhett's sister-like friendship? Why do you feel it was important to incorporate this female friendship into the story?
I think it's the friendship we all want. I am lucky enough to have more than one ride-or-die friend in my life, but the thing Rhett and Jasmine get is to stay together. Life doesn't pull one of them to the East Coast and one to the West, or give one a day job and the other a night job, or one a kid whose needs make maintaining her friendships harder—all things most of us deal with. Rhett and Jasmine have been apart but now they're back and they get to choose to stay that way.

What do you want readers to take away from *In Her Boots*?
I hope we all end up thinking about whether we really are who we show to the people around us, and how we can show up more truly—and how that might help others to do the same, and let us all see and understand each other in new ways.

Without giving anything away, did you always know how the story would end?

I did not! It had a couple of other endings over the process, in particular around Jasmine, but they didn't really fill that need for everyone to become more intensely themselves. My editor (who's the best) kept saying, "But readers will love Jasmine; I'm not sure this is what people will want for her" until I figured out where she would really want to be and why.

What's next for you?

I'm already working on another novel. It's early days to share much, but I think, given *In Her Boots* and *The Chicken Sisters*, that it will once again be about how ridiculously hard it is to figure out what makes us happy.

Discussion Guide

1. Throughout the novel, Rhett has a love-hate relationship with her hometown. Discuss your connection to the place you grew up, and how you feel that shapes the decisions you make as an adult. How is it similar or different to Rhett's feelings and choices?

2. Who was your favorite character in the novel, and why?

3. Rhett and Jas have an almost unshakable friendship that is tested at different points in the novel. What do you think each woman emotionally provides for the other? Do you think they're good for each other?

4. *In Her Boots* is a story about finding yourself again, but also a fun novel about the ups and downs of farm life. What was your favorite scene in the novel pertaining to the farm or animals? Did you learn anything about tending to a farm that you didn't know before? Does this lifestyle appeal to you?

5. What was your favorite scene in the novel, and why?

6. The relationship between mothers and daughters is a special and multifaceted one, especially for Rhett and Margaret. Discuss how Rhett and Margaret are both similar to and different from each other. Do you ultimately think Margaret was a good or bad mother to Rhett, and why? How does Rhett and Margaret's relationship compare to your own relationship with your mother?

7. If you had a superhero alter ego, what would its name be? What qualities would it have?

8. If you were placed in Rhett's boots, how would you have reacted upon learning Margaret was going to be on the *Today* show with you minutes before the interview? If you were Jas, would you have taken your friend's place?

9. Margaret and Rhett have very different opinions when it comes to attending college and how that choice sets you up for the future. What is your opinion on the matter? How did you navigate this choice, and what did you ultimately decide? If you had the opportunity to change the past, would you?

10. Both Emily and Mike want Louisa to follow a specific path for her future, similar to what Margaret had wanted for Rhett. Was Rhett wrong not to bring Louisa's plans to her parents' attention? What is the line you draw between interfering in someone else's parenting and looking out for what you believe to be good for a child?

11. Mike accuses Rhett of running from her problems—is this a fair accusation? Did she owe it to him—or herself—to confront him over what she'd heard way back then? Or now, when she re-met him?

12. What are your thoughts about the ending?